## THE OPEN FIELDS

Chun-Chan Yeh was born in 1914 in a remote Chinese mountain village and is one of the few intellectuals in China today to have received a classical education. The region was an important revolutionary base and in 1929 Yeh went to Shanghai when his village was overrun by Nationalist troops. It was there that he encountered new ideas from the West and began his literary career, writing short stories and articles.

Chun-Chan Yeh pursued his literary activities in Japan (where he was imprisoned for 'harbouring dangerous thoughts'), China, Hong Kong and Chonqing. In 1944 he was invited by the British Ministry of Information to speak to the British people on Chinese efforts against Japanese invasion and after the war he went to Cambridge. There he furthered his relationship with many of Britain's leading cultural figures of the time.

He returned to Beijing in 1949 to work in the field of culture, editing a literary monthly in English and French, *Chinese Literature*. During the cultural revolution he was accused of 'having poisoned the mind of world people' and was relegated to cleaning toilets. He was not fully rehabilitated until the arrest of the Gang of Four. Since then he has devoted his time to his own writing and to promoting new cultural exchanges between East and West through International PEN.

The trilogy *Quiet are the Mountains* consists of three novels: *The Mountain Village*, *The Open Fields* and *A Distant Journey*. The first was written in English in 1946 while the author was in Cambridge and was published to great acclaim in 1947. The other two were written in Chinese in 1984 and 1986 after Chun-Chan Yeh had had the opportunity to revisit the village region of his childhood, the background of the trilogy.

by the same author

**ff**

# THE OPEN FIELDS

## Chun-Chan Yeh

*Translated by Michael Sheringham*

*faber and faber*

LONDON · BOSTON

First published in 1988
by Faber and Faber Limited
3 Queen Square London WC1N 3AU
This paperback edition first published in 1989

Printed in Great Britain by
Richard Clay Ltd Bungay Suffolk

*British Library Cataloguing in Publication Data*

Yeh, Chun-Chan
The open fields
I. Title
823[F]     PR94509.Y43

ISBN 0–571–14171–4

## TRANSLATOR'S ACKNOWLEDGEMENTS

I am grateful to Phil Kidgell, my wife Susu, and my father, Walter, for the time and help given to me in checking my translation, making suggestions and improving the style.

# CHAPTER 1

'Listen, what's that sound outside?' said my mother.

'It's the wind,' I said, 'the autumn wind. Didn't Father say a few days ago that it's the beginning of autumn? "The harvest should be finished, the rice should be dried and taken in, in preparation for winter." After these words, he sighed; I don't know why.'

'Yes,' Mother said, 'I heard him sigh too. You know, he's getting old. When autumn comes, he realizes the year will soon be over. But listen carefully. The wind sounds different this time, so fierce, it frightens me!'

At that moment I was squatting in the courtyard repairing a chair. We were living in a side room attached to the warehouse of my father's employer, Ho Ludong. The house was in the western quarter of the town, and usually there was a storekeeper staying there. Now the warehouse was not being used, as there was a depression in the market and Ho Ludong was not buying or storing anything. As the storekeeper had nothing to do, his employer told him to go to work in his shop in the town centre. (Ho Ludong's own residence was just behind the shop.) When Mother and I arrived, he arranged for us to live there together. He said he would not charge us rent as a special favour to my father, who had been working for him in the shop half his life. He also left us some broken furniture, so ever since we had moved in I was always busy repairing this or that. If we had not moved in then, I am afraid this room would have been left empty and gradually collapsed with all the broken things inside.

'Yes, Mother, you're right, the wind really sounds strange, as if bugles were blowing.' I listened carefully for a bit, and said,

1

'How horrible. They've been blowing bugles all the time recently.'

A sigh was my mother's only reaction. She could not continue speaking. She was rubbing her eyes, as the whole room was filled with smoke, which made them water. She was cooking in a corner of the room, which served as the kitchen. We did not have anywhere to dry the brushwood and grass which we had gathered, and the stove had no chimney. As soon as we lit it, smoke filled the room. The silence was broken by Laipao, our dog, who was crouching in the doorway and suddenly barked twice, startled by the autumn wind – this old companion of ours had come far from the open countryside to this crowded town, and felt as lonely as we did. He sat there aimlessly all day, afraid of being one step away from us, as if we might move again and forget to take him with us. In fact, once separated from us in this big city, he would never be able to find his way home again.

'Why do they blow the bugle?' I asked, just to distract Mother from her thoughts, because I knew that whenever she was silent she was thinking of our village. After we moved to the city she always missed our old home with its undulating hills and winding paths. 'As it's only just getting dark, it can't be bed-time yet. Why did they blow the bugle so early?'

As I asked this question, she stopped rubbing and used her sleeve to wipe tears from the corner of her eyes.

'You don't know,' she said. 'The tune of the bed-time bugle is different. Listen how sharp and urgent this buglecall is.'

At this moment my father pushed open the door and came in. He had been teaching in his employer's house and was carrying a blue cloth bag with his textbooks and students' home-work inside. As soon as he had put down his bag, he lay on a bamboo chair in the middle of the room. This was the only piece of furniture we had bought since moving in, specially for my father. All day he sat in a small room behind Ho Ludong's house and taught the three grandchildren how to read and write. From what my father said to my mother, I learned that these children were very naughty and mischievous, and fond of playing. Their father, though, hoped they would be successful when they grew up. He wanted them to achieve remarkable academic success and win honour for the family. My father seemed to find this a difficult task. Although he had some teaching experience, he found it hard to train the children to be scholars. But he always did his utmost to help his employer make his wish come true. He acted like this out of his sense of moral obligation. He was always a man of strong principle. Of course, the main point was how to support our family. He was afraid that if he failed to satisfy Ho Ludong's wish, he might be dismissed from his job some day. In fact, my mother and I also feared that this would happen. This became a source of psychological pressure on the whole family and made my father age fast. He was sitting on the bamboo chair with his eyes closed and his face sickly pale with exhaustion. His mind, though, was still active, as we could see from his fluttering eyelids.

After a while, the urgent buglecall carried by the wind died away and finally disappeared.

Father slowly opened his eyes, pressed his hands on the arms of the chair and straightened his back. Looking at Mother and me, he spoke quietly.

'You must both be hungry. Why do you always wait for me to come home to have supper? Why don't you eat first?'

'There are only three of us at home now,' said Mother. 'It's nice to eat together, which we can only do at supper-time. You leave home every day before dawn because the boss's house is far from here, and you don't want to spend money on the fare.'

We tried to cast aside our anxious thoughts. Father pretended not to hear the strange piercing sound. When even the dog, Laipao, noticed it, how could my attentive father fail to do so? He just kept quiet.

Silently we started our supper. The wind blew harder and harder, and it whistled around the eaves. Occasionally we heard a noise like something falling from the roof. It was probably a tile coming loose and smashing on the ground. Father sipped some tea after finishing his supper and just stood there, staring vacantly. He waited for mother to clear the table and then he took the three naughty boys' homework and his textbooks from his cloth bag. Every day he conscientiously prepared for the next day's class, as there had to be some progress in the lessons.

Sensing the silence between us, and as if trying not to interfere

3

with Father's work, Laipao snuggled up to me and lay down meekly by my feet. He had just eaten the leftovers which Mother had given him. He shared our lives so intimately that he completely understood our feelings and inner thoughts. He lay there quietly, occasionally raising his head to look at my mother, then furtively glancing at my father and finally turning to me. When he saw that there was no expression on my face, he patted my leg with his paw as if to cheer me up, but as there was still no response, he licked the back of my hand.

'He's really a part of the family,' said Mother after observing the dog's movements, 'except that he cannot speak. Strangely enough, I dreamed of him yesterday. He was holding a piece of paper in his mouth, with a note from Zhao Jue saying that he would try to come and see us soon. Laipao said to me, "Don't worry, Aunt, he's very well now." You see, he can talk, just like a real member of our family! After speaking he jumped up twice like a happy child.'

'Who knows, Ma, maybe one day he'll really come back to see us.'

'If he really does come back, it would be by the grace of our ancestors,' Mother said, sighing gently. 'But nowadays their spirits seem to have gone far away looking for peace and quiet, so how could they look after us?'

I remembered what had happened one day a year ago in my old home when my elder brother, Zhao Jue, came back home. He absolutely refused to marry the child-bride whom my mother had arranged for him and who was already living with us at home. He created a minor revolution at home, refusing to recognize O Ran as his fiancée. He did not care about making her unhappy and took no more notice of her. After he left home he did not get in touch with us for a long time. He used to be an assistant in the branch shop run by Father's employer, but the revolutionary troops of the Northern Expedition entered this big city, and he organized the shop assistants' trade union and became a union leader. He not only stopped working for Ho Ludong, but he also caused some trouble and finally broke up with him. The merchant felt relieved, but my father had to make up to him for the loss of his recalcitrant son. Ho Ludong seemed to have forgiven my father and kept him on and let him continue

4

teaching, though with some qualms about not paying him the bonus that he had promised.

After Father had heard my mother express her feelings, he remarked, 'Times have changed. Zhao Jue had his own reasons for not doing his job well. I've been a shop assistant for most of my life, but I have nothing to show for it. Previously I expected to live on my savings, have some security in my old age and avoid hardship. That was an idle dream. Let young people make their own lives. As for the boss, we cannot blame him for throwing our son out, because he had his own difficulties. He still cares about us as a fellow villager whose ancestors are all buried in the same county. Although he fired all the other employees, he kept me, and even in these difficult times he gave me this job as a tutor and let me move here. Otherwise you wouldn't have been able to come here and live with me.'

Mother didn't say anything to contradict him, but just added, 'It's only a pity that our eldest son isn't with us; we don't even know where he's gone.'

No sooner had she said this than there was a light knock on the door. We immediately tensed. The military police in this city knocked on doors at any time, especially in the evening, so we had heard. Recently they had forced their way into the home of a 'coolie' who lived near by, explaining that they were searching for a criminal. Actually they were looking for a revolutionary involved in underground activities. 'To maintain social order,' they said. Most of the people they were after were workers, young people or students. They often arrested these innocent folk and looted their belongings. Was it these people knocking? We all looked at one another, at a loss to know what to do. When the knocking stopped, Father put his pupils' homework together, unable to keep calm any longer. When two more taps followed, Father came up to us and whispered, 'It doesn't seem to be the military police or security agents. They always knock hard enough to break the door down. Also Zhao Jue hasn't sent us a note for a long time and I haven't joined the shop's trade union, so I don't think they could be looking for me, could they? As for Chunsheng, he's only a country boy and hasn't been to a modern school. How could he have anything to do with those young revolutionaries?'

'Chunsheng' was what father usually called me, as I was born (*sheng*) in spring (*chun*).

Mother nodded and got up, responding mechanically. She went to the door and opened it slowly. In this situation it was safer for an old woman to open the door.

Father had guessed right. Standing outside was not the military police but a young gentleman. We could not see his face clearly in the dark, but we could see that his hair was dishevelled from the wind and that he was scantily dressed and seemed to be shivering. Without saying a word he slipped in quickly through the half-open door. Quietly squeezing past Mother, he turned and closed the door himself, then fixed the latch. He embraced Mother, exclaiming, 'Mother, my dear mother.'

So this visitor appearing in the night was Zhao Jue, my brother.

We were amazed. We had never expected him to come at this time. We had not even dreamed of seeing him in this tense situation. But it was really strange that the news that Laipao had brought in my mother's dream had come true.

'Where have you appeared from?' Mother asked, delighted. 'My child, we missed you terribly. We didn't hear from you for such a long time. We didn't know whether you were still alive!'

'Of course I'm still alive, and living a very interesting life!' my brother said, smiling as he let go of her and looked at her worried face. But his smile accentuated Mother's weary expression.

'Here I am standing before you, blown here by the autumn wind!'

'This autumn wind really frightened us just now,' Mother replied quietly, but with a trace of a smile already appearing on her face. 'We never thought it might also bring you here.'

Suddenly the tension in the room vanished, and Father, who had been worrying in silence all this time, stood up, incredulous. Relaxing, he pulled my brother to the table where he was preparing his lesson and urged him to sit on the bench. By the light of the candle on the table, he studied my brother from head to toe. He could hardly recognize him: he had brought him from the village to this big town to be an apprentice and taught him himself, and now he looked like this, worn out and

6

shabbily dressed like a tramp. He did not seem to care as long as he pursued his own ideas. Father seemed to be dreaming, hardly able to believe his eyes: this was the son he had brought up himself, hoping that he would take over his job. 'The world has changed and people have changed!' he said to himself. After staring at my brother for a while, he pulled himself together and asked, 'Can you stay with us for a time? I suppose you haven't found work yet? Don't worry, stay for a while. There's always something to eat here.'

My brother shook his head. 'I'm terribly busy,' he said. 'I only have one evening, just this evening. Early tomorrow morning, as soon as the night curfew is over, I'll have to leave town.'

'Why?' Mother asked anxiously.

'Because I'm a criminal on the run,' my brother replied calmly.

'Escaped criminal? What do you mean?' Mother demanded, frightened.

'Father should be able to guess,' my brother continued. 'He must have heard a lot at the boss's place. The situation is critical. Chiang Kai-shek is determined to betray the revolution. Many young people have been pursued by the police as "criminals on the run" and I'm one of them.'

'So how did you manage to come here now?' asked Father in an unexpectedly quiet voice. Perhaps because he had experienced so much anguish and suffering, he could keep calm in this very complicated situation.

'Didn't you hear the sound of bugles in the wind?' asked my brother. 'That was the military police trying to terrorize the population. They were taking away a group of young people they had arrested. I'm afraid those poor wretches must be dead by now, because the bugle has stopped. The executioners must surely have been rewarded to go visiting their opium dens and brothels. When they were enjoying themselves, I jumped off a boat in the river – I've been underground for quite a while. I've come here to tell you that I'm safe. As the situation is getting more and more critical, I'm afraid I won't have another opportunity to come and see you. I can't leave tonight as the night curfew has already begun, so let's just have a happy family reunion.'

'How did you know where we live?' asked Mother. 'We've been worrying about whether we'd be able to see you again.'

'Don't be so pessimistic,' my brother said. 'We have nothing but contempt for those people. Although they're riding high now, they will be defeated.'

'You can't leave us again,' pleaded Mother. 'As long as we have any food left, we'll be able to feed you and we can hide you here for the time being. Nobody will think of this miserable room.'

As Mother's words tailed off, a tear flashed in her eye. My brother remained silent, and none of us spoke as we waited for him to respond to Mother's suggestion. He glanced around at us, and replied evasively, 'Mother, I'm hungry. Is there anything to eat?'

'Sure,' said Mother, 'you must be tired, as well as hungry. When you've had something to eat, you must get some sleep. Relax and have a good rest. I'll look after you.'

So Mother started busying herself. As she specially prepared a fresh dish for him, I helped her warm the rice up. Father was still busy sorting out the textbooks and pupils' exercises on the table, but he made room for my brother to have his supper.

After finishing his meal, my brother sat still beside the table. Thinking he had eaten a little too much, Mother made him a cup of tea to help him digest. Then she sat down beside him to make him feel relaxed and comfortable. Father and I sat opposite them. After taking a sip of tea, my brother's eyes suddenly lit up, his spirits revived. Glancing first at Mother and then at Father, he seemed about to say something.

'If you want to stay here, you should know about the unrest here,' he said finally. 'I'm afraid it'll go on like this for quite a long time. What's going on in the countryside is connected with the situation here.'

'It isn't unrest, it's terror!' remarked Father. 'We hear a lot in the boss's house, and it's all bad news. There are people killed every day and they're all young!'

'You're right,' said my brother, forcing a smile. 'It seems you know all about it.'

'But there are still some things I don't understand. Why do

they have to kill so many young people? Why such hatred? Such young people – many are just schoolchildren!'

'I didn't understand at first, either, Father.'

'But now you do understand, do you? How did you come to understand?'

'As early as the days of the shop assistants' evening class run by the trade union, a veteran revolutionary who taught there prophesied that there would be chaos, and he's been proved right.'

'So you were already prepared for this?' Mother added. 'You young people easily believe what anybody says . . . '

'It isn't a question of believing; it's the truth, Mother. That veteran revolutionary was a fellow villager, speaking with a local accent, like our own kith and kin. How could he deceive us?'

'According to my experience,' said Father, 'one shouldn't believe anything too readily; one should wait and see.'

'Yes, now you're still waiting, I'm still waiting – I've seen too much of the truth. It has made me a criminal.'

'You shouldn't have organized that trade union in the first place,' Father continued. 'Look what trouble you're in now!'

'So are you any better off, Father? You've worked for the boss your whole life and now you have to live far away from home just to survive . . . '

Father shook his head, his grey eyebrows frowning.

'Don't say that, my son. I have my own problems and I'm different from you young people. There's nothing I can do about it, can I? I didn't join your trade union, and I still think I was right . . . '

At this moment Mother interrupted Father. She was still looking at my brother.

'Your father is old. It's no use speaking like this now. I can see you're tired, my son, you must sleep. Have a good sleep and Mama will look after you. You really need a rest.'

When my brother looked up from his tea cup, I discovered his eyes were moist. In fact, he was not as tough as he made out. He was as soft-hearted as Mother. He watched her quietly, as if he were not intending to sleep. Suddenly he turned and looked at the bolted door. Outside the wind was still blowing, but not so strongly now. Occasionally it rattled the door.

9

'I'm not tired, Mother,' my brother said, turning his gaze from the door. Suddenly his moist eyes were alert and bright. He turned to Father and said, 'I think I did the right thing. If all young people only thought of their own comfort, our country would have no future. Let them spread terror. I'm not afraid.'

'Not afraid? Tell us why,' said Mother. 'We want to hear. I don't want to sleep now – we've never been able to have a real talk!'

'You're right, Mother,' said my brother. 'Perhaps we won't have another chance to sit here together like this again. I risked coming here tonight, because I knew you were worrying about me.'

Father gazed at him.

'We've been thinking of you all the time, my son,' he said softly. 'You should realize that and you should get clear what you are risking your life for in these days of terror.'

'For everyone, including you old folk!'

Father's eyes opened even wider.

'What do you mean by that?' he asked. 'I don't need your support.'

'But you won't be able to survive for very long,' my brother said and then paused. 'Well, you're still more fortunate than Peifu. I've heard how he died. What a fate for such a decent teacher! What a pity that you took up the same profession! Dad, I'm sad and angry. We Chinese cannot go on like this.'

With the mention of Peifu, his old colleague and friend, Father hung his head, looking depressed. He could not utter a word.

'Oh, don't talk about things of the past,' Mother sighed, trying to distract them. 'Our generation will soon be gone. Rather think about your own future. You're still young, with a long life ahead of you. There's no need for you to risk your life. It's not too late for you to change your ways!'

'Mama, I know you mean well, but what have I got to lose? What have all Chinese got to lose? If we don't destroy the present system, nobody can survive. It even looks as if Ho Ludong will hardly be able to hang on.'

'I don't understand, my child,' said Mother. 'Explain what you mean. Now we depend on him for our living. If even he is finished, then . . .'

Father looked up at my brother, obviously disturbed. My brother cleared his throat.

'He's got rich by purchasing cotton from the farmers, hasn't he? And he has shops to sell it. We were helping him to collect it for the local weaving industry, which wove it into cloth to be sold in various villages and towns. People buy cloth to make clothes. The business went very well for several years, as the foreign powers were involved in the World War and no foreign-made cloth was imported to compete with the cloth produced locally. Now that the World War is over, foreigners have resumed their businesses, not only exporting cloth into our country, but also setting up factories here. They buy our cotton and turn it into cloth locally. The cloth woven by their machines is beautiful and cheap. In less than two or three years it has ruined the boss's cotton trade and the weaving industry here. What's worse, they have concessions and privileges in our country. They also control our customs offices and sell their goods all over our country duty-free or with very little tax. The sale of our own goods is restricted everywhere by government officials and warlords who extract heavy taxes. As a result, our commerce and industry have collapsed! The whole country has been divided into spheres of influence by different foreign powers. In order to maintain their control, they back up various reactionary factions and warlords who serve them. The warlords fought each other for years until they were wiped out by the revolutionaries. Now the foreign powers turn to support Chiang Kai-shek, who is attempting to throttle the revolution by killing people everywhere. Revolution is the only way for the people in town or countryside. How can I, a young man, remain uninvolved?'

Father sipped some tea, shaking his head.

'You have no weapons, what can you do? Chiang Kai-shek defeated the warlords, didn't he? And what happened then . . . ?'

'Didn't I just say, he changed after that!' my brother broke in. 'His troops marched to Nanjing and then Shanghai, both strongholds of the imperialist countries in China. He immediately fell in with that lot and turned his guns on his old

11

supporters. What else could people do but rise up against him? Let's see if he can kill them all!'

Mother interrupted him.

'My child, you're going too far. I feel uneasy when I hear you talking like this. Tell me, what are you planning to do next?'

Ignoring Mother's question, my brother continued.

'These reactionary powers are nothing to be afraid of. Haven't the workers recovered the British concession in Hankow? Like the United States, Britain has also backed Chiang Kai-shek. The Chinese people do not fear Chiang and all his supporters. Mother, don't worry. I'm all right.'

My parents looked at him dubiously, as if to ask: Is everything really all right? They did not seem to want to ask this question directly, because it would lead to some more awkward questions. We all fell silent once again. It was only then that I noticed that the wind had stopped blowing some time ago. The night was so quiet. In the countryside we had usually gone to sleep early. I only remember being aware of the silent night on New Year's Eve, when everyone stayed up talking, so tired that we could hardly keep our eyes open, but still did not feel like sleeping. Of course, the atmosphere of that New Year's Day had gone. Now we sat in gloomy silence.

It was my brother who once again broke the silence, forcing a smile. Patting my head softly, he said, 'Brother, you've really grown up and you've learned quite a lot. How time flies!'

'It's you who've changed a lot, Brother,' I said, smiling bitterly. 'You've learned so much, but this is the first time I've heard all these interesting things! Last time you came back home you were rude and unreasonable and hurt O Ran's feelings.'

'Don't talk about that. What's past is past. People can't help being impatient sometimes,' my brother said. 'However, life and struggle can teach us some sense, especially in hard times like this. Let's say that I was unfair to O Ran. But I didn't get married to that other girl either – she was arrested and shot by the reactionaries.'

'I'm sorry that things have come to such a pass. Ah, it's late, too late . . . O Ran . . . ' Mother sighed, but had to stop suddenly as tears rolled down from the corners of her eyes. She was trying to control her feelings, wiping her tears with her

12

sleeves. Then she continued. 'Are you sure you can't stay with us for a few more days?'

'I'm afraid I can't.' My brother suddenly sounded more determined. 'I've got a job to do and have to leave here at once. But please don't worry about me. There are people to protect me everywhere. Yesterday I slept in the boat of the old fisherman living by the riverside. I felt so safe and comfortable on that boat.'

'Well, you have totally changed!' Father said, sighing. 'Where are you going now?'

'I'm going to Shanghai.'

'Didn't you just say that both Chinese and foreign reactionaries are based there?'

'Yes, that's why there's a lot of work for us to do and the leadership has assigned me to work there. In this place many people know me, so it's impossible for me to operate here –'

'You haven't answered my question yet,' Mother interrupted him. 'How did you know we lived here?'

'Of course, I have ways and means to find out. You see, Mother, naturally I know where you are. I'm also one of the leaders of the shop assistants' trade union. I have to know what is going on in the boss's shop too. At the crucial moment in the struggle we have to be well informed. I have ways to be informed of everything that goes on among the shop-owners. What those ways are, you shouldn't ask, Mother. I found out that Ho Ludong arranged for you to live here, so I came to find you. Of course, I should be thankful for that strong wind. . . It provided me with natural cover.'

'When can we see you again?' Mother pleaded.

'Perhaps not for a long time,' my brother answered. 'But I'll ask my friends here to visit you . . . '

At this point he happened to look up, and, suddenly aware of a patch of light through the skylight, spoke more urgently.

'I must go. The curfew is ending and the street patrols will be dispersing. This is a good time for me to get through.'

Then he hurried to the door, drew the latch carefully and squeezed through the doorway. He was gone without a word of farewell. We three were left gaping at the half-open door. Nobody could say a word for quite a while until Father, the first to recover his composure, stood up and went over to shut the door quietly. He startled my mother out of her stupor.

'He's gone. Arriving unannounced and disappearing without a word – it's all like a dream.'

'This is no dream,' Mother retorted. 'He's our son, my very own son, whom we nurtured and brought up ourselves. He risked dangers to come and see us. He is, after all, our own son . . .'

A ray of light shone through the skylight, the sky slowly turning red with the dawn.

# CHAPTER 2

One evening a few days after my brother's departure, Father spoke to me:

'Since coming to "The Big City", you haven't met my boss, Ho Ludong. He helped us to settle down here. I'll take you to see him, all right? He really cares about us.'

I knew he was trying to test my reaction, but he sounded as if he had already decided. Father was always stern, but extremely affectionate with us children, perhaps because he rarely managed to come home, and then only for very short stays. Still, if he wanted to do something with me, he insisted on doing it. It seemed I had to see his employer, but I did hesitate. I found it somewhat unnatural that I had to bow to the merchant when we met. My father had worked for him for most of his life without a penny to show for it and now depended on being a home-tutor to make a living. Was it necessary for the whole family to be grateful for this? As I was deliberating, Father seemed to sense my hesitation, and he explained firmly why he wanted to take me to see his employer.

'You're not a child anymore. You should think of your future. It's no longer possible to return to the countryside, so you have to learn something and earn a living here. I once asked my boss to let you attend classes in his home. Then you would become a shop assistant, taking over from your brother. My boss, however, didn't agree to this. He said his business had been ruined by foreigners, and as it could never recover he had laid off all the old shop assistants. What was the use of new shop assistants now? Still, he's a reasonable man and he knows that what he pays me can hardly support three people. He said he could support you and let you do a little work in his home to reduce my burden.'

In spite of what he said, I could already sense that this was not really Father's intention. He just wanted to use this opportunity to let me settle down, make a living and later study by myself.

'How does Master Ho Ludong intend to look after me, Dad?'

After a pause, he replied, 'Naturally, he has to cut down his expenses. He has dismissed some of his servants, but he still has all kinds of visitors. He needs a clever boy to clean the rooms, serve tea and offer cigarettes to the guests and run errands. That's what he wants you to do, but at the same time you would have the opportunity to gain some experience, broaden your horizons and in future really learn about business. Like this you should be able to make progress faster than other boys. What do you think of it?'

I just nodded. Mother still sat there beside us without expressing any opinion except by nodding too. So this was how the matter was concluded. The next day, Father took me to see Ho Ludong. In fact, I was employed there after that.

Although Ho Ludong was getting old, with completely white hair, sideboards and a long moustache, he had a rosy complexion and a lively spirit and was as active as a middle-aged man. He had three sons and one daughter. I had not seen the two elder sons, but I heard they were both successful businessmen. They were in charge of buying cotton in two other cotton districts for the two branch shops. Now there was a depression in the market and the peasants' purchasing power had slumped to rock bottom. Also, their customers, who had set up two local textile mills, had long since stopped buying cotton, so their two shops were out of business. Still, they could not close them down, because they were afraid that it would be difficult to reopen them in future. So the two young gentlemen kept their shops and only the youngest one stayed at home. Apparently his father did not want him to go into business too, wishing him instead to be educated to become an intellectual, a scholar. According to traditional Chinese classification – scholars, peasants, artisans and merchants – he himself

16

belonged to the lowest category: a merchant. He wanted to bring up his third son to become a member of the educated élite, so he specially gave him a scholarly name: Ho Shuoru [*shuo ru*: an élite scholar in traditional times, especially Confucian – *Trans*.].

Ho Shuoru was twenty-three or twenty-four, but he had a drooping moustache, because he thought he was cut out to be a scholar. He put on a refined and aloof manner in order to dissociate himself from mercenary businessmen. Most of the time he stayed shut up in his small room, trying to avoid any contact with his father's business acquaintances. He enjoyed having a young lad at his beck and call, because as a cultured man he also needed a secretary. I was reasonably literate and could fill this extra role adequately. I found that he would spend the whole day sitting facing the window, reciting the classics [the Confucian classics – *Trans*.] or poetry of the T'ang and Sung dynasties (AD 618–1278). He seemed to thoroughly enjoy this self-indulgent way of life.

His father, however, was not entirely happy with this situation. He was, after all, a businessman himself and he was rather critical of his son's 'aloof' attitude. Once I heard him talking to his wife about Ho Shuoru.

'He takes no interest in financial affairs. Should I hand over my property to him in the future?'

'You want him to become a scholar and at the same time you want him to be interested in financial matters. How can these things be combined? I really don't understand you!' his wife objected. 'A scholar has to bury himself in his books, a habit which you could never cultivate in anyone, even with the lure of gold. Also, how does this habit of his clash with your financial affairs? He's just in the prime of life. Where could you find another man as thrifty as this young master of the family? He doesn't smoke opium or go gambling with friends, nor does he frequent prostitutes. He doesn't cause you any trouble or lose any of your money. Because of the accumulated virtues of your ancestors we have been favoured with a fine son, whom I cherish with all my heart.'

When he heard his clever wife, Ho Ludong suddenly realized that his third son's attributes far surpassed those of his two elder brothers. After this he started to dote on Ho Shuoru, frequently telling me to obey this young scholar. Whatever he ordered me to do, I had to oblige at once.

Ho Shuoru, however, did not really respond to his father's love, perhaps because he was always preoccupied with the classics and T'ang and Sung poetry. He didn't notice any change in his father's affection for him. On the other hand, his attitude to me changed remarkably, as I spent my days beside him at his beck and call. He started to treat me like a confidant, openly sharing with me his opinions about his family when Ho Ludong was busy entertaining his business friends or planning to revive his business. Behind his father's back, he often exclaimed, 'Mercenary and vulgar!'

Once when he was speaking in this vein, I noticed a shadow passing outside the study window. Looking more carefully, I discovered it was in fact his father. However, the old man had not stopped – perhaps he had not heard anything. I went out quickly to make sure he really had not overheard his son speaking like this in my presence. If Ho Ludong thought that we were talking together like this, the consequences for my father and myself would be disastrous. When I went out, I may have opened the door too abruptly, making a noise that startled Ho Ludong. He stopped in his tracks and turned round to look at me, and I noticed that his face was pale and that he looked depressed.

'What's the matter, Master Ho?'

'Oh, I've just remembered, I was going to ask someone to call you. This evening Chuqing and Guizhi are coming. We haven't met very often recently, so we're getting together. We'll need you to serve dinner and drinks.'

It seemed he had not heard what his son had said about him. Chen Chuqing was his son-in-law and Ho Guizhi was his daughter. Judging from his doleful expression, he seemed to have worries, which he was trying to escape by giving a dinner party. Chen Chuqing was said to be a foreign-educated scholar, who had done his stint abroad and was now well educated in politics and economics. He had become a member of the provincial government and an adviser to several militarists. At the same time he was an agent for foreign banks and insurance companies, and arms broker for the militarists. Perhaps his

18

talent could help to solve Ho Ludong's problems. When the couple arrived at nightfall, the table was already laid in the dining room. As Ho Ludong had instructed, I was serving dishes and pouring drinks, hurrying between kitchen and dining table.

'This is a small family reunion.' Ho Ludong raised his glass in a welcoming toast. 'The world is in turmoil, so we cannot have this kind of party very often. Drink and be merry!'

'Don't say that, Father-in-law,' said Chen Chuqing. 'Whenever there is any unrest you come through it unruffled – you even use it to make a profit. The question is how to exploit the situation.'

Ho Ludong shook his head, frowning.

'This time the situation is quite different. See how the new militarists butcher people pitilessly. They just keep on killing! In the past they only killed ordinary people, but now they also kill the sons of the rich – schoolchildren, students and teachers. Luckily our Shuoru is buried in his books, not involved with those young people. In this respect I don't have to worry about him. We must be grateful to our ancestors for blessing our family with peace. Oh yes, we haven't been back to our native village for a long time to pay respects to our ancestors. Now that we are facing such chaos, we should be even more respectful towards our ancestors.'

At this point Chen Chuqing also raised his glass.

'Blessings to our Ho family's ancestors! Cheers!' Ho Ludong finished his glass in one go. Then he turned to Shuoru and said, 'My son, remember, you must find an opportunity to go back to our old village to sweep the graves of our ancestors. Without their blessings our family could not prosper. You wouldn't be leading such a peaceful life nowadays if it weren't for them, because you're also a young man! Oh, what has happened to your generation!'

'Yes, son, remember what Father has told you,' Shuoru's mother added. 'I'll ask Master Yongsheng to arrange for you to go back to our old home. Is that all right, Master Yongsheng?'

'Yes, of course!' replied Han Yongsheng. 'You're quite right! I'll certainly arrange it for your son. You may count on me!'

Han Yongsheng looked after Ho Ludong's house and also the accounts office of his main cotton store, which had the signboard

'Qing Feng' ('Celebrating Prosperity'). He was forty-four or forty-five years old, but on his head there was already a shiny round bald patch. He seemed to be a capable man. His eyes were very small, but animated, and he moved with an agility that reflected his ability. Ho Ludong employed him both at home and in business, confided in him and treated him as a member of the family, so he also had to attend this kind of 'family reunion', this 'party to forget worries'.

'A toast to the lasting prosperity of the Ho family!' Ho raised his glass.

The atmosphere at dinner gradually mellowed. I carried a pot around pouring out wine, and everyone drank liberally and began to relax, their faces turning red as they talked more freely until they were really uninhibited. Then Ho Ludong suddenly lowered his voice and whispered to his son-in-law, who was sitting on his right, 'Have you solved the payment problem?'

Chen Chuqing nodded slightly, but did not reply. Using chopsticks to stick a piece of sweet-and-sour fish in his mouth, he looked up at everyone as if what he was going to say was both vital and secret. When I heard him mention payment, I remembered what Shuoru had said casually when I was making him a cup of tea in his study a few days ago. He was obviously feeling bored, as he spoke half to himself and half to me as he sipped his tea.

'You're all so simple, with no cares in the world. When you're tired, you just go to sleep – right through until next morning. People like my father worked his way up to seek fortune, but there are always people trying to bother you, even when you're asleep. When the two militarists came to this province not long ago, they extorted money and murdered people at random. They squeezed money from merchants, not even exempting local ones like my father from their taxes. There's this tax today, that tax tomorrow – taxes non-stop. They don't know that nobody grows cotton in the countryside now, so the merchants have no goods to collect. If they have managed to collect goods, they cannot sell them, because the native textile mills are bankrupt. So where can the money come from? Money-grabbers! They've caused a lot of trouble, and it's getting worse. Now

20

there's no cash coming in. I wonder what these people will do next?'

I thought Ho Ludong's reference to 'payment' was connected with his son's complaint about the 'moneygrabbers'. Ho Shuoru and his father were both anxiously gazing at Chen Chuqing, hoping that he would be able to supply the latest news about the 'payment' situation. Chen Chuqing seemed to sense this, and he felt that it would be embarrassing and ill-mannered not to reply as his father-in-law expected. He was influential in the provincial government and well known in the city, so he had plenty of contacts with political and military circles and with the financial and foreign banking world. Not only was he familiar with the present situation, but to a certain extent he could also exert his own influence. He probably also felt that he should do something to help his father-in-law with his 'payment' problem. Otherwise he might also lose face. His father-in-law was no doubt paying so much attention to him because Ho Ludong thought he could help him solve his problem.

'The two army chiefs demanding payment or tribute are from the faction in Guangxi province,' said Chen Chuqing. 'That's a terribly poor province. Generalissimo Chiang Kai-shek sent them here to suppress the communists, and they are doing this with all their might. I need hardly tell you that they are executing people – young people – every day. But they must have a purpose in doing this: they kill communists in order to protect the rich. How could they exempt such a wealthy person as you, Father-in-law? They also have a reason for this: they have to provide for the thousands of troops under their command. Of course, they must also fill their own pockets. Otherwise what's the point of becoming an official? This was their reason for asking for two million silver dollars the first time they spoke to the general trade committee. You have been asked to pay an average amount. So you have to pay on time . . . '

Chen Chuqing suddenly paused, quietly looking at his father-in-law, who was pale, with beads of sweat on his forehead.

'The chairman of the trade committee is so unfair,' he said angrily. 'He knows my business has slumped because of the recession. How can I possibly pay that amount of money?'

'If he wasn't so hard, demanding payment from every

21

business, he would have to fork out himself.' Chen Chuqing, unlike his father-in-law, spoke quietly. 'To put it another way, however much money he has, he would never be able to pay this much. As a matter of fact, it was the members of the provincial committee who made the suggestion to those two army chiefs. They shift the load on to the merchants to reduce their own burden . . . '

Ho Ludong suddenly interrupted his son-in-law.

'You're also a member of the provincial committee. Couldn't you put in a word for me?'

Chen Chuqing smiled unexpectedly.

'Don't worry, Father-in-law. If I hadn't spoken up for you, the money collectors would have come to your shop long ago with armed police. How could we have enjoyed a party here tonight?'

To show how he enjoyed joining the family for dinner, he proposed another toast.

He emptied his glass in one go. Now the atmosphere livened up. Everyone including Shuoru followed suit, draining their glasses. I circled the table with the wine pot, filling everyone's glass.

'To tell the truth,' said Ho Ludong, relaxing a little, 'they only bother about us native businessmen. There are so many foreign-run enterprises, companies and banks in the foreign concessions [areas controlled by the foreign powers – *Trans.*]. They are much stronger than our local merchants. If those militarists are so powerful, why don't they dare touch those foreign enterprises?'

'Who dares touch them?' Chen Chuqing exclaimed. 'Don't you know, the Ching dynasty government challenged them several times, and what was the result? They had to cede territory and pay indemnities every time. Even the control of customs, postal services and salt distribution got into their hands. By the time the republic was established [in 1911 – *Trans.*], every military leader, provincial governor, general and commander-in-chief had to rely on foreigners for arms, ammunition and loans. With foreigners in charge, who would dare to challenge them?'

At this point Shuoru, who had remained silent all this time, spoke out.

'In that case, may I ask how the communists dare to challenge them? Wasn't it the Communist Party that organized the workers to retrieve the concession in this city from the British?'

Chen Chuqing did not react angrily to this riposte. On the contrary, with a knowing smile on his face and in a cautioning tone, he went on.

'Brother, you are immersed in your books. The world is quite different! The Communist Party is just a bunch of ignorant young people. They incited some stupid people to act recklessly, and these poor fools were finally all arrested and executed one by one!'

Someone at the table sighed. It was Ho Ludong's wife.

'How evil!' she exclaimed. 'Executed! Who were executed? Thank God it wasn't my children! It isn't easy to raise children! But to execute them like that! Haven't those executioners got children themselves?'

She covered her face and started sobbing. Her daughter, Guizhi, who was sitting next to her, gently patted her back, trying to calm her. But a shadow was cast over this family banquet. Guizhi also felt that the atmosphere had suddenly changed, and she turned on her husband for spoiling the fun.

'See what you've done! Just when we're all enjoying ourselves drinking a little, you start talking about executing people. What's the point of that?'

Chen Chuqing lowered his head, acknowledging his mistake. Ho Ludong then brought the conversation back to the original topic, partly to wind up the party and partly to make the atmosphere more congenial.

'Chuqing, please tell me clearly, has there in fact been any final decision about the money I have to pay?'

Chen Chuqing raised his head, his confidence restored, because when his father-in-law asked him this question it made him the centre of attention at the dinner table.

'Exempt! I specially went to the general headquarters to find out. They're not demanding any from you. Many other merchants have also been exempted.'

Ho Ludong's face suddenly brightened, like that of a man who is suddenly spared.

'What does this mean?' he asked, amazed. 'Such a quick change!'

Chen Chuqing put on a knowing smile.

'Well, don't they rely on foreigners? The British and Americans are supporting President Chiang Kai-shek financially, and supplying him with a vast amount of arms and ammunition.'

'What's that got to do with the two militarists demanding payment from us?'

'It's got everything to do with it! Chiang Kai-shek is very shrewd. He gave some money to those two militarists in our province and supplied them with more arms. But he also stipulated that they must stop demanding payment from the merchants here, who all have vast estates in the countryside. In fact, they are landlords. They have to co-operate with these people in order to crush the communists. Wouldn't they be digging their own graves if they exacted payment from the merchants? They couldn't do that at such a crucial moment in the campaign to wipe out the communists. People say that Chiang Kai-shek's foreign adviser specially warned him about this.'

Hearing this, Ho Ludong showed great relief after worrying for so many days. Raising his glass, he addressed everyone.

'President Chiang is really a great statesman. He's so far-sighted that he even heeds the advice of foreigners. Cheers! To the health of President Chiang Kai-shek!'

After this toast the family gathering broke up.

Now Ho Ludong's spirit revived and life in his household continued as before. My father and I continued to work as usual in their house. Every day we left home at the crack of dawn and got back in the evening. If there was no special dinner at his house or no extra errand to run, I could usually go back home with Father to have dinner with Mother, who had already prepared it. Over dinner we would chat about comings and goings in Ho Ludong's house. Mother also told us about her daily activities and ideas. At dinner one day she reported an incident.

'A young fellow came to visit us today. He was a stranger, but he seemed so familiar that we talked for ages. I found him very congenial and friendly, so I asked him to stay for dinner to meet you. But he was afraid the curfew would start later and that it would be dangerous on the way back, so he decided to go – he only left half an hour ago.'

Father immediately became pale and agitated.

'We don't know any others here,' he said. 'Where did this stranger come from? Could he be . . . ?'

Father stopped short at this point. I could guess that he probably intended to say two words – 'a spy' or 'agent', because the atmosphere in town was very tense. He always seemed on tenterhooks and had become timid and cautious, especially after my brother came to see us. He did not dare to have contact with anyone.

'What did you and he talk about?' he asked Mother.

'A few things,' she answered.

'What things?' Father asked, more perturbed. 'Wouldn't it have been enough to be polite and then see him off?'

Mother realized what my father was getting at, and she hastened to explain.

'Don't worry. I'm sure he was all right.'

'How do you know?' Father insisted. 'How can you be sure?'

'From what he said. He knows about our son – nobody else could know so much about him. In fact, he's a friend of his and he came to bring a message from him.'

'What message? Tell me, quickly!'

Father's eyelids began to twitch nervously, as if he sensed some mishap. I also began to feel anxious.

'Don't worry,' Mother answered quietly. 'He brought good news which we have both been longing for.'

'So tell me now,' Father urged her. 'You're keeping me in suspense.'

'What are you so anxious about?' she asked. 'It's quite simple. Our Zhao Jue has arrived safely in Shanghai.'

'How does that lad know?' Father kept up his questions.

'That's what I wanted to know,' said Mother, 'so I asked him to stay and have a talk. I'm not such a fool as you think!'

Mother forced a laugh, making Father relax a little. We had not had a laugh in this old room for such a long time, not even a forced laugh like this.

'Come on, tell me,' said Father, also smiling. 'Is that young man also involved in underground activities?'

Mother cleared her throat.

'No, he isn't,' she said, 'but I think he's a trustworthy and honest young man. As he thought I wouldn't believe him, he even told me all about himself. He used to teach Chinese in a secondary school. When Zhao Jue and the others set up the evening class for the shop assistants in the trade union, this young man volunteered to teach there without pay. He was very conscientious about his teaching, so Zhao Jue respected him and they made friends. In turn, this young man admired Zhao Jue, as our son was very hard-working and had learned a lot by himself, even though he was a novice. He had learned much about world affairs, the sufferings of mankind, the future of China and the responsibility of young people. He said that what he had learned from Zhao Jue was much more valuable than the language lessons he gave the children at school. He was very happy to have found a friend like Zhao Jue . . .'

'So they definitely get on well, do they?' interrupted Father.

'I think so,' replied Mother.

'As long as this fellow is a real friend and does no harm,' said Father. 'I've recently heard of young people betraying their friends! If this one is unreliable, it isn't even safe for us to live here.'

'You worry too much. Actually, at first I was as suspicious as you, but from talking to him, I feel he's honest. He didn't hide anything. He sympathizes with Zhao Jue's views, supports the revolution and thinks that our country has become so poor that there must be a great revolution. But he says he himself cannot play an active role, because his father died when he was young. His mother had to struggle all her life to bring him up and even sent him to teacher-training school. Now she's on her sick-bed, paralysed, so he has to look after her and cannot risk dangers outside.'

On hearing this, Father nodded, saying, 'He seems quite a reasonable fellow. I agree with him: he also knows that getting involved in revolution is dangerous.'

'But it's not as simple as that. He's also got something else in mind. He's well read and likes writing poetry, and he has a gentle nature. According to him, he isn't suitable material for revolutionary struggle. If something happened to him, he couldn't stand being tortured by the enemy, so he would be endangering the revolution, his friends and also himself. He doesn't want to harm anyone. He's so kind-hearted. I really liked him.'

'If he's good, so much the better,' said Father. 'In that case, we can trust him!'

'I think that's why Zhao Jue was prepared to tell him our address and ask him to bring this message. He said he had seen Zhao Jue off when he took the boat to Shanghai, and he even bought the ticket for our son. He was worried about Zhao Jue going on the boat by himself, afraid that something might happen. He also said he would bring messages from Zhao Jue again, of course, ordinary messages. He doesn't even need to know Zhao Jue's address in Shanghai. I think he's very disciplined. But Zhao Jue knows his address here, so if he needs anything to be done or has any message to be passed on, this fellow says he will certainly do it. He came here to give us all this information and to reassure us about Zhao Jue.'

Father nodded.

'So we should trust him,' he said. 'It's difficult to find a young person like that nowadays . . . '

'I agree. He said he'll come again whenever we are free. He would also like to help us, because he grew up in this town and knows it well.'

'We don't need his help,' said Father. 'It would only be necessary for him to bring us news from time to time. Without this we would be cut off from our son, since it seems he cannot correspond with us directly – he's probably afraid of getting us into trouble.'

'Oh, when will these troubled times be over?' Mother sighed.

'There are even more chaotic times ahead, Ma,' I said. 'The militarists are just about to send troops into the countryside to go on killing people.'

'How do you know?' asked both Mother and Father anxiously. 'Isn't it miserable enough in the countryside? Where did you hear this?'

'Father, you know that day when the boss had the dinner

27

party,' I said, 'and he told me to stay and serve them? I heard about it then.'

I went on to tell them all that I had heard, and Father kept on nodding. I heard him mutter, 'Chen Chuqing has his own channels of information. I am sure his information is correct and he was telling the truth, especially as he was talking to his own family.'

Father turned pale again, and I could see from Mother's eyes that she was disturbed.

'Oh,' she sighed, 'Chumin and Wang the Lion have already caused enough suffering in our villages, and now troops are coming to slaughter our people. I don't know what will happen to our Uncle Pan, O Ran and Old Liu. So far away, I keep thinking of them!'

The mention of these three familiar names touched us deeply and filled our hearts with sorrow. We could speak no more, and suddenly the room was filled with a deathly silence.

# CHAPTER 3

At this frantically busy and tense time, the days passed very quickly. Without our noticing it, summer had already come, and now it was almost midsummer. Mother slept very little because she was so uneasy. She always got up at five o'clock. On the fifteenth of the seventh month of the lunar calendar* she got up especially early. Father and I got up later, because our employer had given us a day's holiday. When we woke up she had already tidied the room, prepared breakfast and was waiting for us to wash and come and eat. At table she said, 'Last night Grandpa and Grandma came to see me. They're very concerned about us.'

'Oh, old folk always worry about the younger generation!' said Father. 'How are they? Are they well?'

'We haven't cared enough for them!' said Mother. 'They're not so well and they feel very lonely. They've had some difficulties, probably because we're not with them.'

I saw that Mother was frowning in distress. She sounded so miserable that I tried to console her.

'They don't want us to look after them, so it doesn't matter whether we're with them or not.'

'They must be able to understand our situation,' Father added.

Mother shook her head.

'That's not the point. Since coming to this chaotic town, we've forgotten about all our village customs. Do you know that today is the fifteenth of the seventh month? What day is that? Why did the boss give you a day off? They'll do nothing but abstain

*This was the day of the spirits of the dead, observed traditionally in the past.

29

from eating meat, provide charity and pay respects to their ancestors today.'

When Mother reminded us, I also suddenly realized that today was the day when lonely and hungry spirits wandering around the human world were offered food and drink. Some of them have no offspring, ghosts with nobody to pay respects to them. Some have transgressed in some way during their lifetimes and so cannot be transformed into spirits, remaining locked up in hell without hope of being transformed into humans again. Only on the fifteenth day of the seventh month does the King of Hell release them for a while to wander freely about the human world and enjoy our charity. This day is like their festival. In our village on that night people float lanterns in the rivers and ponds to help these spirits cross the river dividing the human world from hell. Then lamps twinkle like stars, floating on the water, producing a mysterious and beautiful dream-like scene on this summer night.

I remembered that Mother was always terribly busy on that night. She had to offer tribute to the ancestors and gifts to those spirits, to make them feel that they had not been forgotten. Generally it was not considered quite fitting for women to perform these important functions. With Father and Elder Brother both away, Uncle Pan was the only male adult in our home. On an occasion like this it was he who usually performed these tasks, so he assumed the role of family head and took on the job of sending off the spirits with my mother. When evening came he would carry some porridge, and I would follow him with a basket of paper money. We would go up the mountain to scatter the porridge as a meal for the spirits and the paper money as their fare to go back to the nether world.

The task of offering charity to the spirits usually went on until almost midnight, after which we went home to pay tribute to our ancestors. Of course, the gifts we presented to them had to be much more lavish than those we bestowed to the spirits. We had to do this, because none of us could be sure whether our ancestors had behaved properly or not in their life-time, or had been captured by the King of Hell and sent to hell. We had to give them a more splendid meal and more for their travel expenses, in case some of them were unfortunate enough to return to the nether world to suffer penal servitude.

'What difficulties have they had?' asked Father, referring to what Mother had said about Grandpa and Grandma. 'What did they say to you? Is it the same in the nether world as in our present living hell, with people trying to arrest and kill them?'

Mother shook her head.

'No, it's not. In the nether world there are no warlords, no Chiang Kai-shek and no foreigners, so who could kill them? Also, they were not communists. They just cursed those spirits who were mocking and taunting them. They said that their progeny were not carrying out their duty to present them with tribute. Those ghosts and spirits blamed Grandpa and Grandma for having brought up these disrespectful offspring. They had to pay for their failure because the spirits couldn't receive their offerings!'

I interrupted my parents' conversation, to ask, 'Ma, how did Grandpa and Grandma come yesterday? How is it I didn't hear them?'

'You couldn't hear them,' said Mother. 'You're not yet old enough to communicate with our ancestors in seance. One day you will have more responsibilities and you'll often be able to meet us – your father and me – and you'll be able to talk to us, even though we won't be in this world any longer.'

I couldn't help laughing. Mother was really fantasizing. She had dreamed this during the night.

'It's not our fault,' I said. 'Where can we go to bestow our blessings? Our ancestors aren't in town, and there are no rivers or ponds for us to float lanterns on, nor our familiar mountain forests, where we could scatter paper money and porridge. And we don't know what's happened to Uncle Pan. Forget about that dream, Ma.'

'It wasn't a dream, it was real. I couldn't forget it, my child,' said Mother. 'I'm sure your father couldn't forget it either. Every year at this time he used to ask the messenger, Sweet Potato, to take some money back home, so that we could buy some paper money and incense to bestow our blessings and pay respects to our ancestors –'

She stopped suddenly. Father averted his gaze from her eyes,

31

which were already starting to moisten. I knew they were both thinking of the same thing: our village home. They said no more. In the silence, I quietly walked over to the oven and filled a bowl with boiling porridge and took it back to the table. I hoped that the sight of breakfast would distract them from nostalgic thoughts of the village and bring them back to reality. At that moment there was an urgent knock on the door, shattering the silence. It startled Father, and he tensed up. He did not know what to do, but Mother kept calm and gestured to him not to be frightened. She walked steadily to the door and opened the latch.

Standing at the door was a young man, around twenty-four or twenty-five years old, with an honest smile on his face.

'Huang Zhuqing, it's you!' exclaimed Mother, smiling spontaneously. 'Come right in!'

Mother stood aside to let Huang Zhuqing in and then immediately closed the door.

'This is the young friend I was telling you about. It was he who brought us news of Zhao Jue. He has really kept his word: he said he would come back to see us and here he is.'

'I haven't yet met Uncle and Little Brother,' said Huang Zhuqing, 'so I thought that if I came at this time you would definitely all be at home.'

When Father heard these friendly words, he immediately brightened up. He was longing to hear news about my elder brother.

'Sit down, sit down!' he urged the young visitor, pointing to an empty chair beside him. 'My wife has told me that you are as concerned about us as if you were one of the family.'

Huang Zhuqing sat down, that honest smile still on his face. This smile of his unconsciously attracted me. Although he was slender and delicate, resembling a scholar, he looked like a lad of my own age. I immediately felt close to him. Like some other young people, he preferred being in the company of older people, just to listen to them. In their presence, though, he could not express his own opinions, only smile affably. When Mother noticed that he was a bit shy, she tried to make him feel at ease.

'You really are reliable. You've come back so soon!'

'This time it was convenient to come early, because the curfew has just ended,' he said, dropping his polite smile. 'If I came any later there would be spies all over the place. On my way here I looked all around me, but I didn't notice anyone following me.'

He spoke forthrightly and was evidently not at all childish, as I had imagined, but in fact quite mature. Father all the while was sizing him up, with a slight frown, as if he were thinking something over. But when Huang Zhuqing explained why he had come so early, he relaxed, his frown disappeared, and a smile even came to his lips.

'I'm sure you haven't had breakfast. Just help yourself to whatever we have. As a friend of Zhao Jue's, you must make yourself at home here. How lucky that we're all together today! Let's eat together, even though it's only porridge!'

Huang Zhuqing seemed to appreciate the warmth of Father's words, as the timid expression suddenly vanished from his face. He stood up, went over to the stove to help himself to bowl and chopsticks and brought them back to the table. Gradually the atmosphere in the room warmed up, and after we had eaten a little hot porridge, we also felt warmer, both in body and in spirit.

After finishing our porridge, we remained sitting round the table, just as we used to do in the village. It was only a pity that Uncle Pan was not with us now – he used to talk a lot and tell us many stories, so it was always lively at meals with him around. Huang Zhuqing did not say much, though. My mother had to encourage him to speak.

'Has Zhao Jue been able to get in touch with you since arriving in Shanghai?'

Huang Zhuqing sat with his head lowered, pondering for a while. Then he looked up, first at Mother, then at Father, and spoke softly.

'There's no more news . . . ' He paused a moment as he swallowed, and then went on. 'I don't know why, Aunt, but when I came here the first time I felt you were so kind, just like my own mother. At night-time I thought of coming here to see you. When I used to chat to Zhao Jue, he told me much about your village home. I heard that on this day you celebrated "seeing off the spirits", presented them with paper money and food and paid respects to your ancestors. We don't have this custom in the city, so I've never seen it, but I can imagine how you feel today. I think you must be feeling homesick, so I've especially come to see you. I hope I can take Zhao Jue's place and have a chat with you to stop you feeling sad – there are many things I want to talk to you about.'

'Well, tell us,' said Mother, her voice revealing how moved she was by his direct and intimate manner. 'Speak freely and don't worry. Nobody else comes here. The city may be full of activity, but we're very cut off here.'

To encourage us to speak freely, Mother went over to the stove to boil water for a pot of tea, even though we had all just finished our porridge. Contrary to my first impression, I found that Huang Zhuqing was not taciturn at all. When he saw Mother pouring him a cup of tea and waiting for him to speak, he suddenly became animated and spoke freely, just like an innocent youngster. He mostly talked about himself, about his childhood, his youth and his present work and life. He really felt at home here and treated Mother as his own relative. He told us about everything and it seemed that he was going to spend the whole day talking about himself. Apparently he wanted to pour out everything he had bottled up for a long time. At the same time he wanted us to understand and trust him, so we listened attentively.

I gathered from his account that, although he lived in town, he had much in common with us. His situation was even worse than ours. In a sense, he was an orphan, because he had been brought up by a distant uncle. Before he was three years old, his parents were divorced, and both had soon married again. His mother took him with her, but her new husband already had three children. At first he could just about tolerate the boy's presence, but soon he began to feel he was a nuisance and started to be hostile towards him. The three children also mocked him, as if he were a hanger-on. When that distant uncle discovered the boy's predicament, he adopted him and brought him up. This uncle was a language teacher in a secondary school, but he was poor and always under threat of being dismissed and unemployed, so he never married. He hoped that Huang Zhuqing would not follow his profession when he grew up. He deliberately trained him as an engineer, so that later he could find a good job. Things, however, turned out differently, because the boy insisted on pursuing his interest in literature. He secretly read almost all the literature which his uncle had in his collection and he dreamed of becoming a poet or novelist. Secretly, too, he started writing a few stories and poems to describe what he had learned about life and to express his own humanistic ideas, which he had formed through witnessing his uncle's hard life. By the time his uncle found out about this development, it was too late to remedy. Before he died, he finally found a job for him: as a language teacher in a teacher-training school – following his own profession, which he had always been trying to give up.

'I feel strongly for those at the bottom of society who suffer injustice.' Huang Zhuqing's low, dry voice suddenly became animated. 'That's why I want to use literature to describe them, their depressing lives, their troubles and pleas, but . . . oh, in this harsh society nobody wants to hear their pleas. So nobody wants to publish my stories or poems! But never mind, if only I can do something practical for these people, I will be happy. That's why I tried to teach in the trade union night-school for poor shop assistants and novices. But, oh . . . ' He sighed. 'The union has gone and the night-school has closed down! I respect – no, I really revere – the union leaders, the organizers of the evening class, but they've all gone now! Only Zhao Jue understands me, so we have kept up our friendship. I'm so happy and proud to be able to bring you news from him. But he's much braver than I and his work is much more important than mine: he is willing to risk his life for the revolution!'

'Teaching in the teacher-training school is also important,' Father said, to console him, but he could not help smiling bitterly. 'I'm in the same profession now, but my work is far less important than yours – I'm a tutor in my boss's home, teaching three mischievous children!'

Huang Zhuqing looked pessimistic.

'But in fact there couldn't be a worse situation than mine. My students' fate is precarious.'

'Zhuqing, what do you mean?' asked my mother. 'I don't understand. Please explain.'

'What can I say?' he said in a more subdued tone. 'Haven't you often heard buglecalls in the streets recently? Now everyone knows what this means: young students are being dragged to the execution ground. Among these martyrs are my students – every few days some in my three classes disappear. Oh, my dear innocent students!'

When he sighed again, we all bent our heads in sympathy, as if we were mourning those who had died and those who were going to die. My heart was full of grief, but strangely, at this moment, I also felt suddenly enlightened. I recalled what my brother had said to us before he left for Shanghai, and it seemed to have a new significance. As we sat in deep thought, we were distracted by a noise. Listening carefully, we realized it was our dog, Laipao, scratching on the door. Every morning he went out for an early run. He had just slipped out when Huang Zhuqing came in. When I opened the door he came running up to me, put his front paws on my shoulders and licked my chin excitedly. He was just as innocent as he had been in the countryside, completely oblivious of human woes and worries. Then he ran up to Mother, shaking his head and wagging his tail, rubbing against her leg. Next he approached Huang Zhuqing and sniffed him, finally cuddling up against Father and settling down there. Father patted his head and then looked up and addressed our young visitor.

'But we still have to go on living, and we still have to teach. The situation is complicated for all of us, however different our problems. Do you have any difficulties at home?'

Huang Zhuqing gazed at Father anxiously. He probably did not know how to answer. When Mother noticed how he hesitated to speak, she prompted him.

'Zhuqing, I'm sure you've got a job and a family of your own. What does your wife do? Does she also teach?'

Huang Zhuqing's lips quivered slightly, almost as if smiling.

'I don't know what to say,' he said in a low voice, hesitating again, looking up at all of us. We were all ears as we waited for him to reply. Seeing our intent expressions, he could only answer shyly, 'I only got married the day before yesterday.'

Mother and Father leaned forward, their interest aroused. They became quite animated again and began to smile.

'Congratulations!' they both said together.

'When you came last time, why didn't you tell us the good news?' asked Mother. 'I could have prepared something for you to celebrate. Why didn't you bring her here? We would also like to meet her!'

'It's not so easy,' he said, his voice so low as to be almost inaudible.

'Why?' asked Mother. 'If you walk in the street as a newly wed couple, those secret agents couldn't suspect you of being revolutionaries. You must bring her here and we'll open a bottle of wine to celebrate – we haven't celebrated a wedding for such a long time!'

Huang Zhuqing nodded, and that half-smile appeared again, but then he looked bitter.

'She, Peng Wanzhen, my new wife, cannot move about. She's sick.'

'What's the matter with her?' Mother asked anxiously. 'What's so bad that she can't move about?'

'Tuberculosis,' answered Huang Zhuqing softly, 'advanced tuberculosis.'

'Oh, dear . . . ' Father sighed heavily. 'Yet you've come to see us! You've come for a chat to help us forget our troubles!'

Huang Zhuqing bent his head low.

'Oh, dear . . . ' Mother breathed a heavy sigh too. 'Advanced tuberculosis, and you still wanted to marry her! How brave of you! Why did you decide to do that? Did she agree? What does she do?'

'She's a writer,' replied Huang Zhuqing, raising his voice excitedly. 'She writes stories, essays and poetry. Like me, she wants to express the feelings of ordinary people in their struggle for life, but she can't find anyone to publish her writing either. Nobody is willing to spend money on printing them, and we have no money. Like me, too, she wants to put all her energy into writing, so she hasn't joined directly in revolutionary activities – she doesn't think she's a fighter. So when Qiu Qunying asked her to marry him, she ignored the disapproval of her family and married him very soon. He was an active young

37

revolutionary, who went around giving lectures. He was really a model for our young generation trying to make revolution. Wanzhen's parents had originally chosen a young gentleman from a rich family for her, but she firmly refused. From then on her family believed that she had gone astray, so they ostracized her. She had nobody to turn to and at that time she became seriously ill!'

Both my parents shook their heads.

'So the situation got more complicated,' remarked Father. 'As she was already married, how did you manage to marry her? What kind of person is Qiu Qunying?'

'Don't mention him. He used to consider himself an expert in literature, but he didn't write a single piece.' Now Huang Zhuqing raised his voice again, speaking passionately. 'At the height of the revolution, he was the most revolutionary, but when there were setbacks he suddenly abandoned her. What was worse, a week ago I saw an announcement which he put into the notice section of *National Daily*. He wrote that he had divorced Peng Wanzhen, that he had nothing to do with her and wouldn't be responsible for her . . .'

Mother interrupted him. 'Run away, all right, but why write in the newspaper?'

'God knows! He might very well have been trying to protect himself by cutting all links with people with a social conscience.'

Father nodded, mumbling to himself, 'This is really very dangerous. It amounts to reporting to the authorities. It's impossible. After all, they were a couple.' Turning to Huang Zhuqing, he asked, 'Hasn't he had some mental breakdown? It has happened to people of his age.'

'He couldn't be more sane!' said Huang Zhuqing, getting more excited. 'When the reactionaries were murdering people he acted like a coward and hid away! Peng Wanzhen mistook a coward for a hero. She felt bitter and angry, so her health deteriorated. She needed someone to care for her and comfort her, but at this time of tension and terror who could look after her? Ah, Wanzhen, what a pure, noble spirit . . . !'

He could not carry on, but my mother took over.

'So you married her – such a quick decision!'

There was no response from Huang Zhuqing, who only hung

his head, holding it in his hands and gazing at the floor with a dazed look on his face. He seemed exhausted, both mentally and physically. My parents could not think of anything to say to revive the conversation, and they had already noticed that our young guest needed a rest. They led him to my bed, made from a door plank, to let him lie down. As if hypnotized, he closed his eyes and lay down straight away. He did not utter another sound, lying there as if unconscious.

The whole day we did not disturb him and tried our best not to make a noise in the room. We did not even call him for lunch, letting him have a good sleep. Only later did he turn over and, noticing that it was already dark outside, suddenly jump off the bed. He rubbed his eyes and smiled in that special shy and innocent, child-like way.

'I'm too bad, behaving so rudely in your house and sleeping most of the day,' he said apologetically. 'I was really tired, as I didn't sleep at all last night. You've really made me feel at home here.'

'If you want to rest,' said Mother, 'just come here any time, and you can also bring Wanzhen. Perhaps to move a bit would be good for her health and spirit.'

Huang Zhuqing looked downcast again and his face clouded.

'She can't go out,' he whispered. 'She isn't strong enough and she's bed-ridden. The situation is even more critical now that Qiu Qunying has written that notice in the newspaper, which will certainly attract people's attention. So she has to hide.'

'Where can she hide at such a time?' asked Father anxiously.

Huang Zhuqing spoke in a hushed voice, as if confiding in us a great secret.

'In a safe place, in a docker's home. I got to know him when I was teaching in the union evening class. He lives in a slum with only his old mother, a kind soul, who wants to look after her. Nobody would imagine a woman writer living in a docker's hovel. As long as I don't go there during day-time, there won't be any danger.'

'You want to comfort her,' said Mother, 'but you're away from her the whole day. How can she get through a day? Have you thought about that?'

'Of course I've thought about it,' replied Huang Zhuqing firmly. 'I married her after thinking it over carefully. She's very sensitive, well qualified to be a writer! But she's also very reasonable, and she understands my situation. We only decided to marry quickly when we realized we could understand one another. Her situation is so desperate that otherwise she wouldn't have agreed to marry me.'

Mother watched him quietly as he spoke so gravely and emotionally. She suddenly saw him in a new light: a young man of principle. She mumbled to herself, 'Ah, our youngsters nowadays!' Her voice expressed amazement and wonder mixed with admiration. Suddenly jolting her out of her reflections, Huang Zhuqing said, 'Oh, it's getting late. I must go; I have to go to Wanzhen. I'll come and see you again!'

He turned towards the door, but when he put his hand on the latch and was just about to open it, he suddenly hesitated, as if he had just thought of something. Noticing his vacillation, Mother stopped him.

'First have supper here. I'm just going to prepare it. It'll be ready very soon!'

He looked at Mother and hesitated a moment.

'No, I have to go to Wanzhen!' He spoke more resolutely now. 'I have to go right away. The curfew's starting soon. Goodbye!'

He opened the door latch and slipped out. Through a crack in the door, I watched him running away in the dusk, as if he were afraid of anyone seeing him and hoped that darkness could protect him. I quietly closed the latch and stood by the door with Mother and Father, all of us gazing at one another. Our minds were drained; we were incapable of thinking. It was Mother who stirred first, with the same words she had just uttered.

'Ah, our youngsters nowadays!'

Three days later, at about ten in the morning, my young master, Ho Shuoru, sent me to Hui Wen Bookshop – the biggest bookshop in town – to buy a history book, *Outline of History*, written by the British writer H.G. Wells. The bookshop was right in the busy centre, crowded with people. Just as I got to the entrance of the shop, I caught sight of a big notice newly pasted on the side wall. The headline read:

#### COMMUNIST RINGLEADER HUANG ZHUQING EXECUTED

I suddenly felt shivery all over, my head spinning and my eyes dazed. After a while, when I had recovered a bit, I read the notice in detail. It was true – the notice stated clearly that he had really been executed. It was indeed the young schoolteacher who had come to our home. He was accused of 'secretly organizing students and plotting against the Nationalist Party and State'. He was 'one of the most important ringleaders of the communist bandits' in the city. On such and such a day he 'slipped out to carry out secret activities before the curfew' and he was 'arrested just in time by our special agents, and thus student disorders were avoided'. The certain day mentioned in the notice was just the day Huang Zhuqing visited our home. Suddenly my heart sank and my legs felt weak. I had no strength to go into the shop to buy the book, so I could only make up a story to Ho Shuoru that the book was not in stock yet and would be available in two days. That day I was so disturbed that I almost dropped the tea cup when I twice served him tea. I could hardly wait for evening to come, and then I dragged myself home. Father did not go back with me, as our employer kept him there a while, asking him what progress his naughty children were making. So I told Mother about the notice.

Her face turned pale, and she couldn't speak for a while. She turned her head away slightly as if to stop me seeing the tears which she was trying hard to control. She mumbled to herself, 'He was a ringleader of the communist bandits!' Then she continued, turning to me, 'My child, according to this, you could also be a "ringleader of the communist bandits!" '

'He shouldn't have left that day,' I said, 'If he had stayed with us for the night, perhaps this tragedy wouldn't have happened.'

'Oh, what's the use of saying that now!' retorted Mother with a sigh. 'Unluckily, it was the fifteenth of the seventh month, just that fateful day when the ghosts wander around freely . . .'

41

Who would have thought that Ho Ludong's family would also meet with misfortune? Our family was the direct cause, even though we were so careful about everything. The person involved was my father – always conscientious in his job, no trouble-maker, an old shop assistant and family tutor with no interest in politics. The incident happened just after I had cleared up Ho Shuoru's study and went into his father's sitting room to do the cleaning there. At this moment two strangers suddenly burst in. Ho Ludong had kept up contact with some businessmen and regular customers, and although his 'shop' had already been closed down and moved to his mansion, the shop signboard was still hanging at the entrance, and during the day the gate was generally left open. So these two men just entered, came right into the sitting room and shouted roughly, 'Where is Ho Ludong? Call him out! We have something to discuss with him.'

One of these men looked like a gentleman, the other rough, but they both appeared very strange. The latter had a pistol at his waist, his hands on his hips, a fat face and arched eyebrows, looking rather like a bandit. The other was wearing a long gown and in his hand was a fan, which he was waving gently. He looked like a scholar or a kind of instructor in an organization for secret agents. His face was waxen, like an opium addict's. I immediately had the feeling that these two were up to no good. I did not want them to stay in the empty sitting room with nobody to watch them. Just as I was hesitating whether to go in and call Ho Ludong, he came straight out himself, probably after hearing them shout. He did not seem prepared, though, as he looked very surprised. He soon recovered his composure, however.

After sizing up these two, he soon guessed what their business was. Then he bowed to them, clasping his hands in greeting, and asked politely, with a smile, 'What can I do for you two gentlemen?'

'We're officers of the special branch of the investigation department of the garrison headquarters,' answered the opium-addict type. 'We've heard that the former secretary of the shop assistants' trade union was an employee in your shop. Is that right?'

'Please sit down,' Ho Ludong repeated several times. 'Chunsheng, hurry up and get some tea for our guests!'

I immediately obeyed his instructions and served tea to the 'guests' and my employer. The two 'guests' displayed bad manners by sitting in the two armchairs, stretching their legs and resting their hands on the arms of the chairs, as if they were going to jump up at any moment. The one with the pistol kept tapping the chair and repeated the question the other had asked, preceded by, 'Did you hear what he said?'

Ho Ludong bowed again and clasped his hands before replying, 'Yes! Yes! But as soon as he became secretary he left my shop and has had nothing to do with it since.'

'Well, that's very simple,' the opium addict said. 'Where has he gone? You must know. Speak up now!'

Ho Ludong swallowed some tea, no doubt to calm himself. Then he glanced at me, indicating, I felt, that I should not reveal who I was or that I was related to the union secretary whom they were seeking. He was, of course, my elder brother, Zhao Jue.

'He's on the move,' Ho Ludong argued. 'The world is so big. How should I know?'

'He can't run away,' said the opium addict. 'He worked for you for so many years, you must know him well. How come you don't know where he is?'

Meanwhile the man with the pistol swayed his hips, lightly patting the butt of his pistol.

'We're very busy people. We have plenty of cases to work on, so we cannot spend too much time here. Just tell us the truth. When can you get hold of him for us?'

Ho Ludong remained silent for a while. He realized that these two thugs were agents of the garrison headquarters, and they might have no connection with the two military chiefs of the Guangxi faction who controlled this province. In any case, he did not have time to get hold of his son-in-law, Chen Chuqing, to contact the provincial leaders. He was already in the hands of these two men and could not move an inch. Now he suddenly turned pale, realizing that the situation was very dangerous.

'My shop has been closed for quite a long time,' he replied. 'The staff have all left and gone their separate ways. How could I get hold of him?'

'So you won't?' said the one with the pistol. 'Just come aong with us to the garrison headquarters and we'll deal with you there. I told you we can't spend so much time on you. Let's go!'

He stood up, as if he were going over to Ho Ludong. The 'opium addict' also stood up, as if they were really going to drag Ho Ludong off to the garrison headquarters. Now his forehead was covered with beads of sweat. Perhaps he was thinking of the recent rumours in town. This had also happened to other local merchants and small entrepreneurs. It looked as if they had been 'invited' to the garrison headquarters, but in fact not far from home they had ended up with a few bullets in their head. If Ho Ludong could not satisfy them, he would probably meet the same fate. So, wiping the sweat from his brow with his sleeve, forcing a smile and bowing again a few more times, he said, 'Please do me a favour. I would come straight to your headquarters, but unfortunately yesterday evening my wife got sick and went into hospital. Today she'll be having an appendix operation, so I have to go there to sign for her. I'll call my son-in-law, Chen Chuqing, to go with you, if that's possible. First rest here for a while.' Then he instructed, 'Make some tea for the guests.'

He headed towards the next room to make a telephone call, but he had hardly moved a step when the man with the pistol leaped towards him, seized him by the collar and glared at him.

'Is that the Chen Chuqing who does business with the insurance company and foreign banks?'

Ho Ludong nodded. 'That's him. He's my son-in-law.'

'Foreign lackey!' shouted the one with the pistol. 'You want to call him to appeal to the authorities for you, do you? I'll just shoot you on the spot!'

He started fingering his pistol with his free hand, making it click, so that Ho Ludong was frightened out of his wits.

The 'opium addict' immediately grasped his mate by the hand that was holding the pistol. Pretending to calm him down, he said, 'Brother, don't get excited. Manager Ho is a clever man. If you get so excited and grab his collar like that, he can't do anything.'

'OK, I'll give him five minutes,' said the one with the pistol, letting go of Ho Ludong's collar. But he immediately stuck his hand in front of the merchant's face and said threateningly, 'Hurry up. Remember, you've only got five minutes!'

At this point, my employer, and I too, realized what these two were up to. He nodded and bowed repeatedly, pleading pathetically, 'Don't worry. I'm going inside and I'll be back in a minute.'

He hurried into the other room and came out promptly, carrying a tray piled with banknotes. Nodding and bowing all the while, he gave the tray to the one with the pistol.

'Please excuse me,' he said ingratiatingly, 'since my shop has been closed for a long time, I have only this left.'

The tough guy with the pistol looked up and clenched his fist in front of the shop-owner's face, shouting, 'Nonsense! Are you blind? There are two of us! I'll give you five more minutes.'

Then he pointed the pistol at Ho Ludong's head. In a flash, gasping 'Yes! Yes!', Ho Ludong went back into his room. After a while – this time it was more than five minutes – he re-emerged with another tray piled with banknotes, which he offered meekly to the opium addict. Perhaps because he was thinner, this one moved more adroitly than the tough guy. He grabbed the money with one sweep and stuffed it inside his gown. Then the two 'secret agents' signalled to one another, turned and left without a word.

Ho Ludong stared after them, as if he had seen a ghost, and then laughed loudly. But he was soon silent again, gazing down and muttering to himself.

'Flown away with one thousand dollars! Who the devil sent two robbers in broad daylight!'

Then, turning to me, he continued, 'If they knew that you and your Father were still in my house, even giving them another thousand dollars wouldn't help. Tell your Father he was lucky not to have been here to witness what happened! I bore the brunt of it!'

Of course, my Father soon heard about the visitation of the two demons. Our employer came to the 'classroom' at the back to tell him about the incident in detail, but he remained calm. Many years of experience in business had trained him. He knew the incident had already happened, so blaming my Father for causing this trouble would not help, but, on the contrary, would make matters worse. Moreover, my father had always been loyal to him and had worked hard for his business half his life. He also knew that Father was rather timid. He only wanted to explain the situation to him, so that Father would understand that, in these difficult circumstances, he must leave. Father listened and nodded, thanking his employer for understanding and not blaming him.

'I must really apologize to you,' said my Father. 'My son has caused you so much trouble, but he's a grown-up now and he has his own ideas, so I have no control over him. Only . . .'

'I'm not blaming you,' interrupted our employer. 'My Shuoru is just the same; he has his own ideas and I can't control him either. These times are so confusing and everyone is changing! Only . . .'

He broke off there, making Father nervous, as he could not guess what he meant by 'Only . . .'. Father could only gape at him awkwardly. His employer must have felt that he could make his point now, so he went on, 'Only nowadays anyone can frighten and harm people by waving the banner of anti-communism. The two creatures who came today could be agents from the garrison headquarters or perhaps simply the chiefs of the criminal secret society: the Blue and Red Gang.* Of course, they are all of the same ilk, hand in glove. I can't offend them, so I have to accept that.'

'Luckily, you have many ways and means,' said Father. 'You could just get rid of them without any trouble. As the saying goes: "When the thief has left, people feel safe." Please think this over.'

This time Ho Ludong gazed at Father, shaking his head as he replied, 'You think we can feel safe? They could come back any time! What do you think I should do when they come next time? They don't yet know that you and your son are still working here.'

Only at this point did Father fully realize what his employer had in mind. He hung his head in silence.

Ho Ludong also remained deliberately silent, while his slit eyes stared even harder at Father, waiting for his response. Father looked up furtively and met his employer's gaze. Then, frightened, he looked down again. I also felt that Father had to say something at this point, but he was at a loss for words. I felt very sorry for him, but what could I say?

'It was we . . . it was we who caused your trouble,' mumbled Father pathetically. 'If we stayed on here, we would get you into worse trouble. I think we should leave . . .'

Father was unable to go on, but his employer seemed to feel that it was unnecessary for him to continue. He only wanted to hear Father utter that word 'leave'. Giving the game away, he simply asked, 'When?'

The question was so abrupt that Father was taken aback. He looked up again at his employer, to make sure that he really wanted him to leave. His eyes were so hard and cold that there was no doubt about his question. Father's eyes had become misty and blurred, but suddenly they brightened, as if his doubt was dispelled. He now spoke with a firm voice.

'Right, I'll leave – and my son Chunsheng too.'

---

* With ramifications all over the country, working in league with government officials to plague the people. It was eradicated after the establishment of the People's Republic.

47

All the frustration so long buried in the merchant's heart suddenly erupted in a single word.

'Fine.'

With this, he turned and stalked out. He did not mention the salary which he owed Father or ask him what he planned to do. Father stared for a while at his rapidly receding figure, then picked up his empty cloth bag and left the house. His textbooks were still lying on the table, as he did not want to take them. He seemed to have decided not to be a teacher any longer.

When we reached the street, he felt weak and started to stagger, so I quickly supported him. He seemed not only physically weak, but also mentally exhausted. He put his hand on my shoulders for support and I began to feel his weight.

As soon as we got home, Mother saw that his face was exceptionally pale and that he had difficulty in breathing, and he was more confused now. She helped him to the bed to lie down.

'What's the matter with you?' she asked Father.

Father opened his eyes slightly, looking at Mother as if she were a stranger, then, as if he had just recognized her, he said, 'I can feel my heart beating fast. My mind . . . is so confused . . .'

Mother quickly poured a cup of warm water and held it to his lips. He took two sips and immediately closed his eyes again.

'What happened?' Mother turned to me, looking frightened.

'Father's teaching is finished and so is my work. From now on we won't have anything to do with the boss!'

'I realized when you came back early today, looking so distressed, that something bad must have happened. But as long as nothing has happened to your brother I can stand any misfortune. You must tell me the whole story in detail later.'

Then she took a blanket out of her wardrobe and put it carefully over Father. She sat down next to the table, and I next to her. Our dog, Laipao, also seemed to sense that something was amiss in the family. He lay silently by my foot, his head raised and his eyes keenly observing us, as if he were waiting to hear what I was going to relate to Mother. She stroked his head as she heard how Father and I had lost our jobs.

Unexpectedly, Mother did not show any surprise or anguish

after she had heard my story. She kept exceptionally calm, although her eyes were moist with tears.

'Don't worry, my child. Your father is obviously ill, very ill, and he is unconscious. We must keep calm. After Huang Zhuqing's death, we didn't want to stay in this place anyway. We don't belong here.'

'So what are we going to do?'

Mother could not answer for a while. But to cover up her distress and to assuage my anxiety, she patted Laipao's head, asking, 'What do you think, Laipao?'

Laipao looked at Mother, then at me, with a vacant expression.

'So, you still can't answer, can you? All right, don't answer just now. I think you're hungry. Chunsheng is hungry too. I'll prepare something for you.'

Mother put on her apron and went to the stove to prepare supper. She did not say any more, her head lowered, her heart heavy. In fact, the casual words she had just spoken to Laipao were completely forced.

By chance, the answer which Laipao could not give was offered by an unexpected visitor two days later. One morning just after the night curfew in town, when Mother went out to throw away the rubbish, this visitor followed her in through the open door. Now Mother was so troubled and desperate about how to cope with Father's illness and all the family affairs, she had not noticed the visitor who had followed her in and was standing in the middle of the room. She only discovered him when she looked round. He looked familiar and yet she was not quite sure. Mother and I looked at him suspiciously and anxiously, asking ourselves: Isn't this an agent from the garrison headquarters? How did he know where we live? But he did not look a bad type. He was about fifty years old, wearing an old blue cloth gown and cap, which gave him the appearance of a small merchant. The flap of his cap was so broad that it completely covered the upper part of his face. We could only see his nose and mouth, but of course he could see us clearly. As he looked at us, a smile crept over his face, and he said, 'Don't you recognize me?'

His voice sounded even more familiar.

'Oh, you can't be Uncle Pan!' my mother suddenly exclaimed. 'How did you find this place?'

When Uncle Pan took off his cap, he smiled even more broadly. It could not be our Uncle Pan! That was really a miracle. Father seemed to have been affected by Mother's cry, as his eyes opened slightly, but immediately closed again. He was already unable to speak and his reactions were very slow.

Uncle Pan's smile suddenly vanished and he hurried up to Father to stroke his forehead, but Father still did not respond.

'Oh, how did he get so ill? I couldn't imagine he was sick.'

'He got ill suddenly,' replied Mother. 'He hasn't vomited or had diarrhoea, but his mind isn't functioning. He's unconscious now. We can't do anything for him.'

Uncle Pan looked at Father and sighed, as he could not think of a solution. As Father was lying peacefully in a sleep-like state, we did not want to disturb him. Uncle Pan left him alone and continued where he had broken off.

'It was Sweet Potato who gave me your address. He's still a messenger in our town, so he often comes to this city. Those rich families in the countryside who do business here still use him as a messenger. Your boss, Ho Ludong, occasionally asks him to run errands, so he sometimes goes there. Since he knows this place, I can naturally get news about you from him.'

'So how does he know where we live?' asked Mother.

'Ho Ludong still has relatives in his native village, where he also has some land, property and particularly his ancestral grave. He has kept up his links with his village. Every time Sweet Potato comes here he has to go to the boss's house, where he has a meal and brings letters or village gossip, which Ho Ludong likes to hear. Sweet Potato has known for a long time that you came here from the village, and, of course, he gets news about you from Ho's family. Bringing news is his job! He also wants to come and see you.'

'Weren't you intercepted by revolutionaries on your way home?' Mother asked anxiously. 'We heard that your beloved little cow was confiscated.'

Uncle Pan nodded.

'Yes, that's right.'

'So, how could you get away again?'

'I've got two legs! Why couldn't I run away?'

'Didn't they capture you again?'

Uncle Pan just shook his head without answering.

'Why did you come to "The Big City"?' Mother continued. 'It's expensive to live here. Country folk don't come here!'

Uncle Pan once again avoided answering this question directly, but added, 'And even more frightening. They kill people every day!'

'Aren't you afraid?'

'I'm already over fifty. Most of those they kill are young!'

'So how can you live here?' said Mother anxiously. 'There are no fields to farm here.'

Once again Uncle Pan just shook his head.

Because of Uncle Pan's inexplicable reticence, Mother and I both suddenly felt strangely sad. Poor Uncle Pan, when he used to live with us in the countryside, he sometimes kept quiet like this for no special reason. His silence now, however, seemed to be different, as if it had some deep significance, and there was even something mysterious about it. Was it possible that Uncle Pan had changed? Yes, people can change. We heard that after he had been captured by the revolutionaries he was sent to a study class. After staying with them and studying for a while, he might have changed. Mother, however, seemed to be thinking of the good old days when we were living a simple life in our old home. So when she spoke, her voice sounded full of regret.

'If it was like the past in our old home, it would be easy: we could live together again. Uncle Pan, I've been thinking of you ever since you left! But now, oh . . .'

Mother sighed. What she wanted to say was: We cannot go back home!

Uncle Pan did not respond directly to Mother's nostalgic reflections. Instead, he addressed me.

'Chun, pour me a cup of tea!'

He sat down on a stool next to the table, as if he were going to have a good talk with us about the past.

'Now, I would like to talk to you about going back to our old home, Ma'am. Yesterday I learned from Sweet Potato something

51

about your life here and what has happened recently – that's why I've come here specially today.'

'What did you hear from Sweet Potato?' asked Mother, startled. 'What did you hear?'

Uncle Pan drank some tea, while glancing first at Mother and then at me.

'It's better if you tell me. You can give me more details. I just got the rough story from Sweet Potato. Come on, after all, we are all one family. I need to know in more detail how Chun's father got so ill. Please, tell me.'

Mother gestured to me.

'You'd better speak, my child. You witnessed it yourself.'

Uncle Pan quietly listened to my account. He listened so attentively and seriously that when I mentioned certain points he stopped me to ask some crucial questions, and I had to answer in detail. It looked as if he were not just listening, but thinking about it carefully. Uncle Pan had indeed changed; he seemed to have become wiser. My mother was forming a new impression of him, surprised at this transformation.

When he had heard the whole story, Uncle Pan drank some more tea and sat with his head down, deep in thought. Then he tapped the table as if thinking even more deeply. After a while he looked up, saying, 'The lackeys of the imperialists, the reactionary armies, spies and thugs are frantically spreading terror. If we don't think of a way, you might also become hapless victims. I think the situation is so critical that you must go back to the countryside without delay. I'll take you back! It's not so chaotic there; there's great hope as the revolutionary forces are growing!'

'Go back to the country? Yes, go back to our native village! I have also been thinking about this problem for the past two days . . .' At this point, Mother suddenly stopped short. She looked at Uncle Pan suspiciously and changed the subject. 'Uncle Pan, how is it that the way you speak now, some words you use, are exactly the same as my elder son's, like "lackeys of the imperialists", "white terror", "revolution" . . .? I simply cannot believe my ears: is this our familiar Uncle Pan talking to us? Where did you learn this language?'

'In that political study class,' answered Uncle Pan, a smile on his lips. 'You just mentioned that I was intercepted by the revolutionaries on my way home. Because of that incident I had the opportunity to study things I wouldn't have dreamed of in the past. I've lived in ignorance half my life, and if I had just gone back home I would perhaps have lived the rest of my life like that. I was born poor, but fortunately, Ma'am, you took me into your home, otherwise I would probably have starved to death. But poverty is not decided by fate, as we used to believe. No, it's inflicted on us by those who spread terror. I've now found the way to change our fate, the fate of all poor people. I'm still not too old; I want to spend the rest of my life working to change our fate!'

'Uncle Pan!' Mother cried out in surprise. 'So you also have become a revolutionary!'

Uncle Pan smiled.

'Call me whatever you like, Ma'am. That's what I am now. I've seen the light.'

'Has the same happened to Lao Liu and our O Ran? Have you seen them?'

'Frequently. They're very well, but extremely busy. In the present circumstances, of course, they're fully occupied.'

'So you've all got involved?'

'That's how it is. We all knew one another well before, but this is a new experience. None of us could have imagined that such a life was possible. Each of us came our own different ways to join together, because we feel that this is the right way for us poor folk.'

'So you want us to go back and join you too?'

'I didn't say that. I just feel that, although life's unsettled now in the countryside, you can go on living there. Your fellow villagers are there, the familiar land – everything you're used to. Living here so isolated, the terror campaign might strike you any time. I cannot let anything happen to you like this again.'

'Can you tell me how bad it is in the country?' asked Mother, now taking Uncle Pan more seriously. 'The more details the better. We've never had any news from home.'

'Yes, I must tell you the real situation.'

He drank some tea to clear his throat. Mother and I kept quiet as we listened to his account. When he noticed how attentive we were, his expression became graver still. It reminded me of the times in our old home. He used to tell us stories as we sat round the low table having supper after working outside the whole day. In those days he always told us stories and anecdotes, embellished with his own imagination. He spoke seriously, as if everything he said were true. This scene from the past was now re-enacted – and Uncle Pan behaved in the same old way.

'When you left the village, Chumin and his reactionary army were just going on the rampage,' he said gravely. 'As we were inexperienced and unprepared, he took the opportunity to gather and expand the Order Preservation Corps, which he had previously used specially to suppress the poor. Then he threatened some of his farm-hands, forcing them to join the Red Spear Society.* That was the game Wang the Lion was playing. He told the Red Spear Society members that if they smashed a communist stronghold or killed some communists, they would receive a reward of one hundred dollars each. Those who didn't join the Red Spear Society would have no land, and if they openly refused they would be treated as communists and shot. He also proclaimed that poverty and wealth were preordained, and that it was unnatural and illegal to accept what the communists advocated – to distribute wealth equally. Not only would they be taken to the county town and executed, but after death they would be condemned to eternal hell.'

Uncle Pan paused for a moment, drinking some more tea.

'Do you remember,' he continued, 'after the Revolutionary Army took the town last year, the revolutionaries also came to our county? The old government office was also changed into a new county government. The first big political decision of the new government was to arrest five landlords who had always oppressed us common folk. They had done so many evil things that all the villagers wanted them to be executed. Finally, one evening, the new county guards took them to an empty spot

* This was a superstitious secret society headed by a sect leader. He had the faculty to draw talismanic figures on a piece of paper which would enable his followers to brave guns and swords without being hurt.

behind Dongyue Temple and shot them. Those who shot them were new recruits with no experience, and when the criminals fell they thought they had accomplished their task. They shouldered their rifles and returned to their headquarters.

'Only when they went back to bury the bodies the next day did they discover that two were missing. By the side there were two bloody tracks leading right up to the wall. Then they realized that these two landlords had not been fatally shot, but only slightly wounded. They had pretended to be dead and in the night crawled up and escaped over the wall. Everyone looked for them all over the place and finally found one of them in a thicket. As he was bleeding too much and couldn't move, he had attempted to hide there for a while. Of course he was recaptured. As for the other landlord, at first nobody could find him. Afterwards we heard that he had found his way to the river outside the town. By chance there was a line of bamboo rafts tied up there for the night. The raftsman, an old acquaintance of the landlord, immediately carried him up to a hut on the rafts to hide. At the same time he released the rafts to float downstream, so that they could escape quickly. In less than two days the rafts reached this town. The landlord was lucky to have survived. He had a friend there, a shop-owner, who immediately took him to a hospital run by the Japanese. The doctors removed the bullets from his body and after a while he recovered. This landlord was the hateful Duan Lianchen, who, as we all know, is a good friend of Chumin.

'When he came out of hospital, he sought refuge in the Japanese concession where he rented a house, living a comfortable life under Japanese protection. But he couldn't forget his big estate in the country and couldn't bear the thought of his former farm-hands farming his land free of rent. After surviving the execution, he became even more conceited. He was still intent on going back to exploit those farmers. He worked hand in glove with Chumin and made connections for him. He linked up with the provincial military lords and corrupt officials and also bought military supplies from Japanese there for Chumin. So Chumin began to be active again in the countryside and his Order Preservation Corps began to display their strength . . .'

'How did you get to know about these events, Uncle Pan?'

Mother interrupted him. She was puzzled, and so was I. 'If we hadn't lived with you for such a long time, we really could hardly imagine that it was you speaking. The expressions you use now remind me of that student who once took refuge in our barn when the spies were searching, and also of that young man who disguised himself as a woman – what was his name?'

'He now calls himself Chang Je-an and he's our political commissar. He still mentions you sometimes and he's very concerned about you.'

'Really, you're together with him now?' Mother asked, even more surprised. 'Where is he?'

'He's still in the countryside, working very hard. Since I left the study class I've been working with him.'

'So you've become a revolutionary too!' said Mother, gaping at Uncle Pan as if he were a stranger. 'Why have you come here now?'

'I have a task.'

'What is it?'

Uncle Pan just smiled. To avoid Mother asking more questions, he resumed his story.

'Duan Lianchen himself also spent a lot of money on bribing a militarist, who then donated a hundred rifles to Chumin over there. Wang the Lion led Chumin's Order Preservation Corps and the Red Spear Society to spearhead the regular troops newly sent by the provincial governor and mop up our revolutionary force. We were inexperienced enough to challenge them in the open fields, with the result that we lost all our weapons. Very soon they reoccupied the county town. There they killed many revolutionaries and then turned their guns on the villagers, killing the leaders of the peasant unions. Those organizations had no weapons at all except a few very old-fashioned rifles and guns left behind by "long-hairs"* many years earlier. These had not been used for a long time, and although some of them fired and could be used to counter-attack, they were all finally

---

* Soldiers with long hair, of the Taiping Peasant Uprising which started fighting against the imperial government of the Ching Dynasty in 1851 and established the Taiping Heavenly Kingdom with Nanjing as its capital until 1864, when they were defeated by the Ching imperial army.

captured by Wang the Lion. We took them on with spears, but how could these match their rifles and guns? I don't know how many of us were slaughtered, but I've never seen so many of our country folk die . . .'

'So you've come here to escape the chaos?' asked Mother.

'No. This sudden attack also taught us a lesson: if we have no strength and no weapons, we farmers will never gain power!'

'How can you gain power by coming here? It's even worse here, the way they kill people. Where can you escape here?'

'You've got it wrong, Ma'am! Didn't I just tell you that I have a task here?'

'What task?' Mother persisted. 'When I asked you just now, you changed the subject! You see, Uncle Pan, it's so chaotic here, I'm worried about you! Can't you trust us, as kith and kin? What's so special that you have to keep it from me?'

'Oh . . .' Uncle Pan hesitated.

'Look, we're only mother, child and an invalid. We have no idea what to do, and we have been longing to discuss these things with someone close to us. You are close to us, Uncle Pan. Why are you so reticent about speaking now?'

'It's not deliberate. I can't explain it all in a moment, and I'm afraid it would even be confusing for you. It's true we're all like one family and trust one another, and there's nothing to hide. To tell you the truth, I came here with a companion, as we have something important to do . . .'

'So you're an important person, Uncle Pan,' Mother interrupted, and smiled to make up for being impatient with him. 'I thought you were still the old Uncle Pan we knew before! I was confused.'

'Not at all, Ma'am. I'm still Uncle Pan, just like before, but now I've learned something and understand the situation better. I've fought a battle against Chumin's lot and have gained some experience, so now the organization has given me different work – "security".'

'Security for what?'

'I can't explain just like that. It's also not necessary for you to understand. Suffice it to say that I've come with this comrade on a security mission. They say I'm good at getting on with people and meticulous in what I do. Also, because I'm older

57

and look like a villager, I wouldn't attract attention like the young students. Don't I look like a minor landlord or small-town grocer?'

'Yes, very much, Uncle,' I replied, 'especially when you wear that long blue gown and hat.'

'That's why we didn't recognize you just now when you came in,' said Mother. 'But what does the man you came with really want to do here? It's bad enough in the country, and here it's even worse. Isn't it asking for trouble to come here in these circumstances?'

'With both town and countryside in upheaval, we must have a clear idea about the next step in our operations. We had to come here to see the provincial revolutionary leaders and get their instructions. The whole country is one huge chessboard. The countryside is not isolated: the upheaval there is part of the upheaval in the whole country – in the whole world. Our revolution is also part of the world revolution. We must have a united command and a co-ordinated policy.'

'Oh dear, Uncle Pan, where did you learn all those new words!' Mother looked astonished, her eyes open wide. 'The way you speak now doesn't sound at all like a farmer.'

'That's not surprising. I gradually learned by working with the revolutionaries every day. We had meetings in which we discussed matters in this way, so I got used to it after using the words frequently. Sometimes I didn't quite understand certain words, so Chang Je-an and Pan Xudong specially explained them to me. They're both learned men with much worldly knowledge. I'm a country bumpkin who didn't know anything before. I was even more ignorant than Lao Liu. But Chang Je-an and Pan Xudong were both so patient with me. When they had any time they explained in detail about the revolution – and, of course, they did the same for other country folk who joined the revolution.'

'What kind of person is Pan Xudong?' Mother continued to ply him with questions. 'Is he a student?'

'Even more erudite than Chang Je-an with his student background,' answered Uncle Pan with obvious respect. 'He went to university. Apparently he has also written articles which were printed in newspapers. This time everyone chose him as a representative to report on the situation in the countryside to the provincial leaders and at the same time to get instructions about the next step in our activities. You know, Chumin and his gang are trying desperately to restore the old order, while we are endeavouring to build a new one – only underground. Pan Xudong is really capable! He's been busy here for quite some time.'

'Has he finished?'

'Just yesterday, otherwise I couldn't have come here today.'

'Does he know you've come here?'

'Of course. He agreed that I should. Sweet Potato also told him about your situation. He said you cannot go on living here, not only because you have no way to support yourselves, but also because it's extremely dangerous – anything might happen within the next few days.'

Mother's expression became animated.

'So he also approved of us moving back to our old home?'

Uncle Pan nodded.

'That's no problem,' he said emphatically. 'Although the countryside is in turmoil, you'll still be among your own folk, after all, like Lao Liu, O Ran and me. However cruel Chumin and Wang the Lion and their gang may be, most of the villagers are not really our enemies. They may be deceived for a while, but they can still be enlightened, not like the Nationalist soldiers here, who cause people such suffering . . .'

Mother hung her head, deep in thought, repeating to herself the two names: 'Lao Liu, O Ran. Lao Liu, O Ran.' Then she looked up to see Uncle Pan's expression. It was grave.

'Uncle Pan,' she asked seriously, 'do Lao Liu and O Ran still remember us?'

'They not only remember you,' Uncle Pan replied vehemently, 'but they also miss you a lot, especially O Ran. Have you forgotten that you brought her up yourself?'

Mother's face suddenly brightened.

'Fine, then, we'll go back to the country!'

Uncle Pan immediately responded in the same way.

'Fine, then, we'll leave tomorrow! We'll come to fetch you at dawn. Comrade Pan Xudong is still waiting for me, so I must leave right away.'

Uncle Pan went up to Father's bed and touched his forehead, but he did not make the slightest sound or react. Uncle Pan's expression suddenly turned grave, and without another word he made for the door and drew the latch. Then he turned to glance at us and went out quietly. After Mother had closed the door, she turned to me.

'My child, Uncle Pan is right, we should go back. He was also right in saying that we have no close friends here. However unstable our village, it's still the place we know best, after all, where our ancestors are buried . . .'

'Yes, Ma. Our few old belongings are easy to pack. I'll do it. You go and see if Father wants to drink anything.'

At dawn the next day, soon after the curfew was over, Uncle Pan came with Sweet Potato, the messenger. They were both carrying shoulder-poles, and they were accompanied by a man with a clean-cut face, aged about thirty-four or thirty-five. He was wearing a grey silk gown and hat, which made him look like a small businessman.

'This is Mr Pan Xudong. He has finished his work here and is going back to the country with us. Have you got everything ready?' asked Uncle Pan.

'We're ready,' Mother answered.

Pan Xudong had already gone up to Father's bed and was observing his expression. Father's eyes were still closed, and he was obviously quite unaware of all the visitors.

'Yes, he's unconscious,' said Pan Xudong. 'Perhaps he got a shock and a blood clot in his brain. We must take him back to the country quickly. Let's move!'

Uncle Pan turned over the small bamboo bed on which I usually slept and tied the two rough bamboo poles to the sides of the bed to serve as a makeshift stretcher. Then he put a quilt on the bed and laid Father on it. He and Sweet Potato then put the 'stretcher' on their shoulders and led the way out. Mother and I had put all our old clothes in two bundles and the ancestral tablet in a cardboard case, which we now carried on our shoulders. Pan Xudong followed, brandishing a walking-stick and wearing sun-glasses to look like the owner of some big shop. This is how we set out on our journey back to the countryside.

Although this dilapidated hut was not our home, we had, after all, spent some time here, so Mother seemed a little sorry to leave. When we left, she turned and looked back several times, walking rather slowly. Our dog, Laipao, pressed close to her, as if he were also somewhat regretful. Only when Pan Xudong reminded her that time was pressing did she quicken her pace. Laipao started wagging his tail, innocently following her. Perhaps he thought we were once again moving to an interesting new place – perhaps a more peaceful place – to settle down.

In the town nothing untoward happened to us. Although passers-by and patrolling soldiers sometimes cast us curious glances, nobody came to investigate, as it was quite common for a family to take a sick relative back to their old village home. After about an hour we came to the outskirts of the town, where there were soldiers on guard. They called to us to stop, and Pan Xudong waved his walking-stick as a signal to us. Getting the message, we stopped, and Uncle Pan and Sweet Potato put the bed down.

Two Nationalist soldiers with rifles came over and one of them asked, 'What are you doing?'

'Carrying my uncle back to our village,' said Pan Xudong. 'He's mortally sick and must be back home within two days.'

'What's your job?'

'He's the boss of Yuqing shop,' replied Uncle Pan, and then, pointing to Sweet Potato, he added, 'We're all shop assistants there.'

Sweet Potato kept quiet, although he had never heard of any such shop. The two soldiers went up to the bed and lifted up the quilt. My father's eyes were closed; he was unconscious. Without a word they covered him with the quilt again, but they questioned my mother:

'And you?'

'She's my aunt,' answered Pan Xudong. 'She has to look after her sick husband on the way.' Then he pointed to me and explained, 'He's my cousin. If something happens to my uncle, he'll have to carry out the mourning rites as a filial son.'

The two soldiers did not pursue their questioning but just exchanged glances. Pan Xudong understood what they wanted and immediately took a handful of banknotes out of the pocket of his grey silk gown. The two soldiers instinctively stretched out their hands. Playing his role of Yuqing shop-owner, Pan Xudong generously divided the notes equally and squeezed them into their open palms, which they clasped around the money, stuffing it into their trouser pockets greedily. Realizing that they were letting us pass, Uncle Pan and Sweet Potato picked up the stretcher and started on their way again. Laipao also seemed relieved to have passed through safely and started wagging his tail, bounding forward freely beside us. After a few steps he suddenly ran up to a nearby mound and lifted up his leg to piss.

Then we heard one of the soldiers say, 'That creature looks good. Tonight we can enjoy a dish of roast dogmeat with wine.'

Then we heard a rifle-shot. Our Laipao fell to the ground before finishing his business. My mother stopped in her tracks, uttering a shriek, and then ran frantically towards the two soldiers, challenging them to save our beloved Laipao. But Pan Xudong quickly grabbed her sleeve and said, 'Don't let's have any more trouble. Let's get going!'

So the following night we returned to our old home – our familiar village. But we had lost our Laipao.

# CHAPTER 5

The county where our village was situated was divided into two parts, north and south. The land in the south was poor and barren, but strangely enough the people were better off than in the north. That was because not many could make a living by farming, so they had to go to other places to find work, mostly to 'The Big City' on the lower reaches of the long river which flowed through our county. That was where the provincial government was situated and it was also a commercial port with foreign settlements. Some of them became coolies at the docks there, rickshaw pullers or street pedlars. Those with a little education became shop assistants, like my father and brother. A small number took to wheeling and dealing, speculating in the market, and thus pushed their way up from being pedlars to small tradesmen, finally becoming wealthy. Then they would send money home to their village to buy land and would become landlords there, trade being dependent on fluctuations in the market and not as stable as land.

It was said that Chumin, who was a big landlord in the southern part of the county, had a grandfather who started off as a pedlar in this town. When he had saved a little money, he went to Szechuan province to buy opium, which he transported here for sale. When he had made a lot of money, he went back to his home town to buy land. By the time his son was born, he had become one of the few big landlords in these parts. Chumin inherited the family property and used his acquired wealth and connections with county officials. He employed all kinds of tactics to grab most of the good land in the southern part of the county, thus becoming a land baron here. After the peasant unions were established in the countryside, he was

63

almost killed by the new revolutionary forces, but he escaped. Soon he developed his own armed forces and took on the revolutionary forces.

'When Chiang Kai-shek attacked the communists with the support of the imperialists, Chumin became bolder.' This was how Pan Xudong had described him on the way back to our village. 'Now he has become even more vicious, but he's counting on his Order Preservation Corps, which has about a hundred rifles, and the Red Spear Society, made up of a group of duped peasants. The vast majority of peasants hate him. His armed forces only hold sway during the day-time, afraid to go out at night. But our men can go about freely at night. That's how strong Chumin is!'

We just happened to be crossing into our county at night. At the north–south border we met two scouts going to the southern part. They were sent to observe enemy activities by the revolutionary headquarters in the mountains in the north. Afterwards I learned from Uncle Pan that even though the southern part was under the control of Chumin's forces, the revolutionary headquarters often sent scouts to observe his activities. Sometimes they even destroyed the base of the Red Spear Society, captured their hated leaders or burned down the houses of the Order Preservation Corps officers. So Chumin's men did not dare go out as soon as night set in. The two scouts stopped us. When they learned that Pan Xudong was with us, they almost jumped with delight, because they said that the 'headquarters' were waiting anxiously for his return. One of them, a man of about forty who looked like a farmer and was called Pan Zaixing, took over the stretcher from Sweet Potato and carried my father with Uncle Pan on our way home. Pan Xudong and Sweet Potato went to the 'headquarters' in the north accompanied by the other scout, Liu Dawang.

It was already midnight by the time we reached our village, so nobody was aware when we entered, except for an old dog which barked feebly at us. But when Uncle Pan gently called to him, he recognized the voice and fell quiet. On the gate of our house there was still a big lock, which Mother touched suspiciously.

'Somebody has changed the lock,' she said. 'It looks as if the house has been occupied.'

'That's not likely,' said Uncle Pan. 'I didn't forget about the house, and O Ran and Lao Liu were also concerned about it. When we sent people out to scout, we asked them to come and check here, if they happened to come to this village. They never said that the house had been occupied.'

No sooner had he said this than we caught sight of a figure coming towards us. In the darkness we made out the faint shape of a woman. Finally we realized that this was She-crow, the widow of Chumin's farm-hand, Mao Mao. Her hair was dishevelled and her clothes shabby. Although we could not see her face clearly, she had obviously changed; she no longer had her powerful physique. She was the first person to come and 'welcome' us.

'Ah, you're back again!' she said. 'Just now when I heard the dog bark, I thought somebody had probably come into the village, so I opened my door to have a look. When I heard Uncle Pan call the dog, I summoned up courage to come and investigate. It's true, it is you! This house of yours has caused me a lot of anxiety.'

She took off a key from a key-ring dangling from her waist and unlocked the door. So it was she who had locked it.

'Your lock was broken by the Order Preservation Corps sent by Master Chumin,' she explained. 'My father wondered what you would do if you came back one day and the door was open. He asked me to look after it.'

'Why should they break people's locks?' asked Uncle Pan. 'Aren't they the Order Preservation Corps? How can they keep order like this?'

'They said that Lao Liu was some propagandist for the revolutionaries,' said She-crow. 'They wanted to check if there was anything left behind here. Didn't he marry O Ran? He's your son-in-law!'

'Did they search for me?' asked Uncle Pan.

'Yes,' replied She-crow. 'They said you were kidnapped by the revolutionaries and must have suffered at their hands, so you must hate them. They're still planning to rescue you and

65

make you an officer in the Order Preservation Corps or Red Spear Society.'

'Well, here I am. But you mustn't tell anyone, under any circumstances. I don't want any position. I'm no longer a villager here!'

'Can't I even tell my father? Chumin made him *Bao* chief\* here. He should know you're still alive and have visited the village!'

'Absolutely not!' Uncle Pan spoke in a warning tone.

After this conversation with She-crow, we went into the house. Only when we lit a candle did we notice that She-crow, who had followed us in, had really got much thinner. She had not only lost a lot of weight, but her formerly full, sun-tanned face had become gaunt, like a dried-up lemon. Her eyes were sunken, strangely set into her bony eye sockets, which made them seem much bigger and brighter than before – only her eyes made me realize that she must still be a young woman. Probably after Mao Mao died nobody did the farming for her, and so she looked half-starved. Now, seeing Father lying on the bamboo bed, she cried out in surprise, 'What's the matter with you, Uncle? How did you get so sick?'

My father was still completely unconscious. His lifeless eyes did not open to look at her.

'I see!' She-crow cried out again, and then muttered, 'No wonder you hurried back now – in the middle of the night!'

'Enough, She-crow,' said Uncle Pan. 'Since it's late you should go back home to sleep. But remember, please don't say a word about my coming back to the village! This good friend of mine is a strong farmer – also a part-time quarryman, and he can beat people, and when he beats you his fist is as heavy as a sledgehammer!'

He pointed at Liu Dawang, and only then did I notice what a strongly built man he was.

\* An administrative system organized on the basis of households enforced by the Nationalist government to consolidate its rule at the grass-roots level. A *Bao* was made up of ten *Jia* and a *Jia* consisted of ten households.

'I've really beaten quite a lot of people in my time,' said Liu Dawang in a low voice, 'especially those who talk too much!'

'I'm going! I'm going!' said She-crow. 'I always keep my word. I definitely won't tell anyone, even my father, about you!'

'Hmm, you silly girl, what secret are you going to keep from your father?'

The words came from outside. Then an old man came in, thin and tall. As soon as he saw us, he stepped back.

'Really!' he said, 'so you've returned! When I realized that my daughter hadn't come back for some time, I came over here to have a look. So you've come back! Ah, Uncle Pan, you're here at the right time. The Order Preservation Corps have been looking for you all over the place. They want to ask you to be an officer. Oh dear, nowadays nobody wants to be an officer under Master Chumin. It's very strange!'

'Not at all strange. I tell you, Zhu the Ninth, I don't want to be an officer either,' said Uncle Pan, 'so I just warned your daughter not to tell anyone that I'm back in the village. Now I warn you as well!'

Zhu the Ninth gaped at Uncle Pan as if he could not believe his own ears.

'What's the matter, Uncle Pan? You're usually so easy-going. How have you become so tough now? You have changed!'

'I haven't put on weight. How could I have changed? I just don't want to be an officer. I'm warning you again, you must definitely not tell anyone about my return. I hear you've now become an official yourself, haven't you?'

Suddenly Zhu the Ninth frowned. He nodded with embarrassment, looking as if he were almost about to cry because of his pent-up grievances.

'Yes, it was Master Chumin who forced me – because nobody else wants to. He gives me three pecks of rice every month as payment. You know, the countryside is now in disorder, so no family distils wine after harvest and nobody employs me to do the job. There's no work for me, so I have to do this! The only thing was to become a *Bao* chief and receive rice from Master Chumin. To tell you the truth, it isn't enough rice, so I had to move to my daughter's place and squeeze in with them to avoid starving. Master Chumin trusts me and thinks I'm suitable to take on this glorious work in the village, because he says I'm the elder relative of a "martyr" – because I'm Mao Mao's father-in-law. Poor Mao Mao was captured by the revolutionaries and jumped into a river on the way and drowned. Master Chumin says he's a "martyr" and instructs all his tenants to learn from Mao Mao.'

'Do you know what the *Bao* chief does?' asked Liu Dawang.

'He protects society against criminals,' Zhu the Ninth said spontaneously.

'And also he fights the communists,' added Liu Dawang.

'I haven't fought them yet.'

'Yes you have,' Liu Dawang corrected him. 'Every time Wang the Lion sent the Red Spear Society to the north part of the county to molest the people there, didn't you help him by mobilizing the villagers whom Chumin forced to join the society?'

'Chumin told me that this was the duty of the *Bao* chief – I have to do something to earn my rice!' said Zhu the Ninth, but he immediately felt that he shouldn't have said this. He suddenly asked, 'How do you know I often mobilize the villagers?'

'If you don't want people to know something, you'd better not do it,' said Uncle Pan calmly. 'Even in the northern part of the county everyone knows what you've done. Of course, I also heard about it. What's strange about that?'

Zhu the Ninth stared into the dark night, deep in thought.

'Yes, I remember now.' He turned to Uncle Pan. 'I remember now. One night someone tapped on my door. When I opened the door, I saw two villagers standing there. They were wearing big straw hats, with the rims pulled so low that I couldn't see their faces. They said to me, "Correct your ways. You'd better not continue following Chumin and Wang the Lion causing suffering to the people, otherwise you're finished! This time we're just warning you." Then they turned and went off. I've been wondering ever since who these people were. I thought they were probably thieves knocking to see if anyone was at home. When they saw I was in, they just tried to frighten me . . .'

'Did you tell Chumin?' asked Uncle Pan.

'I was too embarrassed to tell him. Although I am a *Bao* chief, not even thieves respect me, knocking on my door in the night. What use am I to Chumin? Honestly, Uncle Pan, I couldn't show my face!'

'Your face!' said Uncle Pan. 'Those people who knocked on your door couldn't be thieves. I've heard that the revolutionaries in the northern part of the county often send scouts to the south to find out about the Order Preservation Corps and the Red Spear Society and to observe Chumin and Wang the Lion's activities. I'm sure they were revolutionaries coming to you first very politely to give you a warning. Probably they knew that you had only become *Bao* chief to earn a little rice, otherwise I'm afraid they would have taken you away long ago. You should be a little more astute and keep a low profile. Don't overdo it.'

Zhu the Ninth gaped in astonishment.

'So that's it! Fine, they understand my predicament!' he muttered, staring vacantly. We all looked at him without saying anything, just letting him go on staring. After a while he gradually recovered and turned to Uncle Pan.

'You seem to be much wiser than me, Uncle Pan. You've been to many places and had many experiences, so you've really changed. Please tell me, what should I do?'

'It's just as well you didn't tell Chumin and Wang the Lion about the two revolutionaries coming to you! If you had, it wouldn't be the revolutionaries but Chumin who would cut your head off. So in future don't tell them anything. As I warned you, don't tell them that I'm back with Ma'am and Chunsheng – yes, and instruct the villagers not to tell them either. What are three pecks of rice? You're worse off than an ox-herd. It's ridiculous to go on following them tamely.'

She-crow, who had been standing there gazing and listening to Uncle Pan talking to her father, suddenly became alert. She blinked as if distressed, and tears came to her eyes. Then she suddenly pulled herself together and wiped them away with her sleeve, and spoke in an angry voice.

'Now I understand, Father, what kind of official you are – pathetic!' She stuck out her little finger to indicate that her father's position was only that small. 'You're nothing, so nobody presents you with gifts. No wonder, when you assembled the members of the Red Spear Society to go and fight in the north, they were usually passive and listless. You're a starving official. What kind of father-in-law of a "martyr"! If they really wanted to make Mao Mao into a "martyr", they should first make sure his widow got enough to eat! But these days she has been starving, living only on porridge! Father, you can throw your gong away, and let Chumin and Wang the Lion beat theirs to assemble their forces! My poor Mao Mao died for them!'

'Shut up!' Zhu the Ninth stopped his daughter. 'What do you understand? You only know how to curse others, even your father! You never forget that bottomless pit of yours – your big stomach! Off you go! Get back home!'

Now a smile appeared on Uncle Pan's face and he addressed Zhu the Ninth.

'What your daughter says is quite true. You go around beating your gong, mobilizing people just to earn a living, but she can hardly survive on porridge every day! Now it's very late. Don't quarrel, you two. You'd better go home and sleep. I'll be leaving soon too.'

'Right,' said Liu Dawang to Zhu the Ninth, 'go back and have a good sleep. There's nothing else to discuss. I just remind you not to tell anyone that we've come.'

Zhu the Ninth angrily pushed She-crow through the doorway, but as soon as he was outside he seemed to realize that he had not said goodbye, which was not very polite. So he turned round to all of us.

'I never intended to harm anyone. You must believe me, you know me well. I definitely don't want to harm anyone!' Then he specifically addressed my mother. 'I'm sorry, Ma'am, I haven't spoken to you at all, nor to your husband – he seems to be very ill! If you have any problems, just tell me and I'll certainly help. I'll do everything I can! We haven't talked about the village affairs yet, Ma'am. I'll come and see you tomorrow. Right! Go and sleep now.'

The old *Bao* chief disappeared into the darkness with his daughter.

'I don't think he'll cause us any trouble,' said Mother, watching his vanishing shadow. 'I'm sure he wasn't bad before, but now he's been enmeshed in Chumin's and Wang the Lion's net. Oh dear!'

'Anyway, this is no place for you to live, Ma'am,' said Uncle Pan. 'It depends on Runchi's health, but we must try to move you to a safe place. Every night our scouts come to this area to investigate. I'll tell them to come and see you. Please be prepared to move at any time!'

'It wasn't a mistake to come back now,' said Mother. 'When we left here, I was in such a hurry that I forgot to take our genealogical book. Luckily, when they broke into our house they didn't destroy it. This time I must take our family record with us when we move. Then I'll have carried out my duty and I'll feel at ease.' Mother looked up at the ancestral book on the incense table at the back of the room and then turned to Uncle Pan. 'I'll do as you say and get everything ready.'

Uncle Pan went up to Father's bed and stroked his forehead. Father still gave no response. Uncle Pan looked grave, but he did not say any more before leaving with Liu Dawang.

At that moment, from far away, there came the sound of a gong striking four beats at a time. It came from a temple a mile away, where there was a branch of the Red Spear Society. We could hear it very clearly, because the night was still.

The next afternoon, just when my Mother was washing rice for supper, Father's condition suddenly changed a bit. He seemed to have heard my Mother washing the rice and he slowly opened his eyes. Although there was no lustre in them, he still seemed to recognize Mother as he gazed at her. She immediately noticed this and ran over to him, wiping her hands on her clothes. She thought he might have regained consciousness and she gently stroked his forehead and cheeks.

'Chun and I are both beside you,' she said softly. 'It's very peaceful in the village. You mustn't worry about anything. Tomorrow I'll call a doctor to see you.'

I came right up to his bed too and pressed against Mother.

'Chun,' Mother whispered, 'fetch some warm water. He hasn't drunk anything for days: he's parched.'

I brought a bowl of water, but Father slowly closed his eyes. Mother took the bowl and held it up to his mouth. But he could not part his lips any longer, so the water trickled down from the corners of his mouth. As this was no use, Mother sipped some water herself and then passed it drop by drop into his mouth. Father could not swallow, but he slowly opened his eyes again. He looked as if he wanted to say something to Mother, but he could not speak, so he just looked at her lovingly. After a while, Mother bent down and kissed his forehead, then his eyelids, his cheeks and his chin.

'Just rest,' she whispered, 'and you'll get better. You've experienced so many hardships in your life, but you've always overcome them. I'm sure it will be the same this time. We're back in our old home now, and our ancestors will bless you.'

Just then, Father's eyes closed again. I took his hand in mine and stroked it to give him some warmth, sympathy and hope to encourage him. But his hand felt cold and stiff.

'Ma!' I shouted in fright. 'Feel Father's hand!'

Mother took his hand and pressed it between hers. Her face suddenly turned pale and her lips blue. Her right hand moved automatically to his pulse, which she held as if transfixed. She remained there staring until there was a sudden sound at the door, which startled her, so that she moved her hand away.

'Ma'am! I'm late. I intended to come here earlier to see how your husband was doing and have a good talk with you. But early this morning they told me to go to Chumin's house for a meeting. It's a long way, and I've just got back to the village. I'm sorry!'

It was Zhu the Ninth who had come in. When he saw Mother sitting at Father's bedside, not uttering a word and looking stunned, he asked, 'What's the matter, Ma'am? What's happened?'

'There's no need for you to come and see him, Uncle Zhu,' Mother replied mechanically. 'Runchi has left us for ever.'

Zhu the Ninth stood paralysed in the middle of the room for a long time before he finally spoke.

'So he has really left us so quickly. I've come too late. Poor Runchi, he struggled his whole life, but he has departed so quietly.'

At this point Mother seemed to have recovered from shock. She got up and gently covered Father with a sheet. Then she pulled up a chair and asked Zhu the Ninth to sit down, she herself sitting down opposite him. She spoke in a calm voice, suppressing her grief.

'Uncle Zhu, you are now our village head. What do you think we should do, now that we've met with such misfortune? We're completely unprepared for this, only just back home.'

'Didn't I tell you last night, if you have any trouble, just tell me and I'll surely do my best to help. Although I'm no good at anything else, I can help you in the village. What can I do for you?'

'We cannot give Runchi a proper funeral now – with so much trouble here, it's out of the question. I think it would be better to bury him as soon as possible to let him rest in peace beside his ancestors. Do you think this is possible?'

Zhu the Ninth scratched his bald head and sighed deeply.

'It's possible, possible,' he repeated. 'There's an empty coffin in the temple with three layers of lacquer paint. It was left behind by Grandpa Jianqing – his son was trading and getting rich at the old river port, so he moved there to enjoy the rest of his days. As he's not coming back, he asked me to sell this coffin at any price. He doesn't mind how much.'

'That's fine, Uncle Zhu, so I'll buy it. Now it's impossible to think of burial garments . . .'

'That's right!' Zhu the Ninth interrupted Mother. 'Nowadays it's impossible to find a tailor. All burials have to be simple affairs now.'

'All right, Uncle Zhu, so we'll bury him tomorrow morning. Can I ask you to get some villagers to help?'

'That's easy! No problem!' said Zhu the Ninth, to show how capable he was, that he could do anything for anyone and that he was a suitable *Bao* chief. But suddenly he looked worried and scratched his bald head. Mother looked at him to see if he might be changing his mind. After hesitating a while, he continued haltingly, 'I forgot something, something important. You remember I just told you that this morning Chumin and Wang the Lion summoned the Red Spear Society in Chu Family Village . . .' He suddenly stopped again, hesitated, and then continued in a hushed, secretive voice. 'They've decided to send the able-bodied men of the village to the north of the county. I'm afraid nobody will be available to help . . .'

Mother looked shocked and anxious. Leaving the question of the burial for the moment, she asked, 'What are they going to do in the north?'

'These men have been enlisted into the Red Spear Society. They appointed me to be a group leader responsible for several villages around here, mobilizing the people. We're going to root out the communists!'

'How?'

'By fighting them with all our strength. Master Chumin invited sect leaders of the Red Spear Society to stay in his home, sending them to different villages to instil magic power into the members of the Red Spear Society. Those who swallow the talismanic figures prescribed by them on a piece of paper become immune to swords and guns. The communists flee when they see them.'

'But where is the communists' hide-out?'

Once again Zhu the Ninth scratched his bald patch.

'I'm not sure exactly. In any case, the sect leaders and Wang the Lion lead the way. Wherever they say there is a hide-out we have to believe them. No matter if we ruin the crops or burn people's houses, shattering their lives, it all helps to boost Master Chumin's and Wang the Lion's authority. This is also meant to deter people from making revolution here.'

'So the men here are about to set off,' said Mother, returning to the original subject. 'Early in the morning?'

Suddenly Zhu the Ninth seemed to understand, and the troubled expression on his face disappeared.

'Not so early. We still have to wait for Wang the Lion's men to arrive. That'll probably be after breakfast, and then I'll beat my gong to call everyone to assemble at the end of the village. Then we'll go to the crossroads at Maozhaowu to join forces with other groups of the Red Spear Society – that's a mile from here.'

'So we can bury Runchi early in the morning, can't we?' Mother said hastily. 'Of course, we'll need your help in asking some good, strong fellows to assist. In this emergency, we'll have to do without the ceremony. We'll just have to do our best in the circumstances.'

Zhu the Ninth suddenly became more relaxed and animated, saying, 'As long as you think this will do. I can still do you this little favour, although I'm not sure about anything else. We're fellow villagers, after all. Why can't I help? I'll bring them here early tomorrow morning.'

'So we'll get ready. Oh, it's such a rush!'

'I'm very sorry that I wasn't able to do something for Runchi while he was still alive. I hope he'll rest in peace beside his ancestors. I must be going now. See you tomorrow morning!'

Watching his receding figure, Mother said to me sadly, 'It looks as if we'll have to leave this place quickly. It's not safe here. You're no longer a little child. If Chumin gets to know that we've come back to the village, they'll either arrest you or force you to join the Red Spear Society – to go with them to fight the villagers in the north of the county. That would be wicked! It would also destroy our family and put us in the opposite camp from Uncle Pan, Lao Liu and O Ran.'

'You're right,' I said. 'Our people are in the north. We belong there, so we should move there.'

Now a faint smile appeared on Mother's mournful face. She patted me on the shoulder affectionately, just as she used to pat my head when I leaned against her as a child.

'My child, you're really grown up. You know about things.'

Then we started to act quickly. Mother made a funeral garment from the only presentable gown which Father used to wear when he went to his employer. I just put my belongings together into three bundles. Around midnight we were just about ready.

'This time we mustn't forget our genealogical book,' Mother reminded me. 'Last time we left in such a hurry that we forgot it, and I was always worrying about that. The night before the fifteenth of the seventh month I had such a strange dream, and I'm sure it was because of this. The book wasn't worth anything to those men in the Order Preservation Corps, so they left it unharmed, but it's our treasured family heritage. None of our ancestors committed any crimes; they all worked hard for a living. You should remember that! We must never forget them.'

'I'll never forget. If we put the book in a bundle with other things, I'm afraid it might get torn. I'll put it together with the ancestral tablet in the cardboard case and carry it on my back.'

'That's the right idea, do that then. We must respect our ancestors; we mustn't forget our roots.'

Mother spoke these words very solemnly. She held up the gown which she had just altered into a funeral garment and asked me to see if it was proper for Father to wear this for going to see his departed ancestors and if they would have a good impression of him in this attire.

'No problem. The ancestors will certainly be happy to see Father,' I said. 'And he must be glad too, because as he parts from us he goes to rejoin his ancestors.'

'I hope so, my child. If so, what I have done won't have been in vain!'

The faint smile on her face had changed into a bitter expression. It was only then that I noticed that she was extremely pale. She seemed to have aged years in just one day, exhausted both physically and mentally.

'You should eat something, Ma. It's still hours before dawn. You can sleep a bit, propped up on the bed.'

'I'm not at all tired, my child, but you should have something to eat. There's still some food in the wok. Go and heat it up. I'm not at all hungry either.'

Just as I was about to heat the food up, there was a soft knock at the door. Startled, Mother rushed to the door and listened a moment. There was another tap. This was followed by a soft but audible whisper.

'Open the door quickly! It's me, your O Ran!'

Mother recognized the voice and immediately revived. When she swiftly opened the latch, in walked a young woman – our O Ran. She fell into Mother's arms, crying: 'Ma! Ma! My mama!' Then they both sobbed. When I realized that it was O Ran, who had looked after me as a child, I could not help crying too. I hugged her as I had when we were small, as if I feared she would leave again. Only when I heard a man's voice did I release her, and we stopped crying. I wiped away my tears and looked – it was Lao Liu standing by my father's bedside: he had come in quietly behind O Ran, so we had not seen him. He had closed the door silently and had been looking at Father.

'Don't cry. It's not the time to cry. Look, have you thought about what to do with Father?'

'I've already arranged it with Zhu the Ninth,' answered Mother. 'We're burying him early in the morning. Zhu the Ninth is looking for some villagers to help us bury him – beside the graves of his ancestors. Lao Liu, you've come in the nick of time. We have to discuss with you what to do next.'

'What do you plan to do? Uncle Pan has already told us all about your situation. That's why we rushed here to see you tonight . . .'

'Did anyone see you coming?' Mother interrupted.

'Of course not. We came all the way with our night scouts and entered the village after they had investigated the situation here. They're still waiting outside the village.'

'I'm really relieved to hear that. It's very dangerous here!'

'Dangerous in what way? Uncle Pan has already told our people over there about Zhu the Ninth. Do you have any new information?'

'Yes, we have!' I replied. 'Zhu the Ninth told us that just after breakfast this morning the Red Spear Society here will set off under Wang the Lion's command to attack the villagers in the north.'

Mother nodded, adding, 'What Chun says is quite true. Look, he's grown up and concerned about us all now. We cannot stay here a day longer in this critical situation.'

'Right!' said Lao Liu. 'We've already decided with Uncle Pan to take you there to live with us.'

'The situation can't be as bad over there, can it?' Mother asked, sounding a little hesitant.

'There are some reactionary troops stationed there, with more weapons than here. But the villagers are better organized there, so the soldiers don't dare to come out alone even in the daytime. So they have to dispatch urban troops to disrupt the villages and then get back to town immediately. There they stay at night, afraid to move. So it should be safer for you to live there and we won't feel so anxious.'

'So when should we move?'

'Tomorrow night,' answered Lao Liu and O Ran together. 'Some of our people will come to fetch you. After burying Father, be careful and wait quietly for us, and we'll definitely come in the night.'

'So it's settled,' said Mother sadly. I knew she was loath to leave Father so soon after his burial.

'Time is pressing,' said Lao Liu. 'We have to go back right away and report the situation. Don't take it too badly, Ma.'

Thereupon he pulled O Ran away and they turned and left.

This was the first time that our former story-teller, Lao Liu, had called my mother 'Ma'. Mother watched them as they departed, unable to prevent the tears streaming down her face.

Father was buried on a hill a few hundred yards beyond our village. It was right next to a row of our ancestors' graves in a dense old pine wood. When the villagers got to know about it, they nearly all came to attend the burial, with Zhu the Ninth leading the way, so the scene was quite impressive. No sooner was the grave completed than Zhu the Ninth looked up at the sun already rising above the mountains and hurriedly left for the village. After a while we heard the urgent clanging of the gong, and the villagers streamed back to join him in the village. Mingled with the sound of the gong, we heard a woman's voice, 'Let's go! Let's go! Let's go and fight the communists!'

This was She-crow shouting in the village square, joining her father who was beating the gong to assemble the village lads. She was so intent on shouting that she even forgot what she was shouting about. Since she had lost Mao Mao, no man had shown any interest in her – that was mainly because she sounded like a crow cawing and stirred up too much trouble. Also, she had too much of an appetite, so that not even a hardworking villager could cope with her. She felt hungry all the time. It was said that Wang the Lion deeply commiserated with her, and whenever the village branch of the Red Spear Society set off he would give her an extra half a catty of rice. The condition was that she had to match her father's gong by shouting: 'Let's go! Let's go! Let's go and fight the communists!'

When Mother and I got back to the village, she was still shouting madly, although her voice was beginning to crack. Still nobody paid any attention to her. Partly impressed and partly sorry for her, I filled a bowl of water at home and took it to her. Only then did she stop shouting.

'When you call the villagers to go and fight the communists, do you know what kind of people you're opposing?' I asked.

'They share property, including wives. They want to do away with landlords, relatives, friends and even ancestors.'

'I've heard that they're ordinary villagers in the north not far from here,' I said. 'Have you seen them share wives?'

'No, I haven't, but Master Chumin and Wang the Lion convinced us. If you don't believe it, go and ask them.'

Just then I noticed Mother standing in our doorway, waving to me from a distance. It looked as if she wanted me to come back, so I promptly left She-crow and went back to Mother. She whispered to me, 'We're trying to escape, and you run to have a chat with her. Isn't that inviting trouble?'

Still, Mother did not pull me into the house. She too wanted to watch the activity and developments outside. We hid in a dark corner of the doorway, from where we could watch without being seen.

The clang of the gong gradually faded and She-crow had shouted herself hoarse. In twos and threes the village lads gathered listlessly in the village square. Although they were carrying daggers and fish-nets, they all seemed reluctant, dragging their heels like the proverbial lazy ox. Some of the youths went up to Zhu the Ninth to have a word with him, probably to avoid this expedition with some pretext, such as having a headache. They were carrying rakes to go into the mountains to collect firewood. Afraid that those who had already gathered in the square would disappear, Zhu the Ninth hastily marched them off.

We went back into the house and closed the door.

'I don't think anybody will come and bother us,' said Mother, 'and they won't go and tell Wang the Lion about us. It seems that nobody is interested in these affairs. Today Wang the Lion himself has gone to the north to harass the villagers. He doesn't care about anything else!'

'I just hope today passes peacefully. It doesn't look as if

anything will happen. We can take this opportunity to rest. In the night we have to set off again . . .'

'Yes, you need rest most of all, my child. Go and get some sleep; I'll keep watch here.'

As she said this, though, she couldn't help yawning, but she covered her mouth with the back of her hand to hide it from me. She was obviously exhausted, so we could not continue talking. Our eyes closed and we could no longer prevent ourselves from falling asleep. So we both dozed off sitting on our chairs, we had no idea for how long.

It was already getting dark when we were woken by the noise outside and opened our eyes to have a look. The contingent that had left in the morning had returned. Amidst the hubbub in the village square we could also hear some loud sobbing. Mother and I went to the window and stood on our toes peeping out. Some of the Red Spear Society members were sitting on stones scattered over the square. Their heads bowed, they were all murmuring words I could not hear clearly. Some could not raise their arms; some had wounded legs. Some struggled up, only to sit down again, because they could not lift their feet. Around them were several wives and mothers shouting and cursing at Zhu the Ninth, who was sitting on a tree stump. One wife was raging and crying hysterically. I recognized her as Hongtao, a formidable villager, who was nicknamed 'Pickle' – she was Huang Yongfa's wife. They had married soon after we left the village. Huang Yongfa was one of Chumin's tenant-farmers. He also had a nickname – 'Grumpy', because of his bad temper. Every New Year when the villagers were celebrating with lanterns he used to lead our village lads to go and fight people in other villages, in case the others' dragon lanterns would harm our 'earth spirits'.*

'Why hasn't my man come back?' asked Pickle, jabbing at

---

* Playing dragon lanterns was a collective ritual for the inhabitants of a village during New Year time in veneration of the God of Rain – the dragon. The playing generally took place in the hills where villagers buried their ancestors. If players trespassed the burial hills of other villages, they would be regarded as having defiled the spirits of those villages and fierce fights would ensue.

Zhu's nose. 'Did you hand him over to the communists? How dare you? Please be good enough to get him back!'

Zhu the Ninth raised both hands to hold his head, which had a bloody swelling on top. It looked as if a stone had hit it. He did not utter a word, sitting there like a dummy. When Pickle pressed him, he still did not respond, as if oblivious. His insensitivity angered Pickle even more. She gave him a kick to which he did finally react by moving aside to avoid her onslaught. His passive attitude infuriated this woman, but he gained some sympathy from one man who was watching the commotion from near by. This man, who was nicknamed 'Flat-nose', was the village tailor. He was already getting on in age and he could not find work now, because the village was in such disorder and everybody was so poor. So he often wandered around the village, but because of his age he could not join the Red Spear Society. He did, however, enjoy the position of being 'neutral' in village disputes, in which he expressed somewhat philosophical ideas.

'Sister Hongtao – no, Aunt Pickle,' he consoled this tough woman, 'the *Romance of the Three Kingdoms* mentions several times that victory and defeat are military facts of life. You can't put all the blame on Brother Zhu because your husband hasn't returned from the expedition. Brother Grumpy is so reckless and always wants to be up front. He rushed ahead and the others couldn't keep up with him, so it's not surprising he was captured. Well, he's been captured, but he's still alive! He's got two legs, and probably tomorrow night he'll escape and come back. Then Master Chumin will certainly reward him for his bravery! A defeat can turn into a victory!'

Flat-nose's conciliatory words provided an 'escape route' for Zhu the Ninth, who seemed to have his own grievances. He took this opportunity to put his case.

'Our small village contingent wasn't the only one to meet with losses! Many men were also lost in the big contingent led by Wang the Lion himself. I saw one with my own eyes. His name is Jin Bailong, a very strong man who can run faster than anybody, but he was captured by the communists too – I saw it myself! How can I be blamed for losing one man?'

'Right!' Flat-nose once again offered his wisdom. 'As long as

81

they don't become "martyrs", they'll be able to escape! They have strong legs.'

When Flat-nose mentioned that word, 'martyr', he unintentionally reminded Pickle of Mao Mao's fate – Chumin had honoured him as an anti-communist 'martyr'. The way her husband had been inveigled into the Red Spear Society was very much the same as when Mao Mao 'joined' the Order Preservation Corps. As soon as she thought of this, she flared up again. She lunged towards Zhu the Ninth and dared to give him a slap on the face.

'If my Yongfa has become another of Chumin's "martyrs", don't think you'll get away with it!' she threatened. 'I'll fight you to the death. I'll bring my chopper. Just you wait and see!'

Pickle lived up to her nickname. She was well known in the village as a tough woman, as sharp as pickle. When Flat-nose saw the damage he had caused by uttering the word 'martyr', he just slipped away. Zhu the Ninth took the cue and also hastily got to his feet, covering the bloody swelling on his head with both hands. He summoned up all his strength to run like a fleeing rat to the wood on the hill behind the village to hide there. He could not deal with Pickle and had to admit defeat. When Pickle realized he had already disappeared and that she had no opponent, she went home, crying, sniffing and cursing all the way. By now night had already fallen.

Mother and I withdrew from the window and stood looking at one another until Mother spoke:

'It seems nothing is going to happen today. They're too busy quarrelling amongst themselves to bother about us.'

'Yes, I think Wang the Lion must also be harassed. Apparently quite a few of his own men have been captured. Zhu the Ninth just said that one villager there called Jin Bailong has vanished. How can his wife accept it just like that?'

'You're quite right. Tonight it should be quiet and Lao Liu and the others will probably be able to get here punctually. Let's cook something quickly – you must be hungry. In the bag there is still some rice, which should be enough for you. We have a long journey ahead.'

At about ten o'clock we had finished our meal and prepared the things we wanted to take with us. Lao Liu and O Ran arrived as expected in the quiet village. They simply said, 'Two of our scouts are waiting outside the village and they'll escort us out.' Then, picking up a bundle of our old clothes, they urged us to get going. With our ancestral book on my back, we left our old home. This time we did not lock the front door – we thought it was not necessary, because we did not know whether we would be able to return.

# CHAPTER 6

About two and a half hours later we were approaching a higher stretch of land. The hilly terrain which we were just passing through rose higher and higher, stretching into the distance. In the moonlight we could make out the silhouettes of the towering mountain peaks clustered in the distance. They were as quiet and tranquil as the hills we had been crossing. It looked as if they had been like this for ever, as far back as our ancestors could remember. The night was so still as we looked at this scene – who would have imagined that it was such a troubled land!

'We've already reached the north of the county,' announced Lao Liu. 'When Chumin's Order Preservation Corps came from the south yesterday to attack the villagers here, they took this route.'

'I can't believe this road is so peaceful now,' said Mother. 'If I hadn't seen them myself coming back to the village beaten black and blue, I couldn't have imagined that there could be such a fierce fight in such a beautiful place.'

'It's only just begun, Mother,' said Lao Liu. His confiding tone made us feel that he really was one of the family. 'I'm afraid this struggle will drag on and get fiercer and fiercer. Who knows how long it will go on! But don't worry. With us beside you, you don't have to be afraid of anything.'

Mother sighed.

'I'm not afraid, but I'm worried about the villagers. How will they manage if this situation continues?'

'Mother, even without this chaos the villagers had hard times,' said O Ran. 'We still remember quite clearly how villagers were always sweating their guts out the whole year only to have

84

nothing to eat at the end. Chumin and his lot robbed them of the fruits of their labour. Uncle Pan came to our home when he couldn't make ends meet. You see, he's an old bachelor, but he understands these things now, so he's resolved to fight Chumin's gang!'

'And Chumin didn't stop at forming the Order Preservation Corps,' added Lao Liu. 'He also enlisted the Red Spear Society and, what's more, he got the county head, Yao De-an, to collaborate with Duan Lianchen, who had fled to "The Big City". They called for provincial troops to attack us and terrorize the villagers. We were unarmed when they increased their strength with over a hundred soldiers from the provincial government.'

'But they haven't sent troops from the county town!' said Mother. 'They've sent only the Red Spear Society to fight the villagers here.'

'This is where their ruthless scheme lies,' said Lao Liu. 'They make the villagers fight against one another and create bitter dissension amongst them. This is their first attempt to restore their authority. Very soon they'll use their troops and Order Preservation Corps, but we're not afraid of them. As you can see, they're already in a tight spot; they don't dare go out during the night, and neither do their troops or the Order Preservation Corps. Their strength lies in a couple of hundred rifles. If we can manage to seize these, they'll be finished.'

Mother sighed again, but this time it was probably because she felt that events were happening too fast for her to keep up.

'My child,' she said, 'you understand a lot now; I can't keep up with all of you.'

'You can change too, Ma,' said O Ran. 'It's just that things are changing faster than usual.'

We walked on for two more hours. We came to the foot of a mountain range, which was not so steep, but densely wooded. The trees were very tall, so from afar the mountains looked high. The leaves had already turned red with the early frost, and it was a magnificent sight as the first light of dawn filtered through these trees, blending with the green of shorter pines. At this moment we felt refreshed and relaxed. I heard Mother sigh with relief. Our legs also felt lighter, so we now stepped up our pace, striding towards the densely forested mountains.

'Ma,' said Lao Liu suddenly, 'we'll have to go our separate ways now. I have to attend a propaganda meeting this morning, so O Ran will take you to your new home.'

'Is the meeting far from here?' asked Mother anxiously. 'Don't forget to have something to eat.'

'It's not far, in these mountains. Don't worry, I won't starve. This is not a poor area. There's food available everywhere.'

With this he shifted the bundle off his back on to my shoulder and then left us.

We came to a valley with rice fields on either side and several hamlets around. After this O Ran led us over a hill to an open plain. By this time it was already dawn, and we heard cows mooing and pigs snorting. They had probably been let out to answer the call of nature and graze. An old farmer with a manure fork over his shoulder and a bamboo bin hanging from it was walking towards us. He was following his pig and picking up its fresh manure. When the pig saw us, it turned up a fork in the road. The old fellow looked up and, seeing us, stopped in his tracks and called out joyfully:

'O Ran, what a coincidence! I've just come out and here you are.'

'Well, this is my Mother,' said O Ran, pointing to her, and then, turning to me, she added, 'this is my little brother, Chunsheng. Chunsheng, just call him Grandpa Whiskers.'

'How do you do, Grandpa Whiskers,' I said, bowing to the old man.

'We're relieved that you've arrived safely,' said Grandpa Whiskers. 'This is a woody, mountainous area with a hard-working population, so you'll be safe here.'

'There are also good old people like you,' said O Ran, 'which was why we decided to move Mother and Brother to your village.'

'Since yesterday, Aunt Sunflower has been looking forward to your arrival. She's put your room in order.'

'Thank you for all your help,' said Mother, bowing respectfully to Grandpa Whiskers.

I bowed to Grandpa Whiskers once again, but I could not think of anything to say.

Turning round, he led us on our way.

'Look, that's Red Hill Village,' said Grandpa Whiskers, pointing to a hamlet behind a wood ahead. 'That's our village, where you're going to live too.'

As we approached the village, Mother seemed to revive. It was a small hamlet with about twenty mud-huts and thatched cottages and apparently no rich families. These poor cottages formed a row from the east, with a narrow, long pond in front and a mountain behind, covered with maple trees and shrubs. Stretching from north to south in front of the village was a big meadow, giving an impression of wide open space. Before we entered the village, Mother stopped for a moment to have a look around. Then she sighed again. The scene before her was so peaceful, she was able to relax a bit. We had not enjoyed such quiet surroundings for so long.

Aunt Sunflower was waiting at the edge of the village. When she saw the three of us, she came over quickly to welcome us. She looked under forty, neat and clean and quite graceful for a country woman. When O Ran introduced her to Mother, Mother's face suddenly lit up. She seemed very familiar. Her hair was neatly combed and her face was quite fresh. Although she had the big, rough hands of a country woman, they were not so worn. She seemed to be used to delicate work. Like an old friend, she said, 'You must be hungry and tired. Let's go home quickly!' She grasped Mother's hand affectionately, leading her to her home.

'Fine, you're home now,' said Grandpa Whiskers. 'I needn't look after you. See you later!' With his bin over his shoulder, he went on his way, picking up manure.

Aunt Sunflower's home was quite spacious: in the middle was the hall and on both sides were two adjacent rooms. They were all kept very clean. At the end of the hall was an altar, where the ancestral tablet was displayed.

'You and your son can stay in the two eastern rooms,' said Aunt Sunflower. 'I'll stay with Zizhong in the two western rooms – anyway, he isn't here often. When our elder daughter, Meixiang, was small, we couldn't afford to bring her up, so we gave her away as a child-bride, and now she's married. Her younger brother Jiqing is working in the nearby town, Tanjiahe, like his father. At the back of the house next to the kitchen there's a shed for firewood and hay, where Jiqing has put a bed. He sleeps there whenever he comes back. You see our house is quite big, and it's very convenient for you to stay with us. Just make yourselves at home.'

She spoke very openly and managed to tell us about the whole family in a few words. From this I realized that she was capable and kind. I took a liking to her and felt close straight away.

'Actually this place is better than our home, and it's much quieter!' Mother also spoke very openly. 'By the way, there's something I'd like to discuss with you. I don't know if it would be all right to put up our ancestral tablet somewhere on your altar – or to put it on a small table underneath . . .'

Aunt Sunflower turned towards Mother, and when she saw her serious expression she covered her mouth with her hand. Still she could not hide a friendly laugh as she spoke.

'In these troubled times, you still haven't forgotten your ancestors?'

'Where would we be without our ancestors? My eldest son is still away, I don't know where. I still have to pray for the blessings of my ancestors!'

'OK! But there's no need to put a table there. We are one big family now even though we have different ancestors. I'll put our ancestral tablet a bit to one side. We can place the two tablets side by side symmetrically – that will look good too.'

Then right away she moved her tablet aside, and I immediately put ours on the altar next to it in the right position. Now Mother sighed with relief that she could settle down peacefully in Aunt Sunflower's home.

'Ma, is there anything else you need?' asked O Ran. 'I have to be going. There's so much to do just now.' Then, turning to Aunt Sunflower, she went on, 'Aunt Sunflower, I'll leave Ma and Brother in your hands then. See you later!'

As she turned to the door and left, we went to see her off.

'I'm quite free at the moment,' called out Aunt Sunflower to O Ran. 'If there's anything I can do, just send it to me.'

'I'll send something in a day or two,' O Ran called back. 'Ma and Brother don't know this place yet, so you'd better look after them for a couple of days.'

Coming back into the room, Mother asked Aunt Sunflower, 'What work were you talking about just now?'

'Sewing. You know, she can sew and she has gone into a little business partnership, renting a small shop in Tanjiahe. They have set up a clothes stall, where they also mend clothes. If she's too busy, she sends some to me. Sometimes she brings a whole lot over, so I'm quite busy helping her. But this also supplements our income, because we don't do any farming. She often says how grateful she is that you taught her how to sew when she was a child, so she can be a tailor now. She comes here every few days.'

'I never imagined that she could earn a living by sewing. So you became friends through this, and that's how we've been able to come and stay here.'

As she spoke, Mother nodded with satisfaction. She was also relieved that O Ran did not have to worry about earning a living now.

'I'd like to go to Tanjiahe some day to see her clothes stall,' I said.

'You can also go and see Zizhong and Jiqing,' said Aunt Sunflower. 'Maybe you can find some work in the town too!'

Hearing this, I became even more interested. I really wanted to go into the town to have a look. It was only just over a mile away.

On the third night after settling into our new home, when I was half-asleep, I heard a rustling sound coming from the kitchen. At first I thought it was a rat running around and then I suspected it might be a thief. So I threw on some clothes and went out to look. I saw a lamp burning in the kitchen and a young man looking for something in the cupboard. When he saw me, he turned and asked in a hushed voice, 'Are you Brother Chunsheng? I'm Jiqing. Ma must have told you about me. I've come home late and I'm rather hungry, so I'm looking for some food.'

'Yes, Aunt Sunflower has told us about you. I've been thinking of going to Tanjiahe to see you and Uncle Zizhong.'

'Well, here I am. I'd like to have a chat with you too, but it's too late now and I'm tired. You shouldn't have got up. Sometimes I get home late and Ma knows it's me, so she goes on sleeping. You should go and sleep too. I work as a blacksmith in Shunxing Forge in town. If you come the day after tomorrow, I'll be there waiting for you.'

Saying this, he took a cold pancake and went to the side room next to the kitchen to sleep.

The day after tomorrow soon arrived. That day Grandpa Whiskers was also going to Tanjiahe. He had heard that I wanted to go and see Jiqing, so he came to ask me to go with him. As he was familiar with the area, he took a short-cut, which led through the wood on the mountain behind our village. Soon pine woods met fields of peanuts and sweet potatoes – a typical mountain scene. If one just looked ahead at the endless pine forests, one did not notice the peanut and sweet potato fields. Grandpa Whiskers had spent his whole life in these parts. Although he was now over sixty years old, he was still agile and fairly skipped over the stony path, with me following. He only stopped when an old peasant tilling a peanut field hailed him to have a chat. He was obviously an old friend.

'*Jia* chief, I haven't seen you for several days. What have you been up to?' asked the old peasant with a smile which revealed toothless gums.

'Nothing special, you see, I'm just on my way to Tanjiahe to have a look at the shops.'

'Well, what about your official duties?'

'What offical duties can I have? It was *Bao* chief Liu Qiyu who imposed the title *Jia* chief on me. He lives in that big village to the east of the town. He often goes to the county town, but it isn't so convenient to come to our village. When he comes, he usually traipses behind a dozen armed fellows of the Order Preservation Corps, who fire their guns to frighten the village. He just has a few words with me and then rushes off again. All I have to say is something to reassure him, like "Don't worry, it's very peaceful in the village."'

'How easy it is to be a *Jia* chief!'

'It's even easier to be a *Bao* chief!' said Grandpa Whiskers. 'What's more, he gets paid every month – by County Head Yao De-an, actually by Chumin, and where he gets it from nobody knows.'

'So you'd better retire,' said the old peasant, once again

exposing his toothless gums. 'You're small fry. If the job's no advantage, forget it!'

'Don't think it's useless. As long as I'm here to deal with them, I can keep the village peaceful and stop them coming to disturb it.'

The old peasant laughed, completely baring his toothless gums.

Grandpa Whiskers also burst out laughing.

After this conversation we went on our way.

'Grandpa Whiskers,' I said, 'if you're really the *Jia* chief, then you're an official. But if there's nothing to gain from it, then it's really not worth it.'

'It's very useful. The county magistrate knows each village has a *Jia* chief, who reports on the situation in the village. He's reassured if they report that everything is in order in the countryside under his administration. The people can also be spared trouble from the county office – at least, that's how it is today and how we get along!'

'Why isn't there anyone like Chumin here, rounding up all the village lads and organizing them into a Red Spear Society?'

'Ha!' Grandpa Whiskers laughed. 'It's not so simple here! There was someone here like Chumin. They called him the tyrant, and he lived in Tanjiahe. But he was captured by the revolutionaries and brought to the county town where he was shot together with four others. The tyrant owned many shops in the town and swallowed up all the village land. But after he was shot all his family were scared to death and fled to the concession in "The Big City". The villagers divided up his land amongst themselves, and his shop-hands in town took over his shops. Who would want to join the Red Spear Society and fight the revolutionaries? County Head Yao De-an was furious about all this, but what could he do? Only send troops to terrorize people every so often. But in this mountainous region it's not easy for him: if they were ambushed, they'd probably lose all their guns!'

Chatting like this all the way, we soon reached Tanjiahe.

This small town was surrounded by pine woods and maple trees, so it was hidden from the outside world. It was the centre of this district, however, with a main road leading to the county town and many small roads going to other places. A small river, wending its way down from the mountains, passed by the town and flowed on to 'The Big City'. Even though it was shallow, small bamboo rafts could float on it. Three or four rafts strung together could carry quite a lot. Grandpa Whiskers said that in the past the mountain products of this region were transported downstream on such strings of rafts, which also carried foreign and coastal goods upstream from 'The Big City'. So this small town with only one street used to be quite prosperous. Even today it was still quite well supplied with everyday goods for the villagers. The shops included a cooking oil and salt shop, a general store, a chemist with Chinese medicine, a dyeing shop, pawnshop, fried dough-stick shop, blacksmith, noodle shop and even a cake shop and soy sauce brewery, which sold such things as preserved and pickled vegetables. As soon as we entered the town, I followed Grandpa Whiskers, looking around at these shops. Soon I heard a tapping sound, and after a few steps Grandpa Whiskers suddenly stopped in front of the blacksmith's.

'Didn't you want to see Jiqing?' he asked me. 'He works here. You can go in and see him. I've got other things to do, so you can go back by yourself. Now you know the way, don't you?'

'Don't worry, Grandpa Whiskers,' I replied, 'I'm very good at remembering my way. I can even remember the way we went in the night.'

'Well, that's a very useful skill,' he said, patting me on the shoulder and giving me a meaningful look – at that time I didn't know what it meant – 'especially in these troubled times.'

After this he turned and left me.

As I entered the blacksmith's, Jiqing was just holding an iron hammer with which he and an old blacksmith were hammering a piece of iron. I thought the old blacksmith was probably his employer, because he looked very skilful, holding the hammer in one hand and tongs in the other to grasp a piece of red-hot iron. Turning it on the anvil, the two took turns to beat it rhythmically. The hammer which Jiqing was wielding was much bigger and longer than his master's. He was gripping it hard with both hands as he struck at that red-hot iron. Every time he struck a blow the muscles on his bare arms seemed to burst and almost explode. At the same time sweat broke out on his forehead.

When he saw me come in and greet him, the old blacksmith – later I found out that he was called Ren Daqiu – put down his hammer and plunged the newly forged hoe into a bucket of water next to the anvil, producing a cloud of steam. Then he sat down on a chair by the wall and lit up his pipe. He obviously needed a rest, so Jiqing pulled me over to a bench by the door, where we sat and chatted.

'Did you see how busy the town is now?' he said. 'We can hardly keep up. Since the tyrant was shot, the villagers have been enthusiastically farming their land without having to pay rent. Every day we get a pile of tools to repair. Look at that pile by the wall over there!'

I glanced over at the wall on the right, where there were piles of plough-shares, hoes and rakes waiting to be repaired.

'In that case, the tyrant's family had better never come back again. Then your business can go on flourishing.'

'That depends on how we villagers manage. Of course, they want to come back, but they haven't built up enough strength yet. Now they're in league with Chumin in the south, plotting to come back. We have to organize ourselves against them.'

'Organize?' I asked. 'What does that mean?'

'Organize with the villagers. How can one person stand up to them alone? They have their Red Spear Society, Order Preservation Corps, regular troops and Duan Lianchen, their accomplice, who also fled to "The Big City". They are colluding with Chiang Kai-shek and the foreign powers to come back at any time. Now Chiang Kai-shek is fully occupied fighting his military rivals in other provinces, so they can't cope at present. They'll come back sooner or later, and then there'll be a blood-bath like in "The Big City". But we needn't be afraid, as long as we're prepared!'

'Jiqing, it's amazing. As you work here you're thinking and talking about things just like those students I met.' I couldn't help expressing my admiration for him. 'You're so clever!'

'I also learned from those students. If you have a social conscience and mix with the peasants, you will understand these things too. The situation is changing.'

'I'm now living in Red Hill Village. Isn't that amongst the peasants?'

'Well, that depends whether you think and behave like the peasants.'

'But I'm not involved in farming. How can I be like them?'

'That doesn't matter. Aren't I working as a blacksmith in town? You can also find some work in town, but you can still identify with the peasants. Oh, I've just remembered, the fried dough-stick baker in town is just looking for someone to go and sell his delicacies in the countryside for him – some people in the countryside can still afford to buy their children dough-sticks. Would you like to do that? It's very easy. You only have to carry a basket full of dough-sticks around the countryside every day. If you sell them all, you get twenty per cent of the earnings. What you can't sell you return to him. You're completely free, and you don't need to spend any money yourself. If you have anything urgent to do you can stop working for a while without asking for leave.'

This suggestion attracted me a lot. Also, I should have a job. Doing nothing was really boring; and this job was so flexible. I could go back home every day to help Mother, and just going around could not be too strenuous. So without consulting anyone else, I just took Jiqing's advice.

'Fine!' I said. 'I can start tomorrow!'

'Well, you'd better go and see the baker now. Tell him I sent you. I'm sure he'll be very glad.'

By this time the old blacksmith had finished smoking and went back to the anvil with his hammer in one hand and tongs in the other. Jiqing got up too, and picking up his hammer, which was leaning against the wall, he was ready to begin forging again. I thought I had better leave. Even after a short talk with Jiqing, I found that he had a straightforward manner.

As he suggested, I went to the fried dough-stick shop and found the owner. He was called 'Pockmarks the Sixth', as his face was so pock-marked that it looked like sesame. He was already bald on top, but his lively way made him appear young. He was just standing with his sleeves turned up, frying dough-sticks by a big oil wok. When I mentioned Jiqing's name by way

94

of introduction, he immediately responded warmly. It seemed he was just as spontaneous as Jiqing.

'No problem! No problem!' As soon as he found out that I was willing to go to the countryside selling dough-sticks in the villages, he responded, 'You can start today!'

Without waiting for my reply, he put down the two long chopsticks with which he was frying the dough-sticks. He went into the inner room to fetch a bamboo basket which he handed over to me. There was an oily sheet at the bottom and one covering the basket. As soon as I had taken the basket, he took the oily sheet off the top, quickly counted eighty dough-sticks, put them in the basket and covered it again.

'Well, it's still early; off you go and sell them! You'll be paid according to how many you sell at a rate of twenty per cent of your takings.'

Pockmarks the Sixth was so enthusiastic that I felt a certain pressure; I had to leave the town hastily with my basket of dough-sticks to begin my job as a pedlar, so I gave up my plan to see Uncle Zizhong. During the day I went to several villages and sold all the eighty dough-sticks, thus earning twenty cents. When I got home I told Mother all about it. She did not blame me, but instead praised me for making a prompt decision and not losing the chance of a job.

'As long as you have something to do,' said Mother. 'You're grown-up now. You should have a job, whatever it is.'

From now on I was busy, going into town at dawn and coming home in the dark after working out the accounts with Pockmarks the Sixth. For a long time I could not go to see Jiqing, but I thought I should go and tell him about my work. One day I went into town specially early to see him at the blacksmith's, but he was not there.

'After work yesterday he went home to see his mother and he hasn't come back yet,' said his employer.

'Went home to see his mother?' I asked, surprised.

'That's right,' said his employer, nodding. 'He's been back home every night recently. He told me his mother isn't too well. How come you don't know?'

Of course I did not know, because I had not seen him come home for the past few days. Ren Daqiu seemed to be rather upset because Jiqing had not arrived yet and it was difficult for him to start the day's work. He did not go on talking to me, but concentrated on lighting the furnace for forging. I also felt disappointed and hurried to the dough-stick shop. Pockmarks the Sixth had already fried a big basketful of dough-sticks. I picked up my basket and hurried to the countryside to sell my wares, but I was very disturbed: these days Jiqing had in fact not come home and Aunt Sunflower was quite well. What had he been doing at night? Why didn't he tell his master the truth? Of course, I had not revealed to his employer that he had not come back home those nights, nor that his mother was quite well. I had my suspicions. In fact, I had great misgivings. So in the afternoon, after I had sold the dough-sticks and got back to town, I settled the accounts with Pockmarks the Sixth and went back to the blacksmith's specially to see Jiqing.

He was just forging iron with his employer, hammering with all his might. He was working energetically, as if he wanted to make up for perhaps upsetting him. He had told him he was 'going home' for the night and had come late in the morning. He just glanced at me, and without putting down his hammer, he directed me, 'Go back first. After work I'll come back home too.'

I had to leave. When I got home Aunt Sunflower and my mother were cooking dinner. They were not only in good health, but also in good spirits.

'What's happening in town?' Aunt Sunflower asked.

'Brother Jiqing told me he was coming back this evening.'

'He doesn't always mean what he says,' said Aunt Sunflower. 'Sometimes he suddenly appears in the middle of the night and before dawn he's gone. I don't even catch a glimpse of him. As for his father, he just doesn't come home.'

This time, however, Jiqing really did come back. He did not 'suddenly appear in the middle of the night', but just after we had finished dinner.

He chatted with Aunt Sunflower and my mother for a while, drank a big bowl of tea and then stood up and patted me on the shoulder, saying, 'Let's go out for a stroll and have a chat. Tonight the moon is beautiful and it's not windy. The whole village is so quiet. We rarely have a chance to get together, even though we're both working in town!'

So he took me out. The moon was really beautiful, high in the sky. There was a star apparently following it and winking to us. In fact, after moving to this village Mother and I had frequently witnessed this scene, but, strangely enough, I only really appreciated how wonderful it was this time, when Jiqing pointed it out. We strolled along the road by the pond in front of the village until we came to a wood of scattered willows outside the village. Sometimes I looked down at the moon reflected in the pond through the willow leaves; sometimes I looked up at the distant stars. Enchanted by this peaceful scene, neither of us spoke.

After strolling along like this for a while, it was Jiqing who broke the silence.

'I hear you came to the blacksmith's to see me. What did he say to you?'

'He told me that these days you've often been going to see Aunt Sunflower at night, because she isn't feeling well.'

'What did you say?'

'I didn't say anything. I know you haven't been sleeping at the blacksmith's, so I thought there must be another reason, like a girlfriend. If you meet in the evening and it gets too late, it's awkward to go back to the workshop. It would still be better for you to come home to sleep – I would open the door for you. It's not worth spending the night outdoors and getting ill.'

Jiqing shook his head. Perhaps he was smiling at me, but in the dark I couldn't see his expression clearly.

'You're wrong. I don't have a girlfriend,' he said. 'In this situation, how can one think of personal affairs? There's so much to do that it can't even be finished in the night.'

'So what do you do running around at night? If you don't sleep during the night, how do you have the strength to work at the blacksmith's in the day-time?'

'You're quite right, this work is really important – I have to do it to earn a living. But I also have even more important matters . . . '

He broke off as we emerged from the willows on to a wide meadow at the foot of the mountain. It was bathed in moonlight, suddenly transforming this place into a silvery fairyland. The moonlight reflected in a clear pool near by seemed to be smiling at us. As we approached the pool I was suddenly transfixed by this scene, unable to walk another step. I said to Jiqing, 'Walking in this place at night is like a dream.'

'I don't think so,' he replied. 'Of course this scenery is magnificent, but you have to be happy to enjoy it. Well, that's for the future. Who has the time or the peace of mind nowadays? Look at your family with all the difficulties you've had. Still, with enough to eat, you're not too badly off. How many there are with nothing to eat! For as long as I can remember, all the people we've met and seen have been starving. Your Uncle Pan was starving, but he was lucky enough to meet you. He somehow managed to survive, but he is still single and without any family.'

'Uncle Pan!' I exclaimed. 'So you know him too?'

'Of course I know him. Now he's aware of his condition and he's trying to change it – not only for himself but for all the starving people. He has a clear purpose in life, so he works with all his energy.'

'No wonder he behaves as if he were so young,' I said. 'Ma and I feel that he's changed – well, Lao Liu and O Ran have also changed, but we still can't work out how. They're not like those students who learn so much in "The Big City", where they are introduced to so many new ideas.'

'Now you know,' said Jiqing. 'Please think about this: what should we young people be doing? When even old people like Uncle Pan are so involved, how can we young people remain inactive?'

I had never thought about the question which Jiqing raised. Now that he had brought it up, I really felt it involved something very urgent: Was I going to continue selling dough-sticks for ever, thus frittering away my life? But thinking it over again, wasn't Jiqing doing the same as me, working the whole day? Moreover, forging iron was tough work. He was sweating away with his hammer all the time. How could he be working for the poor people?

When I raised my doubts directly, he could not hide a smile. 'Weren't you puzzled why I didn't come home to sleep? This work can only be done now during the night. What's more, we have to work during the day too. They have armies, Order Preservation Corps, Red Spear Societies, which means they have guns. They have Chiang Kai-shek and foreign powers backing them. You must have seen all this for yourself in "The Big City". As we have no guns, we can only operate at night. Sometimes we are so involved that I can't get back to town or go home. I just have to find somewhere to have a nap and at dawn I go back to work in town.'

'That's why you told the old blacksmith that you were going home to see your mother!' This time I could not help smiling. 'Also, you just said "we". Who do you mean – Uncle Pan, Lao Liu and O Ran?'

'You're very clever!' he said, smiling again. 'That's fine, it's good to be clever! I was referring to many people, including those with not enough to eat. In our rural area it includes people who have no fields to farm, who have no power and who are always persecuted by county officials, troops and people like Chumin in the south. You know, even if we want to overthrow these oppressors, individuals like us who feel strongly about this situation cannot do anything about it. We will finally just be crushed and killed by them, just like many young students in "The Big City". We have to co-operate with other people. That's what I meant by "we".'

Listening to Jiqing, I couldn't help feeling respect: he was no simple young blacksmith. He knew a lot, even more than that poetic young Chinese teacher, Huang Zhuqing, whom I had met in 'The Big City' and who died a tragic death. Because I had so much respect for him, I found his ideas most convincing and enlightening. In fact, I started to think about what I should do in the future. Now that I was already a young lad, shouldn't I join with others and do something with them as Jiqing said? I didn't discuss these thoughts with Jiqing, but only asked him, 'Jiqing, I really admire you. You know such a lot about these big matters. Where did you learn about them?'

'At meetings.' Jiqing sounded calmer now. 'Some learned people joined, who had studied the situation in the world, in our country and our rural areas.'

'I would never have imagined that, in these remote mountains! Where are the meetings? When do they take place? Can I go to listen too?'

'They're not held in any definite place, but they're always at night. We mustn't let those tyrants find out, because we're still not so strong and have only a few guns. As for you going to a meeting, well . . . '

His words suddenly tailed off. We had come back from the foot of the mountain and had reached the space in front of the village, which was now completely silent; everyone was asleep.

'Well . . . well what?' I said. 'Why don't you go on?'

'Right, we're brothers now. As long as you don't tell anyone, I'll tell you.'

'I definitely won't! Didn't I keep quiet when you told the old blacksmith that you'd gone home to see your mother?'

'Good, you are very clever,' said Jiqing. 'That shows you're very reliable. We need people like that. Now you know that our meetings are secret. Only the members of our organization can attend the meetings, and if you do, you have to realize that if the county officials and landlords get to know about it, they might send troops or the Order Preservation Corps to arrest and execute people. Aren't you afraid . . . ?'

He paused again, waiting for my response.

'If you're not afraid, neither am I.'

Jiqing pondered a while.

'Fine!' he said in a firm voice. 'If you're afraid, you can't do anything. If you don't fear those county officials and landlords, they may fear you. You see, they just hide away in the county town at night, not daring to emerge from their fortress – because we operate in the open at night! You don't have to be afraid of anything, as long as you have the courage to resist them.'

Hearing Jiqing talk about being 'afraid' or 'not afraid' made me realize why Zhu the Ninth had got a bloody bump on his head, why his Red Spear Society had been defeated and some of its members captured. I suddenly realized why Lao Liu and O Ran had dared to come in the night to fetch Mother and me and calmly lead us to Red Hill Village.

'I'm not afraid!' I said spontaneously.

Jiqing did not react to my exclamation. He just patted me warmly on the shoulder and raised his head to look at the silent bright moon hanging in the sky. Then, deep in thought, he hung his head and walked on quietly by my side. And so, absorbed in our thoughts, we reached our door-step. Only then did he break the silence, whispering to me, 'It's not necessary to tell our mothers about what we discussed tonight. They'll understand in time. They won't blame us. Be prepared, I'll take you to a meeting some day.'

Jiqing opened the door quietly and I followed him in. It was already nearly midnight, but unexpectedly Aunt Sunflower and my mother were still up. They were sitting and chatting quietly in the moonlight streaming through the window. When we came in, Aunt Sunflower said calmly, 'It's late, you should get to sleep. So should we.'

Thereupon she got up and went over to the door to check the latch. Then she retired to the bedroom with my mother. Aunt Sunflower seemed to be used to Jiqing coming back late at night and she did not seem to worry. My mother would have to get used to it too.

One evening Jiqing came back from Tanjiahe town unusually early. He said he had left as soon as Ren Daqiu finished work, so he had not eaten yet. By chance, we were eating later that day, so we could have dinner together. This was an exceptional occasion in this family. Although Uncle Zizhong and Jiqing were both working quite near Red Hill Village, they found it difficult to get home and have dinner with Aunt Sunflower. So this evening Aunt Sunflower seemed very excited and she specially took out the best thing she had – noodles. She boiled two big bowlsful just for us young lads. While we were eating, our heads down as we scooped the noodles into our mouths with chopsticks, Jiqing glanced at me furtively with his big black eyes. It was a meaningful look, which I understood: Today I have come back so early to do as I promised last time, to take you to our meeting. I did not say a word, but just responded with a smile. Then he looked up at Aunt Sunflower and said, 'Ma, this evening I'm going to take Chunsheng to see some friends, and we'll probably get back rather late.'

Aunt Sunflower smiled at us in a way which startled me and made me wonder whether she could have guessed our plan.

101

Just look at her knowing smile! Still, she did not show any suspicion or make any sign that she had discovered our secret. She just replied calmly and affectionately, 'All right, you can go. On a moonlit night like this, it would be a pity if you young lads didn't go out for a walk.' Then she turned to my mother, saying, 'Don't you agree? Let the young lads go out and have fun, while we stay here and chat. The children have grown up – they have to live their own lives. Jiqing is a smart lad. Yes, I must have a talk with you later about our boys.'

'You needn't worry about Jiqing,' said Mother. 'I'm very happy that our Chunsheng has such a friend and companion. After his father died, I didn't have a definite plan for him. Jiqing has so many friends, and he found him a job to earn his living. Otherwise what would we have done?'

'As they say, boys will be boys,' said Aunt Sunflower. 'Let them go.'

Aunt Sunflower's smile became cheerful laughter, which made my mother laugh too.

So we went out without speaking a word to one another. In the open space in front of the village Jiqing stopped for a moment and looked all around. Nothing was stirring in the village and there was not a soul in sight. Then Jiqing led the way at a faster pace to the end of the village. There he looked all round again and nudged me, whispering, 'Quick!'

We slipped silently out of the village. After going through the willow grove to the east, we took a path which zigzagged up the mountain behind the village. Half-way up we followed another path which branched off behind the mountain. On the other side it led down to a long narrow meadow, where we stepped up our pace, making swift progress.

'The place where we're going is quite far,' said Jiqing. 'I'm afraid we'll only get there just before midnight. If you want to take part in our activities, you'll have to get used to walking at night. If you think you can't get used to it, there's still time to change your mind.'

'I won't change my mind.'

'Are you sure?'

'Sure! But do you go to meetings every time?'

'Not necessarily; there's a lot of other work to do.'

'What work?'

'What I told you about last time – working for the poor. Your uncle Pan and sister O Ran are doing this now.'

'I see. That's why they're busy and working very hard!'

'Yes, they're very busy! If you work with us, you'll be busy too. Can you manage that?'

'Of course! Working with you, I can manage anything!'

'Fine! So the meeting I'm taking you to tonight won't be in vain!' said Jiqing in a serious but also excited tone. 'You just express this determination at the meeting and you'll be able to work with us. The people there are waiting for us.'

We walked on even faster. Jiqing had so much energy and he strode forward as if we were on a forced march. I followed close behind. Although I was already covered with sweat, strangely enough I did not feel at all tired. On the contrary, I felt exhilarated. As this was my first night march, I felt excited, curious and all the more interested. We covered a great distance rapidly and finally reached the bank of a small stream, which came zigzagging down a mountain gully, reflecting the moonlight like a silver ribbon. I still felt fresh and calm.

Jiqing stopped here, turned, patted my shoulder and grasped my hand. He gripped so hard with his strong, rough hand that it hurt.

'Here we are. This place is called Pheasant Nest. Very few people normally come, so pheasants make their nests here. But we don't come here to catch pheasants!'

Both of us burst out laughing, which immediately helped to dispel our fatigue.

Pheasant Nest was next to a stone bridge high upstream. It was not a village, nor a resting spot for travellers, as travellers did not come this way; it just consisted of two mud-huts combined into one. As we approached, Jiqing told me a bit about the place. These two mud-huts were inhabited by two old bachelors, one called Wang Xiangzheng and the other Feng Xinshun. They used to work here for a small landlord called Wang Jincai. When the peasant union here took power into their own hands, this small landlord was paraded through the county by his farm-hands for two days, wearing a dunce's hat to humiliate him. Later, when five big bad landlords were crushed in the county, he was scared out of his wits and fled to a neighbouring county, never daring to return. These two farmhands were now farming his poor plots scattered over the mountainside. Just as we were approaching these two huts, we heard the voice of an old man calling out, 'Who is it?'

Jiqing apparently recognized his voice immediately, and answered, 'It's me, Jiqing, Uncle Wang Xiangzheng. I've brought a friend with me too.'

There was no response, but we saw the old peasant emerge from under a maple tree beside the hut. He gently pushed the door of the hut and it creaked as it opened half-way. We squeezed through, and Jiqing closed the door behind him. Uncle Wang Xiangzheng stayed outside, no doubt keeping watch. There was an oil-lamp on a table at the end of the room, but it cast only a spot of light. Still, I could make out three faces, two middle-aged peasants and one lad of about twenty. The two peasants were both wearing belts and looked like hired hands. Although they looked very tough, they seemed quite intelligent, reminding me of Pan Zaixing and Liu Dawang, whom I had met recently. Just as these two faces flashed through my mind, I suddenly realized that it was indeed them.

'What are they doing here?' I whispered to Jiqing. 'I know them.'

'We know that,' Jiqing whispered back. 'Aren't you determined to help the poor people? Well, we need an organization first. This is a serious matter. The reason I've brought you here today is to introduce you to this organization, so that you can join it. We have to have a formal meeting to admit you. Have you got anything else to say at this point?'

I shook my head.

'No, I've already made up my mind.'

'Good! As you know one another already, I don't have much more to say. That young lad is not much older than you, but his father is a tenant farmer, who is so poor that he sometimes has to work as a hired hand. He's called Pan Mingxun, also attending this meeting for the same reason as you.'

It was only then that I noticed a square white cloth hanging on the dimly lit wall. On it was painted a simple emblem consisting of an overlapping hammer and sickle. Standing in

104

the corner, I suddenly felt the solemn atmosphere, especially when the whole room was plunged into deep silence.

'Now we can start,' said Liu Dawang, 'as the two new comrades have arrived.'

Thereupon Pan Zaixing went up to the table and said to Pan Mingxun, 'Please come over here!'

He pointed to a spot by the left side of the table. Pan Mingxun went over as instructed and stood there. He glanced at Jiqing, who nodded. Then Jiqing said to me, 'You stand by the right side of the table.'

I went over and stood at the spot he indicated.

'Now we'll take the pledge,' said Liu Dawang. 'Comrades Mingxun and Chunsheng, please raise your hands!'

I slowly raised my right hand. I felt that this was an extremely solemn gathering. I would make a pledge and take up a heavy responsibility, but at that moment I did not have a clear idea of how I could fulfil my duty. However, I did feel as if I had suddenly grown up. I realized that I was no longer a child, especially when I raised my right hand and repeated the following words after Pan Zaixing, speaking in a low voice:

> I pledge myself to the revolution,
> to strive my whole life for the communist cause.

Pan Mingxun also repeated this in the same tone. My own voice became loud and clear as I continued:

> I will abide by the Party's discipline,
> keep secrets and carry out my duties.

When I came to the last sentence, I spoke with an even more powerful voice:

> I will never betray the Party!

After repeating the last sentence, for some reason my hand remained raised; I forgot that I was still holding it up. I had only one thought in my mind at that moment: I was now deeply involved in an organization which was working for the poor. It was extremely clandestine, judging by the atmosphere here, at least. Why did it have to be like this? Because the enemies of the poor were afraid of this organization and were always trying to destroy it. Then I recalled what my brother Zhao Jue had told us about the massacre of those young students by the military police in 'The Big City' and the tragic fate of that Chinese language teacher, Huang Zhuqing. This was a cruel world where deadly struggles were going on everywhere, and I was now involved. Then I remembered what Jiqing had asked me just before we came to this hut: Afraid or not?

Not afraid! I said to myself. I can't be afraid! Jiqing is only a few years older than me and he has so many ideas. That's because he isn't afraid of anything. Neither am I!

At this moment somebody held my hand, making me put it down at last. Startled out of my musings, I looked up to see Uncle Pan standing beside me.

Astonished, I asked, 'How did you get here?'

'I'm one of those who recommended you! Yes, I got here a little late, because I had another urgent meeting – the situation is very critical!'

'In what way?' I asked.

'Didn't you see how it was in "The Big City"? Soon the countryside will become the focus of the struggle, which involves "The Big City", the whole province, the whole country and the whole world. Chiang Kai-shek and his followers can only display their strength with the support of world imperialism. We must prepare for a direct struggle with them. When I went to "The Big City" that time, I was escorting Comrade Pan Xudong to get in touch with the party leaders, to find out about the situation in the whole country and to receive instructions about the struggle in our area. Do you understand now?'

In fact I did not really understand, because it was too complicated. Moreover, what puzzled me even more was this: these words came from Uncle Pan, whom I had known so well, but he was very different from the old Uncle Pan. Still, this was indeed my Uncle Pan – his appearance, voice and familiar way with me all proved it. I could only stare at him, baffled. Uncle Pan seemed to have sensed my bewilderment, as he added, patting me on the shoulder, 'You will gradually come to under-

106

stand when you take part in this struggle yourself. I've seen you grow up with my own eyes. I'm delighted that you've decided to help the poor people. In this historic period, young people should be like this. Although I'm old, I still want to learn from you young people.'

Just then Jiqing came over and nudged me, saying, 'I've got to work at the blacksmith's tomorrow and you have to sell your dough-sticks. We must go.'

'Oh, yes!' said Uncle Pan, smiling and touching his head. 'I forgot you're working tomorrow. My poor memory! I'm afraid I can't come with you – I have to hurry back to headquarters.'

When we got back to Red Hill Village, we could already hear the cocks crowing at the dawn.

# CHAPTER 7

Gradually Jiqing became not only my best friend but also my contact in the organization. He came home more often in the evenings. Sometimes, after selling all my dough-sticks and working out the accounts with Pockmarks the Sixth, it got quite late. If I reckoned that he would be finishing his day's work, I went straight to the blacksmith's to see him. I told him about my experiences while selling dough-sticks in the countryside – which villages I had been to, whom I had met, what special incidents I had come across, whether I had heard about any activities of the Order Preservation Corps or Red Spear Society, and so on. If there was a lot to talk about or if it was awkward to talk at the blacksmith's, he sometimes came back with me for the night. To make it easier to talk and not to disturb our two mothers, he suggested that I sleep in his room, so we could talk deep into the night. I not only talked about my daily experiences, but also listened to him talking about current affairs – the state of the nation and county affairs, about Chiang Kai-shek colluding with foreign powers, provincial militarists killing revolutionaries and the activities of Chumin and other landlords. I was amazed how he could work full-time and still be quite well informed about all these things. One evening he came back very early. While we were talking into the night, I asked him, 'Where have you learned about all these things, including the operations of Chiang Kai-shek and the provincial militarists?'

'Some from our night meetings and some from books.'

Then I remembered that he could read. Aunt Sunflower had once told me that as a child he had attended a private school in a nearby village temple until he was twelve, and then he went to work as an apprentice at the blacksmith's in town. In fact,

Aunt Sunflower had also told me that his father, Zizhong, had also studied in a private school for many years, so he was able to become an apprentice in the Revival Pharmacy in town – now he had become the main pharmacist there. He could read the prescription of any doctor and make it up, without making a mistake. Apparently he could still cure villagers' small ailments, although he did not charge for it.

'Where do you get books from?' I asked Jiqing. 'There's no bookshop in town.'

'From here.'

He lifted up his mattress and took out three pamphlets lying in the straw on his bed.

'Well, do you know what this is?' he asked smiling. 'If you want to read it, I can lend it to you, but don't let anyone else know – yes, you should read it! If you don't know revolutionary theory or what's happening elsewhere, how can you work for the revolution? You must know that you've now joined the revolution! Selling dough-sticks is a means of earning your living, just like my work in the blacksmith's – of course, these jobs can also be a cover and enable us to keep contact with people. You still have to study. First have a look at these pamphlets, and when you have read them put them back in the straw under the mattress – never forget to do that!'

I took the pamphlets and flicked through them under the oil-lamp. One of them was called *The Revolutionary Path of the Colonial and Semi-colonial Peoples*; another was *Imperialist Aggression against China*; and the third, *Mobilize the Masses and Smash Counter-revolution*.

'How did you get these pamphlets?' I asked Jiqing.

'Some students at the new school in "The Big City" brought them back. They're all revolutionaries active in our county now. Recently, though, we haven't had students like this coming back – many of them were killed in "The Big City". So sometimes when our comrades go there for a meeting, they buy some and bring them back. Didn't you come here with Pan Xudong? He brought back a big pile. Those who can read all want to borrow them.'

'Then what about those who cannot read?'

'They go to meetings in the evening, and people give them

109

talks. Uncle Pan is illiterate, but he is studying very hard. If there's a meeting and he can squeeze in the time, he always goes. He listens and takes part in discussions – the more he discusses problems, the more deeply he understands things. It isn't enough just to read. You ought to go to meetings too, to listen to talks and participate in discussions.'

'Who gives the talks at the meetings?'

'Of course, they're all educated people who have been to the new schools. Comrades Pan Xudong, Chang Je-an and Wang Jiansheng have all given talks.' At this point Jiqing suddenly touched his head before continuing. 'I almost forgot. Tomorrow you have to go and see Comrade Wang Jiansheng. There's a task for you!'

'Who's Comrade Wang Jiansheng?'

'You'll find out tomorrow. We should go to sleep now. Tomorrow morning at the crack of dawn we have to go into town, but you'll have to skip your job for a day.'

That was the end of our conversation that night.

As soon as I woke up I noticed the daylight through the window. Realizing that Jiqing had already washed, I jumped out of bed. We stuffed some pancakes our mothers had made the day before into our jackets and left hastily. Just as we were leaving the village, Jiqing suddenly reminded me, 'You've forgotten to bring that basket for your dough-sticks. Quickly go and fetch it. You'll still need it today.'

I turned back and went home. After fetching the basket I rushed back. Then we took the usual path over the hill to town, which we reached very quickly. Jiqing took me straight to Revival Pharmacy, where he handed me over to his father, Zizhong. He himself went to work at the blacksmith's.

Uncle Zizhong seemed to be a busy man. After we moved to his house, as far as I knew, he had only come home twice. Both times it was in the night after I had gone to bed, and he was gone the next morning before day-break. This time I looked at him carefully as I stood before him. He was tall and thin, with grey hair, but he was still energetic. He was sitting opposite a young patient by the cash desk behind the counter. After feeling the patient's pulse, he was explaining his condition. Uncle Zizhong seemed to be both pharmacist and doctor. I was not sure whether they were talking about medicine or not, as I could not understand. When they had finished, Uncle Zizhong looked up and spoke to me.

'Today I have to ask you to do something, my lad, but you have to do it properly.' Then he looked around. There were no customers yet. As the shop-owner had long moved to 'The Big City' and would not come back 'unless the situation returned to normal', he himself was actually in charge. He then introduced me to this young 'patient'. 'This is Comrade Wang Jiansheng. Jiqing must have told you about him. What I'm asking you to do today is connected with him.'

I had a look at Wang Jiansheng. He looked like a student, of average build and apparently under thirty. He was even thinner than Zizhong, with sunken, fiery-red eyes, perhaps from leading an exhausting and disturbed life over a long period of time. He stood up and patted my shoulder while shaking hands – his hand was freezing, a sign of malnutrition.

'Comrade Zizhong has told me about you,' he said. 'Carry out your tasks well. Our country and our people are now in turmoil. It's the responsibility of our young generation to work for China's revival. We must create a new society and a new world. The task which our organization has delegated to you today is to take a letter to Long Copse Village. It's in the south of the county, where you come from, so you should have no difficulty in finding it. You have to give this letter to a young woman called Sister Apricot. She'll understand as soon as she sees it – she can read and she knows my handwriting . . . '

He took the letter out of his pocket and handed it to me, but before he had finished what he was saying, Uncle Zizhong butted in:

'Sister Apricot is his wife and they have a little boy. Your task today is not just to deliver this letter, but also to bring them straight back to Red Hill Village, where Grandpa Whiskers can arrange for them to stay. Yes, take your basket to look as if you're going through the villages selling dough-sticks. Now hurry up, and I hope you can get back to Red Hill Village before it gets dark.'

I set off for the south immediately. Even though I had not been to Long Copse Village, I had heard of it, because Wang

111

Taihe, a rich landlord with a big estate, lived there. It was known far and wide, so I had no difficulty in finding the village. As a young lad selling dough-sticks in the villages I could travel around freely, and I reached my destination at midday.

Long Copse Village was quite large, at least twice the size of Red Hill Village, where we were living now. The houses were quite well built, many with bricks and tiles, not like our village with only mud-huts and thatched cottages. I was surprised to find the ruins of what formerly must have been the finest tiled-roof house in the middle of the village. Only some crumbling walls and their foundations made of grey stone slabs remained. A young woman, dragging along a small boy, was just searching there. She was looking amongst the ruins, her head bent down. She appeared to be about twenty-three or -four years of age, with fine features, but she had dishevelled hair and a frown, as if she were burdened with worries. I asked a buffalo-boy where Sister Apricot lived, and he pointed at the young woman searching in the debris, saying that was her. When I went up to her, she looked up startled. Then, seeing me standing there with my basket of dough-sticks, she said, 'Son, I have no money to buy dough-sticks. Don't waste your time here.'

'I'm not selling dough-sticks. Are you Sister Apricot? I've come specially to find you.'

'To find me?' she asked, astonished. 'Why are you looking for me?'

'I've got a letter for you.'

'How come? Even my parents don't care about me. Who would write me a letter?'

I took the letter out and handed it to her, saying, 'It's from your husband.' Then I lowered my voice: 'He sent me to take you to the north of the county.'

Sister Apricot gaped at me like an idiot.

'What do you mean? Is he still alive?'

'Otherwise, how could he have written this letter? First read it.'

She opened it and read it twice. A smile flickered on her lips, but two big tears also dropped on to her husband's letter.

'Am I dreaming?' She folded the letter and put it in her clothing, mumbling, 'Oh no, this is no dream!' Then she picked

112

up and hugged the little boy of about three, who had been standing and staring beside her. 'My Little Baldy,* your dad is still alive! Still alive! You'll be able to see him!' she cried, and then, turning to me, she said, 'Let's go! We have nothing but the shabby clothes we're wearing. Let's go, quickly. Let's leave this place right away! Oh, I forgot to ask you, my boy, what's your name? Tell me and then I'll know what to call you from now on.'

'Chunsheng. Just call me Chunsheng, Sister Apricot.'

She was surprised again, and asked, 'How do you know I'm called Sister Apricot?'

'Comrade Wang Jiansheng told me this morning.'

'So he really is alive!'

I did not answer, as I could see that there were no longer tears in her eyes and the smile on her lips now broadened. She was so excited that a faint red glow also appeared on her waxen face. She was so happy that her husband was safe and sound.

I took her child and held him in my arms. Then I gave her my basket, so that we would look like brother and sister. Thus we left the village at noon, when everyone was at home having lunch. She was not carrying any clothing or anything else, so she could walk quite quickly. As soon as we were out of the village we stepped up our pace, so that nobody near by would notice us. After we had gone a mile or so, we stopped by a small gully in the mountains and drank some water from the clear stream. When I noticed that her face was covered with sweat, I told her to sit down and rest for a while, as there were two stones by the stream. I sat down first and she took her child from me, patting it and looking at me in a friendly way. She seemed to feel more at ease with me now.

'My boy, no, I should call you by your proper name,' she began, just to make conversation. 'Brother Chunsheng, right? It's a nice name.'

'It's not so special – my father invented it. I was born in spring, which is the time of nature's rebirth, so my father called me Spring Birth. And you? What should I call you formally?'

* Intimate name used in the countryside for male child whose downy head looks bald.

'I'm just a woman, so I haven't got a formal name. My father was a teacher and he taught me some characters, so I could understand Jiansheng's letter. I was born when the apricot trees blossom, so Father called me Apricot Face. Now everyone calls me Sister Apricot, so just call me that!'

This conversation was not deep or important in itself, but strangely enough it did help us to get closer. By this secluded stream we were really like brother and sister travelling together towards the same destination, fleeing from dangers to find a safe place to live. I took this opportunity to ask her about her own affairs. I wanted to know, because I already felt close to her.

'Sister Apricot, back there you were ferreting around in that burnt-out, delapidated building. What valuables could there have been in that heap of rubble?'

'There was nothing there, in fact, but I was just looking for anything. My child had nothing to eat, so I wanted to have a look in case some unspoiled rice had been left in the rice chest.'

'Was that your home?'

'Yes, it was my father's-in-law,' she replied, nodding. 'It belonged to Wang Taihe – do you know about him?'

I was shocked. I never imagined that Wang Taihe could be her father-in-law.

'They fled to a neighbouring county to seek refuge with relatives, because they couldn't live here any longer – you've seen it for yourself, haven't you – a pile of rubble?'

'So why didn't they take you with them?'

'Well . . . ' she started, but then swallowed her words.

'Everyone knows about Wang Taihe,' I said. 'He's a wealthy landlord in our county, even if he doesn't match up to Chumin. Where has he gone now?'

Her expression became mournful, and she refused to answer.

'Well, how did the house burn down? Was it an accident or arson?' I asked again.

She heaved a sigh.

'It's a long story,' she said, looking up at the sky and then suddenly becoming alarmed. 'We must leave here at once! How much further have we got – to get to the place were Jiansheng lives?'

'It's still quite far. We have to cross several hills. We're just coming to a hill which we have to climb. It'll be dark and slow-going when we get there.'

'Well, let's get going.'

When she got up, her child, who had fallen asleep in her arms, woke up. I quickly took him again, and we started off. As she had evaded my question, I could only keep silent.

We made our way in silence with our heads down. We took turns carrying the child, who behaved very well. Perhaps he had been frightened in the village, but now that they were away he was calm and quiet. Sister Apricot also seemed to relax gradually as they got away from the depressing atmosphere of the troubled village. After a long period of silence, perhaps because she felt that now it was unnecessary to keep her personal affairs from me, she started speaking freely to me.

'It's really difficult to tell my story in a few words. The destruction of the house was not so important, but what I could not bear was that Wang the Lion and his Order Preservation Corps burned it down.'

At this point she suddenly let herself go, showing that indeed she could not 'bear it'. She talked frenziedly about the circumstances surrounding the burning of her house:

'This was a new house, which Wang Jiansheng's father had built after knocking down his old one just before we got married and I moved in. You probably know that he was one of the wealthiest landlords in this area. Of course, he was small fry compared with Chumin, but he was clever enough not to be swallowed up by Chumin, who always had his eye on his two or three hectares of land. He prevented this by keeping on good terms with Chumin, not giving him a pretext to find fault with him or manipulating officialdom to persecute him. When a new county head took office, for instance, Wang Taihe took the initiative to present him with a valuable gift. Recognizing Chumin as one of the rich gentry in the county, he always deferred to him and never competed. He let Chumin buy all the best land without interfering. Whenever Chumin wanted to do any "charitable" deeds, he supported him. For example, when Chumin organized the Red Spear Society and asked him for a contribution, he complied. Last year, when the Red Spear

Society was established and Wang the Lion came round with a "contribution record book" for a donation, he again agreed, handing over two hundred silver coins on the spot. Wang Taihe had to co-operate with Chumin who was always bullying him. It was really difficult for my father-in-law.

'He had four children, three of whom were daughters – when he married them off, he bought all their wedding clothes, which cost a good part of his fortune. His youngest child was a boy – that's Wang Jiansheng. His parents adored him, so they didn't want him simply to manage the family's land, carrying on their traditional occupation. His father sent him to a new-type school in "The Big City" to learn new subjects. He even put some money aside to send him to university after he had finished school and passed his exams. Father-in-law had his own plan: if Jiansheng got into university, he should specialize in a subject called "law and politics", as he had heard that it was necessary to study this subject in order to become an official. He hoped his son would become an official – even higher ranking than county head. In that case he wouldn't have to fear Chumin. But Chumin wasn't stupid. He himself was just as afraid of anyone in the county surpassing him. He frequently tried to persuade Father-in-law that it was enough for Jiansheng to finish secondary school. It was essential for him to carry on the family occupation. Instead of spending large sums of money to send him to university, it would be more profitable to buy more land. Father-in-law just pretended to agree.

'Jiansheng was intelligent and he studied hard. Apparently the school which he attended was run by a scholar from our county, who had studied abroad. He was very knowledgeable, so the education was very good. Jiansheng himself did exceedingly well in his studies and seemed all set to go to university. Within a year after he left school Father-in-law arranged his marriage. He did this to let his son settle down, then study calmly at university and soon have a child. That's how I joined the family, and that was the year when the new house was built. We got married when he came back home for his summer vacation. I soon discovered that he didn't have the same idea as his father. He didn't want to go to university. In this respect he actually satisfied Chumin's secret hope, which is really ironical. He told me, as the state of affairs in our country was critical and the people were living in misery, young people should do something about it. So university was out of the question. He even criticized his parents directly, calling them misers. When the peasants were suffering so much, they shouldn't collect rent or should at least reduce the rent. He wasn't just talking either – he was very good to the peasants himself. Whenever he had a moment to spare, he went to have a talk with the poor tenant-farmers in the village. He even ran a literacy evening class for them and their children. He taught them himself and bought textbooks for them. He was very serious about his teaching and so he had to go out every evening. His parents, however, were disappointed in him. They tried every way to persuade him not to mix with those rough people. It was useless, because somehow Jiansheng had become quite determined. My parents-in-law also asked me to urge him to "correct his ways", but what could I do? He was much more knowledgeable than others, so it was impossible to persuade him. On the contrary, he persuaded me, because what he said was true: it couldn't be wrong to do something for poor people. Anyway, after that my parents-in-law also became dissatisfied with me. As a woman, what could I do but accept my fate?

'When Jiansheng left school and received his diploma, he was already outstanding in the village, but he was still mixing with villagers around there. That was at the time of the Northern Expedition of the Revolutionary Army, and they set up a peasant union in the county. Then he got closer to the peasants, even asking his parents to distribute the family land among the poor. Even though he was their only son and they doted on him, they could not accept this drastic idea. So they started arguing. They had frequent quarrels, and when he had had enough of it he ran off to the county town. There the Revolutionary Party had taken over the county office in the wake of the Northern Expeditionary Army. The Revolutionary Party consisted of all his former schoolmates from "The Big City", and he got on well with them – I heard later that he organized the peasant unions with them.* Once he came back from the county town and

* Organized by the communists in the late 1920s.

117

quarrelled with his parents again, threatening to burn the house down. He said that with most of the farmers still living in mud-huts, how could we go on living in this new house built wth grey bricks and stone slabs? All his parents could do was to ask some tenant-farmers whom he trusted to prevent him burning down the house, but nobody was willing. So they went to consult Chumin, who was only too glad to be able to interfere in our family affairs. He promised to send Wang the Lion with some tough lads to our house to arrest Jiansheng, keep him in his house to straighten him out and not let him go until he "corrected his ways". A servant of Chumin managed to leak this secret plan, so Jiansheng got out of the village, never to return. After this the peasant unions sprang up everywhere. Chumin became isolated and he was even arrested by men sent by the new county government and brought to the county town to be tried. Unfortunately, on the way he was rescued by a gang of thugs sent by Wang the Lion.

'Of course, you know the rest of the story. The provincial officials and militarists staged a counter-attack, even killing the revolutionary students. They also sent troops to the countryside to kill villagers, who had no guns to resist them. So they were defeated, and some students and leaders of the peasant unions were captured and executed. We had no news about Jiansheng; Chumin was delighted. This time he had learned to be on his guard. He expanded his Order Preservation Corps and worked hand in glove with the new county head, who was fighting the Revolutionary Party. They formed the Red Spear Society and went around arresting and killing people. Now Chumin believes he is more powerful than ever and can lord it over people. Recently he asked my parents-in-law to hand over our new house. He could protect it and jointly manage our fields to force the tenants to pay tax.

'"Let's combine our family properties to fight together against our common enemy!" That's how he tried to persuade my father-in-law.

'This sounded fine and sensible, but my parents-in-law were no fools. They knew that if they agreed to let Chumin "jointly manage" their land, they would definitely have nothing left in the end. All their efforts would be wasted. They could never

118

agree to this "generous proposal", so their discussions came to nothing. Then Chumin changed his attitude completely, saying that Jiansheng was a revolutionary and that our house was a hide-out of the Revolutionary Party. He sent Wang the Lion in the night to burn our house down.

'Ah, Jiansheng was quite right.' She heaved a sigh before continuing: 'If he had burned down the house at the start, I wouldn't have minded so much, but I cannot bear the thought that it was burned down by Wang the Lion's gang.'

'Why didn't your father-in-law bring him to trial?' I asked. 'Why did he burn down your house? You didn't owe him any debt!'

'He's in league with the county officials. How could one bring him to trial?' Sister Apricot asked in turn. 'He said that we were harbouring bandits and that if he captured Jiansheng, he would cut his head off! Now my parents-in-law had a "bandit" son. When they saw the house in flames, they were afraid that Wang the Lion's men would turn on them and arrest them, so in the night they fled to a neighbouring county. At that time Little Baldy was bawling and screaming. Since those thugs of Wang the Lion had taken everything we had, I feared they might kill Little Baldy, as he's Jiansheng's son. So I quickly escaped with him to the mountains behind the village. I only found out later that my parents-in-law had also fled. As the villagers were fond of Jiansheng, they didn't betray us to Wang the Lion but secretly protected us, so that we two could stay in the village for a few days – Wang the Lion thought we had really fled afar with my parents-in-law. Chunsheng – may I call you that? – you came just in time to save us!'

As Sister Apricot came to the end of her account of her family misfortune, she really seemed to have been 'saved'. Far from being exhausted, she seemed to have more energy and walked even more quickly. When I told her that we were coming to the end of our journey – Red Hill Village – she realized that she had escaped from danger. Her spirit rose further and she walked even faster. Soon we had reached Red Hill Village.

Grandpa Whiskers, Aunt Sunflower and my Mother were waiting for us at the roadside as we entered the village. Aunt Sunflower immediately took Little Baldy from Sister Apricot.

119

When she held him in her arms, he started crying, but Aunt Sunflower had brought some sweets, which she stuffed into his little mouth to stop him. Sister Apricot was amazed to see all these people she did not know. She could not have imagined that they would be here to welcome her like this.

'Don't be shocked,' said Grandpa Whiskers. 'These two "sisters" will be your neighbours and friends. You'll be staying in my house without paying rent, as Jiansheng arranged. I'm an old bachelor with one or two empty rooms in my home. It'll be livelier with you and your little boy. Let's go!'

He led Sister Apricot to his home, with the rest of us following. Arriving at his mud-hut, we stood in his sitting room.

'You see, the rooms are empty; you've come just at the right time,' Grandpa Whiskers said to Sister Apricot. 'Just make yourself at home.' Then, pointing to the room on the right, he continued, 'That's your room; you can go in and have a look.'

Aunt Sunflower and my mother took Sister Apricot in. Inside was a big bed, which was already prepared for the night, and also a table with some bowls, chopsticks and a cooking pot. Even though these things were very simple, they were sufficient to meet their daily needs. Sister Apricot had probably never imagined that Wang Jiansheng could arrange everything for her and the boy so well. After all, for so long she had not known whether her husband was still alive or not. Her worn-out, waxen face suddenly lit up with a glowing smile. Then, just as suddenly, she looked anxious and asked, 'What about Jiansheng? Where is he?'

Hearing this, Grandpa Whiskers poked his head in and said with a smile, 'Just before you arrived he asked us to pass on the message that he had to attend an urgent meeting. He'll come after the meeting, so you two had better get some rest first.'

'You must have something to eat,' said Aunt Sunflower and my mother. 'We're going home to fetch you something. The little one must be very hungry!'

Then both women left to fetch some food from home. I went back with Mother too, feeling relieved: I had successfully accomplished my task.

One day I got back home after dark having sold the whole

120

basketful of dough-sticks which Pockmarks the Sixth had given me in the morning. Sister Apricot was there too with Little Baldy, who was playing with a rag ball beside her. She was sewing while talking to Aunt Sunflower and my mother. It looked as if these three mothers were very close now. O Ran had given Aunt Sunflower this sewing work from the clothes shop which she owned in Tanjiahe, jointly with a widow and a tailor. In fact, however, she seldom had time to work in the shop. As she was out most of the time, she usually gave her share of the work to Aunt Sunflower, whom she naturally paid. Aunt Sunflower in turn allocated the work to others, and Sister Apricot was now part of the 'co-operative'. Grandpa Whiskers told outsiders she was a distant relative of his from another county. This seemed quite plausible, and she gradually got used to her new environment, feeling quite at home here. Still her husband, Jiansheng, had not once come to see her, saying that he was 'terribly busy and would come maybe tomorrow'.

Although Sister Apricot had settled down now, the frown which I had seen from the very first day had not disappeared. In fact, she looked very depressed now as she sat with Aunt Sunflower and my mother, sewing and talking in a subdued voice. They must have noticed this too, as they both asked me, 'Have you seen Wang Jiansheng today?'

'I haven't seen anybody for the past two days. Before coming home I specially went to the blacksmith's to ask Jiqing to come back with me, but he wasn't there. I don't know what's happening – I can't find anyone.'

'So Wang Jiansheng is just as busy as anybody else,' said my mother. I knew that she said this deliberately to console Sister Apricot. 'As soon as he's free, he'll come to see you and the child. Don't worry, Sister Apricot.'

Sister Apricot did not say a word. She just put the clothes she was sewing into a wicker basket and took Little Baldy in her arms, stood up and made to leave. She was really miserable, as it was impossible to find out what had happened to Jiansheng.

'Don't go,' said Aunt Sunflower. 'We have a lot of food left over from lunch. I'll put some water and wild vegetables in the rice and boil a big pot of mixed porridge, which will be enough for all of us. Have supper with us, Sister Apricot. The more the merrier.'

My mother took the child from Sister Apricot again, talking to him playfully: 'You're hungry! I know you're hungry! In a minute you'll have two extra bowls to eat. You'll get so fat that your dad will be happy when he sees you!'

Sister Apricot hung her head, probably wondering what had happened to the child's father – if only he were still alive!

Just while we were eating there was a soft knock on the door. I went over at once and cautiously lifted the latch. In came Jiqing, and he pushed the door wide open to let in the group of people behind him. We were all amazed to see them. There was Uncle Pan, Lao Liu, Chang Je-an, Pan Zaixing, Liu Dawang, Pan Mingxun and O Ran. Finally, there was Uncle Zizhong. After greeting them all, we gradually calmed down.

'Oh dear!' Aunt Sunflower cried out. 'Why didn't you tell us first? We would have prepared something for you to eat!'

'When did I ever tell you that I was coming home?' said Uncle Zizhong. 'What times are these? When we come nowadays, we just arrive like a whirlwind. Haven't you got used to it yet?'

'But Aunt Sunflower could never have imagined that so many of you would come together,' explained my Mother. 'Nor could I!'

'We've all come to see Sister Apricot,' said O Ran. 'None of us has met her yet, but we're all concerned about her!' Then she turned to Sister Apricot and asked, 'Have you got used to living here?'

Holding her child, Sister Apricot got up and smiled to thank everyone for looking after her. This forced smile soon vanished as she replied, 'I'm fine, but what about Jiansheng? Have you seen him? Where is he now?'

'He was with us today,' answered Uncle Pan. 'We had a meeting with him this afternoon. Comrade Pan Xudong had a lot to say, so the meeting finished late. Comrade Jiansheng still had something to discuss with Pan Xudong, so he asked me to come here first with everyone. It's a good opportunity for us to come and meet you. We're very glad to see you well settled here.'

'Well, sit down, all of you. We'll prepare something for you to eat,' said Sister Apricot, handing the child to my Mother as she turned towards the kitchen.

'There's no need, Sister Apricot,' said Uncle Pan. 'We've still got another meeting. Jiansheng will be reporting to us and then we'll be discussing Pan Xudong's speech. So he'll definitely be coming, don't worry.'

Just as he finished talking, there was another soft knock at the door. Zizhong hurried over to open it, and who should walk in but Wang Jiansheng.

'How lively,' said Wang Jiansheng. 'What a change since I came back to your home with you that night!'

'Yes, indeed, there are two new guests here!' Uncle Zizhong pointed to Sister Apricot and Little Baldy, asking, 'Do you know them?'

Wang Jiansheng looked up at Sister Apricot and his son, dumbfounded. Sister Apricot and Little Baldy also looked at him blankly. They did not seem to recognize one another. Their faces were pale and thin, so different from before – one the result of her recent trials and tribulations, the other from his tense and strenuous work.

Observing them, Uncle Pan said to everyone, 'We'll go over to Grandpa Whiskers's place first and prepare for the meeting.' Then he spoke to me: 'You come too. According to the regulations, you will also be attending meetings like this.'

'Fine,' said Jiansheng, recovering. 'Yes, you go ahead. I'll have a few words with Apricot and come along after!'

Aunt Sunflower and my mother got up too and went into the kitchen to boil some water. They wanted to leave Wang Jiansheng and Sister Apricot alone to have a moment together, and at the same time they prepared a big pot of tea to send over to Grandpa Whiskers.

We had been sitting on four benches around Grandpa Whiskers's sitting room for a while, when Sister Apricot brought Wang Jiansheng over. She was carrying a big pot of fresh tea. Jiansheng was carrying Little Baldy – the little one seemed to have recognized his father, as he was curled up very cosily in his arms. Sister Apricot put the tea pot on the table, took the child from Jiansheng and then went into her room at the back.

'You didn't have to come so quickly; you could have talked

longer,' said Lao Liu. 'You haven't been together for such a long time!'

'I can't hold you all up.' Jiansheng was standing by a table in the middle of the room. 'I gather you're all here this evening to relay the report made by the leadership at the emergency meeting of the county committee today and to discuss its contents. I didn't come here for personal reasons. Now, let's start the meeting.'

Grandpa Whiskers immediately went out to keep watch outside. I knew his mud-hut was, like Pheasant Nest, a meeting place in the evenings. Because the peasant unions had flourished here in the past, the revolutionary forces had quite a solid base in this area. The counter-revolutionary forces, on the other hand, were relatively weak and more passive at night. Even so, Grandpa Whiskers was worried, and every time they had a meeting there he insisted on standing guard outside himself until everyone dispersed. When Jiangsheng saw that Grandpa Whiskers had shut the door from outside, he continued:

'The developments here have caused concern to Chiang Kai-shek. The leaders of our organization have received information that he's going to send more troops to our county to destroy all our revolutionary forces in one fell swoop, so it looks as if a big extermination campaign is about to begin. We must mobilize the masses rapidly and organize them to fight a revolutionary war against the counter-revolutionary forces. That's what our leaders have decided. From tonight, every district under our control has to carry out this task rapidly. It's already quite dangerous around the county town, so the leaders have decided to move the headquarters and the county committee to Tanjiahe tomorrow. So comrades, your responsibilities will be even heavier. If any of you have points to make, please speak.'

Wang Jiansheng waited for everyone's reaction. Lao Liu cleared his throat and spoke.

'I'm responsible for propaganda, so that's what concerns me first and foremost. We have to mobilize the masses and get them to organize themselves. As for arming them, we should raise their class consciousness even further and make them realize that it's necessary to fight – at this stage, as the leaders pointed out, it's necessary to wage armed struggle. This needs wide-scale propaganda and organizational work has to be combined with propaganda. Both are indispensable! I raised this point at the extra big meeting of the county committee today, but unfortunately it wasn't discussed.'

'Because there wasn't enough time and there were even more important things to decide,' explained Jiansheng. Then he asked Zizhong, 'You're responsible for organization work. What's your opinion?'

Uncle Zizhong saw how Lao Liu was sitting straight-backed, his head held high, gazing at him and eagerly waiting to hear his response.

'I'd like to know first, Lao Liu, how you plan to spread propaganda far and wide,' asked Uncle Zizhong. 'As you used to in your job, by carrying a small drum and clappers, going around all the villages telling stories? Or do you have a better way?'

Uncle Pan suddenly interrupted.

'Telling stories is no longer enough – even though I loved to hear Lao Liu's stories in the past. You need great ability to tell stories and their scope is still limited. Now you have a new role, and the enemies are even more powerful. If you fall into a trap set by their agents and are arrested, you could be executed!'

'Uncle Pan is responsible for security work,' said Liu Dawang. 'He has a lot of experience in this field. We should seriously consider what he says.'

'Yes,' said Pan Zaixing, 'story-telling is unsuitable now, because our enemies are suspicious of story-tellers. I heard that a short while ago plain-clothes detectives sent out by the county government arrested many story-tellers, whose fate is still unknown.'

At this point Lao Liu suddenly stood up and glared at everyone, obviously in a state of agitation.

'I don't know what you all mean,' he said indignantly. 'After we've been together all this time, how is it that you still don't understand me? I'm not the same Lao Liu I used to be! Do you still think I can only tell those old stories . . . ?'

O Ran interrupted him:

'What are you talking about? Who took you for the Lao Liu of former days? Who said you tell old stories? You take yourself

125

too seriously; you're too sensitive! How can you be a committee member responsible for propaganda?'

'He does very well,' Uncle Zizhong put in. 'He's very responsible and enthusiastic. If he wasn't, then he wouldn't be so serious now. Lao Liu, I'm afraid you didn't quite understand what I meant. I'll explain again: although story-telling is one kind of propaganda, there must be other means, otherwise how can you expand it – moreover, with such urgent tasks facing us now, propaganda work must really develop. So I fully support your opinion. I only want to know, what other means of developing propaganda do you have?'

Now Lao Liu sat down, having apparently calmed down. He looked around. Everyone was calmly waiting for some conclusion to this important discussion. Wang Jiansheng was sitting silently by the table. His serious and silent demeanour added to the tense atmosphere.

'I'm sorry, I didn't understand what you meant when you asked me just now.' Lao Liu now addressed Zizhong in a quiet and apologetic manner. 'That was a good question. What I meant was that we need written as well as oral propaganda. In the present circumstances written propaganda is even more important. I propose sticking up posters with slogans, distributing leaflets and even issuing notices. The aim is to call on the people to struggle against their enemies and also to warn those enemies not to carry on their evil ways. This kind of propaganda has a wide scope and can have a big influence.'

'That's quite right. I think you've got the right idea,' said Chang Je-an. 'Lao Liu, you're really an artiste; you're full of imagination. By doing this we can strengthen our own will and undermine our enemies!'

'I agree.' Pan Zaixing and Liu Dawang spoke together. 'When we go out at night on some mission, we can stick up posters all over the place and distribute leaflets right under the noses of the enemies. They'll be frightened out of their wits, imagining that we have vast forces and strength. They'd better think twice if they intend to start a "mopping-up" operation.'

'I can go out at night too to distribute material,' said Jiqing.

'I can go too,' said Pan Mingxun.

'So can I!' I shouted.

'We can't have everyone doing this,' said Zizhong, and then he addressed me. 'We have liaison work, which is also very important. But now we haven't got enough people for this work. After consulting with the district committee, we've decided that this will be your main task. I will contact you later about the details. If we can't meet, Jiqing can inform you too.'

Lao Liu got up once more, looking worried again. Using the two words he had so often used when telling stories, he said, 'Hold on!'

Everybody now focused their attention on him, waiting for him to continue. He coughed to clear his throat.

'The question of extending our propaganda mainly relates to written propaganda.' He raised his voice: 'I haven't finished giving my opinion. I am grateful that you agree with me, but it isn't as easy as that. First, who is going to write the posters and leaflets? No, to be more precise, I don't mean copying with a brush or handwriting or formal script. I mean, who is going to compose or write these posters and leaflets? Writing a leaflet is like writing an essay. Writing posters is even more difficult. The language has to be concise and the contents clear. They should be easy to understand, inspiring and easy to remember – I think that's almost more difficult than writing poetry . . .'

'Stop! Stop! Stop!' Pan Zaixing interrupted Lao Liu. 'Just now you blamed me for talking too generally. Now you're drifting from the subject. Here you are talking about writing essays and poems. We country bumpkins don't understand all that stuff. You used to be a story-teller, so you can make up stories, moving stories, what's more. You'll have no difficulty in writing posters and leaflets. You've chosen the wrong place, the wrong time and audience to discuss this topic. Let's finish here. We have to go right away to mobilize the peasants, artisans, women and children too. Time is pressing!'

'No, no, no!' retorted Lao Liu anxiously. 'I haven't finished yet, and it's a most important problem connected with propaganda: how many posters and leaflets can one man write in one day, if he writes nice and clearly? Even ten people cannot write many. So how can we expand our propaganda? We have to print it – only by printing can we solve this problem. We need at least a mimeographing machine. But with this machine, another more serious problem will arise. We'll need paper and ink – in fact, a whole set of things for printing!'

When Lao Liu mentioned all these 'needs', everyone was at a loss, unable to respond. It was Zizhong who broke the silence again:

'You're really a born story-teller with a very rich imagination. You've thought of so many things, from expanding our propaganda to all the things we would "need". Nobody wants to contradict you, but you know too what a difficult situation we're in. Chiang Kai-shek is planning to send more troops to wage his extermination campaign, while we only have a few pistols and old rifles. What do you think we can do?'

This time Lao Liu could only stare dumbly at Uncle Zizhong.

'I admit that guns are a vital "need",' he mumbled, 'but I'm responsible for propaganda. Naturally, I considered this problem first. I was born with a rich imagination.'

'It's good to have a rich imagination,' said Chang Je-an. 'We have to think about things. The reason why we held the meeting this evening was to get everyone to think about problems and express their opinions, so that we can act on them. Propaganda serves the struggle, and the struggle needs guns – the time has come when we need guns to fight the enemy. So both your opinions are quite right, and the problems you raised must be solved, because they are urgent. We must report the situation to the leadership, and I'm sure the problems can be solved. They must be solved – and solved quickly. So you see, I have also put forward two "needs". We need all our different kinds of work!'

'You're right, Comrade Je-an,' said Wang Jiansheng. 'I agree with you entirely. Let's go ahead straightaway.'

This marked the end of the meeting. It was already late at night. Jiqing opened the door carefully. Grandpa Whiskers was still standing there like a statue under a Chinese scholar tree about ten feet from the hut. When he saw us emerging from his home, he turned and blocked Jiansheng's way.

'You can't go!' he said. 'You have to stay here tonight. Sister Apricot has been waiting for you for so long. You must know how she feels!'

'I wasn't planning to leave. The leadership also instructed me to stay here!' Then he turned to us and continued lightheartedly, 'You see, Grandpa Whiskers has added two more "needs" – the last one was the need to "be human". The government office and the landlords are inhuman towards us peasants, and that's why we've joined the revolution.'

We could not help laughing. As the night was so still, our laughter must have carried quite a distance. The thugs of the county government and the landlords, however, did not dare go out at night, so the noise did not matter.

The others wanted to carry on with their various tasks, so they all went back to their posts, except for Chang Je-an who received a new assignment. Under cover of darkness, he was to pass through the area under Chumin's domain en route to the neighbouring Machen county, where he would be engaged in underground activities right under the nose of the Nationalist garrison headquarters in the county town – no longer as a fortune-telling woman in disguise as of old, but as a learned geomancer. Uncle Zizhong, Uncle Pan, Lao Liu and O Ran did not come back to our house, as they had so much to do. Only Jiqing and I went home for the night, and we found our mothers fast asleep.

The following morning, after the cock had crowed three times, Jiqing crawled out of bed and woke me up. He was going to town to work at the blacksmith's and I was going to sell my dough-sticks in the countryside, at the same time finding out what was happening in the villages. As we stepped out, we saw Wang Jiansheng coming towards us. He wanted to go with us to Tanjiahe. Before leaving for other places to carry on with organizational work, he wanted to spend a day in town delegating all the work to be done here, so he was in a great hurry. I calculated on my fingers that he had hardly spent four hours with Sister Apricot and Little Baldy, as it was past midnight by the time our meeting had finished.

# CHAPTER 8

It was a sunny day and the whistling west wind had subsided. The whole landscape of fields, mountain ranges, woods and villages appeared extremely peaceful. In this stillness any sounds would carry far. The most striking were the cocks crowing and some singing coming from the valley and fields. It was very unusual, because people in this mountain district and, in fact, in the whole county had long since forgotten the sound of song, and even children no longer sang. This singing rekindled their thirst for life and aroused their hopes. For some reason I too felt in high spirits, and my legs seemed stronger than usual. That day I went around a dozen villages, carrying my basket of dough-sticks. In the afternoon, when the sun was still high in the sky, I had already sold a whole basketful, so I could go home early.

On the way home, I saw two people walking ahead of me, one fat and the other thin. The fatter one was wearing a faded blue padded jacket with a belt. He looked like a peasant of middle age, a butcher or even an accountant in a pawn-shop. The thinner man was walking behind him. He was younger, but from the way he was strolling lazily along, he was definitely not from the countryside. On the other hand, he did not seem exactly like a shop assistant either, but rather like a good-for-nothing idler. I followed them for a while until they came to a fork in the road, where they suddenly turned off to the right along a path leading to Red Hill Village. Since we had moved to this little village I had never seen such strange people there. Out of curiosity I hurried to catch up with them to see what they were up to. I noticed that there was something protruding behind the thin man, making his gown stick out two or three inches. This was a pistol, I guessed. In the countryside this was a terrifying weapon, because the villagers did not have anything but knives, lances, spears, hoes and spades. Why were these two coming to our village with this weapon? I thought I should find out what they were up to. Then I could take a short-cut back to the village and warn the villagers to prepare to defend themselves. Perhaps I was walking too quickly, and when I got nearer to them I was out of breath. The thin one noticed me and immediately asked, 'Who are you?'

'I sell dough-sticks,' I answered.

'Why are you following us?' asked the thin one again.

'I'm going back to my village. This is the way to Red Hill Village.'

Then the fat one turned round and I immediately recognized who he was. As soon as he saw me, he smiled in a cunning way, baring his nicotine-stained teeth, and said, 'So it's you, Little Brother. Do you have any dough-sticks left?'

'Quite right, it's me, Uncle Qiyu. As the weather was fine today, everyone was in a good mood and so I sold all my dough-sticks quickly. That's why I can go home early today.'

Liu Qiyu frowned and that strange smile disappeared. He was the *Bao* chief in this district, Grandpa Whiskers's superior. He lived quite far from here, in a village called Three-arch Bridge nearer the county town. By the bridge there was a temple to the God of the Earth. It was said that when the movement to set up peasant unions was in full swing and the peasants were fighting superstitions, they threw the clay idol statues from the bridge into the river. As the temple had been emptied in this way, the *Bao* chief converted it into his office, where he did his 'security work'. He installed a table and chair there, and a stove in the corner to boil water for tea. He often sat at his table 'working'. In fact he had no work to do, but because Three-arch Bridge was on an important road leading to the county town, there were always all sorts of people coming through. Sitting there, he could show his authority and collect information about what the peasants were doing in the countryside. He reported to the county government and to the military officers stationed in the county. In this way he could show that he was a loyal 'county official' and gain some rewards. He felt happy and secure sitting behind that 'office desk' enjoying his tea. The armed plain-clothes agents sent by the county government to keep a watch around pretended to be his friends and sometimes sat there with him, drinking tea and chatting. One of the tasks Zizhong had given me recently was to visit him frequently to 'pay my respects'. He was always in good spirits and when he saw my dough-sticks he always chose two or three crisp ones to go with his tea. Sometimes he paid for them, but usually he just expressed his appreciation – 'Very good! Very crisp!' – as I was about to leave. To be friendly, he often called after me, 'Come again tomorrow, Little Brother!' He seemed to be addicted to dough-sticks.

Now he glared at me. 'You just said that everyone was in good spirits. How's that?' he asked. 'Was that why they were singing so nicely?'

'How do I know?'

'Didn't you hear?' he persisted. 'Now there's singing everywhere. Even the peasants hoeing the soil are singing. Do you know what they're singing?'

'How should I know? If you want to find out, you'd better get close and listen.'

'But as soon as I get to the village the singing suddenly stops!' he said, showing frustration.

As he mentioned it, I just realized that the singing had suddenly stopped, perhaps because he was approaching the village. The peasants working in the fields here were from our village or other villages around. They were obviously inhibited by the arrival of the Bao chief. The sudden silence made him rather nervous. 'But the singing has suddenly stopped!' he repeated, hoping to get an explanation from me. I deliberately kept silent now. The Bao chief's questions reminded me of a chat with Jiqing. He had told me a story about the previous Bao chief. As soon as the peasant unions had been broken up, he thought he could recover his lost power and start to lord it over people again. He went around investigating the leading members and activists of the peasant unions. One day he disappeared on his way from Tanjiahe on 'official business'. Three days later his body was found floating in the river by his village, downstream from Three-arch Bridge. Liu Qiyu learned a lesson from his predecessor's fate, so he did not dare visit Tanjiahe very often – it was under his jurisdiction, but became a kind of 'liberated town'. He was afraid to go alone to any village in the course of his duties, so he always took an armed guard with him. The thin one with him must have been sent by the county government to protect him as he went through the countryside. Now he must have grown very anxious, remembering the fate of the previous *Bao* chief.

'Are you going to our village?' I asked, not wishing him to suspect my silence.

'Yes. Is Grandpa Whiskers at home?'

'He's a very quiet old man, who always stays in the village. He's concerned about all the village affairs, so the villagers like him and follow his example.'

'That's fine,' said the *Bao* chief. 'I'm just going to visit him, as I haven't seen him for a long time.'

'I'm going to see him too. He asked me to buy some pills for his heart trouble.'

'Have you bought them?'

'No, they were sold out. We'll have to wait for four or five days.'

'Why are you going to see him then?'

'To tell him I couldn't get them, because he is a very serious person and the village *Jia* chief. If you cannot do what he wants, you have to report to him. We villagers are all polite and correct.'

In fact I was very worried about this strange official and this ruffian-type carrying a pistol. I decided to follow them to Grandpa Whiskers's place, so that, in case anything happened, I could immediately report it to the villagers. Liu Qiyu probably accepted my explanation, as he agreed to let me go with him. The thin one just gave me a nasty look, but he could not object.

Grandpa Whiskers was standing at his door gazing at the sky, so he saw us approaching. He promptly extended both arms in greeting, welcoming his senior into his house. He poured tea, offered cigarettes, addressed the thin man politely, displaying all the necessary respect and courtesy. Liu Qiyu and the thin one sat down at opposite sides of the table at the end of the room, putting on a superior air. After the preliminaries, Liu Qiyu took out two silver coins and put them on the table, saying to Grandpa Whiskers, 'County Head Yao De-an is very concerned about his subordinates, and he has specially sent me to give you some money to buy half a kilo of meat, so that you can enjoy some soup. Life has been hard these recent years, so there hasn't been much opportunity to taste meat.'

'Yes, *Bao* Chief, all too little,' responded Grandpa Whiskers. 'Some of the villagers haven't even been able to taste meat for New Year.'

'They're too frugal. People should eat some meat at New Year and other festivals. By the way, how are the villagers doing nowadays?'

'Very well. They're always busy with farming – recently they've been so busy, starting to collect manure, that they hardly have time to eat!'

Liu Qiyu's mouth twisted with anger. He evidently didn't like what Grandpa Whiskers had said.

'How can you say that they have no time to eat? Since Landlord Mao Dehou left this area and never returned, nobody has collected the tenants' taxes. They must all be eating very well!'

'Are you talking about that "Living King of Hell"?' Grandpa Whiskers retorted. 'Yes, since the old landlord left Tanjiahe, nobody has paid taxes, and they're relieved.'

Liu Qiyu frowned again.

'They will still have to pay taxes. You can tell everyone to save up and pay all the taxes together later on. He has recorded these debts, so the county head and I cannot neglect this – that's the law. I must also remind you that "Living King of Hell" is a nickname which troublemakers have given Landlord Mao Dehou. As a village official, you cannot talk so irresponsibly!'

'Everyone calls him that, so I've also got used to it,' said Grandpa Whiskers. 'You're quite right to point it out.'

At this point Liu Qiyu turned to the subject he seemed to be most anxious about and which obviously was the main purpose of his visit:

'Recently a singing craze has been spreading all over our county. Of course, that's a good sign, showing that social order prevails and everyone is living in peace and contentment. Is your village the same? Does anyone sing here?'

'Yes indeed!' replied Grandpa Whiskers.

'What kind of songs?' asked Liu Qiyu anxiously. 'Sing one to me quickly. What are they about?'

'I'm too old to sing. I can't sing well. If you insist, I can only recite one for you.'

'Then recite it please. I'm not much of an expert on songs; I only want to know what they're about.'

'All right!' said Grandpa Whiskers, clearing his throat and putting on a serious expression. 'Listen carefully:

> Blacksmith Zhang,
> Blacksmith Li,
> Made some scissors for a lady,
> She asked me to stay,
> I did not stay,
> I had to say:
> I was making iron night and day!

It's pretty good, isn't it?' added Grandpa Whiskers.

Liu Qiyu frowned again, mumbling, 'That's an old song which children sing. I used to sing it as a child too. Doesn't anyone sing new songs?'

Grandpa Whiskers nodded.

'Yes, it's an old children's song. I used to sing it when I was small too.' Then Grandpa Whiskers shook his head, replying, 'Nobody sings new songs. Have you heard any?'

Liu Qiyu also shook his head and answered hesitantly: 'Well, no, I haven't heard any . . . '

Then he looked out of the window at the distant mountains. The sun was setting in the west above the peaks.

Liu Qiyu, obviously nervous again, turned to his thin bodyguard and said, 'It's getting late. Let's get going!'

Grandpa Whiskers accompanied them all the way to the end of the village, and I followed. We continued waving to them until they disappeared into the distance. Then Grandpa Whiskers turned to me, bursting out laughing.

'We've seen off the evil spirits. It's still all right, nothing happened!'

The peasants in the fields were just stopping work; some were already making their way back to the village, carrying their farm tools on their shoulders. Probably realizing that the 'evil spirits' were already far away, they once again took up that song, which had recently become so popular:

> 'The peasants farm but have no food!
> And what they grow they cannot sell,
> So now they think they might as well
> Climb the hills to cut firewood.
>
> We get up early before dawn,
> And feel our way along the road,
> Today there's snow on our road:
> Take care, don't slip or you'll fall down.
>
> Today we're really out of luck,
> We go to town to sell our wood,
> But the streets are full of firewood,
> We cannot sell, so let's go back.
>
> But soldiers and the corps today
> Take our firewood without pay.
> Arise, villagers, don't delay!
> And listen to what we have to say:
>
> Unite as one with all our might,
> With the army and the corps we'll fight,
> Let us strike and we will smash
> Corrupt officials, and all that trash.'

The singing gradually faded away as the sun set behind the mountains. We made our way home to have dinner. In every household they had a lively conversation over their meal, because they all knew that Liu Qiyu, who had kept away for a long time, had come to see Grandpa Whiskers today. Some were not sure what was going on, so they went to see Grandpa Whiskers to find out. His sitting room became a noisy meeting place for a while. Sister Apricot in the next room was disturbed by all the uproar, so she came to our house with her child in her arms. Aunt Sunflower and my mother were also discussing this affair, and Sister Apricot gave them more details.

Since I was curious, I left the elderly ladies to see what was going on in Grandpa Whiskers's house. Unfortunately, it was all over when I got there, and everyone was just about to leave. I only heard them laughing, but when they came out the laughter suddenly stopped, as Grandpa Whiskers warned them, 'I know this incident was funny, but there was something behind it. It was rather ominous, so we must never relax our vigilance!'

Grandpa Whiskers's warning was obviously necessary, as I discovered as soon as I got back home. O Ran suddenly appeared. She had apparently been running quite a way, as she was a little out of breath, her face was haggard and pale and her hair dishevelled – perhaps from the evening wind, which was blowing hard that evening. Aunt Sunflower and my mother had not yet cleared the table after dinner. When she saw Sister Apricot there too, O Ran nodded to her, smiling affectionately, and then sat down at the table. She wanted to get her breath back and she was obviously hungry.

My mother was quite surprised to see O Ran, as if she had fallen from heaven. Perhaps Mother missed her; she had not come round recently. She went up to O Ran and combed back her dishevelled hair, which reminded me of the days when she was a child-bride in our home. Mother used to treat her as her own daughter and every morning she would comb her two plaits, which looked like pigs' tails. She wanted her to look neat and tidy, so that people would not say that she was an orphan with no parents to look after her.

'Do you want something to eat?' Mother whispered into her ear. 'There's still some food in the wok.'

'Yes, please, Ma,' O Ran whispered back. 'I haven't had anything since noon.'

Their whispering seemed like something private between mother and daughter, but Aunt Sunflower and Sister Apricot could hear too. So Aunt Sunflower hurried over to the kitchen to heat up some food, and Sister Apricot poured a cup of tea, which she put on the table for O Ran. Very soon Aunt Sunflower came out with a big bowl of stew. Mother also combed her own hair. Then she sat down opposite O Ran and watched her hungrily devouring the stew – which also reminded me of how hungry she used to be as a child-bride in our home. After watching her for a while, she looked as if she had suddenly remembered something. She asked O Ran in a surprised tone, 'How is it that you've come alone? What about Lao Liu? Wasn't he worried about letting you come by yourself on such a dark night?'

'He did come with me, but only half the way, because a comrade caught us up, saying that something urgent had happened and he had to go back immediately to see to it.'

'You should have gone back with him!' said Mother. 'How can a young woman go by herself in the night?'

'I'm used to going alone at night, Ma. When there's work to do, it doesn't make any difference whether you're a man or a woman. Women have to go out at night if it's necessary. In the present circumstances it's much more convenient and much safer to carry on activities in the night than in the day!'

'But it wasn't convenient today,' said Mother. 'This afternoon the *Bao* chief came to the village with a scoundrel carrying a pistol. They've only just left. What if you had bumped into them on the way?'

At this O Ran laughed softly.

'I couldn't have,' she retorted. 'We knew they were coming. We were informed as soon as Liu Qiyu left his small temple in Three-arch Bridge for his activities all over the countryside. We wouldn't take the same road as him, so how could we meet?'

Aunt Sunflower and Sister Apricot stayed at the end of the room, listening to O Ran's conversation with Mother. They were interested in O Ran's account, and Sister Apricot asked, 'Why did they come to the village today? They came all the way for nothing. What was the point?'

'Luckily they couldn't do anything here,' said Aunt Sunflower. 'Whatever they do will cause us trouble!'

O Ran looked at all three of them and then her expression became grave.

'They didn't come here for nothing,' said O Ran. 'How could they? It was also risky for them to come now. As Ma just said, they left the village just a short while ago. If they couldn't get back home before dark and met our people in the night it would be most unfortunate for them. Of course, they have guns, while we only have knives, so we have to be on our guard against them. They didn't come only to our village today, but Red Hill Village was the last place they investigated. Haven't you heard many people singing in the fields and village these days? These songs have annoyed County Head Yao De-an and the militarists stationed in the county town. They're afraid that the villagers are going to cause trouble, so they sent the *Bao* chief to some villages to find out who composed these songs, who spread them around and who's singing them . . . '

'Yes, I've heard them!' Mother interrupted O Ran. 'The villagers sing in the fields and children have started to sing too. But their singing suddenly stopped this afternoon – now I know, that was just the time when *Bao* Chief Liu Qiyu arrived.'

'So he couldn't discover anything,' said O Ran. 'Let's see what he reports when he gets back!'

'But I'd like to know who composed these songs,' said Sister Apricot. 'They're very good and inspiring too, because they express the villagers' feelings.'

'I'm delighted to hear that, Sister Apricot,' said O Ran, glancing shyly at Mother. 'Guess who made them up!'

Aunt Sunflower rested her chin on her hands, thinking hard.

'Well, this morning when I went to White Stone Stream at the foot of East Mountain, I heard a song about selling firewood,' said Aunt Sunflower. 'I heard every word clearly, and it was nice and powerful. Only a good story-teller could compose such a fine song!'

My mother had apparently guessed, as she kept on nodding.

'I know,' she said, 'it must be Lao Liu.'

O Ran could not help laughing. She was so proud of him. Now she had finished eating, and she wiped her mouth to cover her laughter.

'Yes, it was definitely he who wrote them,' said Aunt Sunflower. 'I heard that he's been terribly busy recently. I still don't understand how he's had time to compose these songs.'

'This is the urgent task which he's trying to accomplish – he brought it upon himself too. He wants to broaden propaganda,' said O Ran. 'But this work has caused a lot of trouble. For the past two days the *Bao* chief and his men have been going round all the villages investigating, and this does not bode well. If they cannot find anything out, it will naturally make the county officials angry, but that won't help them. They'll only get more frightened when they come to hear about it. So will Chumin and his lot in the south of the county. But this time they won't stay in the county town, because they must show their strength. If you don't believe me, just wait – I'm sure very soon they'll cause havoc in the countryside!'

'They can't come and disturb us, can they?' asked Sister Apricot anxiously. 'We've just settled down peacefully here . . .'

'There's nothing to fear,' said O Ran. 'It's no use being afraid, but we should be prepared – all the villagers should be prepared, including us women, of course. That's why I hurried here today to talk to you about this.'

'What can we do?' asked Sister Apricot. 'Jiansheng is so busy, he doesn't even have time to come and see me, while I have nothing to do here. I'm really ashamed! I would also like to do something useful.'

O Ran's and Aunt Sunflower's eyes lit up.

'Fine, Sister Apricot, that's a good idea! You can do plenty of things, like making shoes, sewing emblems and making red flags . . . there's so much to do!'

'I don't need to make those things. I've already got enough shoes!'

'They're not for you, they're for the villagers, for everyone!' said O Ran. 'Our village lads need these things. They'll be going into action, and so will we. You'll know about it all very soon.' Then, turning to Aunt Sunflower, she continued in a louder voice. 'I've come to tell you to mobilize the women in the village as fast as possible, Aunt Sunflower. It's extremely urgent to act quickly. So many troops have come to the county town, and they're not there for nothing. We can't sit around waiting for them to come and slaughter us!'

My mother looked up and stared at the ceiling, pondering. She seemed to have understood what O Ran was talking about, but she looked carefully at her as if she still wondered how this girl, whom she had once brought up as a child-bride, could have become such an energetic woman, an activist. What's more, the way she spoke was just like those revolutionaries and Aunt

Chrysanthemum's husband, whom we had almost forgotten. She looked at the lively, excited expression on her face. O Ran seemed to be worked up, and suddenly she bent down, clutched her stomach and looked as if she was going to vomit.

The other three women were astonished to see O Ran change so suddenly, with her face twitching in pain. My Mother hastily took her in her arms and stroked her, just like when O Ran was sick with malaria as a child. She patted her back and whispered into her ear, 'Relax, don't worry. When you were eating just now, you spoke too much. You'll be better in a minute!' Aunt Sunflower went to fetch some hot water, and Sister Apricot quickly brought a bowl in case she was sick. She just retched, trembled and coughed, without vomiting. My mother frowned, but all she could do was go on patting O Ran's back maternally. Suddenly she thought of something and gently laid O Ran back in the chair and hurried into the kitchen. There she got a small cup of vinegar, poured it into the bowl of hot water which Aunt Sunflower was bringing and put it to O Ran's lips.

'Drink some, my child,' said Mother. 'You'll probably feel better if you drink a little.'

O Ran now looked very weak, perhaps from the strain of retching. She watched Mother's worried face as she offered her the water mixed with vinegar, and her eyes moistened. O Ran had become so soft now, like when she was living with my mother in her childhood. She knew that everything Mother did was for her good, so she just gulped down the vinegar-water. She leaned back, her face pale and worn, and Mother immediately supported her head, resting it against her shoulder. She gently stroked her forehead and at the same time slowly straightened her dishevelled hair.

O Ran closed her eyes and stopped retching. After a while she opened them again and gazed at Mother, whose face was already quite wrinkled and her hair grey. Then she whispered, 'I feel much better now, Ma. Don't worry.'

Thereupon Mother helped her to sit up and withdrew. Her worried expression was suddenly replaced by a happy smile. She spontaneously clapped her hands, crying out with delight, 'O Ran is pregnant! My O Ran is pregnant!'

Aunt Sunflower and Sister Apricot both got excited too, also clapping and shouting, 'This is wonderful news! This is a great event!'

By this time O Ran had completely recovered. When she saw how happy these three mothers were, she smiled bitterly. Pursing her lips, she said, 'It's most unfortunate to be pregnant just when there's so much to do!'

'What are you saying?' Mother responded easily. 'Your child will be my grandchild. You have to look after yourself for your child's sake. Whatever work you have I can do for you. Didn't you want everyone to make shoes, sew those emblems and make red flags? I can do all that; I can work day and night for you!'

'So can I!' said Sister Apricot.

'Fine,' said O Ran, 'but there are some things you can't do for me. Oh dear, I have to get up early again. The time has passed so fast!'

'Yes,' said Aunt Sunflower, 'you should go to bed. There'll really be a lot to do tomorrow.'

Just then there was the faint sound of a dog barking outside. I knew this was only the old dog in the village. It was not usually bothered about human affairs and just slept through the night. Perhaps it had woken up and discovered that someone was there, and so it barked to show that it could still be useful. O Ran's hearing had become extremely acute through these two troubled years, so she immediately noticed this sound. She stood up and said to me, 'Could it be Lao Liu coming back? Go and have a look, but be careful!'

She probably knew that, apart from officially selling dough-sticks for Pockmarks the Sixth, my real work now was liaison, sentry duty, being a guard and sometimes scouting. So she thought I should be able to cope with this situation. I carefully unbolted the door and slipped out to a tree beside the house. Indeed, there was a figure approaching. Looking carefully, I recognized from his gait that it was Lao Liu after all. Then I noisily pushed the door wide open and stood in the doorway, so that he would realize that there was no danger and I was waiting for him.

'O Ran told me to wait for you here,' I said when he disco-

142

vered me. 'You've come at the right time. The three mothers are still here, so this will be a surprise for them.'

'I also had a surprise after I parted from O Ran,' said Lao Liu as he stepped into the sitting room.

'What surprise?' asked my mother anxiously.

'We captured a young gentleman. He's very refined and seems to be quite well educated. So they called me back immediately to investigate and make some arrangements for him.'

'Did you have to make all these arrangements and come back so late?' asked Aunt Sunflower. 'O Ran has been waiting for you all this time. You two can stay here tonight.'

'No, that's impossible! We have to go straight away to discuss things with Grandpa Whiskers.' Then he turned to O Ran. 'You have a certain responsibility in this matter, as you are the liaison officer in this village. Let's go together, right away. We have to report to the leaders at dawn! This is an urgent task.'

'Task' or 'duty', I had already discovered, was almost like an absolute order for Lao Liu, O Ran and even Uncle Pan. I was also gradually being influenced by their attitude. Without a word, O Ran immediately stood up to go with him to Grandpa Whiskers's place.

'I was just going back too,' said Sister Apricot.

'That's fine,' said O Ran. 'We'll go together.'

My mother stared after them as they departed. She apparently could not believe this. It took her quite a while to recover, and then she said to Aunt Sunflower, 'They're so busy working hard, and O Ran asked us women to help more. As a woman, I don't think I can refuse. I have to join everyone and make my contribution.'

Aunt Sunflower did not reply, but just smiled. She apparently agreed with my mother and was happy to see how she had changed.

Our small village of Red Hill Village started bustling with activity. Our family was the first to get involved. Aunt Sunflower was busy for several days after Lao Liu and O Ran visited us that night. She went around the village seeing each family and having a talk with all the women. Soon they were busy sticking rags together to make shoe-soles and flags . . . Of course, they did all this secretly at home, without anyone outside the village knowing. As soon as everyone had finished housework, they all worked frantically with needle and thread. The atmosphere was warm and friendly, because they showed the enthusiastic spirit which came from a sense of purpose. Grandpa Whiskers appeared to be very busy too. These days he was also going round the village to see the men. These villagers, old and young alike, had become much more active than usual. After farming every day, they were busy repairing – old knives, guns, swords, garden forks, fishing forks and bird traps. From where they came they did not know, but they seized every moment to repair them. Their work reached fever-pitch, and the air also seemed to carry a whiff of gunpowder. Outwardly, however, the village still appeared peaceful – as still as dead water, so people could not sense it.

As for me, as dough-stick vendor in Pockmarks the Sixth's shop in Tanjiahe, I did not originally have much to do with our village life. Still, I became involuntarily involved in this frantic activity. Grandpa Whiskers pushed me into it, asking me to tidy up a spare room, which had always been empty in his house. This room had originally been intended for his adopted son, a distant relative, as his bridal room, but before the date of the marriage had been arranged, his son had been seized by passing government troops and pressganged into the army. From that time, many years ago, he had never come back and nothing had been heard of him. As the room had been vacant for such a long time, it was very difficult to clear up, and I spent ages working on it. By chance, Pockmarks the Sixth said that for the time being he was busy with something urgent and would have to stop working for a while. I need not sell dough-sticks and could have a break at home during this time. Little did he know that now I was busier than when I was selling dough-sticks for him.

It took me three days to put Grandpa Whiskers's spare room in order. Not only was it very dusty, but the walls were broken and had to be replastered and the windows had to be repaired too. Although the room was small, it needed more cleaning and repairing than any other room in the whole village.

'A guest is coming from "The Big City" to stay soon and he

might find conditions poor here,' said Grandpa Whiskers when he came to check the room after I had finished putting it in order. 'But we must do our best to accommodate him here for a while. I've already spoken to Sister Apricot and asked her to cook for him and wash his clothes.'

'Who is this guest?' I asked curiously. 'How is it I have never seen him here or heard you mention him?'

Grandpa Whiskers stroked his beard and smiled mysteriously.

'I don't know him either. That night when Lao Liu came here – actually it was in the middle of the night – he told me about him and asked me to do this. The next day Uncle Zizhong assigned me the task of looking after this guest – feeding him, giving him lodging and making sure he's safe. You see, now I have this new responsibility. But you can't take it easy either . . .'

'What has it got to do with me?' I asked, surprised. 'I've finished what you asked me to do. I don't think there's a cleaner room in the whole village now.'

'That's just the first step,' said Grandpa Whiskers, laughing. 'He's not an ordinary guest. He's used to living comfortably, so he needs two people to attend to him. Apart from Sister Apricot, you'll have to be at his beck and call – that's your duty.'

'Don't I have to sell dough-sticks? I only came here to help these days because Pockmarks the Sixth closed the shop during this time.'

'Even when he opens up again, you still have to come here to carry out your duties – we've consulted him about it, and he agrees.'

'So you arranged all this in advance! Was he fibbing when he spoke to me about closing for a while – was it a pretext?'

'Pockmarks the Sixth, like you, really does have other urgent things to do, so he had to close the shop for a while. The old fellow was not deceiving you.'

Just as I was going to ask a further question, Sister Apricot came in, panting. She was carrying some clothes, which were still dripping wet. Apparently she had just been washing them in White Stone Stream, but she had run back to the village before she could even wring the clothes out.

145

'It's terrible, terrible!' she shouted hysterically. 'The troops and Order Preservation Corps have arrived.'

'Where?' asked Grandpa Whiskers.

'In the fields,' she replied desperately. 'They're coming here. Go and have a look! You're the *Jia* chief. You should deal with them!'

'Yes, I am *Jia* chief. I have to deal with them!' mumbled Grandpa Whiskers, raising his right hand to his forehead to shield his eyes from the sunlight. A contingent of armed soldiers was coming towards us. Suddenly he said to Sister Apricot, 'Hide quickly – hide in the hay in the kitchen! I'll deal with them!' Then he turned to me and said, 'Quickly go and inform all the villagers and tell the women to hide! Hurry up!'

I started running at once, calling on every household to warn the women. Suddenly the whole village became as quiet as a tomb. Only children and old folk like Grandpa Whiskers were to be seen. The arrival of the troops and Order Preservation Corps aroused my curiosity. Since I had been frequently participating in night activities I had naturally become bolder and more enterprising. I did not run away from people with guns or from troublemakers – on the contrary, I wanted to get a closer look at what they were up to. After I had done as Grandpa Whiskers had instructed, I went back to his place. I wanted to see what was happening and how he was dealing with these armed soldiers, who had suddenly disturbed our peaceful fields. He was standing at the end of the village, looking in the direction of the approaching soldiers. These fully armed men must have an important mission, but from their leisurely pace they seemed rather to be rehearsing for a parade or a review of the troops.

As they had arrived so suddenly, the peasants working in the fields had no time to hide. They acted as if nothing was happening and carried on calmly with their work. The soldiers too seemed to enjoy the peace and quiet here. Not wanting to disturb it, they did not interfere with the peasants. They just strode along proudly, taking the track leading from the road towards our village.

'The purpose of their expedition seems to be to demonstrate their power,' whispered Grandpa Whiskers. 'With more troops in town, they have to show off to the villagers. They have

146

brought the Order Preservation Corps – this bunch of good-for-nothing idlers – to boost their image and make a big impact. Since they've come in broad daylight they probably won't cause any trouble. Let's wait and see!'

'Isn't it crazy of them to appear from nowhere and put on a show of strength in these fields?' I exclaimed. 'Look how weak they are! Apart from carrying a few guns, how could they possibly frighten anyone?'

Laughing, Grandpa Whiskers patted my shoulder affectionately and said, 'So you aren't afraid of this lot now. Fine, they are ridiculous, but with those guns they're still a force to be reckoned with. We still have to take those things seriously. We cannot do much without them; the reason they can operate effectively is because they have guns. Recently the villagers have been singing new songs, and the county officials and Chumin and his lot have taken up arms to scare us and close our mouths.'

'One day we'll take the guns from them,' I said, 'and use them ourselves!'

'Good! Very good!' responded Grandpa Whiskers excitedly. 'You're very clever now, and brave too. I agree, we have to seize these weapons!' Suddenly he lowered his voice: 'Look, what are those? There are some men amongst them without guns, in ragged clothes, and they don't look like soldiers. Look!'

I looked very carefully. The nearer they came, the more clearly I could see them. Indeed, in their midst were five men in peasants' clothing, and their hands were bound behind their backs with ropes. These were clearly prisoners or criminals, but we had news that the Order Preservation Corps or troops had recently been sent from the county town to clean up the countryside. Where were these prisoners from? Just as we were wondering about this, the soldiers reached the outskirts of the village, and we could see them more clearly. Some live chickens, geese and ducks were hanging from their rifles – no doubt these creatures were also prisoners! Suddenly Grandpa Whiskers nudged my back, indicating that we should hide.

We went behind a thicket from where we could still see their movements.

When the soldiers came to the big road in front of the village leading to Tanjiahe, they halted and looked around. Probably our Red Hill Village was the smallest and poorest of all the villages they had passed through. As all the women were hiding and the children were quiet, the hamlet was absolutely silent, as if it did not exist or had been completely abandoned. So these soldiers stood there gazing and then set off again, round the corner towards the next place. After a few steps, however, they changed their minds and came back. It looked as if they were going to enter the village. Grandpa Whiskers suddenly tugged at my sleeve, saying, 'I have to go out and deal with them. If nobody talks to them, they may cause trouble.'

'I'll go with you. I can't let you tackle them alone. What if . . .?'

'OK, but be sensible,' said Grandpa Whiskers. 'If they're rude to you, tell them you'll bring them some tea and cigarettes. You can use this excuse to slip back to my home. From the back door you can climb up East Mountain and disappear into the woods.'

Now the soldiers entered the village. Grandpa Whiskers barred their way, but not with his hand. Instead, he hastily bowed to them, repeating, 'Welcome! Welcome!'

The soldier in front was probably an officer, as he was not carrying a rifle on his shoulder but had a pistol with a tassle hanging behind him. He was wearing a very neat uniform, too. A thin man, wearing the uniform of the Order Preservation Corps, came running up to stand beside him. He also had a pistol hanging behind.

'Who are you?' asked the officer.

'I'm the *Jia* chief of this village – I was appointed by *Bao* Chief Liu Qiyu,' answered Grandpa Whiskers. 'Welcome! Welcome all of you!'

The officer glanced inquiringly at the thin man, who responded at once, 'Yes, he is the *Jia* chief of this village. I met him here a few days ago.'

Then I realized this thin man was the one who was guarding *Bao* Chief Liu Qiyu when they came to investigate the village a few days before. The officer-type nodded, acknowledging Grandpa Whiskers was on their side, and asked, 'Does anyone sing in this village?'

'This is a small, remote hamlet, hidden away in the mountains. Nobody here knows anything about the outside world,' answered Grandpa Whiskers. 'Everyone is so busy farming the barren fields, and still they live on the breadline. Nobody is in the mood to sing!'

The officer again glanced at the thin one, who nodded, confirming what Grandpa Whiskers said: that when he came here a few days ago with *Bao* Chief Liu Qiyu they had not discovered anyone singing. The officer glared at Grandpa Whiskers, changing the subject.

'Just now you welcomed us very warmly! But how are you treating us?'

Grandpa Whiskers promptly instructed me, 'Chunsheng, quickly fetch some tea and cigarettes!'

Just as I left, I heard the officer talking to the *Jia* chief.

'I'm a straightforward man, and I don't like others welcoming us with empty words. "Welcome" must mean some concrete action. You've done that; your attitude was very good. You were very polite to us, bowing and smiling. But what have you given us to show how sincerely you welcome us?'

'If you're talking about money or grain, we've all handed it over to the authorities according to the regulations, keeping nothing for ourselves. Now there's a shortage of grain, so we have no more to hand over.'

'Does that mean you have no chickens, ducks or geese? Tomorrow our soldiers are going to have a feast. Couldn't you treat us with a little respect? If our soldiers weren't protecting you, would you be living in such peace and contentment in this mountain valley?'

I did not hear the rest of their conversation, as I was already in Grandpa Whiskers's house, getting tea and cigarettes.

When I got back to the edge of the village with these offerings, the village was in pandemonium. The five peasants with their hands bound behind their backs were tied to two trees, so that they could not move. The soldiers and members of the Order Preservation Corps were running all over the village catching chickens and ducks, while their officer and corps chief were giving the 'battle orders' – it was like the end of the world. Grandpa Whiskers did not utter a word as he watched these armed men struggle with the chickens and ducks. He looked completely resigned to all this, and when I came up to him he smiled wryly and whispered to me, 'Why did we feed the chickens and ducks so well? But it's no good having them all skin and bones either – that's the problem!' Then he pointed to the bound-up peasants and continued, 'Go and ask them where they come from. Quick!'

I went up to them. When they saw that we were also in a mess, they told me directly about their predicament. They had been captured at night by the Order Preservation Corps in the south of the county two days before. The big landlord, Chumin, was afraid that the tenant farmers under his control would be influenced by the peasants in the north and would also start singing those 'seditious' songs which gave him such a headache. So, as a warning to others, he seized five of the peasants whom he thought had wayward ideas. They were dragged to the north by these soldiers to try to stop the villagers singing! One of them was a 'northerner' whom they suspected of having instigated the singing. He was treated as a more serious case, so he had been beaten. He could not walk easily, as he was still wounded.

'This villager from the north is really suffering,' said one of them, with protruding eyes and a rough neck. 'When he couldn't walk, they prodded him from behind with their rifle butts, so that his wounds have got worse.'

'Will they release you and let you go back?' I asked.

'That depends what they want to do,' said the peasant. 'If they intend to make us go back and tell our fellow villagers never to sing those songs which they hate so much, then the corps will probably take us back. Or they might lock us up here.'

'Why has the corps come from the south?'

'Why not?' said the same peasant. 'When Chumin saw that there were more troops stationed in the county town, he also wanted to show his strength and prove that he could still take personal command, so he sent a corps troop here to join in a combined operation with the soldiers. I hear the county officials intend to give them a feast tomorrow. Oh dear, they're coming back. You'd better go quickly!'

When I was with Grandpa Whiskers, I had seen the soldiers chasing chickens and ducks right up the hill behind the village. Now they were coming back triumphantly, with chickens and ducks in their hands or hanging from their ammunition belts.

Luckily they were coming back fully laden, with no hands free for anything else. Otherwise it is quite likely that they would have burst into the villagers' homes to seize other 'spoils of war'. As a 'farewell' gesture, the officer kicked Grandpa Whiskers on the backside and then knocked the big tea pot which I had brought on to the ground, where it broke into pieces.

'As this is the first time,' said the officer, 'I'll forgive you. In future, if you ever "welcome" our troops like this again, I'll use my pistol.'

He patted the pistol hanging behind him, ordered his men to untie the five 'criminals' from the tree and swaggered off.

About half an hour after they had left, we heard some shots coming from the mountains to the west. Soon after this we got some news from the peasants who were coming back from their work in the fields: the soldiers had shot a peasant on the path. After dark Grandpa Whiskers specially took me to the mountains in the west to investigate. We did in fact find the body of a peasant who had been shot by the mountain path. As it was now night-time, there was not a soul around. Nobody had yet dared remove the corpse, because they were all afraid that the troops and Order Preservation Corps would arrest them. Looking more carefully, we recognized the victim as that wounded prisoner who had been crippled. His death was the 'climax' of the 'military show'.

The county committee's decision had been quite correct. Our villagers could no longer tolerate such killings. As Grandpa Whiskers looked at this unfortunate wretch, he seemed to be pledging himself or promising the dead man: we will certainly arm ourselves immediately!

Next day two visitors came to our village. One was Liu Dawang and the other Pan Mingxun. They had come to attend a meeting called by Grandpa Whiskers as *Jia* chief. Altogether, twelve village lads came to the meeting. Liu Dawang, who was chairing the meeting, reported that troops from outside and the local Order Preservation Corps had started killing villagers, so they must get organized for self-defence immediately. Finally he announced that our district had formed two peasant self-defence teams, the sixth and seventh teams. The county committee had appointed him leader of the seventh team and Pan Zaixing leader of the sixth team. Our village lads were to make up a small team affiliated to the seventh team. It was to be led by Pan Mingxun, because he had been a farm labourer who had suddenly been fired one winter's day. As he had nothing to eat he had gone into the snowy mountains with a hunter to hunt rabbits, so he had learned to shoot. Since I was also almost as old as these village recruits, Grandpa Whiskers spoke to me after the meeting.

'As you have no other task at the moment, you can also join this team. If there's some particular task, Zizhong will decide what's necessary at that time.'

Now I realized that I was already an adult. I also understood that O Ran had come to the village to organize the women to make shoes and flags because we were forming our own defence force.

# CHAPTER 9

One afternoon Grandpa Whiskers said to me, 'After dinner tonight, you have to go to Pheasant Nest. We're having an emergency meeting there. You may have to stay there for a couple of days.'

Grandpa Whiskers came to my home to tell me this. At that time I was staying at home, where I was doing some household chores for Mother and Aunt Sunflower. He had told me to be prepared to take care of that 'new guest' who would be coming to stay in his house. I was just cutting firewood, and Mother and Aunt Sunflower were also sitting in the doorway, basking in the sunlight and busy with the sewing which O Ran had given them to do. I was still puzzled about the instruction which Grandpa Whiskers had brought all of a sudden, and I looked at him inquiringly. So did Mother and Aunt Sunflower, who both put down their sewing at the same time. He must have felt that he had not explained enough, so he filled in a bit.

'Uncle Zizhong asked me to tell you this. I've just been to Tanjiahe, where I sat in his pharmacy for a while.'

Grandpa Whiskers glanced across at Mother and Aunt Sunflower. As he was an old man now and could not do any farm work, he often went into Tanjiahe, and the villagers asked him to buy matches, salt and other such things. It was different with Uncle Zizhong. He had a certain authority, as important notices from the leadership were transmitted to the grass-roots through him. So we automatically accepted his instructions, feeling that they must be correct and had to be obeyed. Aunt Sunflower gave Grandpa Whiskers a meaningful smile, and my mother did not express any opinion. Only I asked, 'Uncle, what about the guest you want me to look after?'

'Don't worry, he'll come,' answered Grandpa Whiskers with a laugh. 'When the time comes for you to take care of him, of course you'll be informed. When there's other work to be done, then do it. There's a lot to do and too little time for everything. Have dinner earlier and leave after dark, so that nobody sees you.'

Thereupon he patted me on the shoulder affectionately and left for home.

When I left the house it was already pitch dark. The two mothers were not worried about me now, as it was not the first time I'd gone out at night. When they saw me off at the door, Aunt Sunflower said reassuringly, 'If the meeting ends very late, or if there's anything else to do, just stay there overnight. You've just about chopped all the firewood, so there's nothing else you have to do at home tomorrow.'

Outside the village the countryside was so dark that one could hardly see one's own hand. Pheasant Nest had left a deep impression on me, and I could still remember the way there very clearly. The night was so quiet that I could hear any slight sound: the rustling of rabbits in the grass, the cry of hedgehogs, the scream of predatory birds as they attacked their prey . . . these sounds all made the peaceful night like a battle-field. This might have alarmed me, but I had enough experience to know that the troops stationed in the county town and the Order Preservation Corps under the control of the landlords did not usually dare to go out at night – if they did, they formed a conspicuous contingent of troops. Night travellers like me could easily discover them and escape in time, so there was nothing to fear. My hearing seemed to be more acute, my eyes sharper and my legs stronger than ever. So I covered several miles in a flash. Surrounded by the sounds of hunting animals, I felt suddenly confident, as if nothing could stand in my way. Then I relaxed and my pace gradually slackened.

As I slowed down, I was suddenly overcome by a strange sensation, as if completely alienated from the present. I fell into memories of my childhood. On such a night as this I had once forgotten everything of the real world. We – O Ran, Uncle Pan, some villagers and myself – were all crowded in the open space in front of the village. We were watching the stars while listening to Lao Liu telling stories, gradually being drawn by his voice into the remote world described in his story. But the actual Lao Liu, Uncle Pan, O Ran and me, walking along in the night . . . I could not help laughing to myself.

Suddenly I felt a hand on my shoulder. I was taken completely by surprise and broke into a cold sweat.

'How come you're laughing? How bold you are!'

The voice sounded very familiar. Looking round, I saw it was Jiqing.

'How did you get here?' I asked, astonished. 'You gave me such a fright!'

'I came straight from town after dinner. I've taken another path to Pheasant Nest. As I knew you were coming too, I was looking out for you on the way. And here you are!'

'Why didn't you call me?'

'We can't shout or laugh on our way at night. That's a rule. Even if nobody told you that, you should know it yourself. Luckily, it was me! If it had been an enemy . . . '

'I've never come across an enemy,' I said, trying to defend myself. 'To tell you the truth, I would like to meet one, at least to see what they're like.'

'So cocky!' said Jiqing, but he did not sound reprimanding any more. 'You sound quite experienced now. Let me ask you what you would do if you really met an enemy agent.'

'Since I've never met one, how do I know? Have you met one?'

'Several times,' answered Jiqing, setting off again.

'How did you deal with him?' I asked, following him.

'It wasn't "him" – it was "them", two of them. But we were also two – Liu Dawang and me. We were going to a meeting too.'

'Who were they?'

'Agents of the landlords, of course. They knew that we operate at night, so they also tried to spy on our movements at that time. They wanted to get definite information, so that they could send the Red Spear Society to harass us in the day-time.'

'Did they discover you first, or was it you who noticed them?'

'If they had discovered us first, it would have been tough. So I have to remind you not to shout or laugh at night!'

155

'Did they teach you this lesson?'

'That's right. They had guns: long rifles, short ones – pistols. They had pistols on them, while we were only carrying kitchen knives – now we aren't even carrying kitchen knives. So they were swaggering along, talking, laughing and even smoking as they came towards us. Their lit cigarettes provided us with a good warning signal.'

'You should be grateful to them for giving you this warning and the chance to escape.'

'Yes, we first heard them laughing and then noticed their smoke signal!'

'What did you do when you noticed them? Did you hide?'

'Yes, we dashed into a thicket beside the path and waited for them to pass . . . '

'So they passed without seeing you?'

'It's not as simple as that!' replied Jiqing in a grave tone. 'These agents are our deadly enemies, who come out at night to kill us. If we don't destroy them, they'll destroy us. They're different from those villagers who have been tricked into joining the enemy. They're rascals who have joined of their own accord. When we come across them, how could we let them get away so easily?'

'So you two decided to kill them? But how could you manage bare-handed against their guns?'

'We were prepared – that's the difference.'

He sounded more excited now, like a story-teller about to tell an exciting tale.

'Also, you cannot shoot accurately in the pitch dark – but we didn't even give them a chance to touch their guns! As they swaggered along, talking and laughing, they could hardly imagine that there was a blacksmith and a former stonemason hiding behind the bushes by the path. You know that when you are forging iron you have to lift the hammer and smash it down with enormous force? You have to strike the iron exactly when it's red hot. A stonemason has to use the same strength. Liu Dawang is a very strong stonemason, as you can see from his arm muscles. We both jumped out, me first and Dawang behind. We tackled them separately: I smashed my fist down on the first one's head, and Dawang kicked the second one in the groin.

The two agents were on the ground in a flash, and we pounced on top of them and grabbed the pistols hanging behind them. Before they could even call out, I smashed the first one's head in as if it were a piece of red hot iron. Dawang shattered the other's head like a piece of rock. We sent them to hell instantly, without even a drop of blood.'

'Very efficient – but what did you do with their bodies? Did you leave them on the path like the peasant they shot that time?'

'Do you think it's so simple?' asked Jiqing. 'We're not so strong yet; we can't expose ourselves! We undid their belts and tied a big stone to each of them. Then we carried them to a dark pond near by and threw them into the deep water. They sank like stones with just a "plop", and there was no trace left of them.'

'So that's how those two agents disappeared?'

'Yes, disappeared mysteriously. Keep their chief guessing! Keep them all guessing! The longer they're kept in the dark, the more frightened they get. So now neither their agents nor even their Order Preservation Corps dare go out during the night. The land is ours at night!'

They had done really well, I thought, otherwise I would not be able to travel at night so easily. But then another thought immediately came to me: What would I do if I came across an agent like that? I was not as strong as Jiqing or Liu Dawang – also, I had never killed anyone. My heart missed a beat. But I had to take part in these activities, and they could only be organized at night. For me, this was a new problem which I had never faced or thought about before. Now, preoccupied by this problem, I did not feel like chatting with Jiqing. I went on pondering silently about my position: How could I carry out my duties like this without harming myself or our work?

'What are you thinking about?' asked Jiqing, interrupting my thoughts. 'We're almost in Pheasant Nest.'

'I'm thinking, thinking . . . '

'What about?' Jiqing interrupted, sounding concerned.

'I was just thinking that for this kind of work you have to be courageous, resolute, adaptable and clever. It's no easy task.'

'You should have thought about that earlier. For a big cause you have to devote yourself entirely to your duties. You should have considered this when you joined the organization, but it's still not too late.'

'Right, I'm not as strong and courageous as you or Liu Dawang. It looks as if I'll have to get some more experience, train myself and get more involved in the struggle.'

Jiqing could not help laughing softly.

'You think too much,' he said. 'When the enemies come to kill our people, they don't give it a thought. You've seen this in "The Big City" and you saw it a few days ago, when they came to our place and shot an innocent villager. Enough said on that point. As for strength, you don't necessarily have to fell an enemy with one blow like Liu Dawang and me. Just think of Wang Jiansheng, Lao Liu, O Ran, my father and even Uncle Pan, who has been farming for so many years. How much strength have they got? But they have more work and responsibility than we do and often go out at night as their activities demand.'

Jiqing suddenly tugged at me to stop and whispered in my ear, 'Look! Look in front!'

I craned my neck, looking ahead. There were the dark shapes of the two mud-huts in Pheasant Nest. As we stood there silently watching out for any movement, a person appeared from behind that old tree in front of the huts. After he had advanced a few steps, we did the same – that was our pre-arranged signal. Gradually we could recognize one another. He was the tenant, Wang Xiangzheng, who was just keeping watch. He beckoned to us and then went up to the door of the left hut, which he gently pushed open to let us in.

Inside were many people seated on benches along the walls of the room: Wang Jiansheng, Pan Zaixing, Liu Dawang, Feng Xinshun, Lao Liu, Pan Mingxun and two peasants whom I seemed to have met before. I could not see clearly, because the light from the small oil-lamp on the incense-table at the end of the room was so dim. I sat down with Jiqing on an empty bench beside the main door. It took a few seconds before we could see the room clearly. All were sitting silently with solemn expressions on their faces. It was obvious that we had interrupted their discussion when we came in, as they always had to pay attention to any noise at the door. Apparently we had arrived a little late, as the first item on the agenda was over. They could excuse us, as we lived quite far from there. I noticed a white cloth hanging on the wall behind the oil-lamp. On it was the emblem I had faced last time, when making my oath of allegiance: an overlapping hammer and sickle. Beneath it were the two villagers I seemed to know, with Wang Jiansheng sitting beside them. On closer inspection I recognized them at last. One was Huang Yongfa, the husband of Hongtao who was nicknamed Pickle, and a former tenant-farmer of Chumin in the village where we used to live; the other was Jin Bailong, who usually worked half the year as a farm labourer and the other half cutting firewood in the mountains. They had joined the Red Spear Society organized by Chumin, but they had disappeared without a trace during the expedition to the north. It was their wives who had kicked up a fuss with the head of the village branch of the Red Spear Society, Zhu the Ninth. How had these two lost lads turned up here? Had they come to pledge their allegiance under the flag with the hammer and sickle? That would really be incredible! Just as I was pondering over this, Wang Jiansheng stood up, looked at all of us and spoke.

'I am delighted that there are two new comrades joining our forces. We've investigated their background. Like the rest of us, they work for a living. After a year's work, they always go hungry for half a year. This is the basic reason for their joining our organization. It's true that they joined Chumin's Red Spear Society, but it wasn't done voluntarily. They were deceived. All of us villagers have at one time been duped by Chumin and his acolytes. That's an undeniable fact. The question is, now that we know we've been deceived, what do we do? It isn't good enough just to have learned how to avoid being tricked. We have to destroy those swindlers, so that they'll never be able to deceive us again. We must fight them tit-for-tat, and we must hit them harder. Just to match them in strength will not do, otherwise how can we destroy them? These two comrades were tricked by Chumin into coming here to fight us, and we captured them. After that they lived with us for a while and we taught them. Gradually they came to understand that the "enemies" they had come to fight were their own people, villagers who were suffering like themselves. They learned that the real enemies are Chumin and his lot.'

Then he pointed to Huang Yongfa, sitting on his right, and continued.

'He was a tenant-farmer who had been poor all his life. However carefully he planned together with his wife, Pickle, they never had enough to eat. Now he knows that he cannot go on living like this. He has decided to work with us and operate right under Chumin's nose. That's a great decision!'

Now pointing to Jin Bailong sitting on his left, he went on, speaking emphatically:

'He wants to do the same. This new comrade was employed as an ox-herd when he was a boy and then he became a hired farm-hand. After the harvest every year, he was discharged and had to go up into the mountains to cut firewood. He was up there all day, so he only had coarse cakes to eat for lunch and sometimes there was no water to drink. Still, this bitter experience is also valuable: he's been all over the mountains, so he knows all the paths. He also knows many people from carrying firewood for sale. We need this kind of valuable information, especially about the southern part of the county. He comes from a different village from Comrade Huang Yongfa and joined another branch of the Red Spear Society, but he was also captured during that combined operation. These two will be very valuable to us and they'll have very important responsibilities after they've taken the oath today.'

As Wang Jiansheng finished his speech he looked at us all again. We were silent. I was wondering how he knew so much about Huang Yongfa and Jin Bailong. He must have spent a lot of time with them after they were captured – talking to them about the situation, about their past harsh life, about how people like Chumin had oppressed and deceived them and about finding a way to escape their hardships. So they had finally decided to join forces with the 'northerners' to change their own lives. That time when Uncle Pan was leading his so-called 'daughter' – our family calf – on his way back to his village, he had been 'captured' too. The change that came over him in 'captivity' must have been similar, except that it had been Pan Xudong who had talked things over with him that time. Wang

Jiansheng had been a scholar like Pan Xudong, but now he was very close to the tenant-farmers and farm labourers. He himself must have been through an even more complicated process of ideological and emotional transformation. Looking at him, I thought he still seemed calm and gentle, like an educated man, and he still sounded like a scholar, with the words he used.

When he saw us all looking at him attentively, he went on speaking in a louder voice:

'Chiang Kai-shek has once again obtained a large amount of loans and weapons with the support of the foreign powers, in order to suppress the people. Our small county in this mountain region has become a focus of this campaign. Their action is quite natural, as they want to recover their old power. The landlords who fled are now coming back one by one, planning to counter-attack and retaliate. They are particularly active in the south. Even though they have not completely recovered their authority, they have already started threatening us. They're not even allowing people to sing . . . '

At this point Lao Liu suddenly stood up, interrupting Wang Jiansheng's speech, and spoke defiantly:

'The more they forbid the villagers to sing, the more songs I will compose! Let's see what they do about it!'

'You've been doing your propaganda work very well,' said Pan Zaixing. 'Of course it makes them worried when we rouse the people. Sending their troops to the countryside to display their strength, I think, also shows that they're afraid.'

Hearing this praise, Lao Liu became more excited. Now he spoke even more passionately:

'I want to make them afraid, so that they can't sleep at night! I want to print thousands and thousands of leaflets and posters, and stick them on their doors, scatter them over their graves and throw them into their bedrooms!'

Liu Dawang, who was not accustomed to speaking in public, was affected by Lao Liu's rousing words. He also became excited as he added his praise.

'You aren't just a story-teller with a rich imagination. You make suggestions and also carry them out yourself. Still, there's one point I don't quite understand. Just as we have no guns, you have no printing machine, so how are you going to print your thousands of leaflets and posters?'

'You don't have to worry about that,' replied Lao Liu, full of confidence. 'You should all know that I'm no longer a story-teller who simply uses his imagination to tell tales. I'm a member of the propaganda committee, so I do what I say I'll do!'

'If you can do it, I'll go out and stick up posters and distribute leaflets for you!' announced Pan Mingxun.

'I'll go too!' shouted Jiqing.

In this exciting atmosphere I could not help blurting out, 'So will I!'

Lao Liu looked at me calmly and spoke quietly.

'No hurry, Chunsheng. We need you. Be patient!'

I did not say another word. Nobody else said any more on this topic, so Wang Jiansheng went on speaking:

'I must now formally report to you about our tasks in the present situation. We must start our work immediately, and there are three important things we must do right away. First, we must mobilize the people all over this county, especially in the southern part where our popular base is rather weak. Apart from this, we must also strengthen our cooperation with our neighbouring Mazhen county; second, we must make every effort to get new weapons, such as rifles. If we want to stage an effective counter-attack, out-of-date spears, javelins and sharpened bamboo poles are no longer much use, because our enemies have regular armies and the Order Preservation Corps, armed with modern weapons. Third, as Lao Liu said so rightly, we have to expand our propaganda, especially written propa-ganda. We have already agreed on this point. We must issue notices, distribute leaflets and stick up posters. We have to do this work in the county town too, under the very noses of Chumin's gang, so that they cannot guess our strength. Lao Liu will still be responsible for this work. The leadership will help us solve any difficulties. All the comrades responsible for this area must work actively to accomplish these important tasks. Do you have any more ideas?'

At this moment Wang Xiangzheng pushed the door open quietly and put his head in to have a look at how far our meeting had progressed. His duty was not only to stand guard outside, but also to pay attention to the time. Coming in to look at us was a sign that it was getting late. We should all be getting on our way, so that we could try to get a little sleep before dawn, to enable us to go on working next day. When we all saw Wang Xiangzheng indicating this, we all got up at the same time. Wang Jiansheng looked around and said, 'If none of you has anything else, we'll end the meeting!'

Just as he was about to leave he cornered me and whispered, 'Since you're from the same place as Huang Yongfa and Jin Bailong and you haven't met for a long time, would you like to have a chat with them? If so, you can spend the night here. They're staying till tomorrow. They'll be leaving for the south of the county, where they'll carry out new activities. As for you, it's been arranged that you work with Lao Liu for the time being.'

I nodded in agreement, but as Wang Jiansheng was leaving with all the others, I asked him, 'But Uncle Zizhong asked Grandpa Whiskers to tell me that during this time I will have to look after a guest. So how can I also work with Lao Liu?'

'Looking after the guest is the same as collaborating with Lao Liu. That's how our work is: flexible, according to the needs of work. I might have to ask you to work with me for a while too. You can read quite a lot and I've heard you're good at remembering the way: you even remembered the whole way you went at night!'

After saying these words he went out.

Jiqing had heard Wang Jiansheng talking to me, and now he whispered, 'As you're staying here for the night, I'll go straight back to town. Early tomorrow morning I want to start some new work at the blacksmith's. Every minute is precious!'

'What new work?' I asked.

'To make guns: flintlocks and pistols. Have you forgotten what Comrade Wang Jiansheng just instructed us? He was appointed as the leader responsible for our district by the county committee. We have to follow instructions and carry them out immediately!'

He followed the rest of them out. As I watched them all hurrying away, I felt that the situation was getting more and more serious.

Huang Yongfa and Jin Bailong seemed to want to have a chat with me. They had probably been given a hint that I might meet them this evening, so they stayed in the room, waiting to see what I would decide to do after the others had left. Before I had a chance to speak, Feng Xinshun said to us, 'Your bedroom has already been prepared; it's Wang Xiangzheng's room but he's coming over to my room to sleep. There's a big bed and a small one there, so it's no problem for you three to sleep there. What's the matter? Come on!'

Without waiting for our reply, he led us out to the right and after a few steps we came to a thatched hut. The door was open and a lamp was already burning. There was actually only one sitting room inside, and nothing else. Three bricks against the east wall in the corner of the room served as a kitchen stove. They stood there like the legs of a tripod, on which was an earthen pot for cooking, and underneath a heap of ashes. Wang Xiangzheng was standing by the door to welcome us. There was a simple, honest smile on his face as he pointed to the two beds by the east and west walls of the room, saying, 'Please come in. Everything's ready!'

Then they went back to Feng Xinshun's hut, as they were both very tired and wanted to sleep. In fact, nothing was prepared here. There were no quilts on the beds and no sign of a quilt or any clothes elsewhere in the room. It seemed that those Wang Xiangzheng was wearing were his only worldly possessions. Still, the straw on the beds was quite thick and loosely spread, looking warm and soft. I imagined that as soon as Wang Xiangzheng got into bed, he would be completely covered by the loose straw. If he did not undress, he could sleep cosily. We could not sleep, however, even though we snuggled into the straw. We three room-mates felt strange, meeting like this in an unfamiliar place, and not like sleeping. Huang Yongfa was sitting on the edge of the big bed, smoking a pipe, and Jin Bailong filled his pipe with tobacco and followed his example.

'I never expected to see you here too,' said Huang Yongfa. 'When did you come? Did your mother come with you? What are you doing here? What do you do for a living?'

'What's the point of asking that?' Jim Bailong interrupted Huang Yongfa. 'Uncle Pan, Lao Liu and O Ran are all here –

one big family. Of course they can manage. I wanted to ask what the people in our place said when we two didn't return. What did Chumin and his lot say?'

'What could they say?' I replied. 'When the Red Spear Society set off they were so proud, but after one battle with two of them captured alive, they lost spirit. But – '

'But?' Huang Yongfa interrupted, asking anxiously, 'But what?'

'But Aunt Pickle raised hell with Zhu the Ninth and beat his head.'

'What did old Zhu say?' Huang Yongfa went on asking anxiously.

'What could he say?' I replied. 'He mentioned Jin Bailong to protect himself, saying that if even a fighter under Wang the Lion's direct command couldn't help being captured, what better could he do? Your wife, Pickle, urged him to find you, otherwise she'd have no husband and your children would have no bread-winner. That was no laughing matter!'

'So the villagers must all be upset?' said Huang Yongfa. 'No, they should be angry! How were they inveigled into the Red Spear Society to go and fight villagers like themselves?'

'They were deceived,' said Jin Bailong. 'Chumin and his people have been deceiving us for years! Now they're making us fight for them, so that we'll kill one another for their sake!'

'But we'll never be fooled again,' said Huang Yongfa, and then he spoke to Jin Bailong. 'So, it's good that we two were captured by the "northern" villagers. As the people back home have had no news about us, they'll surely think again about following Wang the Lion. That will make our work easier when we get back.'

'Yes, this crazy episode must be a lesson for us,' said Jin Bailong. 'What do you think, Little Brother?'

'I think you've both become very clever!' I said. 'How did you come to realize all this?'

Both of them laughed softly.

'It wasn't so easy, Little Brother,' said Huang Yongfa. 'We two were so stupid, as if we had been drugged. We carried our spears, marching with the Red Spear Society all the way to the "northern" border. We were the first to be captured . . . '

'It was very dangerous,' said Jin Bailong, butting in. 'They immediately bound us head and foot and handed us over to two strong young lads to guard us. When they gave a shout, the villagers came running from all sides. The Red Spear Society is such a rabble, they couldn't possibly resist. Zhu the Ninth is a coward. He was the first to flee and leave us two here. This creature knows how to pay lip-service to Chumin and Wang the Lion, but when they ask him to fight for them he knows how to escape.'

'What do you want him to do?' Huang Yongfa asked Jin Bailong. 'Do you want him to sacrifice himself for Chumin? If he just pretends to fight for Chumin from now on, that will be quite good, in my opinion.'

'Only we were too stupid, taking the lead.'

'Looking at it with hindsight, that was also quite good,' said Huang Yongfa. 'If we hadn't taken the lead, we wouldn't have been captured. And if we hadn't been captured, I'm afraid we would still be muddle-headed and would eventually sacrifice our lives for Chumin!'

'It was also dangerous,' said Jin Bailong. 'After we were arrested, didn't those tough young lads want to hang us on the spot?'

'You must thank that creature Zhu the Ninth for that,' said Huang Yongfa. 'If he wasn't a coward and hadn't led the Red Spear Society in retreat, we would probably really be dead.'

'What do you mean?' I asked. 'You're talking in riddles!'

As he had used up the tobacco in his pipe, Huang Yongfa scraped out the ashes inside it, laughing as he spoke.

'You've been here so long, and you've studied more than us. How come you don't even understand this?'

'I actually arrived here a few days after you. I left the village with my mother soon after you were captured. Otherwise how would I have known that your wife fought Zhu the Ninth so fiercely to get you back? He was under such pressure that he could do nothing but simply kneel down and beg for mercy!'

'Fine,' said Huang Yongfa. 'If he hadn't suffered a bit, he would still think that he was very clever, that he could handle Chumin's gang and continue tricking us villagers. Let this be a lesson to him! When I mentioned just now that we should be thankful to him, it was because he realized that his situation was hopeless, and fled with the group of the Red Spear Society under his command. This gave the leaders here a free hand to deal with us. Do you know who the leader was, who fought back against the Red Spear Society's sudden attack?'

I shook my head.

'It was none other than Pan Xudong,' said Jin Bailong. 'We were very lucky to meet him as soon as we got here! Do you know who he is? He's a big scholar. He studied at university in some big city, but not to become an official or get rich. Instead, he came to the countryside here to do something for us villagers . . .'

'You've strayed from the point, Bailong,' Huang Yongfa interrupted him. 'To get back to the story, Comrade Pan Xudong is an astute man. When he got back from the fight, he came to see us straight away. At that moment we didn't know whether we would live or die, and we were standing there with bowed heads, as if we were attending our fathers' funeral. The boy who was keeping watch on us was looking at us with hatred and holding a thick cudgel so that he could hit us any time. The returning villagers surrounded us, cursing us as Chumin's lackeys, shouting that we should be beaten to death or hung on a tree for everyone to see what happens to lackeys!'

'Some of them actually got two ropes to hang us on a tree!' added Jin Bailong. 'But just at that moment Pan Xudong came and stopped them.'

'So you weren't hanged,' I said. 'I know the villagers here are very tough. If they really intended to hang you, you couldn't count on your luck.'

'That's right,' said Huang Yongfa. 'They were very angry. They wanted at least to beat us to vent their anger. There are educated people like Pan Xudong and Wang Jiansheng here helping and teaching them. When they learn how to behave, they're not so rough. Pan Xudong told them: "What's the use of hanging them? Only the reactionary troops in the county town and the big landlords and their Order Preservation Corps would be pleased. Look at these two! Are they different from us? Their hands are as rough as ours, with thick calluses. They're also bald like us. Look at this tough fellow," he said, pointing

167

at Jin Bailong, "he has no hair left at all! He had scabies when he was a child. Why? Because he was poor! Just think, do the young sons of the landlords have scabies? These two are villagers like all of you. They came to fight us because they were tricked. How should we deal with such people?" He paused and looked at everyone. His words had silenced them all and they were at a loss. One of the villagers spoke on their behalf.

' "They're not our enemies. What's the use of punishing these two who have been deceived? Whoever tied them up, release them."

'The two rough young lads who had been guarding us looked around at everyone to see if they all agreed with what the old villager had just said. All of them fixed their eyes silently on the two lads, who had to untie us. Seeing this, Pan Xudong went on speaking:

' "Now we know why Chumin and his lot trick the villagers into coming here to fight us and sow hatred and dissension among us. They have a pact with the county officials and the troops stationed in the county town! When we villagers have exhausted ourselves fighting and killing each other, they'll deal with us together and wipe us out. We'll never let them carry out their plot!"

'By this time the ropes which had bound us had all been untied and were lying all over the place, a really funny spectacle. We stared at the ropes, not knowing what to do. Should we go back? We didn't dare. Should we join them? We had just come to fight these people. How could we look them in the face? The old villager who had first addressed them spoke to the two young lads again.

' "You tied these people up and then took it upon yourselves to hang them. What have you got to say for yourselves?"

'The two lads looked down at the ropes on the ground. Finally, the shorter one came up to us and said in a subdued voice, "I'm sorry, fellows, we made a terrible mistake. We've learned a lesson."

'The other lad knocked his head and said to himself, "You fool, why couldn't you think for yourself?"

'Witnessing this scene, I didn't know whether to laugh or cry. In fact, we just cried, understanding now that nothing stood

168

between us. At this point Pan Xudong addressed the old villager again:

' "These two lads haven't eaten, and they've come a long way – they must be hungry. What do you think? Here, they are our guests. Will you look after them, Uncle?"

'The old villager nodded and smiled, saying, "Fine, come with me!"

'So we went back with the old villager to his home, where there was only his wife, as his son and daughter were both grown up and married. They lived in a mud-hut on the mountainside, opposite a stream flowing from a mountain gully. It was a pleasant spot, but very isolated, just like this place, Pheasant Nest. There were no fields there, so their children had moved away to make a living as soon as they married. They had a spare room, where we slept that night. The next day, however, the old couple didn't let us leave, saying this was what Pan Xudong had instructed them. As they insisted, we agreed to stay there for the time being. Who would have thought that we would end up staying so long!

'The old peasant had to keep himself, so he went up the mountain every day to cut firewood and carried it to other places to sell – there aren't many cultivable fields, so selling firewood is the main occupation here. As we had the energy, we joined him cutting firewood on the mountain and helped him carry it for sale. In the evening we had nothing to do, and Pan Xudong sometimes came to see us. He chatted with us about this and that, but mostly he talked about how the poor people could change their own lives. As he's a man of learning, we found it strange that he knew so much about the lives of us villagers. When he heard that we two were Chumin's tenant-farmers, he was even more friendly to us, treating us like relatives. Nobody had ever shown us so much concern before. If he had no time to come himself, he sometimes sent others to talk to us and help us learn. Wang Jiansheng came, Uncle Pan, Liu Dawang, Pan Zaixing and also the owner of a pharmacy in town, Zizhong. They told us about many ideas, and we learned a lot. If it were not for our wives at home, we would have liked to settle down here. Of course, we have our duties now, so we have to go back . . .'

'What duties?' I asked, interrupting Huang Yongfa.

Jin Bailong answered for Huang Yongfa, smiling:

'Little Brother, it isn't possible to tell you. Uncle Pan knows, but I don't think he can tell you either. You'll know when the time comes. Uncle Pan is very close to us. He's changed completely and understands a lot now. It was he who persuaded us to do something to help our fellow villagers. One individual isn't strong enough by himself, so he has to collaborate with others, which means that there must be an organization. That's why we pledged ourselves at the meeting this evening. We expressed our determination!'

'So you're going back?' I asked.

'Yes, we're going back tomorrow,' replied Huang Yongfa. 'If you make up your mind to do something, you have to do it immediately. Otherwise the pledge would be wasted words.'

I felt that I understood them completely now. They too had been totally transformed.

'But you've been away from your villages for so long,' I said. 'Won't they think it strange when you suddenly turn up there again?'

'What's strange about it?' Jin Bailong retorted. 'Nobody reported back to the village that we'd died. Zhu the Ninth himself saw us being captured. When Wang the Lion came to the village to talk to the Red Spear Society, he said we had fallen into the hands of the revolutionaries in the north of the county and would be killed. Won't it be good to surprise them when we come back alive?'

Huang Yongfa had his head down as he lit a newly filled pipe and inhaled deeply. He was pondering, but after a moment he looked up and said, 'We cannot be as stupid as before. We can't go back to our villages in broad daylight. We'll leave tomorrow night after a good sleep here and get back to our villages at daybreak the following morning, just when everyone is getting up to go to work.'

'Why do you want to do it like that?' I asked. 'Zhu the Ninth had a rough time with your wife, who demanded that you be rescued. He'll be so delighted to see you that he'll congratulate you for coming back safe and sound. He'll also be thankful to you for making things easier for him.'

'But Chumin and Wang the Lion aren't that stupid. They may be suspicious. If we get back to the village just at dawn, we can say that we escaped during the night, after great difficulty and risk. Why did we try so hard to escape? Because we're loyal members of the Red Spear Society!'

'So do you still want to go back to the Red Spear Society?' I asked.

'If we don't rejoin it,' replied Huang Yongfa, 'how can we carry out our work? That's what Zizhong talked to us about this morning, and we discussed the problem together.'

'Oh, I've just remembered,' put in Jin Bailong, 'Chumin and Wang the Lion both announced that those who led when the Red Spear Society went on the expedition should be hailed as heroes and rewarded!'

Huang Yongfa could not help laughing.

'But we really were captured by the villagers here!' he explained, and, laughing even louder, added, 'It was Zhu the Ninth who betrayed us. When he saw us being captured, he didn't come to rescue us. Instead he led his forces in flight, thus making us look courageous. Now escaping and returning, we'll be heroes twice over and we should be rewarded accordingly!'

We couldn't help laughing. This was the first time in the recent troubled period that we had had a good laugh. It was also the climax of this unexpected 'reunion' between us three fellow countrymen. As if echoing our joyful mood, a cock crowed in the distance.

'It's late,' said Huang Yongfa. 'We could go on chatting for ever, but we should get some sleep.'

'Tomorrow we don't need to leave for home until after sunset,' said Jin Bailong. 'We can sleep right till the afternoon, as we have nothing else to do.'

'I have nothing special to do tomorrow either,' I said. 'I can go with you to see you on your way.'

Then the three of us lay down on our beds without undressing and snuggled into the straw. Perhaps because we were exhausted, we slept very well, without dreaming at all.

I saw off these two fellow countrymen when they left Pheasant Nest at dusk the next day. Their parting words were,

'We certainly won't tell people back home that we met you here!'

I never heard any more about the task Grandpa Whiskers was going to give me. One afternoon I went to ask him about it.

'How is it that the guest you mentioned hasn't come yet, Grandpa Whiskers? I've been waiting to hear from you.'

'I was just coming to see you! The guest will be coming soon. I specially went into town about this today. Your Uncle Zizhong told me that the guest is busy with other matters at the moment, but he'll be coming in two days. This has already been settled, because he needs a quiet place to work. Just you wait and see how busy you'll be! Pan Mingxun has asked me to tell you to go to Pheasant Nest tonight. He'll be waiting for you there.'

'What's going on?' I asked, surprised. 'Why do I have to go there again?'

He stroked his long beard and smiled.

'You'll find out when you get there. As *Jia* chief I'm just responsible for liaison and I don't have to know everything. Go there after supper. Eat a bit earlier – and have plenty! Don't get there later than nightfall.'

When I arrived at Pheasant Nest it was getting dark, the time when they light the lamps up. Old Feng Xinshun emerged from behind a big tree beside the path leading into the village. When he recognized me, he let me pass. I could make out two dark shapes in the open space in front of the village. The first one to come up and greet me was Jiqing. As we had often gone together in the night, he could recognize me at a glance in the dark.

'What are you doing here again?' I asked.

'I came straight from town. We have an urgent task. Look, forty strong villagers have already gathered over there.'

'What are they doing?'

'Can't you see? Our self-defence corps is assembling. Your team leader, Pan Mingxun, can tell you more about it.'

'Are you a team leader too?'

'Yes, the leaders recently assigned me to lead the second group of the seventh team. Mingxun is leader of the first group, as you know. Quick, he's waiting for you!'

He pointed to a group of about twenty villagers assembled on the right side of the open space and prodded my back to send me in that direction. Pan Mingxun saw me immediately and led me over to his group, whispering, 'That time when the troops from the county town came to the countryside with the Order Preservation Corps to put on a show of strength, you must have seen their guns. To tell you the truth, we all had a careful look and we were terribly jealous of their superb rifles! Tonight we're going to seize them – in our hands they'll surely make a difference!'

My heart skipped a beat. I really wanted to get those guns, but I was afraid that their combined troops and Order Preservation Corps would be too strong for us. How could our two teams of villagers armed with only kitchen knives and daggers possbly seize their guns? I put my doubts directly to Pan Mingxun.

'That's a very good question,' said Pan Mingxun, 'and everyone is wondering about it. So we made a thorough investigation. We really cannot go about it in an amateurish way, just rushing rashly to take their guns. Things aren't so easy in this world! It's a pity you came a bit late, because we've just arranged the whole plan to seize the guns. We're still too weak to confront the regular troops in the county town. In any case, our leaders have already investigated the situation. The rifles of Chumin's Order Preservation Corps are really good and quite new. They were bought by Duan Lianchen, who's living in the Japanese concession in "The Big City" downstream. He procured them from the Japanese there. They'll be very useful for us. You're good at finding your way at night, so your first task today is keeping guard. Your second task will be liaison work for our group and Jiqing's group. Corps leader Liu Dawang has approved this arrangement. Listen, they've started marching. We're off!'

'Comrades, off to the south!' This was Liu Dawang's command.

We left Pheasant Nest on a rapid march.

In the middle of the night, after marching for about three hours, we came to a big road which led to an imposing building. As I had wandered around this area when I was a child, I remembered it quite clearly. I knew that this was the Wei family ancestral hall. Here Liu Dawang suddenly ordered us to halt. Twelve to fifteen yards away there was a village called Wei Family Village. Inside was another grand building, which everyone in the district knew was the residence of Chumin's steward, Wei Jingtang. It also looked awesome in the dark. Wei Jingtang obviously could not live here in these troubled times. He had to live somewhere near his master, Chumin, but people still talked about him here.

'Don't bother about him this time,' said Liu Dawang. 'Our task is to take the rifles from the hall.'

Pan Mingxun had scouted around this hall a few days before, as he had told me on the way. He had come disguised as a pedlar with a pole on his shoulder to spy out this area himself. There was only a path leading from the hall to the village behind. There were no houses along it, so the villagers could not hear what was going on in the hall. A team of Chumin's Order Preservation Corps, his 'crack troops', were billeted in this hall. They were proud, and, because the rifles they used were the newest Japanese product, they caused the most trouble, exacting money and robbing people.

'You have to hit where it hurts,' explained Pan Mingxun. 'If we want to beat Chumin's corps, we must first strike at this team!'

Liu Dawang allocated our two teams two different functions: Pan Mingxun's team would go straight into the hall to deal with the soldiers; Jiqing's team was deployed around the hall to support the team inside and coordinate with them. I was placed between the two teams to pass on messages under the direct command of Liu Dawang.

Liu Dawang divided our teams into three sections, the largest of which contained half of all our forces. This section would stand at the main door of the hall preparing to enter, while the two other sections would cover the two ways out of the hall to deal with any problem outside and also to attack the soldiers fleeing from inside. I would go into the hall to keep contact with those inside and outside. When all had been arranged, we advanced quietly under Liu Dawang's command and spread around the hall according to plan. The village behind was completely silent now, with everyone asleep, and nobody had discovered us.

The door of the hall was closed. We were amazed to find that there was no guard outside, perhaps because these 'crack troops' were over-confident. They felt that their weapons were superior and the local village lads had all joined the Red Spear Society, which was in their hands. Although the northern villagers who had been 'duped' by the revolutionaries had some military organization, they could only cope with the Red Spear Society and definitely would not dare attack the troops. So they did not think it necessary to post a sentry there. Although the main door of the hall was firmly closed, there was quite a wide crack between the two halves. The paint on them had long since peeled off. Fortunately, there were many lamps burning inside, so that those inside could not see anything going on in the dark outside and those outside could see part of the interior through the crack. The soldiers were scattered all over the big hall: some slouching with their heads on the table; some leaning against the wall, with their eyes closed and mumbling some nonsense; some lying on floor mattresses by the wall and snoring. It looked as if they had enjoyed a big feast that evening, with plenty of meat and wine, so they were now stone drunk and incapable of moving.

In the middle of the hall there were two square tables on which were seven or eight heaps of bones. There were also wine flasks, cups, plates and soup bowls scattered all over the table. Perhaps these 'crack troops' of Chumin had been wreaking havoc in villages all over the south these past few days, in order to put on a show of strength. On the way they had stolen many chickens, ducks, pigs and sheep, so they could have this kind of sumptuous feast.

After Liu Dawang had peeped through the crack, examining the hall within for a while, he stepped aside and let Pan Mingxun have a careful look. Then Pan Mingxun turned round and gestured to us that we could prepare for action. It looked as if our previous plan would have to be altered, as the situation had changed. This did not look like the corps headquarters, but more like a club after a party. The door was firmly closed and the guests dead drunk. Pan Mingxun tapped on the door twice

175

and then looked in again. None of the drunkards inside stirred; they just went on sleeping. When he tapped a few more times, there was still no response. This time Liu Dawang came up and kicked the door softly twice. Still not a sound from within. Finally, he whispered to Pan Mingxun, 'We can pry the door open, but we must be careful that there's no guard behind it.'

Then Pan Mingxun took a dagger from his belt and stuck it in the crack. The men of our group, who had gathered on both sides of the door, took out their kitchen knives, grasped their spears or held out their fishing forks, ready for action. Pan Mingxun moved the dagger up and down until he found the bolt. He turned his head and whispered to us, 'It's easy. Tell everyone to be prepared!'

I immediately whispered this order to all of them.

Then Pan Mingxun pressed the point of the dagger against the bolt and pushed it slowly to one side until it stopped moving. After this he slipped the dagger down and pushed the lower bolt in the opposite direction. Everyone held their breath as they watched him moving the dagger. His movements were so adept, swift and agile, probably just like when he was hunting with the hunter and skinning the game in those days. When he had finished pushing the two bolts open, he whispered another order to me.

'Tell the vanguard to come up!'

I immediately passed on this order to those in the vanguard team.

Ten members of this team rushed up to the doorway, with weapons in their hands. Pan Mingxun gently pushed the door wide open. Unexpectedly, the first to enter was Liu Dawang. Instead of bursting into the hall, he turned to look behind the door on the left. A moment later we heard something falling on the ground. He picked it up and put it in my hands. As he moved, Pan Mingxun also rushed in. He turned to the right and picked up a gun from behind the door there. In fact, there had been two guards standing there, but they were sitting on the ground leaning against the wall and had fallen asleep with their heads down. They were sleeping so soundly that when we hit them over the head they could not even shout 'Help!'

Then we all rushed into the hall. What we most wanted to

get our hands on were those new Japanese rifles and bullets standing against the wall. We did not waste a second, and in a flash these weapons were all in our hands and we had passed them out. The group led by Jiqing, which was originally ready to play a supportive role when the need arose, also changed their plan at this point. They took the rifles, and we armed ourselves too. We tied all the extra rifles together, so that some of us were suddenly carrying two rifles on our shoulders. Although this action was quick and skilful, we could not help making a little noise, finally waking up these drunken men. One of them, who had a slightly crooked mouth, jumped up and shouted, 'Brothers, pick up your rifles – quick – enemies – shoot!'

At the same time he felt behind for his pistol, panic-stricken. Jiqing was quick-witted and leaped forward, kicking him ferociously in the back, so that he fell on his face, sprawling on the ground. Then Pan Mingxun sprang towards him, kicking him in the mouth with one foot and treading on the hand behind him with the other. I swiftly grabbed his pistol, which was the last weapon we seized during that night attack.

'Who are you?' asked Liu Dawang, pulling him up by the ear.

'I . . . I . . . I . . .' this creatured stammered, reluctant to speak.

Liu Dawang looked around the whole hall. We had seized all their weapons. Then he faced the men who had by now awoken from their drunken slumber. They were gaping at our self-defence corps, hardly taking in the fact that we had seized all their weapons.

'Tell me, who's the creature with the pistol?' he asked them. 'If you speak up, we won't kill you!'

As he spoke, one of the Self-defence Corps stamped his foot on the ground. At the same time he shoved the butt of his captured rifle into the backside of one of the men to show that he could easily shoot him.

'He . . . he . . . he's called Old Hei the Harelip,' stammered this one. 'He's our . . .'

Liu Dawang laughed coldly, saying 'Ah, Old Hei, you have quite a reputation in both north and south of the county. It wasn't so easy to visit you today. You'd better see us off. We have to go now!' Then he turned to the rest of them, who were still standing there bewildered, and commanded, 'Stay standing here, just the way you are! Don't move for one hour. We won't hesitate to shoot anyone who moves.'

I handed him the pistol which I had just taken, and he waved it in front of them. At the same time the others in our corps banged their rifle butts down, making a frightful din. The soldiers stood there transfixed and dumbfounded, as if they had suddenly taken sedatives.

'Tie up Hei the Harelip and take him away!' Liu Dawang ordered us.

Only at this point did Hei the Harelip come to his senses, kneeling down to beg for mercy and to show repentance, but it was too late. He had also commanded that expedition of the Order Preservation Corps with the troops from the county town. The memory of that incident was enough to rouse the hatred which had long been burning in our hearts. Within two minutes our men had bound his hands behind his back and hauled him out into the dark night. Even though he dragged his feet, they still managed to pull him up to the road in front of the hall.

It was getting late, and we had to get back to the north quickly to scatter and hide there. So we all thought that it was a burden to take this corps leader back with us. By chance there was an elm tree beside the road, and everyone agreed to hang him there as a warning to Chumin, Wang the Lion and the other leaders of the corps. So we tied a rope around his neck and hanged him. By the time those terrified soldiers started looking for him, after our stipulated hour, he was already dead.

I got home before dawn with aching legs. I went straight to bed and slept right up to the evening. When I woke, Mother told me that Grandpa Whiskers had called, but hadn't wanted to disturb me as I was fast asleep. He had left a message that I should go and see him later that evening.

I went after supper. In fact, he did not have much to say, only to tell me, 'The guest you've been waiting for is coming. Go to Uncle Zizhong tomorrow to fetch him. Oh, there's something else which might interest you. Last night Pan Zaixing also led his self-defence team to seize the rifles of another team of

Chumin's Order Preservation Corps. They seized them all, so that our two self-defence teams seized altogether over a hundred guns in one night. That's half of Chumin's regular troops, which isn't bad!'

Then he laughed cheerfully, and I laughed too.

# CHAPTER 10

Aunt Sunflower and my mother knew that I was going to Tanjiahe to fetch that 'guest', and they were well informed about it. Perhaps Grandpa Whiskers had told them when he came to see me. The day after he passed on this instruction to me, Mother said at breakfast-time, 'I've heard that a guest has arrived and the leaders have arranged for you to look after him, so that he feels secure in our village. That's a good arrangement. You can stay quiet in the village too for the time being, and we two can see one another every day.'

'As there's nothing else special for you to do, you can stay put here for some time – a rare opportunity these days,' said Aunt Sunflower.

'After breakfast I have to go to town to fetch the guest, as you know. I mustn't delay! When he's settled down here, I'll be settled for a while too.'

Aunt Sunflower smiled.

'Take it easy – wait a moment! You've done all kinds of work with Jiqing and the others. Didn't you go with your self-defence team the day before yesterday to seize Chumin's guns? That was at night-time. It's really not so safe here. In the day the enemy can come at any time. That's why you have to do so much during the night. You must wait till it gets dark before fetching your "guest". Also, your Uncle Zizhong is very busy. Since the proprietor of the pharmacy left, he's never been back home. He has to do everything himself, so he can only see you after work. When he hands the guest over to you, he'll tell you what to do.'

I understood what she was talking about. Jiqing had told me that Uncle Zizhong had recently been entrusted with a new task, very important work. It was quite likely that the 'guest' I was going to receive was an important person. As Aunt Sunflower had advised, I left for town just before dark.

When I got to the pharmacy, it was already closed. One of the front doors, however, was still open, which Uncle Zizhong may have done deliberately so that I could come straight in without any noise. On entering, I could see that Uncle Zizhong was still busy. He was just preparing for the next day, putting all kinds of medicine into the appropriate drawers. As soon as he saw me he dropped his work, came over, patted my shoulder and said, smiling, 'Good, you've come punctually. Come and see who's waiting for you. You'll understand why we wanted you to come and fetch him.'

He led me into a small room at the back, facing a courtyard. There were flowers and medicinal plants growing there, providing a quiet and secluded atmosphere. I heard that the pharmacy-owner, Li Jiuzhang, often came into this room to have a rest and do controlled-breathing exercises. Originally he had been a scholar, as his parents ran a bookshop in 'The Big City'. They had saved some money, and he fancied himself as a scholar, believing in Taoism and Buddhism so he could live a leisured life in retirement. Later he found it boring simply staying at home in scholarly retreat, so he chose to move to this rural town. It had the advantages of being a small town, and because it was near the countryside he could go out for a walk any time and enjoy nature. He set up a pharmacy here, because he knew something about Chinese medicine. Then he asked Zizhong to be his assistant, as he too was educated. Uncle Zizhong had worked diligently in this shop for over ten years, gaining his complete trust. In recent times his quiet life had been shattered by the chaos in the countryside. He was so upset that he handed over the pharmacy to Zizhong to manage on his own, while he returned to 'The Big City' with his wife to become a 'scholar' again. So Uncle Zizhong in fact became the occupant here, and this room, which had been the owner's recreation room, became his sitting room for receiving 'guests'.

Uncle Zizhong led me into this 'guest room'. On entering, I saw Lao Liu and a young man sitting opposite each other at a square table, on which were a pot of tea and some cakes. Lao

Liu was beaming all over, full of beans, as if he were entertaining a long-lost friend and having a most interesting discussion. I had never seen him so amiable and happy – these days, he was always busy with his propaganda work, often frowning and worrying about it.

The young man was shocked to see me, staring in amazement. He was wearing a bright yellow venetian gown. He had a fair complexion and close-cropped hair with a ridge in front, as was the fashion with young men of well-to-do families in 'The Big City'. One could tell at a glance that he was not a country lad, nor was he from a rural town – because country folk all shaved their heads, including all the landlords and gentry. When I looked at him closely, he did seem familiar. After a few seconds we recognized one another and were both astounded.

Who would have imagined that we would meet in this pharmacy! He was in fact Ho Shuoru, the son of my father's old employer, Ho Ludong.

'How did you manage to get here too, Chunsheng?' he asked me at last.

'That's what I was just going to ask you. I'm a local here. As we couldn't survive in 'The Big City', we naturally came back to the countryside. How are you, Master?'

'What do you mean, "Master"?' retorted Ho Shuoru, but with a smile playing on his lips. 'How can you still be so old-fashioned? I've been captured!'

At this point, Uncle Zizhong butted in, also smiling. 'That's right, he really was a captive, but now he is our honoured guest. We knew you were well acquainted, so we were not really asking you to fetch him, but rather to give him a special welcome. Lao Liu will take him to your village. It's too confusing here and he needs a quiet environment, so we've decided to put him up in Grandpa Whiskers's place. You already know one another, so look after him well and follow all his instructions!'

'I'll certainly obey Master Ho. I know the way he's used to living.'

'What do you mean, "Master"!' said Ho Shuoru, rather seriously. 'My name's Ho Shuoru. In future you may only call me Shuoru! Will you remember that?'

'Yes, I will. It's just that I feel rather uneasy not to call you "Master".'

'Fine, it's getting late,' said Lao Liu, laughing as he stood up. 'Anyway, you'll have plenty of time together. It doesn't matter what you call one another. Let's go now! O Ran has probably arrived and she may be waiting for us outside.'

'Has O Ran come as well?' I asked. 'We haven't seen her for ages.'

'She's been going round the villages recently, encouraging the women to support the Self-defence Corps, so she hasn't had time to go and see her mother. She misses her very much, and so do I. We'll take this opportunity to go and see her – and Aunt Sunflower too.'

As we went out, there was O Ran just coming into town. We could recognize her as soon as she came through the town gate – the town had only one little street. She looked exhausted, but as soon as she saw Ho Shuoru and me she seemed to recover.

'This is . . . ?' Ho Shuoru asked Lao Liu.

'Ah, I forgot to introduce you,' said Lao Liu apologetically. 'This is O Ran, Chunsheng's elder sister. She is now a well-known tailor in this town and she's very good at it. She's just back from the villages, where she's been taking back the clothes she's finished for her old customers. Now she's coming back to see her mother at Red Hill Village, where you'll be staying.'

'Chunsheng's mother?' asked Ho Shuoru.

'Yes, really. She grew up in Chunsheng's home, and she learned how to sew from his mother.'

'Well, we're all kith and kin!' said Ho Shuoru. 'That's interesting. No wonder Zizhong urged me to come and stay in Red Hill Village for a while. So many people I know!'

'That should make you feel at home,' I said. 'You'll be very comfortable there.'

Ho Shuoru burst out laughing. I had never seen him laugh so freely. He had left his home in 'The Big City', that 'money-seeking' family, and had come to this small town, where people had no class prejudice. He seemed to be 'spiritually liberated' here. We all began to feel relaxed together.

We four strode out of the town, heading for Red Hill Village. We were like a happy family as we walked along, talking and laughing. Now I realized why Uncle Zizhong and Grandpa Whiskers had asked me to go and fetch Shuoru. On the way I told him how we had left home, how Father had died and why we had moved to this remote mountain area to settle down. When he heard my story, he was angry about the situation and blamed Chiang Kai-shek who was responsible for it.

'If it weren't for that monster arresting young people, shooting students and extorting money, you wouldn't have had to move back to the country and your father might not have died an untimely death. Well, now we're together again – I'm glad we'll be staying together.'

'When you're in Red Hill Village, I'll be looking after you like old times. That's why I've come to fetch you. Isn't life strange?'

'Yes, yes!' He laughed again. 'Strange, very strange!'

Lao Liu suddenly asked, 'Master Shuoru, just now you mentioned extorting money. Extorting whose money?'

'Our family's!' replied Ho Shuoru angrily. 'The first time they said our family was harbouring Chunsheng's elder brother, so they extorted one thousand dollars! This made Chunsheng's father ill and forced them to go back to the country. After you'd gone, they said we'd allowed the family of a revolutionary to get away and they extorted more money from us.'

'How much was it the second time?' I asked.

'Two thousand five hundred dollars!' he replied, even more angrily. 'They wouldn't accept bank notes, only silver coins!'

'That's terrible!' said Lao Liu. 'You shouldn't have paid up. Chunsheng's family originally came from the countryside and now they've moved back. Is that a crime?'

'How can you reason with that gang under Chiang Kai-shek's command?' said Ho Shuoru, getting furious. 'They're warlords, spies, vagabonds, "Blue and Red gangsters" and thugs. They sat there in our house, flaunting their pistols and threatening to take me hostage. They insisted on the money, and it had to be in silver coins. Then they could go to brothels, smoke opium and smuggle goods, while disrupting people's lives. These creatures dare to talk about their "party" and "nation". It's a bankrupt "party" and a rotten "state".'

By now Ho Shuoru could no longer contain his anger. We did not want him to enter our village in such a rage, as he was actually our 'guest'. So, as Red Hill Village was now in sight, we did not pursue the topic. As we kept quiet, he also gradually calmed down. He just mumbled to himself to vent his anger.

'Money, money, money! What's the use of worldly possessions and stinking money? These parasites just frequent brothels and smoke opium. It's intolerable!'

We did not respond to his monologue, because we were already approaching Red Hill Village. Grandpa Whiskers was waiting for us at the end of the village. We did not see him at first as the moon was still hidden, but only some shapes under the trees in front of the village. He approached us and immediately recognized the 'guest'. He quickly came up to Ho Shuoru and bowed to welcome him as village *Jia* chief and also as his host.

'Honoured guest, I welcome you on behalf of the villagers!'

'This is Grandpa Whiskers, whom we told you about. He's *Jia* chief of Red Hill Village,' Lao Liu introduced him. 'He's an excellent host. You'll be very happy living in his place.'

'Thank you, Grandpa Whiskers,' said Ho Shuoru in a gentle voice. 'I'm really sorry that you had to come out to meet me so late in the day at your age.'

'I'm just worried that it will be difficult for you to get used to this place,' said Grandpa Whiskers. 'This is a very quiet village. But you must be tired and hungry. Come to my home right away; everything's ready for you.'

'Fine, Master Shuoru, we'll leave you here,' said Lao Liu. 'I'm going with O Ran to see Mother. See you later!' Then, turning to me, he went on, 'You go with Master Shuoru and see if there's anything you can still do for him today.'

Grandpa Whiskers took us to his house. When we came into the room which I had put in order for Ho Shuoru, the lamp was burning brightly with a welcoming glow. Grandpa Whiskers treated this as a special occasion, so he put two extra wicks in the lamp for Shuoru. Now it lit up the newly made bed and the clean quilt. Grandpa Whiskers had also prepared a set of writing implements for him to use.

Ho Shuoru looked around with a satisfied smile.

'It's really idyllic here! I always wanted to get away from the money-mad "Big City" and now I've found the perfect place in this little village. This is a real indulgence! Ha! Ha! Ha!'

His laughter immediately put us all at ease. Now Grandpa Whiskers looked at me, indicating the kitchen, where I should fill a basin of hot water for Shuoru to wash his face. He also told Sister Apricot to bring in the dinner she had ready. So I went out straight away.

I came back soon with a basin of hot water, and Sister Apricot brought in a tray full of dishes, which she placed on the table. After Grandpa Whiskers had introduced her to Shuoru, she went out.

There were four dishes – peas, cabbage, scrambled egg and stewed chicken. I had never witnessed this kind of reception for a guest in the countryside, especially in these hard times. Sister Apricot had cooked these dishes so well for our 'guest'. This was also a surprise, because she was usually very quiet, with a worried expression on her face. She did not seem interested in anything, so we thought she could not really do much. But seeing these dishes, I realized that she had made a great effort for this 'guest' and understood why his stay here was important.

'This is hardly adequate for you,' said Grandpa Whiskers, racking his brains to find the most 'refined' language. 'Compared to what you're used to at home, this country fare is very simple. Now Chunsheng will be staying here to attend to you as he used to in your home. Don't hesitate to ask him for anything!'

'That makes me feel awkward,' said Ho Shuoru. 'I'm neither an official, nor a VIP.'

'We don't consider you an official. If you were . . . ' Grandpa Whiskers suddenly checked himself. I could guess that what he was going to say was probably: If you were an official, we wouldn't treat you so politely.

'All right, help yourself. If there's anything you'd like to eat, just tell Sister Apricot any time. Now I won't disturb your meal.'

Then Grandpa Whiskers left us. I went to the kitchen to make a pot of tea. When Shuoru finished his dinner, I poured him a cup of tea and then cleared away the bowls and chopsticks.

'Have a good rest,' I said to Shuoru. 'See you tomorrow!'

Just as I was going out, he stopped me, saying, 'From now on, please don't address me so politely. I know where I am now. "Master" indeed! That's only suitable for despots, who have been overthrown here. Please tell Grandpa Whiskers and the others to stop being so polite. Are you coming tomorrow?'

'Of course! My duty is to attend to you and make sure you're comfortable here.'

'Thank you!' he said humbly. 'From now on we'll be friends, confiding in one another. I can only feel at ease like that. The former "master-servant" relationship was a product of the rapacious society and it must be ended now! Right, you must rest too. See you tomorrow!'

When I got back home, Lao Liu and O Ran were having a lively discussion with my mother. They were going to spend the night here. As they were always separated because they were busy, tonight was the first time for ages that they had had an opportunity to be together.

The next day we got up very late, because the evening before my mother thought that we should have a good chat. It was a rare occasion for a 'family reunion', but without Uncle Pan, who was always so busy. So we had talked well into the night. When we awoke, the sun was already high in the sky. O Ran automatically hurried into the kitchen to make breakfast, as if she were still used to being the child-bride at home. Mother promptly stopped her, as it was now quite obvious that she was pregnant. Noticing this in the morning sunshine, Mother was both happy, and worried that she might have a miscarriage. Funnily enough, I thought it would be best if Mother made breakfast, because we were used to her tasty cooking. This taste could remind me of the days when I was little and we used to eat together in our old home – only today Lao Liu was here instead of Uncle Pan, but this made it even more interesting. There was, in fact, something special about this breakfast which Mother prepared, even though it was very simple: a pot of porridge and a bowl of pickles.

After breakfast, Mother asked Lao Liu and O Ran to stay longer.

'If you don't stay, Lao Liu, she won't either – and she needs to rest. Last night she didn't get any sleep!'

Lao Liu thought it over a bit.

'All right,' he said. 'It's not good to leave in broad daylight anyway, and I can spend the time writing some propaganda material.' Then he spoke to me. 'Quickly, go over to see Ho Shuoru. He's new here and probably still unfamiliar with things. You should be with him and see if he needs anything. I want to get on with my writing, so I won't go to see him. If he needs anything, just come and tell me. We'll expect you back in the evening.'

I went to Shuoru immediately. He had also got up very late, but Sister Apricot had already prepared his breakfast. I asked her to take it to his room.

'Come here,' he said to me as he started his breakfast. 'Please sit there facing me, and we can have a good chat. It's so cosy here.'

'Whatever you like. What do you want to talk about? Do you want to know about the situation here?'

He shook his head.

'No, I'm sure you're wondering how I come to be here. I know I've appeared out of the blue.'

'Yes, I have been wondering. I knew that someone was coming, but I don't know why you've come to this poor place.'

'I also feel it's strange to be with you again,' he said, chuckling. 'How odd life is!'

'Yes, there are many strange things which we cannot explain. Our home is in the south of the county. As we couldn't survive there and we have relatives here, we moved to this village.'

'My forebears used to live in the south too, but I have no relatives in this place. Don't you think it's strange that I've come here?'

'Strange! Very strange!' I said. 'But however strange it might be, there must be a good reason. Even though your old home was in the south, that doesn't mean you would necessarily want to go back. But you have even less reason to come here. Didn't your whole family move to "The Big City" long ago?'

Ho Shuoru put down his chopsticks and sighed.

'It would take a long time to explain,' he said.

'That doesn't matter. Anyway, we both want to stay in today. Even if it's a long story, you have time to tell it.'

'You are very curious. Didn't I tell you I was a captive?'

He smiled again.

'How could that be?' I asked. 'They're all giving you such special treatment here!'

'Don't you really know anything about it? If I have to tell you, it'll really be a long story.'

Actually, I really wanted him to talk for a long time, because it had been arranged for him to spend the day resting. I didn't have anything else to do, apart from keeping him company. We would both feel bored if we didn't pass the time chatting.

'Go on, tell me. It doesn't matter how long it takes,' I urged him. 'As we haven't seen one another for such a long time, there must be a lot to talk about. Also, my father spent most of his life working for your father, so we have something in common. We often think of your family!'

'All right, I'll tell you exactly how it happened,' said Shuoru. He had already put down his chopsticks, having finished his breakfast. 'I only hope you have the patience to listen.'

'Hold on a minute. Wait till I've cleared the table.'

I took the bowls and chopsticks back to the kitchen, where I also boiled a pot of tea. After pouring him a cup, I placed it in front of him, saying, 'You can start now!'

After clearing his throat, he started his story.

'As I already told you on the way here, those creatures extorted some money from my father. It's said that misfortunes never come singly. I was nearly arrested. You know that they especially like to arrest and execute young people. Well, I'm young too!'

'They probably wouldn't have dared to arrest you. Your father is a shop-owner with some prestige in the commercial world. You certainly couldn't have anything to do with the revolutionaries.'

Shuoru quickly sipped some tea to cover a wry smile.

'It's not so simple,' he said. 'They dared to extort money from my father, not only once, but twice – perhaps they're now extorting money for the third time! Why wouldn't they dare arrest me? If they arrested me and held me hostage, they could extort an even higher ransom! They could say that your brother worked in our house for many years, that as a young man I was naturally influenced by him and joined the Revolutionary Party. Which of those young students they shot didn't come from a well-off family? Otherwise, how would they have been able to study?'

I could not help smiling bitterly too.

'That's really ironic,' I said. 'They claim to maintain social order for the rich, but they execute their children . . .'

'Yes, it is indeed ironic,' said Shuoru. 'I've been thinking about it a lot lately. Before I came here I read a book on the May Fourth Movement,* which was very interesting. It was your brother's. He had left it inside the desk in the shop, when he used to work for my father. Our steward, Han Yongsheng, discovered it when he was clearing away some subversive literature, which your brother might have left there. Just as Hang Yongsheng was about to burn it, I saw it and took it away and then I read the whole book secretly. Would you belive it, all the revolutionaries at that time were academics and high intellectuals. For instance, Li Dazhao was a professor at Peking University. How could he have gone to university and become a professor if his family were not wealthy? But they strangled him to death just the same. I'm a nobody compared to him. They could arrest me any time and execute me, just as they've done to other young people . . .'

'But now you can have a quiet life here,' I said, smiling. 'Isn't that strange?'

'Yes, I would never have imagined it!' he said, laughing again, but then lapsing into silence, as if he had just thought of something. 'On the other hand, it's not so strange. It depends how you analyse this question.'

'I don't quite understand what you mean. What is there to analyse?'

---

* A patriotic movement, starting with the demonstration of students in Peking on 4 May 1919. They were protesting against the weak and corrupt government and demanding democracy and modernization for China.

He closed his eyes slightly, as if still thinking about something.

'It's partly fortuitous and partly inevitable,' he said, opening his eyes again and sipping some tea. It looked as if he were going to explain the meaning of 'fortuitous' and 'inevitable'. 'Fortuitous, because my parents were pestered by those creatures. They sent my brother-in-law, Chen Chuqing, to ask the provincial government and militarists why they sent such thugs to our house to extort money from us. And what did they say? "These are exceptional times. We must execute all revolutionaries and those who have connections with them. Whoever wants to work with the government to eliminate the revolutionaries has the right to take action, as long as they have guns: rather kill a thousand by mistake than let one revolutionary escape!" It's no use for scholars to try to reason with soldiers. Now it's even more hopeless for shop-owners to try to reason with the armed hooligans sent by the authorities – because it's a matter of money! Money, money! Even if you have good connections with the provincial leaders, in the end only money counts. Faced with this situation, my parents became miserable and pessimistic. Trying to find a way out, they thought: We got rich because of the blessings of our ancestors, but after this we were carried away by success and forgot about them. We neglected their graves in our old home in the countryside, not making offerings to them or keeping their graves in good repair. Our ancestors must have been annoyed by our disrespectful behaviour. So business in our shop slackened, and then they came to extort money from us. Still our ancestors tried to protect us, especially my life, and I wasn't arrested by those thugs like other youths. So, after many sleepless nights and discussions, my parents decided to send someone back to our country home to make offerings to our ancestors and repair their graves.'

Shuoru paused at this point, smiling as if to console himself. Then he sipped some more tea.

'So you went back to the country to offer blessings and repair your ancestors' graves?' I asked, smiling too.

'You guessed right. This is an expression of filial respect and nobody else can do it. To tell you the truth, I was fed up with my little room at home. I wanted to leave "The Big City" and go to the countryside to see what life was like there. Also, I was the only one in the family who could go. My elder brother had gone away, my parents couldn't leave the house and my elder sister was married and lived away from home. Who could represent the family personally except me? After two more nights of discussion, my parents decided to send me back to the country. There was another episode involved here. When my parents were discussing this, they both had the same dream one night. They dreamed that my grandparents came to see them and told them that they had secretly protected one of their grandsons – that was me. That was why I had not been arrested and shot by those villainous politicians. They hoped that their young grandson would come to see them at their graves. That's how it was decided to send me back to the village.'

Shuoru started tapping the table mechanically, as if he were considering how best to describe the situation after he got back to the countryside.

'Now the "inevitable" occurred,' he went on. 'The countryside wasn't as peaceful as it used to be. We had already considered this, and I knew I had to be careful. But I was young and I could dress simply, disguised as a shop assistant. Also, there was a distant uncle living in our village, and we had kept contact with him. The best thing would be for me to go to his home, where there would be no danger for me, to stay for a few days. There I could arrange everything perfectly for offering blessings and repairing our ancestors' graves. So my father gave me two hundred silver dollars and his rickshaw puller – he was also disguised as a shop assistant. Thus we went off to the country-side. The first day went well and we travelled over twenty-five miles through the neighbouring county. We spent the night in a rural inn. The next day we reached our old home county after another twenty to thirty miles without a hitch. But before we had reached my uncle's house it was already dark. So we hurried on, hoping to get there before midnight. You see, the scene was set for the "inevitable" to occur.'

He suddenly laughed and gulped down some tea, as if he wanted to finish telling this 'inevitable' story quickly. Then he continued:

'If you thought that you'd be safe once you came back to the countryside, then you were naïve. But on reflection, our family were also naïve. It was inevitable that something would happen to me, because your forces were too well organized . . .'

'What do you mean by "your" and "our"?' I interrupted him. 'Who do you mean by "your"?'

Shuoru laughed again – this time heartily.

'Little Brother, you needn't pretend,' he said in an affectionate way. 'Now you've joined the revolution like your brother. Otherwise, why would you have come to look after me? It's quite clear to me. You're all working together – your brother-in-law, Lao Liu, and your sister, O Ran – can I call them that? And Uncle Pan too. All right, now I'll tell you about my experience – perhaps you know about it already, but never mind if I repeat it. In any case, we have the whole day to rest and chat.

'The night was very still, and we were walking quickly, so we were rather conspicuous. Suddenly two tough village lads jumped out from behind a tree by the path.

' "Halt!" they ordered.

'We had to stop, as they were blocking our way. One was holding a chopper, while the other frisked us from top to bottom. We had no weapons.

' "Who sent you to spy?" they asked. "Tell the truth, otherwise we'll use this chopper!"

' "We're shop-assistants," I replied.

' "Nonsense, the shops closed long ago. What are you doing running around at night-time? Come with us! Not another word from you. We've warned you, this chopper's not for decoration!"

'What else could we say? All we could do was follow them. On the way we came to a hollow with some peasant huts. They locked me up there and asked me to confess. It was no use concealing the truth now. These two peasants hadn't harmed us, and I guessed they must be revolutionaries. In the afternoon of the following day three men came to see us. Two looked educated and the third was an old peasant. The two educated ones interrogated us, but very politely, with no rough talk. I'm an upright, educated person, who doesn't collect taxes or owe debts. Nor am I an official, so why should I be afraid? So I told them the truth about why I was going back to the village, what

I was interested in, my family's situation, the people I knew – including you and your father. Strangely, these two were polite to us, and the peasant spoke affectionately.

' "In that case," he said, "we're old acquaintances! What a coincidence! Then we don't have to be so formal. It's very poor here, so I must apologize for the poor reception!"

'Actually this old peasant was your Uncle Pan. After he had explained how he was connected with you, I was no longer anxious. As for the two educated gentlemen, one was called Pan Xudong and the other Wang Jiansheng. Although they were dressed like country bumpkins, they were well read. I found out that Pan Xudong was especially learned and broad-minded and was much more knowledgeable than me. I thought his family must be wealthy, otherwise he couldn't have studied so much – afterwards I heard that he'd graduated from university. I couldn't compare with him. He and Wang Jiansheng urged me to stay and see how things were here. They sent back the man who had accompanied me from home and asked him to tell my parents that I was quite all right. I would be staying on a few days in our country home for a change of air.

'As they were staying in the countryside to help the villagers, I thought why don't I do the same, at least for a while, to see how things are going there? So I stayed on, and then Lao Liu arrived. He really has a rich imagination and is a very good writer, which he can use well in his propaganda work – no mean accomplishment! I've also read some books and I know something about philosophy, but it's all abstract and idle theorizing. To tell you the truth, I feel quite inadequate in his presence. He said it's not so difficult to make use of theoretical knowledge and he would help me – we could learn together.

'I agreed with Lao Liu and we studied together. After a while I felt I couldn't go on living in a country retreat having leisurely talks, but should do something practical with him. So they invited me to Tanjiahe, and I stayed in the "sitting room" behind your Uncle Zizhong's pharmacy for a few days. Zizhong is a very practical man and he also talked to me about many things, including what work I could do. He really taught me a lot! Then you brought me here. Now I'm getting special treatment, so I'd really be embarrassed if I didn't do some work!'

I wanted to laugh again. The young master I used to serve had really changed. Of course, even though he was from a rich family, he had always been amiable with me. Now, however, he was treating me like a friend on equal terms, talking to me openly about himself. I discovered that I had changed too. I did not consider him my 'master' as in the past, but rather as a friend and equal. I respected him as a guest and wished to look after him – but I felt that 'looking after' him was not a duty. As he had finished talking about how he came here, I asked him casually, 'What about the two hundred silver dollars you brought with you? Do you still plan to have the graves repaired?'

'I've donated it,' he said, laughing. 'After I became your captive here, how could I repair the tomb, burn incense and paper money or bow to my ancestors? Even if you agreed to let me do this, wouldn't it be ridiculous! Since you need money here, wasn't it better to donate it to you? Also, Uncle Pan told me about the situation in the south of the county. If I hadn't been captured by you and had been discovered by Chumin's men instead, I could have been detained by them. That would have been tricky. Chumin could get my father into his web. Very dangerous!'

'It's also dangerous for you here – at least, your father might think so. So in the end you couldn't go back.'

'Didn't our rickshaw-puller go back?' he retorted. 'He could see for himself that I was in no danger here; I just couldn't go back for a while. Finally I wrote a letter to my father, telling him that I was quite safe here and urging him to do something useful – what was the point of hoarding his stinking money?'

'How could you send the letter?' I asked. 'There's no postal service to places outside here.'

'Don't you know? Well, perhaps you don't. Your Uncle Zizhong and Lao Liu arranged it. They told me that my letter reached home, and I got a letter back. My parents obviously miss me, but they want me to be safe and well. Anyway, they just have to accept this situation. Oh yes, I must write to them today; I must write a long letter straight away! I'll tell them that I've settled down here together with old friends. Life is funny! Ha! ha!'

Shuoru seemed to be really happy, judging by the way he

laughed. So I left him to write his letter. Sister Apricot had told me to go into town to do some shopping, so that she could cook some tasty dishes for him and make him feel at ease and comfortable here.

On the third evening after our reunion Uncle Zizhong unexpectedly came home from town. As he was always busy, it was not easy for him to come home for the night, even though it was not so far. I thought he must have something else to do, and I was right. After having a bowl of tea, he asked me how Shuoru was getting on. I told him that he was in good spirits and that he had written a long letter to his parents, telling them that he was safe and well.

'Very good!' said Zizhong. 'Tomorrow you can deliver the letter for him.'

'Me?' I exclaimed. 'You want me to deliver the letter?'

'Yes, tomorrow! Your present task is to attend to him, which naturally includes delivering his letters. Don't worry – you don't have to deliver it to his home in "The Big City". All right, that's all for today. You'll find out more tomorrow. I still have to see Ho Shuoru.'

Aunt Sunflower served him a bowl of boiled noodles, which he ate hurriedly before going to see Shuoru.

Uncle Zizhong and Ho Shuoru talked until very late that night, but Zizhong still got up early the next morning. After having some porridge, he took me into town. Shuoru had given him the letter. He said he had told Shuoru that I was delivering the letter for him, and he had asked Shuoru to excuse my absence.

When we got into town and arrived at Zizhong's pharmacy, I was surprised to see our long-lost messenger, Sweet Potato, waiting for me. In fact, we were both responsible for delivering this letter. I never thought that he would be working with us. He didn't look surprised to see me, perhaps because Uncle Zizhong had already told him that I was coming. He had come to town the evening before and had stayed there overnight, looking after the shop. He gave me an understanding smile, indicating that he knew that I was going with him to take the letter.

'This time I have to put you in a difficult position,' he said, laughing. 'You'll have to be my apprentice, pretending to deliver messages with me.'

'I can pretend anything, if it's necessary.'

Thereupon he pointed to two empty baskets on the floor, saying 'Right, carry this. We must hurry. I've brought a lot of pancakes – they're in the baskets. So don't worry, you won't starve.'

We set off, me carrying two empty baskets balanced on a shoulder-pole. He followed me along the path, this time empty-handed as the master, through the mountains until we came to a river bank, from where a straight road led all the way down-stream to 'The Big City'. Now that we were on this road, nobody would suspect that we had come from the north of the county.

'You're a messenger, familiar to everyone around here,' I said. 'Now I'm your apprentice, taking letters and sample goods to some merchants. But we're not going to "The Big City", are we?'

'Are you pretending to be stupid?' asked Sweet Potato. 'Didn't Uncle Zizhong tell you where we were going?'

'He only told me to deliver a letter. I don't understand why it needs two people to deliver it or why I have to carry baskets.'

'Well, let me explain,' he said, laughing a little. 'You're my apprentice, so you have to obey me today. You don't need to know everything beforehand, because the situation can always change at any time. Now I can tell you that we are going to Zhongguanyi, where there's a small tea house called White Cloud Pavilion by a bridge. That's where we're heading, and it's half-way to "The Big City". We have to pick up some things there, which is why we've brought these two baskets.'

'What things?'

'I'll only know when somebody comes from "The Big City" to give them to us. We've arranged to meet there.'

'Who could bring us things from "The Big City"?'

Sweet Potato was silent for a while before turning to me with a smile.

'Don't worry about it for the moment,' he said. 'It's no use telling you now; you'll understand when the time comes.'

I could not help smiling too as I spoke.

'I never thought you were so secretive and strict. When did

you become so cautious? I thought you were still running errands for merchants to earn your living.'

'Yes, that's right, I do earn a living by running errands, as I've been doing for many years now. People used to consider me a stooge of the landlords, rich men and shop-owners. But they didn't know that our family has had no land for three generations. My grandfather was a sedan-chair bearer, my father a porter and I did better as a courier. This way I felt free, although I couldn't buy any property or find a wife. I'm still a bachelor living alone in a thatched hut! This "stooge" was unfortunate. When the peasant unions were being formed, they really took me for a "stooge" and wanted to struggle against me! Luckily, Wang Jiansheng heard about this and explained to them that we were all the same – we all did tough work, either as rich landlords' tenant-farmers or as messengers for shop-keepers and merchants. I also took messages for the exploited shop assistants and their families, so I was doing something useful. After hearing Wang Jiansheng, they all began to consider me on their side, so I started working for the poor under his direction. Still, I can't do anything else but carry messages, as I don't have much ability. But now it's for another purpose and the messages are completely different too . . .'

'For example?' I asked.

'For example, I went to "The Big City" to take the first letter which Ho Shuoru wrote to his family, as I told you. What I didn't say was that I also brought them a letter from Zizhong.'

'Does Uncle Zizhong know Ho Ludong too?' I asked.

'No, he doesn't. He wrote the letter in the name of the Revolutionary Party. He told Ho Ludong that his son was in the hands of the Revolutionary Party, but that he shouldn't worry about his safety. They were looking after him very well. He asked Ho Ludong to help by making a donation, and if things went well he would definitely be reimbursed in future, with the additional interest . . .'

'What kind of donation?' I interrupted him again.

'That's a secret which I can't divulge at present,' replied Sweet Potato, laughing again. 'You'll know very soon and you'll see it with your own eyes. Just be patient.'

'You're really brave!' I expressed my amazement. 'What if the letter was discovered by the secret agents in the street? Everything would be finished, including your own life.'

Sweet Potato laughed again.

'That's the advantage of being a "stooge". How could a messenger of the landlords, rich merchants and shop-keepers possibly be carrying a letter like that? Of course, I had to hide it very carefully.'

'But wouldn't Ho Ludong be frightened when he received a letter like that? How could he dare to see you again? He might have reported you and had you arrested!'

'Just like that?' asked Sweet Potato. 'However threatening he seems, he would have to think about it calmly and coolly. His son is in our hands. If I'm arrested, Ho Ludong may be arrested too, on the grounds that he's connected with "bandits". So the thuggish agents would have another excuse to come and extort money from him again and they might ruin his family. He has to keep quiet, for both his sake and ours. Also, I was doing him a favour: I brought him a letter from his son.'

'What did the letter say?' I asked. 'Do you know?'

'Of course I know,' replied Sweet Potato, quite self-assured. 'How could I dare deliver the letter if I didn't know the contents? If it insulted us or betrayed me . . . but Ho Shuoru doesn't seem to be that sort of person; he's very clever. His letter was very simple, only three sentences: "Dear Parents, I'm living very comfortably now, just like at home. Please don't worry. Best wishes! Shuoru."

'I gave these two letters to Ho Ludong personally, but I didn't tell him one thing: where Shuoru was staying. I said I didn't know anything about the affairs of the Revolutionary Party. My job is running errands. I work for whoever pays me or employs me. I'm willing to do anything, as long as I get paid. I'm without a family, running errands for a living. I go wherever there is work for me, including the area controlled by the Revolutionary Party or Chumin's territory.'

Sweet Potato laughed again.

'So you did very well last time.'

'I guess so,' he said. 'I went all by myself. Of course, you couldn't go, and it wasn't necessary. He knows that I have to be flexible to earn a living, because as a businessman he has to do the same. He gave me five silver coins for my service and then asked me to take two letters back: one for our organization and the other for Shuoru. This time we're bringing back more of their correspondence. We'll see the result tomorrow – we'll still have to travel half a day tomorrow before we reach Zhongguanyi.' Then he exclaimed, 'Oh dear, we got carried away talking and time has slipped by. It'll soon be dark.'

I looked up and saw that the sun was already in the west. Then I suddenly felt hungry. We sat down in the porch of a temple to the God of the Earth and ate two big pancakes before going on our way. Now we hurried on, our heads down and without speaking.

At nightfall we came to a small roadside inn. The owners were an old couple with whom Sweet Potato was very familiar. He went over to the stove himself to make a pot of tea and fry the pancakes which we had brought with us. When we had finished eating, we just went to sleep, fully clothed, on the straw spread on the floor. We slept right through until dawn, as we were so exhausted from walking the whole day. When we got up, the sun was already out.

After having a bite to eat, we hurried on our way. We reached Zhongguanyi at noon and headed for White Cloud Pavilion tea house above the bridge. As there was a sedan chair at the doorway, we guessed there must be somebody important inside having tea. When we entered we looked round and saw a familiar-looking man, dressed rather neatly, sitting at a corner table. He was Ho Ludong's steward, Han Yongsheng. There were three others drinking tea with him: Ho Ludong's two sedan-chair bearers and his private rickshaw-puller. Han Yongsheng recognized us immediately. He got up, gestured to us and quickly walked out, and we followed him to the sedan chair.

'Have you been hired to fetch things from here?' asked Han Yongsheng quietly.

'That's right,' replied Sweet Potato. 'Can't you see our two baskets and my new apprentice?'

Looking at me again, Han Yongsheng asked me in astonishment, 'What! You're doing this kind of work now?'

'There's no other way,' I replied. 'I have to earn a living.'

'He's very good at this work,' put in Sweet Potato. 'He can

walk fast and he can remember the way, so I've taken him to work with me.'

Han Yongsheng glanced at me again, but said nothing more.

'Right!' He turned to Sweet Potato, lifting the curtain of the sedan chair, and said, 'Quickly, put these in your baskets!'

Then old Fu, Ho Ludong's personal rickshaw-puller, also came out of the tea house, obviously aware of what we were doing. The four of us rapidly transferred the load from the sedan chair into our two baskets. We covered the baskets with some old clothes, as if we had just taken them off because we had sweated on the way. After this, we rested to recover our breath, and Han Yongsheng asked Sweet Potato, 'Didn't the letter which Master Ho Ludong asked you to take back state clearly: the goods will be exchanged for his son? Where is he then? We can't go back with the sedan chair empty!'

Sweet Potato bowed and smiled respectfully, saying, 'I'm afraid you have to go back with an empty sedan chair again. The young master could not come back this time. He's just got used to living in that place and he's interested in the people there, so he wants to stay for a while – of course, this is what I've heard. I haven't seen him myself.' Then he turned to me and said, feigning ignorance, 'What would you say? You should know much more than I.'

'Yes!' said Han Yongsheng, facing me again. 'How did you think of doing this work? Does your mother agree? Just now I forgot to ask you.'

'What can Mother do about it? We have to earn a living. We have no land and nobody wants to hire me as a farm-hand, so all I can do is help Sweet Potato deliver messages and carry things.'

'Can't you read a little?' asked Han Yongsheng. 'That means you're educated. Why do you need to be a porter?'

'A messenger also needs to know how to read a little. Otherwise Sweet Potato wouldn't have taken me. If you carry letters and other things, you have to carry a basket to put them in. Now, getting back to your question, I did once meet Shuoru on the way and we exchanged a few words. He told me he was living very comfortably, sometimes going for walks in the countryside, sometimes going into town to sit in the tea houses or listen to story-tellers. I heard that he's made friends with a story-teller. They really get on well and sometimes both of them make up stories together! He says this is much more interesting than reading old books in his study at home. Maybe that's why he wants to stay there for some time!'

'With all this talking, you still haven't told me where he's staying. Can I go and see him?'

I shrugged my shoulders, looking helpless.

'I don't know. He was shut up in his study for too long. Now that he's free, he's interested in everything around. He goes everywhere, one day here, the next day there, so it's difficult to keep track of him. It's really too far to go there. It took us one and a half days to get here!'

Han Yongsheng sighed and turned to Sweet Potato, hoping to get some concrete news about Ho Shuoru. Realizing this, Sweet Potato quickly took out Shuoru's letter to his father and handed it to Han Yongsheng, saying, 'Please take this letter from Shuoru back to his father. He describes his situation clearly in the letter. He misses his parents and looks forward to getting a letter back from them. The gentleman who gave this letter to us – perhaps it was the story-teller – told us that we have to come back and fetch his parents' letter on the thirteenth of next month. Please give this one to Ho Ludong, and we'll come back to this place to fetch their letter then. See you next time!'

'So this time we can't take the young master back with us?' old Fu asked. 'What should we say when we get back?'

Han Yongsheng raised his hands in despair.

This was the moment to pick up our baskets and depart. They were really full and heavy, but we had to get away quickly from Ho Ludong's old steward. We covered about two miles in the first half-hour, so I was sweating all over.

The way back to Tanjiahe was uneventful. We carried the two baskets balanced on a shoulder-pole in turn and went straight to find Uncle Zizhong. He was not in his pharmacy but had left a message that we should carry our load straight to Yuewang Temple at the eastern end of the town. There used to be a monk looking after this temple, but when the peasant union encouraged the peasants to get rid of superstitions, he had fled to another place with the temple valuables. Then the temple became the headquarters of the local peasant union. When this was disbanded, the owner of the dough-stick shop in town, Pockmarks the Sixth, took it over. He paid a monthly rent of two silver dollars to the town's commercial association. Inside they arranged several tables and set up a big stove for boiling water and frying dough-sticks. He employed a lad to do this, setting up a tea house in the front porch of the temple, where peasants going to market would come for a cup of tea, a dough-stick and a chat with fellow farmers. He himself also took this opportunity to collect information about the situation in the countryside. The back part of the temple was separated by a partition, and entry was strictly forbidden – actually it was used as the meeting place for the underground Revolutionary Party. As Uncle Zizhong asked us to carry the load to the temple, we knew immediately that he must be having a meeting there.

I had often come here when I was doing liaison work, so I knew that the meeting would be in the former monk's big room in the courtyard behind the temple. We went straight to this place, where they were indeed having a secret meeting. We recognized Pan Xudong, Wang Jiansheng, Pan Zaixing, Liu Dawang, Zizhong, Uncle Pan and Lao Liu. There were also some peasant representatives from the villages in the two nearby districts, including Feng Xinshun and Huang Yongfa. I was interested to see Pockmarks the Sixth and the blacksmith, Ren Daqiu, there. As I approached, Jiqing and Pan Mingxun suddenly blocked my way. I knew that they were standing guard here. I might have been doing this job if I had not been 'serving apprenticeship' with Sweet Potato. As soon as they recognized us, they relaxed, of course. When we swaggered into the meeting room with our two baskets, they immediately stopped the meeting and gathered round us. Lao Liu uncovered my baskets: in one there was a new-type radio transmitter, in the other a hand-operated generator.

'Excellent!' exclaimed Pan Xudong. 'With these we can have contact with the headquarters and the provincial committee!'

'Wonderful!' the others cheered. 'We won't be isolated any longer!'

Only Lao Liu stood silently, pouting his lips. Probably

guessing what was bothering him, Uncle Zizhong gently uncovered the other basket. Lao Liu's face suddenly brightened. His eyes were agape as he looked at the things in the basket containing a big, brand-new mimeograph machine, ink, paper and other stationery.

'Fine! Fine!' he exclaimed joyfully, just as if he had reached the climax of a story he was telling. 'Now the hero can display all his talents! Wonderful!'

The assembled crowd were stunned by his sudden outburst and watched his excited expression in silence. Finally, Pan Xudong spoke out, warning everyone, 'Now that we have at last got these two things which we have been wanting so urgently, we have to use them properly without delay.' Turning to Zizhong, he said, 'You take this radio transmitter and the accessories. Please organize a group to establish contact with headquarters.' Then he turned to Lao Liu again, continuing: 'You know how to use this mimeograph machine. You must make full use of it, it'll help to continue mobilizing the local people . . .'

'Not help,' Lao Liu cut in, 'it'll arouse them and scare the pants off the landlords, county officials and troops stationed there!'

'I hope this machine will prove as effective as that,' said Pan Xudong again, 'but it's not the same as telling stories. You can't just rely on the gift of the gab, you have to be gifted in writing. What we need is someone who can write. Can you get a writing group together?'

'Sure!' replied Lao Liu excitedly. 'Ho Shuoru is good at writing.'

'Are you sure he'll agree?' Wang Jiansheng and Uncle Pan asked in unison.

'Give him to me!' Lao Liu responded confidently. 'Having the gift of the gab is still useful in this work! With the two of us working together, this beloved mimeograph machine can come to life and play a vital role. Chunsheng should help with this – he has some literary ability too.'

Smiling, Pan Xudong added, 'He's also a good guide. He always remembers the way, even where he's gone at night. We should also make full use of this special gift. Do you agree that he can be transferred to this work whenever necessary?'

'I agree!' said Lao Liu, looking up at Pan Xudong, 'but may I ask to be excused from the meeting now? I should take the machine to Red Hill Village with Chunsheng. We have to set it up and start work this evening.'

'Agreed!' said Pan Xudong, who had been chairing this meeting. 'We cannot have all our activities here. As we planned originally, we'll do the mimeographing in Red Hill Village and operate the radio transmitter in town. But we must be vigilant. You two go first. It's getting dark, so it's just the right time to be on your way.'

I shouldered Sweet Potato's baskets, still covered with some old clothes, and we headed back to Red Hill Village. When we got there it was already dark, so nobody noticed us. We went straight to Grandpa Whiskers's place. When he saw this mimeograph machine and the accessories, he laughed excitedly. Shuoru also perked up immediately and he even seemed proud to be able to make a contribution to our work. He was especially pleased that his father could buy such a useful machine with his 'filthy money' and that it could be delivered here. Grandpa Whiskers had already cleared out the firewood shed next to his house to use as a printing workshop, which I would look after for the time being. Shuoru's room was going to be used also as graphic design room, and so they had put in an extra little desk for Lao Liu to use.

We were so excited by this new development that we did not feel at all tired. When night came and everyone was asleep in the village, we went to the hill at the back with hoes and spades. There we dug a big pit in a hidden place, which Grandpa Whiskers had chosen. Shuoru excitedly and enthusiastically joined us in this work. Afterwards we covered the pit with a big stone slab, on top of which we spread some earth and turf to conceal it. If anything happened, we could quickly hide the machine and accessories in the pit.

When we had finished and checked it carefully, we felt quite satisfied. We stood there silently admiring our cover-up job. Jokingly, I teased Shuoru to make him respond.

'No comment, Master Shuoru?'

'Master again!' He suddenly seemed angry. 'I'm one of you now, and you still call me "Master". In future, call me "Comrade" if you think I qualify as such.'

We all burst out laughing. We were so excited that we decided to try out the mimeograph machine that very night. Lao Liu had aleady designed many posters, slogans and leaflets calling on the people to resist the troops stationed in the county, the Order Preservation Corps and the Red Spear Society. Shuoru volunteered to write the stencils, Lao Liu mixed the ink and I operated the machine. We went on working until the cock crowed twice, and the machine proved its worth.

Our leaflets and posters really spread like wild-fire. After a few nights' effort they were scattered throughout our county and right to the furthest border of the neighbouring county. There were leaflets printed on red and green paper stuck on all the gates of the county town wall, on the wall around Chumin's house in Chu Family Village, in the places where his Red Spear Society assembled and on the door of the temple in Maozhaowu. The villagers all over the county and the county head, Yao Dean, the commander of the troops stationed in the county town and leading local figures like Chumin and Wang the Lion all woke up to find a different world when they emerged from their houses. The red and green posters and leaflets had already started a spontaneous movement. People had started to talk in small groups at the end of the village or in the fields – to discuss the contents of these posters, leaflets and printed bulletins about the Chinese and world revolutionary movements. This unprecedented movement threw the whole county, both north and south, into complete turmoil.

The county officials and heads of the Order Preservation Corps in the county town posted two sentries at each of the gates and they started to search the country folk coming into the town. The corps were doing more training and Chumin personally took charge of reorganizing the Red Spear Society. This was just a storm in a teacup, but it stimulated us into action.

# CHAPTER 11

When one is busy, it is easy to forget about one's environment. Although my original responsibility was to attend to Ho Shuoru, he was so busy with his work that he could not enjoy a quiet life in this idyllic village of Red Hill. The work of writing and printing posters, leaflets, notices, declarations and announcements increased by the day. I had neither the time nor the inclination to be his attendant. Another factor was that Lao Liu was also too busy to come to work with us every day. He had to attend many meetings and organize propaganda work. Moreover, his proposals to expand propaganda and get a mimeograph machine were already bearing fruit, so his duties had changed and he now had even more responsibilities. Who would have imagined that the situation in this mountain district would develop so quickly? With the radio transmitter we could have direct contact with the provincial leadership, so that now the leaders could keep up with this development. As a result, the provincial committee decided to strengthen the leadership of this area by setting up a special committee, with Pan Xudong as secretary and Wang Jiansheng, Lao Liu and others as committee members. The area controlled by the 'special committee' did not only comprise the county, but also two or three surrounding counties in order to facilitate co-ordination and combined operations. As Lao Liu was busier than ever, all the printing work was left to Shuoru and myself.

One night at about five o'clock, when I was half-asleep, I heard three taps on the door. That was the signal which Lao Liu had arranged with us. It could save us a lot of trouble. He often had to come, as the propaganda work was done here, but he usually came after midnight to avoid people seeing him. First he came to Aunt Sunflower's and after having something to eat he would go to Shuoru. By this time Shuoru would have finished breakfast and would be getting ready for another day's work. I jumped out of bed and carefully opened the door. When Lao Liu came in, he saw that Aunt Sunflower and my mother were still in bed, so he gestured to me to be quiet so as not to disturb them. On tiptoes he led me to my room, where he asked me about Shuoru, as usual: was he satisfied with his life here, was he homesick, what did he think about his present work, and so on.

'He hasn't requested anything,' I replied. 'On the contrary, he apologizes for putting us to so much trouble and says that Sister Apricot gives him twice as much to eat as Grandpa Whiskers. Yesterday he asked me, "As a youngster, how can I eat better than an old man?" As for work, he's working on your draughts, getting more and more interested and energetic every day. Sometimes he expresses admiration for your work, saying it's very well worded. It's not only convincing, but it can move people and stir them to action.'

'So he's really putting all his energy into the work?' asked Lao Liu, with a little pride in his voice.

'I should say so. Sometimes he reads a moving sentence aloud with as much feeling as if he were reading a T'ang dynasty poem.'

'Good!' said Lao Liu, still sounding pleased with himself. 'Propaganda should be like that; it cannot be dull and dry, but full of feeling. Like when I used to tell stories – propaganda can only be of any use if it moves people, but . . .' Lao Liu seemed to feel that he had been carried away and should get back to the subject – 'but doesn't he feel bored? He spends the whole day doing propaganda work or printing it with you – I'm really sorry, I can't find the time to come and work with you now. I'm just too busy.'

'As far as I can see, he's not at all bored. Sometimes he's even extremely excited!'

'Excited about what?' asked Lao Liu. 'Isn't it monotonous? Cooped up in a little room, like me, he has no time to enjoy the scenery outside. Of course, it's best if he doesn't go outside and expose himself to danger in these circumstances. That's the main reason we've brought him to this small village. But what's there to be excited about?'

'He finds that he can make a contribution in this work. When those young lads come here keenly every evening to pick up the leaflets and posters to stick up all over the place, he feels very important. So many people see his handiwork, and they're encouraged – to use his own words, "influenced". That makes him happy, as he says himself. It's only a pity that he can't see the situation outside for himself. Of course, he hasn't said so directly, but I can tell that he feels it from the way he speaks.'

'So, does he complain?'

'Not exactly. Although he has produced the propaganda, he cannot see the effects or the response of the people. Even I feel frustrated at times.'

'You – you've also been "influenced" by him!'

'Don't you feel like that too, Lao Liu? When I just mentioned that Shuoru praised your scripts, didn't I detect some satisfaction in your voice? How is it that you can't understand how he feels?'

'I'm different from him; I'm a story-teller, or, you may say, an artiste,' he explained. 'I like to hear people's reactions – that comes from my profession. You, you and Ho Shuoru. . .'

'We also feel like artists. You forget, now that we're working with you, an artist yourself, we must have been "influenced" by you, a bit at least!'

It was already light by now, and in the sunlight streaming through the window I could see a smile of satisfaction playing on his lips.

'All right!' said Lao Liu, slapping his thigh. 'In that case I'll satisfy his wish. I'll take him to town to have a look right away! If he's really so enthusiastic about the work we're doing, everything will be all right. I've been worrying about this all the time.'

'Why have you been worrying?' I asked.

Lao Liu lowered his voice somewhat secretively, as if he were going to say something confidential.

'Zizhong asked me to tell you that there's some other work he wants you to do, and I have to leave for a while too. I'm just worrying about who'll do this printing with Shuoru if you leave.

Now you say he's not fussy about what he eats and he's completely involved in the work, so he won't want to give it up even if it's difficult. So he probably won't object, will he, if we ask Sister Apricot to help him with the printing? Then he can keep up with the daily work when you leave. Sister Apricot is very capable, so it'll probably only take her one or two hours to learn to help him mixing the ink and working the mimeograph machine. To tell you the truth, we had a little meeting yesterday to discuss your transfer. Wang Jiansheng suggested that Sister Apricot should replace you, as he needs you.'

'Why does he need me?' I asked.

'You'll know when the time comes. I can only tell you this much now,' he said. 'Right, now it's getting late. Let's go and see Shuoru to talk to him about this and see how he reacts.'

By this time Aunt Sunflower and my mother had got up and made breakfast in the kitchen. After Lao Liu and I had had two bowls of porridge each, we went off to see Shuoru.

When we reached Grandpa Whiskers's house and went to Shuoru's room at the back, my former young master had finished breakfast and was just bending over the table, working on some scripts which Lao Liu had given him last time. Lao Liu came straight to the point.

'I hear you'd like to go out and see what effect the material is having outside. If you'd like to, let's go now, as I have some time to spare this morning.'

Shuoru glanced at me and then at Lao Liu as if to see whether he was joking or serious – they were already familiar enough with one another to make frivolous remarks or jokes. But Lao Liu wore a serious expression this time.

'All right! Let's go now. Although I've got quite a lot of work to do just now, I really do want to have a look around. I'll finish this work tonight.'

'There's some more,' said Lao Liu, putting a handful of scripts which he had just drafted on the table. Now he continued in a lighter vein. 'I'm afraid you'll have to do a few night-shifts, as there's a lot of this material. I also spent two nights rushing to produce it. Chunsheng won't be able to help you printing either, as he has to leave here for a while.'

Shuoru gaped in astonishment.

'What! You want to wreck my work and send me packing?'

'Don't take it like that,' said Lao Liu, surprised. 'We're now working in full spate! How about asking Sister Apricot to take Chunsheng's place for a few days? She's very practical and will be able to do it as well as Chunsheng.'

'Will she agree?' Shuoru asked anxiously.

'With this important work, wouldn't anyone agree? To tell you the truth, we've already discussed this, and Grandpa Whiskers agrees too. Even he can help you, if you don't mind him being slow. If you need anyone else to help, you must say so. You're one of us now!'

Shuoru's face lit up.

'Will you really treat me as one of your comrades? I'm really glad to hear that. So let's go and have a look around. I'll come back in the evening and work through the night.'

We entered Tanjiahe through the eastern gate of the town, but outside there were crowds of people thronging in from the countryside. Some were carrying shoulder-poles, bringing their home-made products into town for sale; others were carrying empty baskets, planning to buy daily necessities. They were, however, distracted by the colourful leaflets and posters pasted above the gate and on the walls on either side. Shuoru was immediately excited to see this scene. Before seeing the light of day and being placed on public view for these people from all over the countryside, every single leaflet and poster had been produced by him. When he stood behind the crowds, Lao Liu and I, of course, had to stop too, even though we were in a hurry. I was impressed to see the amazed expression on Shuoru's face and could not help staring at him. Shuoru was not enthralled only by these posters on red, yellow and blue sheets, but also by the comments of the people discussing them. He might have been asking himself: Is this real? How could I, the young master of the old Qinfeng store have learned to communicate so well with these country folk? They were paying such attention to these posters, even though most of them must have been illiterate or semi-literate. Among them, though, there were some literate people, such as doctors, fortune-tellers and tutors. They may not have had the same reaction to this material,

211

as their lives and circumstances were different from those of the peasants. Still, they read it very carefully, some reading it aloud. They must have appreciated the literary style, which was Ho Shuoru's vital contribution. He watched the expressions of these rural 'intellectuals' as they read the leaflets. When they came to passages which they found meaningful, they could not help nodding in appreciation:

'. . . We working people create history; we are the masters of the world. If we unite, we can eliminate the corrupt officials, the local tyrants and evil gentry and their main agent Chiang Kai-shek and his foreign masters all of whom are oppressing us. However threatening and tyrannical they may be now, their days are numbered. Their present barbarism is their last act before the finale!

'The future belongs to the working people, but the bright future will not fall from heaven. It depends on whether we struggle, on whether we strive for it. Fellow countrymen, let's arm ourselves and join the struggle for a bright future!

'We will create a new world, which can only be created by us. In this new world we will never suffer from starvation and cold or be humiliated. Everyone will have work and all will be equal. Everyone will be literate and all will be educated. . .'

One of those reading or reciting these posters was a middle-aged man, looking like a village tutor. He was reading with great feeling and force, with a full voice, swaying his head as he read, as if reciting T'ang essays. Especially when he read the last part, 'We will never suffer from starvation. . .', his excited tone revealed passionate feelings. Perhaps he had been humiliated and despised as a tutor, his scholarship neglected and his learning unrecognized. His emotions seemed to strike a chord among some of the peasants around, even though they were different. Their children never had the opportunity to study. Only the children of the landlords and wealthy could study, thus creating the situation which Confucius described: 'Intellectuals rule and working people are ruled over.' Those who teach, however, like this tutor, are also oppressed by the landlords and wealthy, and some go hungry like the peasants. Shuoru now saw many peasants and artisans vowing on the spot to take up the fight against all these injustices. Their faces got redder and redder and their eyes were ablaze with anger. Some young peasants even raised clenched fists as if they wanted to smash this unjust society straight away.

Shuoru was moved by this scene, and Lao Liu was nodding to himself, gratified with the results of his own hard work. At the same time he was observing how the expression on his colleague Shuoru's face was changing: as if he were now enlightened by the script he had edited. So when we finally entered the town and sat facing Uncle Zizhong in Revival Pharmacy, he vividly described the scene at the east gate and finally expressed his renewed determination.

'I've just realized that the work I'm doing is extremely important and serious. I'll put all my efforts into it and do it for the people – without the people my work has no purpose!'

Zizhong smiled and patted him affectionately on the shoulder, saying, 'Now we can understand each other better. I've been trying to find an opportunity to come and have a long talk with you, but I've been so busy recently. Now you've come just at the right time.' Then, turning to me, he went on, 'So have you. They're having a little meeting in Dongyue Temple, and some of the matters involve you. Go there quickly!'

'Yes, I almost forgot,' said Lao Liu. 'One of the reasons I brought you into town was for this meeting.'

I rushed straight to Dongyue Temple. At the entrance there was a young lad apparently keeping watch. On approaching, I realized that it was Jiqing, and he nodded to let me in.

Everything seemed to have changed drastically inside. The Buddhas on the altar had been covered with some big rush mats. Two long tables were placed together in the middle at the far end of the hall, with many benches around them. It looked as if this big hall had become an office or meeting room. This was the first time the revolutionary forces had dared to set up an office in town – the first time since Chumin and his gang had thrown the villages into turmoil and Chiang Kai-shek's troops had been stationed in the county town, suppressing the villagers together. This showed that the revolutionary forces now had a relatively secure base among the people of this small and remote mountain region, and this small country town could become a revolutionary base. There were a dozen men seated

213

on the benches around the long tables. I recognized the special committee secretary, Pan Xudong, committee member Wang Jiansheng, security officer, Uncle Pan, and the heads of the sixth and seventh teams of the Peasant Self-defence Corps, Pan Zaixing and Liu Dawang. When I arrived it seemed that they had just about finished their discussion, and Pan Xudong was making some concluding remarks.

'Apparently the factional squabbling between Chiang Kai-shek and the Guangxi faction troops stationed in the provincial capital has ended. Now he can send his own troops to replace them, and he'll suppress people even more harshly. That's how our leaders have evaluated the recent situation, and the instructions which Comrade Zizhong heard on the radio receiver yesterday morning confirm this. We have to get prepared immediately, as our county may take the brunt of their attack. Also, our propaganda has succeeded in rousing the people. The troops in the county town, County Head Yao De-an and Chumin cannot resign themselves to being restricted in their actions. They must be preparing for new operations. Uncle Pan, watch their movements, and if you see any sign of action, report it immediately. Apart from this, today we'll be making contact with Huang Yongfa and Jin Bailong from the south. Someone has to go right away to find out about the situation there.'

At this point Uncle Pan glanced at me, and Wang Jiansheng said to him, 'We've already decided to send Chunsheng – he's here now.' Then he turned to me standing there at the side and said, 'Your task today is to go to Goat-horn Gully, where they'll be waiting for you. You must get there at noon, when everyone will be having lunch at home and there won't be anyone on the road. You know your way, so go there and come back quickly! I'll be waiting for you to report back here.'

It was now clear to me why Lao Liu had asked me to attend this meeting. Wang Jiansheng had explained my task clearly. Without asking any questions as usual, I set off immediately. I gestured to Uncle Pan that I would definitely get to Goat-horn Gully in time and would make every effort to get back before dark. He gave me an understanding smile, indicating that he trusted me.

Of course, this was not the first time that I had gone to Goat-horn Gully to meet Huang Yongfa and Jin Bailong. Since these two had returned to their villages, I had been there about once every five days. The duration of our encounters depended on what we had to discuss, but it was never more than half an hour. We had to avoid people noticing, as Chumin had inveigled quite a lot of layabouts into his Red Spear Society to be secret agents. The society had agents in almost every largish village, keeping an eye on the situation and reporting to Chumin. These agents were all pleasure-seeking idlers, whom the villagers naturally did not trust. When they got involved with the society, nobody told them the truth, so that the information they gave Chumin was either trivial or pure fabrication. They mostly reported only 'good news' and no 'trouble', and their 'good news' was sometimes so ridiculous that even Chumin could hardly believe it. What he had to believe was the continuous flood of posters and leaflets which had been appearing recently under his very nose. He believed the revolutionary forces in the north of the county were expanding – expanding into his own territory. He could no longer doubt it; he had to take measures immediately.

I took some small mountain paths to Goat-horn Gully, as this would shorten the distance and be safer. Even so, I did see some people – of course, I did not let them see me. I hid in the trees or bushes on the hillside as soon as I saw them, only proceeding after they disappeared. They were not carrying farm tools and always appeared in groups of three to five. From this I concluded that they had just come from training in some temple or shrine to the God of Earth under instruction from the sect chief, and they were just on their way home. It also showed that Chumin and Wang the Lion were quickly expanding their Red Spear Society forces and developing these collective 'training' sessions in preparation for some operation in the north. My speculations were proved correct when I met Huang Yongfa in Goat-horn Gully.

Goat-horn Gully was not far from our native village, just a mile away. This was where Huang Yongfa lived. A small stream flowed through the gully from the distant mountains, zigzagging into a mountain hollow here, forming a triangle. From here it flowed through a mountain gully below to converge with the big river by our village. People imaginatively called this triangle 'Goat-horn Gully'. There were no fields, so people did not often come here. The place where I was going to meet Huang Yongfa was at the tip of this triangle, where there was an old maple tree. When I got there, however, neither he nor Jin Bailong were there waiting for me. I looked up at the sky and the sun was indeed right above. How come they were not here on time? As I had hurried here and was thirsty, I used this moment to squat on the bank of the stream and drink some water. Then I sat down on a stone by the stream, just beside a thicket. There was not a soul around, probably because everybody was at home having lunch. It was absolutely quiet here, apart from the occasional magpie flying past. Their calls did not break the still-ness, but, on the contrary, made it seem more silent. I could not help remembering the childhood which I had spent in these peaceful surroundings. In those days, in the slack season when there was nothing to do in the afternoon, I used to come here with O Ran. Carrying two baskets, we came to the bank of the stream to pick wild vegetables and water chestnuts; when evening came we went with Uncle Pan to the village square to hear Lao Liu telling stories. Just as I was lost in my memories, I was startled by some light footsteps. I immediately became vigilant and looked all round. It was Huang Yongfa.

'What happened? You're late this time,' I said.

'Practising magic arts in the temple,' said Huang Yongfa. Spotting a stone next to me, he sat down there. 'These past few days Chumin has been pushing very hard, calling all the heads of the Red Spear Society in each village to meetings in his place. He's stepping up the training of the society. Zhu the Ninth in our village beats the gong to call everybody to assemble after breakfast and dinner every day. There we pray to the sect founders of the society, swallow magic charms and make pledges. Then the sect leaders test our strength to see if our muscles are as strong as iron, so that bullets cannot penetrate and knives cannot cut us. Even more of a nuisance. The day before yesterday Chumin appointed me vice-head of the village branch. I have to help Zhu the Ninth train our village lads to resist knives and bullets and become brave vanguard fighters. That's really driving me crazy.'

'How does Chumin trust you so much?' I asked, puzzled. 'You were a captive in the north!'

'But I escaped in the night. Doesn't that prove how loyal I am to the Red Spear Society?' replied Huang Yongfa, laughing. 'Of course he was worried and sent Zhu the Ninth to interrogate me several times. Zhu was afraid something might happen to me again and my wife, Pickle, would not forgive him, so he flattered me and vouched for my loyalty to Chumin. He also said that, with my wife and child in the village, I would be true to him. This finally set Chumin's mind at rest, and he sent me three silver dollars as a consolation for having been captured – quite amazing for a miser like him! As I was still loyal, Jin Bailong must be too. He also received three silver dollars. In Chumin's opinion, we must hate our captors and we'll fight even harder when we attack them again.'

This really was a new development. Huang Yongfa had become a leader of the Red Spear Society.

'That's good news. The county headquarters will surely be delighted to hear it – I'll report to them when I get back. As one of their leaders, you must know more about the movements of the Red Spear Society. What's the latest news? Before I came here, the county headquarters were holding an emergency meeting, and they're very anxious to find out about the latest situation here.'

'I'll tell you about it,' said Huang Yongfa. 'That's why I was a little late in getting here. Just now, when the Red Spear Society finished training, the sect instructor specially kept Zhu the Ninth and me behind to tell us to organize the village lads well. They must have the fighting spirit of army troops, so that they don't disintegrate in battle.'

'So they're going to set off for the north again?'

Huang Yongfa nodded.

'And it's getting critical,' he said. 'The Order Preservation Corps will form a rear-guard. According to the instructor, the best members of the Red Spear Society will be selected to make up a contingent which will directly attack Tanjiahe – Chumin clearly believes that this small county village is the base of the

217

revolutionary forces. Their influence has already spread to all the surrounding villages, so the troops stationed in the county town don't dare come out alone to deal with them. They only dare take action in collaboration with the Red Spear Society and Order Preservation Corps from the south.'

'Doesn't that mean a double-pronged attack?' I asked.

'I'm afraid their aim is not just to attack,' replied Huang Yongfa, staring vacantly as if contemplating. 'They probably won't just pass through places on their way. They will no doubt burn the villages and kill people in a campaign of terror to teach the villagers a lesson.'

'Do the Red Spear Society members want to do that? They're also villagers. Why should they hate the villagers in the north?'

Now Huang Yongfa looked at me clearly.

'That's just what Jin Bailong and I are concentrating on nowadays. We want them to understand this and we've convinced some villagers – of course, we do this secretly. We tell them that the enemies are not in the north, but close at hand. They are Chumin, Wang the Lion and the Order Preservation Corps under their command. When they've accepted this, they, in turn, influence other villagers. Most of the villagers here are now preoccupied with this problem, even if they don't talk about it in public. They keep their opinions from Chumin, because he's the main culprit.'

'So they won't all follow his instructions and join this campaign?' I asked.

'I can't say for sure. If they all feel like this, but don't dare to speak out, how will they act in practice? A lot of organizational work has to be done before ideas can be translated into action, like in the north. But we haven't got so much time or so many people who are capable of this work here. Jin Bailong and I are afraid that we'll have to go with all the others as soon as Zhu the Ninth beats his gong. If you just hesitate a little, you may be finished. The corps agents may just shoot you. If we don't get organized, we might end up like that – that's what Jin Bailong and I have realized recently. In any case, the good thing is that most of the people now know that Chumin is our enemy. What we two have been thinking about these days is how to turn this to our own advantage. When you get back, please tell

Pan Xudong to think about it. After the training session, Jin Bailong was held up by the instructor, so he couldn't come here, but he thinks just the same as me.'

'Can you be sure that the corps and Red Spear Society will come and cause havoc in the north in a few days?' I asked.

'Judging by their behaviour,' said Huang Yongfa, 'they won't be more than a couple of days. If the situation becomes critical, we won't meet here in five days as arranged. In that case, either Jin Bailong or myself will try to find a way to come and inform headquarters in time.'

We had, in fact, been talking for over half an hour. Huang Yongfa had to hurry back to the village in case Zhu the Ninth became suspicious. I also had to get back to Tanjiahe as soon as possible before it got dark, so I left Goat-horn Gully promptly. Once again I took the small mountain paths and did not meet a soul, apart from a few old men cutting firewood.

It was already dusk when I reached Tanjiahe, but the town gate which I wanted to enter was still open. I knew this must be because some big reconnaissance operation was going on in the countryside, as the gate was only kept open for those involved. This was quite different from the officials and troops stationed in the county town. They closed the gates firmly as soon as it got dark and took refuge within. Here in Tanjiahe, of course, there had to be guards on patrol at the town gates under such circumstances. By chance, Jiqing was on guard duty that evening. We just patted one another on the shoulder and parted, without a word. I went straight to Uncle Zizhong's pharmacy.

Zizhong had not gone to bed yet. As far as I could tell, he went to bed very late every night, and sometimes he did not go to bed at all. He was sitting in the small room in the courtyard behind the pharmacy. There were two familiar faces opposite him – Wang Jiansheng and Uncle Pan, all looking very tense and apparently not talking. It seemed that they had been waiting for me quietly. When they saw that I did not look at all tired – travelling was no problem for me – their worried expressions disappeared and their faces immediately brightened.

'You didn't have any trouble?' asked Uncle Zizhong.

I shook my head.

'Fine,' said Uncle Pan. 'You must be hungry.'

219

Thereupon he handed me a plate of pancakes, which had been placed on the table, and Wang Jiansheng gave me a big cup of tea. I was really hungry, so I grabbed a pancake, my favourite kind, and devoured it ravenously. At the same time I began to report what I had learned about Chumin's activities and what I had talked about with Huang Yongfa. They listened to me quietly.

When I had finished they remained silent for quite a long time. They were obviously pondering the situation. It was Uncle Zizhong who finally spoke.

'The situation over there has indeed developed unexpectedly fast, and they'll soon be moving again. The villagers have changed their attitude to Chumin, which, as Huang Yongfa said, should be a great advantage. The crucial problem is this. How can we deal with this double-pronged attack of Chumin's armed forces and the county troops? How can we tip the scales and defeat them? We have to take rapid measures to prepare for the attack.

'There are enemy forces on both sides and time is pressing, so we have to get fully mobilized straight away. Our forces are pressed between Chumin's armed forces and the troops stationed in the county. This may not be altogether a disadvantage. If they plan to attack us from both sides, we can also cut them off in the middle. Uncle Pan has thought it out very well and has taken the initiative to make all the necessary preparations within his field of authority.' Turning to Uncle Pan, he asked, 'Have all the men been deployed?'

'The gates are all open. If there's any sign of action, we'll be informed immediately.'

'It's not enough just to wait for news,' said Zizhong. 'We have to mobilize and organize our forces immediately to be prepared for action. We've still got time. Let's go to discuss it with Pan Xudong. He's just organizing the Peasant Self-defence Corps about three miles from here. Let's go now!'

Just before leaving, Uncle Pan touched my head affectionately, whispering 'You just stay here for the night and look after the pharmacy. There's no need for you to go back to Red Hill Village for a day or two. Just wait in town for your new assignment. Don't worry about Ho Shuoru. Uncle Zizhong and Wang Jiansheng have already explained the situation to him: Sister Apricot is taking your place for the moment, helping him with the printing.'

'Right, you just sleep on the bed where Ho Shuoru was sleeping,' Uncle Zizhong added. 'I'll probably be back before dawn to see to the shop.'

'There's something else I wanted to say,' I called after them frantically. 'If the situation becomes critical over there, Huang Yongfa won't wait for the usual meeting, but he'll come to report here immediately.'

'Fine!' said Zizhong. 'We need somebody here, so just stay where you are.'

They disappeared into the dark night.

In fact, we did not need to wait for Huang Yongfa to report on developments. Thanks to Uncle Pan's foresight and diligence, we had already heard about it here. He had specially instructed the scouts he sent out to speak to reliable people they met while carrying out their duties, including the members of the Peasant Self-defence Corps, informing them that if they came across any suspicious characters – meaning Chumin's spies – they should act immediately. The next day two members of the Self-defence Corps caught a spy while they were raking the soil in the fields. That night the spy was taken to Pockmarks the Sixth's dough-stick shop, which had been temporarily closed. There he was put in a storeroom in the back yard and blindfolded with a black cloth, so that he could not see anything. Uncle Zizhong and Uncle Pan came back after having consulted with Pan Xudong, and joined Jiqing and Pan Mingxun to interrogate the spy. The two young men spoke roughly, and when they threatened to torture him he finally took a note out of the lining of his jacket. On it were written two lines from Chumin to County Head Yao De-an, as follows:

His armed forces, the Red Spear Society and the Order Preservation Corps, would set off on such-and-such a day at dawn for a 'mopping-up' campaign in the north. The troops stationed in the county town must also set off on time, in order to join forces in Tanjiahe. After further interrogation, the spy also revealed that he had already been to the county town twice with specific plans and documents concerning their 'rendezvous'. This time he was just taking information about the date. Huang Yongfa's report came one day later than the spy's information, but it proved that the date written on the note was quite correct: Chumin's Red Spear Society and Order Preservation Corps were already getting prepared for their offensive and would be setting off soon.

The fact that this spy had slipped through the net twice showed that Uncle Pan's and Zizhong's security work had deficiencies. This also spurred us into immediate action. We sent the spy to the home of a member of the Peasant Self-defence Corps deep in the mountains. In this way he would be under strict supervision and cut off from the outside world. At the same time this would keep County Head Yao De-an and the county troop leaders waiting in vain for the specific date of the 'rendezvous' with Chumin's forces. Uncle Zizhong then gave me another mission: to go and tell Pan Xudong about the developments here and to pass on his proposal – that they should immediately hold an emergency mobilization meeting of the Self-defence Corps in Dongyue Temple.

I went and fetched Pan Xudong straight away, so the meeting took place that evening. As Jiqing, Pan Mingxun and I were familiar with the terrain and fast runners, I stood on guard at the entrance of the temple while the meeting was going on, Pan Mingxun patrolled the street and Jiqing kept watch at the east gate, which was the only one open during the night. The meeting went on until late at night.

On the evening before Chumin was going to set off in full force for the 'mopping-up' campaign in the north, Wang Jian-sheng and I had a good dinner in Uncle Zizhong's pharmacy. Afterwards we quietly slipped out of town through the east gate. I was accompanying him as his liaison man, hurrying to a place called Ox Head Mountain, not far from the border with the south. At the foot of the mountain there was a hamlet with only four households, one of which was Li Chengbao's, the leader of the ninth team of the Peasant Self-defence Corps. He had always been Chumin's tenant-farmer. Chumin's land was very scattered and he even had an estate in the north, but at present it was out of his control and he could not go there to collect taxes. As everyone knew, however, he was keeping records of the debts, so Li Chengbao was afraid that he would come to settle accounts some day. Li, though short in stature, was agile, brave and clever in leading his team. He kept a close watch on the border between north and south, thus preventing Chumin from operating here. Wang Jiansheng's purpose was to establish in Li's house a temporary command post for the front line of the resistance against Chumin's 'mopping-up' campaign. Wang Jiansheng was appointed commander of the resistance operation, because he was from the south. He had led the peasant union there, so he was familiar with the situation and still had considerable influence among the villagers there. I was accompanying him because I was also from the south and knew the terrain.

As we reached Ox Head Mountain, we heard a cock crow. Chengbao was waiting for us in the open doorway. Wang Jiansheng's first words were, 'How have you arranged things?'

'As soon as we got the message from headquarters yesterday afternoon, we had a meeting after dark. It was mainly with the members of the Self-defence Corps, but we also asked other tough peasants to attend. After the meeting I went with the corps members to Changlingang village to observe the terrain. We reckon that Chumin's forces must pass through there, planning to join forces with the county troops in Tanjiahe on the same day. Then they would be able to ravage numerous villages on the way, and it would be a real 'mopping-up' campaign. Unfortunately, we don't have enough rifles, and only a quarter of our men are armed. The others can only use their farm tools – mainly hoes and weeding tools, those kinds of things.'

After reflecting for a while, Wang Jiansheng said, 'That can't be helped. Where can we get so many rifles? The only ones we possess come from the Order Preservation Corps, which we attacked that night, and they have to be divided into three. Pan Xudong is personally leading three teams of the Self-defence Corps, whose task it is to intercept and attack the county troops. When they come out of the county town, two other teams will be patrolling Tanjiahe to be prepared for any contingency.' He reflected for a while again before looking up and asking, 'Who's the best shot in your team?'

'Wang Jingxian. He also farms Chumin's land, but by wintertime every year he's starving. Luckily, he can run fast and he has good eyesight. He knows a hunter who has agreed to take him up into the mountains to hunt wild animals, so he's learned to shoot well.'

'Has he been given a rifle?' asked Wang Jiansheng.

'That's no problem; he has a good one and three bullets more than everybody else.'

'Does he know Wang the Lion?'

'He's Chumin's tenant-farmer. Of course he knows Wang the Lion.'

'Fine!' Wang Jiansheng suddenly seemed excited and said in a serious tone, 'Put him in a strategic spot to look out for Wang the Lion – he's the "commander", so I'm sure he'll come.'

'I've already thought about that,' said Li Chengbao, laughing. 'Great minds think alike! I'll take you to see the terrain, but you must have something to eat first. I've prepared some dough-drop soup. Please wait a moment while I heat it up.'

Li Chengbao disappeared into the kitchen.

Wang Jiansheng took out of his belt the pistol which I had taken from one of Chumin's corps leaders that time in the temple. He could only practise with an empty pistol, never with real bullets, so as to save them. This time, though, he loaded it to try it out, but he did not pull the trigger, as he just wanted to practise the sequence again.

'I'm really sorry I still haven't got a gun for you,' he said to me. 'This time your task is to be a messenger. You have to follow me, but you can hide in a safe place and come out when I call you. Of course, you should have a pistol too, so that you can carry it on any mission. Jiqing and Pan Mingxun should also have some, but for that we'll have to see what luck we have this time.'

'When we were chatting, Ho Shuoru told me that he could ask his father to send us some new-type pistols,' I said. 'The headquarters could think of a way to make him supply them, just as he had to supply us with the mimeograph machine and the radio transmitter.'

'We've already thought about that,' responded Wang Jiansheng calmly. 'Ho Shuoru has already written to his father about it, and we added a letter. Sweet Potato delivered it, but that time we didn't send you too, as you had other duties. Whether he likes it or not, Ho Ludong must buy the pistols and send them to us. In future, he must be our supplier. Ho Shuoru has, of course, helped us greatly in this respect. He's changed a lot recently and become even friendlier towards us, don't you think?'

'Yes, he has. After Uncle Zizhong spoke to him some time ago, he told me that he now feels that life has some meaning and that he can use what he's studied. He really wants to do even more for us. I don't think he felt compelled to ask his father to send pistols. He said that his father's dirty money would only serve a purpose if it were spent on something worthy. What a pity if it were extorted by gangsters!'

'No, it isn't easy for his father to get pistols for us, much more difficult than the mimeograph machine or the radio transmitter.'

'That doesn't matter,' I said. 'I know that his brother-in-law, Chen Chuqing, is a member of the provincial government and knows some top officials and military leaders. As long as he's willing to pay for them, the pistols can be obtained. Pistols are easy to hide and transport – perhaps Sweet Potato has already brought them.'

Wang Jiansheng was so delighted that he could not help patting his pistol, which he had just cocked, and he almost touched the trigger.

At last Li Chengbao came out with two bowls of hot dough-drop soup, which his wife had prepared the evening before, and said, 'Two members of the Self-defence Corps of this village joined the corps members of other villages. Shortly after midnight they all hurried in advance to various spots in the area around Changlingang village. They found these places themselves without disturbing the old folk, women or children in the village, so that they could go on sleeping and get on with their normal work in the morning. These two also had something to eat here before they left. Do have these two bowls of soup and you'll get energy. Even tough-guys need food to sustain them.' Li Chengbao laughed.

As the area where he lived was very near Chumin's power base, he often had to deal with Chumin's men, sometimes openly and sometimes guardedly. He always had to tackle them skilfully, and so he was able to keep calm and composed about this 'mopping-up' campaign, however big it might be.

'Do you mean Pan Zaixing and Liu Dawang?' asked Wang Jiansheng while having the soup. 'It won't do to feed them like this – even if all four families in your hamlet offer hospitality, it's impossible. The number of men in these two teams is many times more than all those in your hamlet!'

'They came here at dawn and stayed for a while,' said Li Chengbao. 'They couldn't stay long, because they had to leave before daybreak for those areas, as instructed. The men they were leading went straight on without entering the hamlet. I just gave these two the coded messages. Of course I couldn't offer them anything to eat. Both of them took out a big pancake of their own. But you're a committee member, so I can't neglect you!'

Li Chengbao laughed again, this time even more heartily.

'We've enjoyed your hospitality – I've completely recovered now,' said Wang Jiansheng, putting down his bowl and chopsticks. 'We have to get going without delay. The cock is just about to crow for the third time!'

Li Chengbao took a three-foot-long blunderbuss from behind the ancestral tablet which stood on the altar. This he pushed into his belt, before ushering us out first; he followed, closing the door behind him. So we started our 'forced march' again, heading for Changlingang, four to five miles away. We took about an hour and a half to get there, and by that time it was already starting to get light.

Changlingang was not, as its name indicated, a long wooded mountain ridge. It was just a rather high knoll with many pines. One could see the open land all around from here, as it was relatively high. On the right-hand side, on a stretch of land below, there was a rather wide road, which led all the way from the south to the north. The three of us squatted in the pine wood on the knoll overlooking the open land. Li Chengbao commanded his ninth team from here, as they were hiding on a hill near by. As soon as his team started moving it would be the signal for the forces led by Pan Zaixing and Liu Dawang and the village lads working in the fields to start operations too.

By Wang Jiansheng's side, Li Chengbao could co-operate with him in carrying out the instructions of the headquarters.

It gradually began to get light in the east. The white sky soon became tinged with a layer of red. The birds in the woods on the hill began to sing, as if welcoming the rising sun. Indeed, the semi-circle of the sun was soon creeping out of this red glow above the distant mountain peaks. It grew gradually, first into a fiery-red ball, and then, rising imperceptibly, into a dazzling bright orb. Now it dispersed the veil of mist covering the flat fields. There were no crops but only rice stubble left over from the autumn harvest. Now was the time to remove the stubble while turning over the soil in preparation for manure. When the sun had climbed high into the sky, the labouring peasants appeared in dribs and drabs in these patchwork fields, with their farm tools on their shoulders. Scattered as irregularly as the fields themselves, they started working on the yellow soil, which was as ancient as the mountains beyond. From a distance the whole scene, with the peasants and the wooded mountains near by, presented a vast tableau.

Gazing at this broad landscape, I could not help asking myself why we had rushed here through the night so urgently, only to be squatting here in the pine wood. Had we got stuck here only to enjoy the peaceful scenery? Had we come here to settle in this insensate pine wood, to become part of nature? Seeing such energetic men as Wang Jiansheng and Li Chengbao squatting here quite still and hardly daring to breathe, I really felt like laughing. Before I could laugh, though, a roaring sound came from the distance. I shuddered for a moment, feeling that it was the end of the world. Strangely, though, we remained absolutely immobile, like a still-life. My eyes were more alert than ever, first staring ahead, then looking around the pine wood and next at Wang Jiansheng and Li Chengbao, trying to guess their intentions. I noticed that Wang Jiansheng had already taken out his pistol and Li Chengbao was holding his blunderbuss upright, with his finger on the trigger. Before the roaring sound in the distance a cloud of dust swirled up on the road through the fields. It was produced by a long line of peasants, advancing en masse like a snake. They were carrying all kinds of old weapons, such as big knives, spears, daggers and even fishing forks. So these were the forces attacking the north. Close behind them were soldiers with new-type rifles and grey uniforms. Li Chengbao and Wang Jiansheng glanced and nodded at one another, as if to confirm that the ones in front were Chumin's Red Spear Society, followed by the Order Preservation Corps. They would soon be passing the foot of Ox Head Mountain.

'Shall we give the signal to attack?' Li Chengbao whispered to Wang Jiansheng.

Wang Jiansheng shook his head slightly and moved forward a couple of steps to get closer to the edge of the little pine wood. He observed the movement of the two forces below through a gap in the pine trees. Li Chengbao and I moved up beside him. Then he whispered to Li Chengbao , with his eyes still fixed on the aggressors below, 'Is Wang the Lion with them?'

Li Chengbao was holding his blunderbuss, which he had already lifted up, with his right finger on the trigger. At the same time he was shielding his eyes with his left hand in order to make out the figures below in the dazzling sunlight. Suddenly he whispered to Wang Jiansheng, 'There he is. Look! That ruffian in the black shirt, leading the corps. Look, he's raising his pistol, about to fire into the air. He must be giving them orders and commanding these two forces.'

'Give the signal!' said Wang Jiansheng.

Li Chengbao's blunderbuss immediately boomed. This was promptly followed by the sound of another gun-shot, which was much fainter but loud enough for us to hear in this small pine wood. The effect of this shot was incredible. The pistol which Wang the Lion was brandishing fell to the ground and he collapsed. Probably realizing that they were being ambushed, the corps behind him immediately scattered in all directions, seeking cover. But it was already too late. The three teams of the Peasant Self-defence Corps, who had been hiding in ditches in the fields, at the foot of the hill, behind bushes and in dried-up ponds, appeared from every direction and surrounded them. The peasants in the fields now stopped working and came to reinforce the ambush with their farm tools as weapons. Even more farcical, the Red Spear Society forces who had already passed suddenly turned round, shouting battle cries, and joined the peasants surrounding the enemy. After closing in, a shattering cry burst out.

'Attack Chumin's old den! Capture the old fox alive!'

By this time we three had rushed down the hill, with Li Chengbao in the lead, brandishing his gun. Wang Jiansheng and I followed closely as he squeezed into the circle surrounding the enemy. Recognizing us, the Self-defence Corps immediately held their weapons high as a sign that victory was already theirs. When the enemy saw three lines tightly surrounding them and heard the battle cry of their 'allies', who had completely betrayed them, they were dumbfounded. Even the fingers holding their guns seemed to be frozen stiff. Li Chengbao, still holding his gun up to show that he was in command, shouted, 'Surrender your weapons or you'll be killed!'

Looking round at the members of the Self-defence Corps, Wang Jiansheng added, 'Take their guns and ammunition belts! Quick!'

That was just what the members of the Self-defence Corps had been dying to do. They acted even quicker than it had taken Wang Jiansheng to give the order. Those without rifles immediately armed themselves with the rifles they took from the enemy. Seeing this, the former members of the Red Spear Society again roared, 'Attack Chumin's den! Capture the old fox alive!'

This slogan was echoed in a roar by our forces. The members of the Red Spear Society who had joined us now responded with another slogan.

'Villagers are all on the same side! Chumin is our common enemy! Fellow countrymen, unite!'

With these calls, the villagers from both south and north forgot the antagonism and animosity between them. The Red Spear Society disintegrated on the spot, as they put down their weapons consisting of hoes and rakes, old spears and daggers. They started to chat with the villagers from the north about family and village life and about the close ties between them. Wang Jiansheng, Pan Zaixing, Liu Dawang and Li Chengbao were extremely busy, and I got involved too, having to pass on many messages and instructions between them and from them to the villagers. The most serious problem was the men whom we had taken prisoner. Apart from collecting all their guns and ammunition, we had to make a preliminary assessment of each of them. They were not definitely all real 'enemies'. Just when we were about to start this work, however, a gun-shot suddenly startled us all. All eyes turned to the man who had fired the shot. He was still holding the gun, but the bullet had already been fired. It was Wang Jingxian.

'Did you fire the shot?' Li Chengbao asked him.

'Yes,' Wang Jingxian replied.

'The enemies have already surrendered their arms. Why did you still have to shoot?'

'Because their leader was still alive,' said Wang Jingxian. 'My first bullet only hit his pistol and broke his right shoulder. He was trying to crawl away and escape, while we were preoccupied. I had to shoot him.'

We all looked in the direction in which his gun was pointing and saw a body lying by the road through the fields. Half his head had already been blown off, but from the rest of his body we could recognize that it was Wang the Lion.

'He couldn't have escaped,' said Li Chengbao. 'You wasted a precious bullet.'

There was some disapproval in Li Chengbao's voice. To smooth things over, Wang Jiansheng went up to Wang Jingxian and patted him affectionately on the shoulder. Then he said consolingly, 'You're a good shot. You played a crucial role, but there's some truth in what Li Chengbao says – bullets are as precious as our lives!'

At this moment an unexpected sound distracted us.

'Spare me! Please spare my life! I admit my crime!'

I was shocked. It was Zhu the Ninth from my old village. I did not know what to do, but Jin Bailong came running up and pulled him to his feet, saying, 'Spare what? Your life is in no danger. Get up!'

When Wang Jiansheng turned round and saw this spectacle, he laughed and said, 'We didn't intend to take your life. Of course, we'll spare you this time. But if you follow Chumin in future, we won't be so lenient!'

Then he turned to face the crowd, and shouted, 'Fellow countrymen, what do you think we should do next? Speak up. Now we've removed one source of our oppression, you can speak freely!'

'Attack Chumin's den; capture the fox alive!'

The members of the Red Spear Society had first shouted this slogan, but now the forces of both south and north joined in.

'Right!' Wang Jiansheng shouted even louder. 'We'll advance with this victory behind us! Fellow countrymen, use your own strength to capture your mortal enemy, Chumin!'

The counter-offensive of the Self-defence Corps was almost over. Pan Zaixing, Liu Dawang and Li Chengbao led their forces back to recuperate. Wang Jiansheng decided to continue leading the forces from the south to follow up their victory, as was previously arranged. Huang Yongfa and Jin Bailong naturally became front-line commanders of the new expedition because of their successful secret work among the members of the Red Spear Society. They had also earned considerable prestige during this period. Harnessing the basic antagonism of the rebels against Chumin, they led them back to 'capture that old fox alive'.

'Time is a decisive factor in winning victory. First we must proceed at top speed to prevent the news from spreading,' said Wang Jiansheng to Huang Yongfa and Jin Bailong. 'I guess Chumin still doesn't know that his two-pronged attack has completely failed. We have to rush to his place, while he is waiting for "news of victory" from Wang the Lion, and capture him alive in a flash!'

Huang Yongfa and Jin Bailong immediately prepared to carry out this instruction. First they announced that the dismantled Red Spear Society would join the Peasant Self-defence Corps. They confirmed that the former members of the Red Spear Society had been deceived by Chumin. The new leaders of the Self-defence Corps would be elected on the spot by a show of hands among the members of each section. The result was that almost all those elected were active opponents of Chumin, whom Huang Yongfa and Jin Bailong had secretly contacted and trained. Then the new Self-defence Corps sorted out all the former local heads of the Red Spear Society, including Zhu the Ninth, the leader of Huang Yongfa's and Jin Bailong's section. They were handed over to a group of men to be temporarily kept in custody, so that they would not leak out any information. The rest of the former Red Spear Society and the Order Preservation Corps, which now made up the new Self-defence Corps, advanced at top speed under Huang Yongfa's and Jin Bailong's command. We were heading for the old headquarters of the Order Preservation Corps in Chumin's family village, where he lived. As Wang Jiansheng was temporarily commander-in-chief, I remained his liaison officer and messenger, following the troops. Although we were in the rear, I could run to the front when necessary, as I was a fast runner. I could pass on his instructions or I could take back the information which the two section leaders, Huang Yongfa and Jin Bailong, gave me.

Even though we moved as fast as possible, we could not prevent the news from spreading. The country folk we passed on the way were all astonished that the Red Spear Society had been transformed so suddenly. When they heard that the aim of these troops who had changed sides was to smash Chumin's headquarters and capture him alive, some of them, including even women and children, spontaneously joined the forced march. They all wanted to see Chumin's empire collapse and him captured. Nobody could control the people's enthusiasm. Wang Jiansheng also changed his own attitude, now considering this development to be a movement to mobilize the people and promote the revolution – 'to build up our own spirits and break the enemy's authority,' he said.

When our forces had covered about six miles, the ones in front suddenly stopped, blocking the advance of those behind, so they all had to halt. I didn't know if this was caused by the villagers joining our ranks on the way, rapidly expanding our numbers with a snowball effect, or for some other reason.

'What's happening?' Wang Jiansheng asked himself. Then, turning to me, he said, 'Quickly, go to the front to find out and report back immediately!'

At the front there was a group of villagers blocking the way. I watched Huang Yongfa and Jin Bailong negotiating with them. I did not interrupt them, but just stood there listening.

'Wang Taihe encouraged us to expand our Red Spear Society this very morning,' said a tough young villager fiercely. He stood there blocking the way, with his arms outstretched, as if he wanted to challenge us. 'What do you say?'

'What do you say?' shouted a group of young lads standing on either side of him to back him up.

'When did Wang Taihe come back to the village?' asked Huang Yongfa.

'Yesterday, at dawn, he slipped back into the village,' said the tough-guy. 'Wang the Lion and some of the Order Preservation Corps brought him back. This time it was not the same as when he slipped out of the village – he came back proudly, flaunting his authority.'

'What authority?'

'Wang the Lion promoted him,' replied another tough-looking young lad. 'He and Wang the Lion stood together at the edge of the village like long-lost brothers, telling us to stand there in front of them and carefully listen to their instructions. They said that Chumin and Wang Taihe had revived their relations and were collaborating against a common enemy – the Revolutionary Party. We've heard that the two have a tacit agreement: Chumin has promised to get his burned-down house rebuilt, and he's promised to be responsible for expanding the forces of the Red Spear Society in all the villages in the vicinity. He himself will be the commander of the Red Spear Society in this area.'

'Is he still in the village?' asked Jin Bailong.

'Yes, but when we heard that Wang the Lion had been killed, we arrested him.'

'So what's the problem?' asked Huang Yongfa. 'You hate Chumin and his lot, so come with us to capture him. Don't let's waste time here quibbling over trifles.'

'Go with you?' shouted the tough-guy and the crowd of young lads around him. 'We've heard that Wang's son, Wang Jiansheng, is your commander now. Are you following him blindly to capture Chumin?'

Huang Yongfa and Jin Bailong were astonished, as were all those up front. They had obviously forgotten the close relationship between Wang Jiansheng and the wealthy landlord, Wang Taihe. Now I realized what was happening. I looked up and saw a familiar village a few hundred yards ahead. I had been there before when I went to fetch Wang Jiansheng's wife, Sister

Apricot. So these lads were from this village. Instead of waiting for instructions from Huang Yongfa and Jin Bailong, I just wanted to run back to the rear to tell Wang Jiansheng immediately. I thought this was my duty as a member of the revolutionary forces and as a reliable messenger. Just as I was about to turn round, though, I saw that Wang Jiansheng had come up to the front. He had squeezed into the crowd and was listening from there. I was shocked again.

As I stood there, dumbfounded, the crowd of young villagers blocking the way shouted out, apparently having lost their patience, 'What do you say?'

'Crush Wang Taihe!' shouted Wang Jiansheng suddenly, as if giving an order. He had already stepped out of the ranks and pulled his pistol out of his belt. He strode up to the strong lad who was in the front blocking our forces, handed him the pistol and said, 'Do it immediately. That's an order!'

The lad took the pistol, turned and sped back to the village. After nearly twenty minutes we heard two pistol-shots in succession, whereupon the villagers barring our way dispersed. They joined our ranks and marched ahead with all of us. When we passed the village where Wang Taihe lived, the tough young lad came running back. He handed the pistol back to Wang Jiansheng and joined our ranks too, as we headed for Chu Family Village.

That was the end of this incident, but it cost us precious time. It frustrated Wang Jiansheng's plan to 'move as quickly as possible to prevent the news from spreading'. When we reached Chu Family Village, we discovered that Chumin had gone, leaving an empty house and the headquarters of the Order Preservation Corps. Having got wind of our march, he had fled with some body-guards. The wrath of the villagers had reached bursting point, but all they could do was set fire to these two dens of vice.

# CHAPTER 12

'Go back to Tanjiahe as fast as you can. You've seen everything that happened here with your own eyes. Report it all to our headquarters in detail. There are so many things that I have to see to urgently, so I can't leave here for the time being. Then quickly bring back any new directives from the headquarters. I'll be waiting for you here.'

These were the instructions which Wang Jiansheng gave me the morning after Chumin's house had been destroyed. He was in the temple of Chumin's ancestors at the edge of Chu Family Village. This temple had been transformed overnight into our branch headquarters in the south of the county. The evening before, Wang Jiansheng had called a meeting here to discuss the next plan of action. It was attended by Huang Yongfa, Jin Bailong and anti-Chumin activists who had been secretly trained by them in all the branches of the Red Spear Society. As the meeting went on deep into the night, Wang Jiansheng had made sure that I went to bed first – because he planned to send me to report to Tanjiahe early the next morning.

As I left Chu Family Village, a gong sounded in the open space in front of the village to call the villagers to a meeting. On my way back to Tanjiahe I heard the sound of gongs clanging again in some villages around, no doubt also to call the villagers to a meeting. In fact, I had already seen a number of villagers coming out of scattered hamlets to gather in bigger villages. Unlike in the past, when they usually looked depressed, they now looked animated, as if they were going to participate in some exciting activity. I stopped a middle-aged villager who was passing, and asked him, 'Uncle, what's happening? Where are you off to, walking so fast?'

'I'm going to the joint meeting of villagers which Zhao Dagui has called.'

'Who's Zhao Dagui?'

'A young lad in the Red Spear Society. Nobody knew that he was in fact a secret member of the Revolutionary Party opposing Chumin. Now he has come into the open to take part in revolutionary activities with Wang Jiansheng.'

'Wang Jiansheng – do you know him?'

'No, I don't, nor does Zhao Dagui, but he's a man we villagers trust. He's so firm in opposing the wealthy landlords that he even ordered his own father, Wang Taihe, to be crushed! Now he's directing us to divide up Chumin's land, helping us to get organized and warning that old fox never to come back again to oppress us. We villagers are determined to follow him!'

When I heard this villager, I understood why Wang Jiansheng had said, 'I can't leave here now.' His main task at present was to consolidate this new base. As his messenger, I also felt that it was my duty to make sure that he could communicate rapidly with headquarters, so I hurried on my way, trying to get to Tanjiahe as quickly as possible.

I reached there at noon, going to the Revival Pharmacy to find Uncle Zizhong. I thought I could immediately make contact with the people at headquarters through him. It was just lunch-time, so the streets were empty and the market-goers had already left town for home. There was nobody in the pharmacy except an old door-keeper sitting on a bamboo chair at the entrance, watching the comings and goings.

'Where's Uncle Zizhong?' I asked him.

'He's just left for Dongyue Temple, as there's no business here at this time of the day. He'll be back in a short while. If you're thirsty, there's some tea on the table inside. Just help yourself!'

'I won't wait here, Uncle, I'll go back to the temple to find Uncle Zizhong and I'll probably come back with him soon.'

When I reached Dongyue Temple, Uncle Zizhong was indeed there. I was happy to find Pan Xudong, Uncle Pan and Lao Liu there too. If I reported to these people, the others involved would find out very soon, and I could complete my mission. Their faces were grave, as they were no doubt discussing

236

something very serious. As soon as they saw me, they stopped their discussion. They were anxious to hear the news I was bringing, so all eyes were on me. I concentrated very hard to report to them in detail what I had seen and heard myself, including the conversation with the villager on my way back to Tanjiahe.

When they heard my report, they did not react immediately, remaining inscrutably silent. Only Lao Liu could not keep quiet for long. He was not used to awkward silences and always kept talking, which he had got used to as a story-teller during all those years. He broke the silence, saying to me, 'Your account was very vivid, which shows you're observant and you've got a good memory. You're already a well-qualified messenger. In future, when we've got rid of these corrupt officials and rich landlords and the land is peaceful again, I think you can become a distinguished story-teller.'

'Lao Liu,' Zizhong reminded him, 'I want to use a phrase which you often liked to use as a story-teller: "Let's get back to the main theme!" In this rapidly developing situation, we should consider what propaganda work you can do next. I think the work Wang Jiansheng has done has been very successful.'

'He did personally order his father to be shot, though,' said Uncle Pan. 'I wonder what he felt like – after all, we all have human feelings.'

'If he hadn't done it, he wouldn't have been able to rouse the people – this action was necessary for the revolution,' said Pan Xudong, raising his voice. 'He was resolute, just as a revolutionary should be at the crucial moment. Right, the problem is the next step.' Then, he looked into the dark corner on his right and said, 'Old Sixth, go on with what you were saying!'

It was only then that I noticed the person sitting in the corner. Peering at him, I realized it was Pockmarks the Sixth, my employer at the dough-stick shop. After disappearing for so long, how had he suddenly turned up here at such a crucial moment? I stared at him in surprise. Seeing how puzzled I was, Lao Liu came up to me and whispered, 'He has hurried back from the county town. He arrived half an hour before you to report on the situation there. He was speaking when you came in. We were waiting for your news about the south. It seems that the situaton there is fine, which is a relief.'

'But, as far as I can see, the situation here is not so good.' Pockmarks the Sixth was continuing his report.

'As I told you, the troops stationed in the county town have been on the alert for the past few days. They've reinforced the guards on all four town gates, and the two battalion commanders have twice inspected the soldiers' weapons. Yesterday morning they also paraded on the drill-ground, as if they were going out on a raid. After going around to find out what was happening, I heard from their water-carrier, Yi Changjiang, that they're planning to join forces with Chumin's Order Preservation Corps and Red Spear Society in Tanjiahe. They've been waiting for a messenger from Chumin, informing them what time both sides should set off – '

'A messenger was sent, but the message never arrived,' Uncle Pan interrupted Pockmarks the Sixth. 'He was intercepted by us on the way. His information was very useful; without it the situation would not be as good as you just heard.'

'The troops suspect that,' said Pockmarks the Sixth. 'The two battalion commanders are also getting very impatient, afraid that something has gone wrong. Now they're preparing to send a battalion on their own to occupy Tanjiahe.'

'Have they fixed the date?' asked Pan Xudong.

Pockmarks the Sixth shook his head.

'I'm not sure yet. I heard that they're just sending an agent to make contact with Chumin.'

Uncle Zizhong glanced at Uncle Pan, who got the message and spoke out confidently.

'We've already deployed people for that. The agent they've sent most probably won't have any better luck than Chumin's agent.'

'But the county troops have other means of communicating with Chumin,' Pan Xudong warned us all. 'They have bigger transmitters and receivers than we do, with which they can contact their division headquarters in Mazhen county town. Chumin's headquarters are near Mazhen county town, and he often communicates with the troops stationed there. They work hand in glove. The division headquarters in Mazhen also keeps constant contact with their military headquarters in "The Big City", which keeps in touch directly with Chiang Kai-shek. They have an extensive and complicated network, so we must not lower our guard.'

'In any case, judging by the atmosphere in the county town,' said Pockmarks the Sixth, 'if the troops there are going to act, it'll be in one or two days.'

'Yes! We must be well prepared,' said Pan Xudong. 'First, we must make the Self-defence Corps effective in combat. Second, we must expand the peasants' volunteer forces; and third, we must arouse the people, in order to be able to cope with the impending crisis. Old Pockmarks, leave for the county town as soon as possible, so that you get there before dark. Try as hard as you can, through whatever channels, to find out about the latest situation and report back immediately.' Then he turned to speak to me. 'You must have some rest. Go back quickly to Zizhong's place and have a good meal.'

'Then how can I report back to Wang Jiansheng?'

'That's the third point I just mentioned,' replied Pan Xudong. 'Tell him to go all out and take the responsibility for his own operations. He must also co-ordinate his activities with those of Chang Je-an in Mazhen county, as they're now in a position to have direct contact. As for the situation in the county town, tell him what you've just heard. His work over there is extremely important and will demand all his energy. If we need to consult with him, we'll ask him to come here. But you'll have to bring news back and forth, at least once a day.'

'I want to say a word,' added Uncle Pan. 'When you come next time, don't come here. Go to Red Hill Village and see Grandpa Whiskers, who will be able to tell you where we are. It doesn't matter if you can't find us, as we can communicate through him. Do you agree, Comrade Xudong?'

Pan Xudong nodded.

'Make preparations immediately,' he said to everyone. 'Report the situation to all the teams of the Peasant Self-defence Corps. If we're prepared, we can cope with any sudden contingency.'

Then we all dispersed. When Uncle Zizhong and I got to the pharmacy, the old janitor had already prepared our meal. While we were eating, I asked Uncle Zizhong about Pockmarks the Sixth.

'He originally said that he was closing the shop for a while, as he had something else to do. It seems he's not closing temporarily but changing his profession.'

'I don't need to tell you what you don't need to know,' replied Uncle Zizhong. 'Just now he's not frying dough-sticks in Tanjiahe, but of course he's just closing his shop temporarily. He's an old hand in the trade, so how could he give up his business? He's still going on with it in the county town. He comes from an established dough-stick family: his father and uncle were both "masters of the art". After they died, he and his cousin inherited this family business. While he opened his shop in Tanjiahe, his cousin started one in the county town. With more and more troops stationed there, those idle soldiers and their officers often come to buy dough-sticks there. His cousin is so busy that it's best for Pockmarks the Sixth to close down his shop here and go to help his cousin. That's also a good way of getting news from those soldiers and their officers. It's a golden opportunity!'

'So he's also on our side?' I asked.

Uncle Zizhong smiled and said simply, 'Jiqing originally introduced you to him to work in his shop because he's reliable.'

I could not help laughing. Soon I had finished eating, and Uncle Zizhong pressed me to go back to Chu Family Village as quickly as possible. As I was leaving, he patted me on the shoulder affectionately and said, 'I'll ask Jiqing to tell your mother that you're very well and that she needn't worry. When you come back in two days, you can go and see her. I can also tell you that Ho Shuoru is working enthusiastically, and that Sister Apricot is co-operating with him very well. Now the two of them are responsible for almost the whole process of producing the propaganda, from writing to printing. Like your Uncle Pan, Lao Liu is running around the whole day, so he cannot stay in one place writing propaganda or attending meetings.'

Now that everybody was working harder than ever, I also felt that I had a heavy responsibility, and I reached Chu Family Village in a flash. When I got to the ancestral temple which served as the branch headquarters, an activists' meeting was just finishing. Wang Jiansheng immediately called me to hear my report. Afterwards he said to me, 'The situation here matches that over there. We've sent many search teams to track down Chumin. He's fled to neighbouring Mazhen county and slipped into the county town, where a division of Chiang Kai-shek's troops is garrisoned. As soon as he got to the division headquarters, he told them about the situation here and probably asked for help. Of course the situation over there in the north will become critical.' He stopped and muttered to himself, 'Time's running out; there's so much to do!'

Then he drank some tea and fell into deep thought.

After a few days away, I returned to a completely transformed village. Red Hill Village was bursting with activity and there seemed to be more people about. As Uncle Pan had instructed me, I had come here instead of going to Tanjiahe. I had been with Wang Jiansheng for five days, because he was terribly busy and I had to help him. Apparently the general headquarters were letting him work independently in the south without interfering with him, so they did not put pressure on him to report back. Before I left, Wang Jiansheng had instructed me to come on the mountain paths to save time and avoid people. I had left Chu Family Village just before dawn and reached Red Hill Village quite early – just before midday.

I went straight to Grandpa Whiskers's place, where I found him in the sitting room, talking to Ho Shuoru. They seemed to be discussing a serious problem, as their expressions were very grave. Once again, they stopped talking when I arrived. I was going to take the opportunity to go and see Sister Apricot in the back room to tell her a little about her husband, Wang Jiansheng. Ho Shuoru, however, grabbed me to sit down next to him.

'I've been missing you,' he said. 'You've come in good time. I know what you've been doing. You're really lucky to be able to do something important. You mustn't think it futile; it's connected with the fate of our country. Compared to you, I'm inexperienced, completely inexperienced.'

I had to smile.

'What are you talking about?' I said. 'You're still like you were at home, with all your knowledge! I'm uneducated; all I can do is take messages. If you wanted to talk about theoretical matters with me, you'd be wasting your time. Ha, ha!'

'Don't laugh,' he said, still in a very grave tone. 'You haven't changed; you treat me in the same old way! Now I want to reject my past and the empty knowledge I learned from books. You're all living such a hard life and working with a will. I feel very embarrassed living amongst you!'

'Are you homesick?'

'If I were homesick, would I speak to you like this?' he asserted most adamantly. 'I'm not longing for that mercenary family. I want to live just like you and do the same things as all of you. You all look down on me, treating me like the pampered boy of a wealthy family and asking Sister Apricot to make me special dishes.' At this point he looked up at Grandpa Whiskers and spoke in an even more serious tone. 'I've already been doing this propaganda work for quite a while. Do you still think I'm a pampered boy? Please all give me your opinions!'

I could not give any opinion; I just felt awkward. All I could do was look up at Grandpa Whiskers too. With both of us looking up at him, Grandpa Whiskers deliberately smiled to make the atmosphere more relaxed. Then he explained to me what was happening.

'The situation has changed here now. It's no longer safe in this small village; we're asking Shuoru to go and stay in a quiet place – Pheasant Nest – for the time being. Sister Apricot also wants to go there to look after him. He can continue doing the propaganda work there, but he doesn't want to go. He wants to be with us, live and work exactly like us, but . . .'

'But you're treating me like an outsider!' Shuoru interrupted Grandpa Whiskers. 'So I refuse!'

I had never seen Shuoru expressing himself so wilfully. I really did not know how to react. Seeing how awkward it was for me, and realizing that it was not necessary for me to take part in their conversation, Grandpa Whiskers said, 'There's somebody waiting for you at Aunt Sunflower's. Your mother also wants to see you. Go there quickly!'

This was an easy way out of the predicament, so I rushed back to my mother. She was sitting in Aunt Sunflower's room, sewing. As she had not seen me for quite a few days, she was delighted that I had arrived, but she did not put down her work at all. Neither did Aunt Sunflower, who just looked up and smiled at me affectionately. They seemed to be so frantically busy that they must have had some specially urgent task.

'Are you skipping your work to come back?' someone asked me.

The voice sounded very familiar and warm. Looking up, I saw O Ran, whom I had not noticed when I entered the room. She was sitting in the dark corner by the window, and I could only see her hand working on her sewing in a ray of sunshine.

'I was missing Ma,' I said in a mischievous voice, as if we were back in our childhood. 'I was also missing you! You never come home these days. What's brought you here today?'

Aunt Sunflower answered for her.

'Haven't you noticed? Her confinement will be starting soon, but she keeps working.'

It was only then that I noticed that she was indeed big with child and could not move easily.

'Yes,' said my mother, 'she should take it easy, so I asked her to stay. I don't have a say in anything else, but I must take responsibility in this matter. She has to obey me.'

'I am obeying you, Ma,' said O Ran. 'Haven't I been staying with you for the past few days?'

'But you certainly aren't taking it easy,' I said. 'You're busier than anybody else. What are you doing?'

'Look, I'm stitching a red flag,' said O Ran. 'Mother is sewing a red ribbon and Aunt Sunflower's sewing a cartridge-belt.'

She spread out the red flag she was sewing and showed it to me. On top there was a five-cornered star, and below the hammer and sickle.

'Why are you preparing these things in such a hurry?' I asked. 'There's still time.'

'No, there isn't,' O Ran contradicted me. 'Can't you guess why the leaders sent you to report here and not to Tanjiahe?'

'How can I guess? I just have to carry out my duty without questioning what the leadership have decided.'

'But you have to use your brain!' said O Ran. 'The situation is changing all the time. Can you follow old instructions if the situation changes? In fact, Tanjiahe has been occupied by the enemy troops. They originally planned to have a "victorious rendezvous" there with Chumin's Order Preservation Corps and Red Spear Society. They never expected their contact agent to "disappear" and their plan to fall through. The county head and the leaders of the county troops were furious and decided to dispatch a battalion to occupy Tanjiahe. Two or three hundred soldiers have been stationed there, preparing to raid the countryside . . .'

'Kick them out!' I was so angry that I interrupted O Ran. 'Our Self-defence Corps is strong enough; why should we be afraid of them?'

O Ran smiled.

'But we have too few guns,' she said, 'and they're well armed. They have new-type rifles too, specially shipped from abroad by foreigners who are supporting Chiang Kai-shek. How can we resist them? The few dozen guns we took from Chumin's corps were all made in Hanyang and they're not very good. Those guns made by our blacksmiths are all right for hunting, but they're hardly suitable for fighting soldiers in uniform. So as soon as we heard that they were coming, we withdrew immediately, leaving them a deserted town. We retreated in order to avoid open confrontation.'

'Now that we've allowed them to capture Tanjiahe, are we letting them come to assert their control over the countryside?' I asked.

'They still don't dare to come into the countryside. As soon as they get into the open fields they start to panic. Who knows, any time they march along the road, a bullet may suddenly come whizzing from a ditch in the fields and smash their heads. They're afraid of being killed . . .' She suddenly stopped, propping herself up with her hands on the arms of the chair. Standing up, she went on, 'Our comrades have come back. Didn't you want to report the situation in the south to them? Come with me.'

I hastily took her arm to support her. She looked as if she found it quite difficult to walk, as the baby was due soon. We could hear the babble of voices in the sitting room, and when we went in, there were Pan Xudong, Uncle Zizhong, Uncle Pan,

Pan Zaixing, Liu Dawang, Lao Liu and many people whose names I did not know, but who looked quite familiar. They were all team heads of the Self-defence Corps. As soon as Lao Liu saw us, he quickly pulled over a chair and gave O Ran a hand as she sat down. Uncle Pan patted me softly on the head, as if I were still a child.

'You've come earlier than we expected,' he said, 'You're really quick!'

Seeing that I was now sitting on a bench with Lao Liu, Pan Xudong directed his attention to me, asking, 'What news do you have from Comrade Wang Jiansheng?'

'First, they've already formed five self-defence teams there, all led by anti-Chumin activists. Huang Yongfa is team leader and Jin Bailong vice-team leader,' I reported. 'Second, other villagers who are capable of fighting have formed a peasant volunteer force. Third, all the property of Chumin and the rich landlords connected with him, like Wang Jiansheng's father, Wang Taihe, has been confiscated. All their land is also being distributed to the landless peasants or those who have little land. Fourth, the villagers there have set up an "investigation committee" to track down Chumin and his followers. Unfortunately, that old fox has fled to Mazhen county town. Apparently, he's become an "adviser" to the division headquarters stationed there.'

After hearing this, Pan Xudong nodded and mumbled, 'Now I can really understand why the county troops occupied Tanjiahe so quickly.' Then he looked up at me and asked, 'What's the spirit of the villagers there like?'

'Extremely enthusiastic. They have a strong fighting spirit and are all determined to defend themselves with arms, to distribute the land and destroy the remaining forces of Chumin and his lot – they've already executed eleven heads of the Order Preservation Corps and Red Spear Society.'

'Did they hold a public trial?' asked Pan Xudong.

'No, they were too quick. Every time, before Wang Jiansheng got to hear about it, the villagers had executed them. He was rushing all over the place and couldn't keep up with the situation!'

245

After nodding to himself again, Pan Xudong looked up and spoke to the assembled company.

'He's had a hard time. We couldn't spare anybody here to go and help him.'

'It looks as if we'll have to keep Chunsheng here for the moment,' said Uncle Pan. 'We haven't got enough fast and experienced messengers here . . . we'll need him tonight.'

'Yes, now we must discuss tonight's operation,' said Pan Xudong. 'Comrade Chunsheng, don't go away. Stay and listen – we're just going to discuss tonight's operation!'

Then they all started their discussion. I was not very clear about it yet, so I could only listen.

In fact, 'tonight's operation' was arranged by afternoon. Those who had been discussing this in Aunt Sunflower's sitting room during the morning had no time to eat. They just left disguised as shop assistants, artisans, teachers and fortune-tellers – Pan Xudong was very realistically dressed as a teacher and Lao Liu as a fortune-teller. As I was actually a member of the second team of the seventh Peasant Self-defence Corps section, I also returned to my team for the time being – at least for that night. In fact, I did not go as corps member, but as liaison man for Pan Zaixing and Liu Dawang, as they were leading these local forces of the Self-defence Corps. They had to keep close contact with each other and with a large contingent of peasant volunteers supporting the Self-defence Corps in the rear.

I had supper early that evening. Mother gave me an extra padded waistcoat, as she was afraid I would feel cold during the night. She was used to my going out at night now. She trusted my ability to run fast and to find my way in the dark, as nothing had ever happened to me. This time she felt even better, because she had O Ran to keep her company. The assembly point was under an old maple tree a few hundred yards behind Red Hill Village. Liu Dawang was waiting there for his forces, which were just converging on him on various paths through the fields. When I got there, he asked me to go over a hill to another valley and find out about Pan Zaixing's forces, who were assembling there. These two forces were going to set off from two separate points and converge on Tanjiahe in a pincer-like movement, to enter by the east gate. Their action had to be synchronized, so that they would reach the east gate at the same time and prepare an ambush on both sides.

This operation had to be executed rapidly. We would attack Tanjiahe simultaneously while the battalion of troops inside were still asleep. Then we would steal up on them, before they had time to emerge, and capture their weapons. As for those who slipped through our net, we would intercept them at the four town gates. Now I fully understood. The main purpose was to destroy their forces and seize their guns.

'We need guns and ammunition most urgently,' Pan Xudong had reminded us in Aunt Sunflower's room at the planning meeting. 'Now they're showing these things off, which gives us a wonderful opportunity. We mustn't let it pass! We can only carry on the revolution if we have weapons. The main reason we've lost so many young students in "The Big City" and let them kill at random in the countryside is that we didn't have arms. But now we're going to seize them, so that they can serve the people, instead of harming them.'

Pan Xudong's speech had raised our fighting spirit and courage. Pan Zaixing and Liu Dawang were particularly inspired. They were used to catching the enemies unawares and seizing their weapons to arm themselves. The prompt decision to carry out this operation was just what they wanted. Seizing guns was the most effective way of expanding and strengthening the self-defence forces under their command.

'But this time they have many troops,' said Liu Dawang.

'But they have many guns too,' said Pan Zaixing. 'Those handy foreign guns are far superior to our own blunderbusses!'

Liu Dawang had licked his lips, as if already relishing the taste of the captured 'handy foreign guns'.

'But don't have any illusions,' Pan Xudong had warned. 'Don't forget that our weapons are mostly old guns and still more are farm tools like hoes and spades. We have to defeat them with our brains, wisdom, strict organization, discipline and good co-operation. The only factors in our favour are that we're locals, so we're familiar with the terrain, and, in addition, that the walls of Tanjiahe are low and not too thick. We can scale them with high ladders. We must try our best to make use of these factors.'

Pan Xudong's ideas made a strong impact, spreading to the ranks very quickly. Therefore, when the self-defence forces and volunteers from all directions assembled under the maple tree, they were extremely disciplined and alert, not making any noise. When I went over the hill to the other valley to find out about Pan Zaixing, I saw that his forces were the same. They were also coming to him along different paths through the fields from various places scattered around.

I stood beside Pan Zaixing for a while, watching more and more people gathering here, until finally the stream of people coming along the paths trickled off. Before counting their numbers and ordering their ranks, Pan Zaixing said to me, 'Quickly go back and tell Dawang that we're ready to set off. We have to advance in parallel columns at the same time until we reach a spot a third of a mile from the town. Then we'll send another message and close the distance between us until we squeeze the east gate in our pincers. Be off, quick!'

When I got back to Liu Dawang, his troops were already lined up and about to set forth. By now the stars had come out and were silently winking at us. I looked back and saw a long line of men starting to follow us in the moonlight. In front was the whole of the seventh team of the Peasant Self-defence Corps. Some of them were carrying rifles over their shoulders, but those without were carrying the same as the peasant volunteers behind them: all kinds of farm implements, including hoes, carrying-poles, spears, blunderbusses and fishing forks. They also had two mules and a horse, carrying several locally made cannon. Although they were not in uniform, they were marching in step and maintaining strict discipline. There was not a sound from any of them – not even a cough.

After we had been going for about two hours, we climbed over a hill and saw Tanjiahe ahead of us. Liu Dawang halted, turned and waved to the troops behind. The long, snake-like line of troops immediately came to a stand-still. Although we could see Pan Zaixing's forces dimly in the distance, Liu Dawang told me to run there as fast as possible with a message for Pan Zaixing. They were level with us, but to make sure that we would co-ordinate our actions he wanted to tell them that we had arrived and could proceed simultaneously. As I knew this area like the back of my hand, I took a short-cut to carry out Liu Dawang's instruction.

'We could see the outline of your forces very clearly,' Pan Zaixing told me. 'I was just waiting for your message. You came very promptly. We'll move right away!'

He started to move forward with his forces. Liu Dawang could obviously make out this movement by the light of the stars shining in the sky. All the shapes on the ground were faintly discernible. He immediately co-ordinated his movements, leading his forces forward too. As the two forces approached the east gate, they began their pincer movement to attack. Now I more or less flew over a field between our two forces to get back to Liu Dawang. On the way I suddenly heard a horse neighing in the distance. This was followed immediately by the sound of gunfire.

The shooting meant that the troops in the town had discovered our night attack – the neighing had woken them up and alerted them. Our two forces each carried out their own plan, taking emergency steps to complete our pincer-attack on the east gate. Now we were already a step behind. The troops inside had already opened the gates and were fleeing and firing their guns. In fact, they did not dare scatter into the countryside, as they did not know the strength of the Peasant Self-defence Corps or the volunteer forces. As soon as they fired their guns, the self-defence forces fired back and rushed into the darkness, shouting a battlecry. As they surged forth boldly from all around the town, they terrified the soldiers, who looked strong but who were actually cowardly. For these troops, it was the most natural thing on earth to open the gates and flee. Our two forces outside the east gate could no longer surround and annihilate them, as most of them had already escaped into the open country, where they found the road. They were heading towards the county town to join the troops stationed there. All our forces had to follow various paths to try and intercept them, so that we could still seize their rifles in the fray. The self-defence forces kept firing their guns to confuse these fleeing soldiers and frighten them out of their wits.

This skirmish lasted for almost an hour, after which the sound of gun-fire gradually died down. The horses and mules, however, continued neighing, as they were only used to working in the fields or hauling on the road. Having never seen a battle, or experienced a night-march, they were obviously alarmed. We later found out that the packhorse carrying cannon in the first team of the Peasant Self-defence Corps had been the first to neigh. It had stumbled on a stone and this completely ruined our night attack. The self-defence and volunteer forces, who had been pursuing the fleeing troops, came back to the east gate of Tanjiahe only at daybreak and assembled on a hillside near by. Each team counted the rifles they had captured: there were 139 rifles and 3,123 bullets – quite an impressive haul, after all.

Pan Xudong, standing on the top of the hill, made a brief speech to sum up our experience.

'We must definitely all remember not to use packhorses or mules again when we go on a night-march. They can only be used for farming work, not for battle – they are draught animals, after all. The county troops occupied this town, where our head-quarters are now located, to intimidate us. Now that they have learned a little about our strength, they certainly won't give up. They'll surely increase their forces to carry out even bigger operations against us. We cannot lower our guard; we must also step up our training. That's the second point. That's all. You can all go back to have a rest. You must be exhausted after a sleepless night. Will all the team and group leaders stay behind. We're going to Dongyue Temple for a meeting to plan the next step. Dismiss!'

Just as he was about to leave for Tanjiahe, he noticed me sitting on a rock beside Liu Dawang. He came up and said, patting me on the shoulder, 'This is also good training for you – that's one of the reasons I brought you here. You can go and give Wang Jiansheng a full, eye-witness report of the situation. He'll understand what the next step will involve and make the necessary preparations. But you must also remind him to get in touch with Chang Je-an as soon as he can to discuss the new situation. They're not so far from each other now. Right, there's nothing else for you to do here, so go back to Chu Family

Village. Wang Jiansheng must be waiting desperately for your news!'

Chang Je-an, who had been transferred to neighbouring Mazhen county some time ago, managed to build a number of secret party nuclei. Their influence had been expanding rapidly, with the result that a sizeable force of peasant volunteers was formed, without the slightest knowledge of the garrison head-quarters in the county town. But Chang Je-an and Wang Jiansheng were in touch with each other and co-ordinated their activities. When I reached Chu Family Village at noon that day, Wang Jiansheng was just having a meeting with some of the leaders of the newly formed Peasant Self-defence Corps and volunteer forces. They were discussing how to consolidate and strengthen their links with the volunteer forces in the neighbouring county, to prevent an attack from the troops stationed in the county town over there. When I went into Chumin's ancestral temple, I sat down quietly in a corner to listen, so as not to interrupt the meeting. But Wang Jiansheng had already noticed me. After a quarter of an hour, he concluded the meeting and called me to give him an account.

'I have to ask you to run another errand. Go to Green Pine Hollow right away and ask Chang Je-an to come here,' he said, after he had heard my account. 'With such a big development here, he should know too, because it involves his situation there.'

Green Pine Hollow was a mountainous hamlet north of Mazhen county town. Like Pheasant Nest, it had no more than five or six households. Chang Je-an often went there, and I had been there several times too. It was not more than seven miles from Chu Family Village, so I could be there by midday.

# CHAPTER 13

The news of these events spread like lightning. On my way to Green Pine Hollow, I could see that things had changed, including even the fields and hills. The whole area seemed to have taken on a new lease of life and to be buzzing with activity. There were groups of people everywhere – on the ridges, in the fields, on paths and hillsides. They were beating gongs and drums as if they were going to join in some festive celebration. Looking more carefully, I could see that they were really villagers taking part in a parade. In every group there were one or two who were clearly being pushed or pulled along, dragging their feet as they advanced despondently. Some of them were wearing tall paper hats, with such words as 'RICH LANDLORD' or 'EVIL TYRANT' written in large characters. Others had both their hands tied behind their backs, with someone pulling them in front and someone shouting to urge them on behind. Judging by the slogans which the paraders were shouting, these prisoners were the heads of the Order Preservation Corps or the Red Spear Society. This parade demonstrated how weak the former powers controlling this whole area were. All of Chumin's armed forces had been defeated and he himself had fled. The atmosphere now was similar to when the peasant unions had been formed in the early years of the struggle. Now the villagers seemed to be in even higher spirits and even more confident.

When I crossed the county border into neighbouring Mazhen county, I realized that this atmosphere was widespread. There was no longer any clear dividing-line at the border. Some of the paraders were actually shouting slogans like 'Peasants of the world all belong to one family!' and 'Workers of the world unite!' As I was passing through a rather big village, I saw many villagers carrying baskets full of grain on their shoulders. They were coming out of a tall grey-brick building and joyfully making their way home. The tall building was a landlord's manor house and the grain they were carrying came from his granary. The peasants were now taking back the rice which they had handed in to the landlord. This had not even happened in the days of the peasant unions; in fact, it was unprecedented. The peasants had probably never even dared to imagine such a scene, but now it was reality. They were acting so boldly in broad daylight, in spite of the fact that a division of Chiang Kai-shek's troops was stationed in the county town.

'This is a result of the conflict between our two forces.'

This is how Chang Je-an explained this historic situation to me, when I told him what I had seen on the way. I had found him in a peasant's thatched hut in Green Pine Hollow.

'This time we had a show-down in Tanjiahe. They had new-type rifles and guns; we had mostly locally made guns and hoes and shoulder-poles. Weapons, however, did not decide the outcome, but the human factor, the spirit of our men. That's what's new about this situation. This is a very inspiring and valuable new experience.'

'In that case,' I said, 'it must also be very exciting for the villagers to seize the landlords and their military heads, open the landlords' granaries and divide up their property. Don't you think so?'

Chang Je-an nodded.

'Yes, the people have really become active. Now you know how to analyse things quite correctly. You've changed a lot.'

He burst out laughing, but immediately checked himself. He stared at me, his eyes blank, as if he had succumbed to nostalgic reminiscences of his visit to our village disguised as a woman. I too had always retained a vivid memory of him. Now we were talking in his room in the little thatched hut where he lived and worked, which consisted of only a bed and a shaky table.

'You've also changed a lot,' I said.

'Changed in what way?' asked Chang Je-an, returning to reality.

'You have many wrinkles on your forehead, and your hands are rougher. Just look at all your clothes, too – your worn-out

padded jacket, your cloth belt and your cotton padded shoes –
you look just like a country bumpkin.'

A faint smile appeared on his lips, and he livened up again.

'Now that I'm working among the villagers, of course I have
to be like one of them. As for the wrinkles on my forehead,
that's because I have to think much more than when I was a
student – much, much more. This region used to be remote
and backward. In order to mobilize the villagers and raise their
consciousness, it's necessary to do a lot of investigation, make
a lot of contacts and friends and have many personal talks with
people – in a word, to do a lot of thinking.'

'But now the villagers are dynamic and enthusiastic, so your
work should be easier.'

Chang Je-an smiled again.

'It's easy to say that! It's not a matter of finishing one task,
like running an errand or delivering a message. Mass work isn't
so specific or cut-and-dried. There's no end to it.'

'For example?' I asked.

'For example, as you've witnessed, the people are spontaneously distributing the landlords' property and opening up
their granaries. Now they want to divide up the land – that's
quite natural. But distributing land isn't like opening the landlords' granaries. When every peasant carries away two baskets
full of millet, that's the end of the matter. Distributing land is
much more complicated and needs thorough planning. I think
this must be what's keeping Wang Jiansheng busy and worried.'
Then he suddenly changed the subject, asking, 'What message
have you brought this time?'

'It's very simple. Please go to Chu Family Village and from
there to Tanjiahe with Wang Jiansheng – I'll probably go with
you as your messenger.'

'I know you learned several Confucian classics by heart when
you were a young boy in the village. So you're looking after
your young master, Ho Shuoru again – I've heard that he's
performing very well now. Is that right?'

'Yes, he doesn't need me to look after him now,' I replied.
'He gets on very well with Lao Liu. They're doing propaganda
work together and they're doing a good job.'

'Yes, he has also contributed a lot towards our successes. He should be considered one of our comrades.'

'There are signs of this,' I said. 'Perhaps he already has . . . the situation has been changing so fast these last few days!'

'Right, let's get back to what we were saying. If you hadn't come, I was planning to go to Chu Family Village in a day or two and then go with Wang Jiansheng to Tanjiahe to report on developments here. Have you seen the pile of paper on my table? I'm just writing a memorandum, which I have to send to Wang Jiansheng in case I cannot get away. There are still many urgent tasks to do! I have to arrange things here first. Tonight there's a group meeting for us leaders, and tomorrow there will be several nuclei meetings, so I won't be able to leave. I can only leave when everything has been properly arranged here. What do you think?'

'Well, I'll go back and report that,' I said. 'I'll go to Chu Family Village tonight. I really like to go in the night, when there's nobody about; I feel free and easy then!'

'You don't have to be in such a hurry. As the situation has changed so drastically here, it must be even more hectic over there. With so many problems, Wang Jiansheng needs time to get organized too. He won't be able to leave Chu Family Village straight away either. I'm sure the special committee will understand that. It would be wrong to abandon our post here without proper arrangements for the next move. Stay here tonight and have a good rest. If you aren't tired, you can also come to our core-group meeting tonight – it could also help you to understand the situation here, so that you'll be able to report it more fully. You can leave before dawn tomorrow morning and I'll leave at the same time the day after and go to Chu Family Village by myself.'

Chang Je-an's proposal seemed very reasonable to me, and I also felt deeply moved that he was no longer treating me like a mere village boy, as in the past, but as a mature adult, a 'comrade'. I suddenly felt very close to him – as close as to Uncle Pan, O Ran and Lao Liu, even though we did not have much opportunity to meet nowadays.

I decided to stay with Chang Je-an that night and to go to the core-group meeting with him.

When I got back to Chu Family Village the next day, it was already midday. As Chang Je-an had predicted, Wang Jiansheng was up to his neck in work. He was no longer in his provisional office in the temple. The only clue as to his whereabouts came from the sound of rousing slogans in the distance, where a mass meeting seemed to be going on. I thought Wang Jiansheng must be there, so I followed the direction of the slogan-shouting. I climbed over a hill behind the village. Facing the valley was Chumin's former threshing ground, where his farm-hands used to thresh millet and lay it out to dry. Now, however, it had become a place for mass meetings. Hence the slogan-shouting coming from here. Approaching the place, I could see that every slogan was accompanied by countless fists being raised. I could also feel the ground shaking, like a strong earthquake.

I went in, but it was so crowded that I could not find a space. When a younger villager acting as an usher noticed me, he asked the people beside me to make room and let me squeeze in. This young villager must have known I was Wang Jiansheng's messenger and thought I might have something to report to him. Although there was a hubbub, the atmosphere of the meeting was very formal, different from the usual mass meetings: there was a high platform in the middle of the meeting ground – perhaps it was to ensure that the audience could hear the speakers and also see their faces. This kind of meeting had only been held in the short period when the peasant unions were flourishing before Chiang Kai-shek started to crush the revolution. Then the revolutionaries and popular leaders had to go underground and in the daytime could only go out in disguise. I was fascinated to see them all on the public platform now. To find out what was happening, I squeezed up to the platform, as the audience let me through.

Wang Jiansheng was actually sitting up on the platform, beside a villager who was sitting in the middle. Evidently, this villager, not Wang Jiansheng, was chairing the meeting. Now I recognized him as Li Chengbao, the head of the ninth team of the Peasant Self-defence Corps of this region, whom I had met a few days earlier. He was no rough country bumpkin, a man of medium height, with a slightly waxen complexion. He looked as if he had not slept for several nights, but his eyes were bright.

Like Wang Jiansheng, he was watching the meeting attentively and listening to the villagers, who were spontaneously coming up to the platform to speak.

'My whole family, from what my grandfather remembers right up to now, have never had enough to eat,' a middle-aged villager was saying. 'Why? Because as soon as the grain came on to the threshing ground it was collected by Chumin's steward. They still said this was charitable, as they had given us a little land to till and we had porridge to eat and didn't starve. At that time we hadn't seen through them, so we really thought that we couldn't survive without them. We did whatever they asked us to do. When they asked us to join the Red Spear Society, we did so, thinking it was the right thing to do! We never thought we were fighting our own people. We must unite and fight back!'

'We're farmers, but for generations we've had no land!' said another young villager. 'Chumin never did any farming, but he owned all the land. He sat idly at home, while we had to obediently fill his granary. How crazy and stupid of us! At the time of the peasant unions we were all shouting 'land to the tillers', but in no time he sent Wang the Lion with his Order Preservation Corps to suppress us! Now we cannot be duped again. We've already picked ourselves up and hit back. We have to go on fighting until we defeat them, so that they'll never recover their power again . . .'

This villager had just finished his speech when another young lad came up on to the platform. He stood legs akimbo, his hands on his hips and his back straight, just as if he were facing Chumin and Wang the Lion and going to knock them down with one fatal blow. The chairman, Li Chengbao, was listening silently, as if he were deliberately giving the villagers the platform to vent the anger and bitterness which they had suppressed so long. Wang Jiansheng, sitting beside him, was equally silent, listening to the villagers express their views – views they had never dared to express openly.

'If we want to make sure that they never recover their power again, we have to know how,' said the young lad. 'That means we have to have our own armed forces. How did Wang the Lion manage to suppress us? Because he had organized the Order

Preservation Corps. How did he dare to raid the north? Because he had formed the Red Spear Society, getting the villagers to fight and kill one another. How did we manage to annihilate them this time? Because we also had armed forces – the Peasant Self-defence Corps and volunteer forces. How were these armed forces formed? They were organized. Only if we villagers get organized can we have armed forces. But organization needs leadership. Who are our leaders? It's the Revolutionary Party which is leading us in the struggle and working for the interests of the vast majority of people. Fellow countrymen, now that the situation has developed favourably, what is our next step?'

This question immediately alerted everyone, and the assembled crowd suddenly hushed. All their eyes were fixed on this young lad. Quite evidently, the question which he had raised was just what they were all thinking about but could not answer. This problem, however, had to be solved immediately, in order to prevent Chumin and the troops stationed in the county town from returning. Everyone was gazing at this young lad as if he were a stranger. In fact, he was somewhat different. He was not a regular farmer, but a hunter. He was Wang Jingxian, who had dispatched Wang the Lion. When he noticed everyone concentrating on him, he appeared somewhat awkward, so he just left the platform quietly, without another word. Li Chengbao, the chairman, waited for a moment to see if anybody else was coming up to speak. Then he stood up, came to the front of the platform and spoke in a sombre tone.

'Brother Wang Jingxian's question was very good – in fact, essential! But he has already answered it. We must have armed forces, the bigger and stronger the better. So we must rapidly strengthen and expand our Peasant Self-defence Corps and volunteer forces. Even that is not enough. All of us, men and women, must get organized. And the organization for poor people is the Revolutionary Party!'

Now Wang Jiansheng, who had remained silent throughout, came up to the front of the platform. He cast his eyes over the whole audience. All were still, looking silently and intently at him and Li Chengbao as if these two had all the solutions to their problems. Wang Jiansheng coughed to clear his throat and began to speak in a quiet tone, which, however, the audience could still hear clearly.

'Brother Li Chengbao's right. The only way is to have an organization, a strong organization. If we're not strong, we can get strong; if we have no guns, we can get guns; if we have no power, we can seize power! Haven't we defeated the armed forces of the wealthy landlords? Haven't we opened Chumin's granary? Aren't we going to distribute his land? Where does this power come from? It comes from ourselves. Why didn't we have it in the past? Because we had no organization. If we want to create our own power-base, and become masters of our own lives, we must have an organization, a strong organization. That's the crucial question. Let everybody think about it!'

Wang Jiansheng remained standing at the front of the platform, as if he were waiting for some response. Everybody remained absolutely silent, though. Wang Jiansheng and Li Chengbao stood there looking at them, and they gazed back. All of a sudden a husky voice broke the silence.

'I want to join this organization, to join the Revolutionary Party!' he shouted towards the platform.

The shout came from an old villager with a greying beard, reminding me very much of my Grandpa Whiskers. He was wearing a short, padded jacket, with a belt made of straw, but he looked stronger than Grandpa Whiskers. I guessed he might be an artisan: a stonemason or bricklayer. Following him, another voice cried out, 'I want to join the Peasant Self-defence Corps. What happened? How come I never heard about it, when the Self-defence Corps was spreading all over the countryside? Now I know, and you must let me join!'

This came from a young-looking man. Judging from the strong hand which he had raised, he was a farm-hand of some kind. Next, a faint but determined voice came from behind him.

'Although I'm not so young, I can still run. I could be useful to the peasant volunteer forces!'

A bald villager had spoken these words. Now another voice, a woman's piercing voice, reached our ears.

'Don't we women have any role to play? Why is there no women's self-defence corps or volunteer force? Why do you men have to decide everything? You quiet gentleman up there

259

on the platform, you seem to be a learned person and you must certainly know about principles. Please would you talk about them! What "leaders" are you, not to have mentioned women at all?'

The 'quiet gentleman' she had referred to was Wang Jiansheng. Since he had been mentioned, he had to respond.

'What you say is quite right! We're still full of old ideas, and we often forget about women. That's a mistake. You're daring enough to speak your mind. In the past, women didn't dare to speak out, and neither did men for that matter. Now all of you dare to speak out. That shows you have minds of your own. That's very good! Just now somebody said that nobody knew all this time that we had formed the Peasant Self-defence Corps or the volunteer forces. That's true, but we couldn't tell people. If Wang the Lion had got to know about it, he could have captured our people and executed them. So many of our good comrades were killed like that. Now we've gained the upper hand, so we can do things openly and speak our minds to all of you. You've all just been giving us your opinions. We'll certainly do as you've all requested. But so many people have come together – we cannot do it all at once. If all of you want to join the Self-defence Corps and the volunteer forces, you should enrol one by one in proper order. Am I right, Brother Li Chengbao? You know this place and the people and situation here well, so I'll give you this task. As for the women, there is plenty to do! For instance, making shoes for the Self-defence Corps, sewing red flags for them and the volunteer forces and taking over the farm work when they go off to fight. Tonight we'll have group meetings in every village to organize and discuss matters systematically. In this way we can expand our forces day by day, and our power will increase. What do you think?'

'Fine!' The thunderous reply rang out from the assembled crowd. 'Peasants of the world are all one family!'

The mass meeting ended with this loud response, whereupon they all went back to village and home in good order. They strolled along, which showed that for the first time they were full of confidence and proud to be masters of their own lives.

Wang Jiansheng had seen me from the platform earlier on.

He had deliberately let me observe this scene to absorb the lively atmosphere. He had not paid any attention to me, but let me watch and listen to everything. Only now, when the crowd was dispersing in every direction, did he hurry up to me. He patted me on the shoulder and told me to go back with him to his small 'office' in Chumin's ancestral temple. He let me lead, while he followed, listening to my account on the way. By the time we arrived I had finished telling him everything I had witnessed, including what I had seen on the way and about the mass movement going on in Chang Je-an's area.

'It looks as if the people in the whole area have become active, and in the north they must be even more active,' said Wang Jiansheng. 'We never expected the situation to develop so quickly. The comrades over there must be as busy as we are here. General headquarters will certainly understand us. We have to take advantage of this situation and strike while the iron's hot. We must arrange everything properly here, and it probably doesn't matter if we go there a day later. Do you think Chang Je-an will definitely come here today?'

'If he doesn't get here tonight, he'll come early tomorrow morning.'

'Well, we'll wait for him then,' said Wang Jiansheng. 'Go and get some sleep now. You must be tired after coming so far.'

Chang Je-an kept his appointment, arriving at dawn the next morning. Wang Jiansheng still could not open his eyes, as he had been attending group meetings all through the night. He rubbed his eyes a few times, first with his fingers and then with a cold towel, at the same time picking up the rice balls that had been left over from the previous evening. He handed over the work to be done to Li Chengbao, who had not gone back home after attending the group meetings that night. Then he left for Tanjiahe with Chang Je-an and me. I followed behind them, as they were talking on the way, discussing the situation in every district and their ideas about the next step in their work. I could not hear them clearly, as they were speaking quietly. Only when we reached Tanjiahe did they raise their voices, concluding, 'The revolution has reached a new stage not only in this region, but also in the whole of China – this will influence the whole world!'

All the group leaders of general headquarters were gathered in Dongyue Temple. They included Pan Xudong, as chairman, Uncle Zizhong, Uncle Pan, Lao Liu and all the team leaders of the Self-defence Corps except Li Chengbao, the group leaders of the peasant volunteer forces and of several underground party groups in the villages and country towns. Some were smoking and some talking quietly. As soon as we arrived, they all hushed.

'I guessed you might come around this time,' said Pan Xudong, beckoning Wang Jiansheng and Chang Je-an. 'Come and sit here! You must have rushed, so just get your breath back.'

Wang Jiansheng and Chang Je-an went up to a long table at the front and sat down next to Pan Xudong.

'We're having a special meeting,' added Uncle Zizhong after they had sat down. 'We were just waiting for you.'

'I'm very sorry,' said Chang Je-an, 'the situation over there has been developing so fast during the past few days, and new problems have been cropping up one after another. We had to organize our work in good time, so we've been delayed a day. Jiansheng's situation is just the same, isn't it, Jiansheng?'

Wang Jiansheng just nodded.

Pan Xudong responded with a smile.

'That's quite understandable. We would know even if you hadn't come to report, as it's the same here too. Everyone made a special effort to come here today, because our meeting is very important. Right, let's start.'

Now everyone was quiet, and those who had been smoking put out their pipes. I was sitting in a corner, having a look at all the people present. I noticed the leaders of various teams and groups and the old master of the 'temporarily closed' dough-stick shop, Pockmarks the Sixth. What was even more interesting, my other 'young master', Ho Shuoru, was also there, probably because he had now become 'one of us'. This was really a 'special' meeting.

'What I want to report is this,' said Chang Je-an. 'The villagers in my part of the region are generally organized, and demand action. But we can't act alone, with the military strength of the enemy growing steadily. To cope with them we need the co-ordination of the revolutionary forces here.'

'Yes, this is the very purpose of our meeting today,' Pan Xudong responded directly. 'Zizhong has already received the secret code from the provincial committee for transmitting and the radio transmitter, which Shuoru's father sent us, is still working properly and powerfully! The provincial committee was fully informed of what happened here. It has instructed us to set up a revolutionary committee for this region, to co-ordinate the work of the various counties around and to carry out the directives from above. Is that satisfactory, Comrade Je-an? What do you think about it?'

'Yes,' Chang Je-an said. 'I for one fully approve of this decision. I discussed this question with Jiansheng on the way here. I think this directive has come just at the right time.'

'Any more ideas?' asked Pan Xudong, facing the others.

A solemn silence filled the hall.

'All right, in that case, we'll carry out this directive,' said Pan Xudong. 'There's some more urgent information, which I'll ask Comrade Zizhong to announce.'

Uncle Zizhong got up from a bench near me, and spoke.

'Last night I received a radio message from the provincial committee. Developments here have scared Chiang Kai-shek, so he plans to strengthen his military forces in this region and wage a large-scale "mopping-up" campaign. We must keep a close watch on the movements of the troops stationed in the various counties around.'

Chang Je-an promptly added, 'Yes, I'm also informed that the civil and military leaders in Mazhen county town are scared out of their wits and have asked the provincial government to send them an army to strengthen their forces. It seems certain that they're preparing a "mopping-up" campaign.'

'It's not a question of "it seems". They must have already decided,' said Pockmarks the Sixth. 'Perhaps the "army" which you mentioned has already come, while we're holding this very meeting. In the county town yesterday afternoon, I saw the troops starting to move residents and shopkeepers out of their houses and shops to billet the newly arrived soldiers from the provincial capital – I heard that they're bringing in a new battalion. Only my old cousin Cuiba's shop hasn't been occupied, because the soldiers and their officers like to eat dough-sticks. So they don't want to close it down.'

'So can you still work there?' asked Uncle Pan.

'Of course,' replied Pockmarks the Sixth. 'After this meeting, I have to hurry back. There are so many soldiers that business is flourishing more than ever. It's really strange. I only hope they'll pay for their dough-sticks!'

Pan Xudong coughed, and the meeting quietened down again.

'The situation is critical,' he said. 'It's certain that Chiang Kai-shek has sent an army, which is about to start a massacre. The question is, are we going to sit here waiting for the "mopping-up" campaign? Or shall we attack them before their reinforced troops set forth, and organize our own counter-attack?'

'Counter-attack!' shouted Pan Zaixing, startling everyone. 'Enough of our villagers have already been killed. How can we wait for them to come and massacre us?'

'I agree,' said Uncle Zizhong. 'We must organize our revolutionary forces to attack them.'

'Attack?' Lao Liu stood up to express his views. He spoke somewhat hesitantly. 'If a new battalion of troops has come into the county town, that would make one regiment altogether. One thousand five or six hundred guns, mortars and machine-guns. It won't be the same as fighting the Order Preservation Corps, no fun at all. How many guns have we got?'

'All in all, hardly three hundred,' replied Pan Xudong in a calm, cool tone. 'Some of these may not fire, or if they do fire, there won't be enough bullets. As for machine-guns and mortars, I'm afraid many of our men have never seen these, let alone fired them.'

Silence reigned again in the hall. Everyone was looking at one another, wishing they had a military expert who could appraise the emergency. The silence was unfathomable, making everyone even more aware of the grave situation.

The silence dragged on for several minutes.

'I have an idea.' This was Liu Dawang's voice, sounding

especially resonant, as he had broken the silence. 'If we take on the enemy directly, we'll obviously meet with swift defeat. Fighting these soldiers with guns, we should make use of our favourable conditions. Doing scouting operations in the night these past few years has taught me a lot. Sometimes there were only two of us scouting around, but we caught spies all the same. Even though the Order Preservation Corps had guns, just a few of us prevented them from coming out at night. They just stayed inside their walls. Why? Because we're familiar with the terrain, and we're brave. Even though we don't have guns – we usually only have choppers – we can still transform this whole plain, in fact the whole countryside around here, into our own domain. Just now Comrade Pan Xudong said that we only have about three hundred guns. Where did they come from? We seized them from the corps and from the troops who occupied our county town. Now the troops in the county town have suddenly increased the number of their guns from a thousand to one thousand four or five hundred. With machine guns and mortars, these soldiers seem formidable. But if we take the initiative and attack in the night before they mobilize, they may be caught off balance. Also, with so many guns – well, it's really tempting. If we are to get hold of them, there's only one way. Get them during the night!'

Everybody sat bolt upright, their spirits revived. Only Lao Liu looked somewhat depressed, staring blankly at everyone. This surprised Pockmarks the Sixth who felt some camaraderie with the ex-story-teller, because story-telling and running the tea house where he fried dough-sticks for the customers were complementary occupations. He felt sorry to see Lao Liu looking so despondent now, so he tried to console him by explaining things in an affectionate way.

'Old Brother Liu, you're a man of letters. Your propaganda work has been brilliant. Without all your propaganda I don't think we could have gained the initiative so fast. But as the saying goes, "Scholars are no match for soldiers." As for taking on the enemy, you're still no military expert, so you only view things from the weapons angle. That's very natural, and we know that you're not trying to be negative. I agree with Dawang. In battle, sometimes timing, terrain and the human factor are more important than guns. His view is based on experience in this field. If you could join a battle, I think your views would also change. Fighting is not the same as telling stories, which depends on imagination and the gift of the gab. Sometimes it's not quite like real life – '

Before Pockmarks the Sixth had finished, he was interrupted.

'Who'll give us the chance to fight? We spend the whole day cooped up indoors, racking our brains. We have to use our imagination, otherwise how could we print so much propaganda every day? Can you try and answer that, any of you?'

The speaker was another 'man of letters', Ho Shuoru. His sudden outburst was enough to startle everyone. They had all ignored him, forgotten that he was also doing propaganda work and that he had obtained the machine for printing the propaganda from his father, free of charge. Now they began to pay attention to him and to take his question seriously. They thought his question was quite right, but they did not know how to answer. Once more the hall became silent. It was Pan Xudong who broke the ice again.

'What you've all said is true. I've learned a lot from you. We must admit that we've not paid enough attention to Comrade Shuoru. According to what you all say, we should be confident, confident that we can cope with this challenge. We should get hold of the tempting guns which Dawang mentioned just now. Of course, we should let Lao Liu and Comrade Shuoru join in this time – that's also necessary for their work!'

'So now we must prepare for action!' said Pan Zaixing. 'We've mobilized all the villagers in this county and also Mazhen county. When can we find the right conditions of "time, place and personnel"? If we don't act now, then when? We must take this opportunity to defeat these troops and seize their guns. With guns in our own hands, we'll be more secure!'

Lao Liu suddenly stood up. His doubts dispelled by Pan Zaixing, he was now inspired again.

'I think guns are still vital! Otherwise why are we going to seize theirs?' He spoke with full self-confidence. 'Only with guns can we be victorious! On the other hand, these guns are nothing formidable in the hands of the corrupt enemy soldiers

– now I understand this, thanks to your explanation, Brother Zaixing. I agree with you!'

At this point, Wang Jiansheng got up and shouted, 'Yes! Quite right! I also completely agree. I suggest that we act immediately. But at the same time we must also do something else – '

'What else?' asked Pan Zaixing. 'The enemy have already arrived. What else should we do?'

The meeting was plunged into silence once again.

'We have to continue mobilizing the people,' said Wang Jiansheng in a quiet voice. 'We have to make them understand that this campaign is theirs and not a campaign with just a few hundred armed men of the Self-defence Corps and volunteer forces. If that were the case, then the regiment in the county town would be really formidable. We're not afraid that they have so many weapons, because we have all the villagers behind us. This is a vast peasant uprising, a campaign to destroy the enemy's armed forces and smash their political power – this is an uprising!'

Pan Xudong got up too, his face infused with excitement.

'Fine! You all have the right idea!' he said. 'I just want to make one more point. The Revolutionary Party is also the peasants' own party. If we didn't have this party to lead us and were as disorganized as in the past, with all the enthusiasm and determination in the world, we still couldn't be successful. Through this uprising – this word is most appropriate – we'll also expand and consolidate our party. The uprising will certainly produce many capable, bold and courageous people, whom we must use to strengthen our party. Right?'

'Right!' There was a unanimous response – so loud and clear that even this old temple seemed to reverberate with the sound.

At that moment Jiqing, who must have been standing on guard outside, hurried in with a short, skinny young lad. They went straight up to Pan Xudong. On looking closely, I realized that it was Sweet Potato, who was still running errands. After he had whispered something in Pan Xudong's ear, the latter immediately banged on the table, asking everybody to pay attention.

'There's some urgent news, which I will ask Sweet Potato to report to you all!'

267

Sweet Potato cleared his throat to call everyone to listen to the 'urgent news'.

'It's very simple,' he said. 'I've been carrying two baskets of letters and things for customers. I came from "The Big City" to Mazhen county town, from there to our county town, and I've just rushed here. With my own eyes I saw Chiang Kai-shek's army enter Mazhen county town, and from there they sent a battalion to reinforce the garrison in our county town. They're fully armed and look aggressive, ready for battle. Yesterday and today I haven't had a drop to drink or a bite to eat, so that I could get here as fast as possible to report this to you. That's all!'

'That's the situation. All reports have now confirmed this,' said Pan Xudong in a conclusive and firm manner. 'We have no time to lose. We must act immediately!'

'Yes,' said Liu Dawang, 'we must attack them before they get a chance to move.'

'But we must organize it. Don't forget that they have one thousand four or five hundred guns,' said Pan Zaixing, turning to Pan Xudong to ask, 'What's your plan?'

'I have a very simple plan,' replied Pan Xudong, his voice still firm. 'We must have a unified command, so we have to set up a general command-post immediately. We also have to unite our armed forces into a military organization which will be easy to command. As we all said just now, we are no longer a spontaneous insurrection, but a planned uprising by all the peasants!'

'Rise up!' Wang Jiansheng shouted. 'Rise up!'

Those present at this meeting had begun to realize that what they were embarking upon was of extraordinary significance. They were about to turn over a new leaf in the history of this region, which for centuries had been ignored, poor, backward and remote. They all remained silent, imbued with a sense of a grave responsibility which they had never shouldered before.

# CHAPTER 14

Sweet Potato's 'urgent news' finally proved to be quite correct. The auxiliary troops sent by Chiang Kai-shek stayed in the division headquarters in Mazhen county for a short while. Then they came to our county and camped down in the county town. We heard that the county town was thrown into chaos as soon as they entered. Most of the premises of the shopkeepers and citizens were occupied, and in the process their property was looted. The citizens just streamed out of the town to seek refuge with friends and relatives in the countryside. Naturally all the shops were closed down, except for the dough-stick shop run by Pockmarks the Sixth's cousin. The soldiers would not allow them to close it. Their petty officers could not find any better enjoyment than a cup of tea and some dough-sticks since the citizens had deserted the county town. So the shop had to stay open as usual.

As it was the only shop in this little county town, business was flourishing, but the customers here were unusual. After eating their dough-sticks, they swaggered off, usually without paying. What was also strange was that the temporary shop-keeper here (the original owner, Cuiba, was afraid that the soldiers would take liberties with his wife, so he had fled to the countryside with her), Pockmarks the Sixth, did not complain. In fact, he was working more energetically than ever. As he did not have enough assistants, he asked for some, including Jiqing, Pan Mingxun, myself and some other young and agile people. We all wore oil-proof aprons, like real masters of the profession, some kneading dough, some carrying water, some making dough-sticks, fried dough-twists, biscuits, crisps and other fried things. We were all terribly busy every day until the soldiers and their petty officers returned to their billets.

One night, however, we did not rest at all. According to foreign superstition, this was the most unlucky day, because it was connected with the number '13': the 13th of November. Strangely enough, though, that night was particularly beautiful. There was no wind, all was quite peaceful inside and outside the town, with not even a dog barking. Quite naturally, we did not feel like sleeping on such a beautiful night. Nor did Pockmarks the Sixth, so he treated us to a 'banquet' to enjoy this beautiful night and forget our troubles. The food was delicious, but we only had strong, refreshing tea, as there was no wine.

At the 'banquet' there were also some young lads who had slipped into town during the day. Pockmarks the Sixth had hidden them in his firewood shed. They were all strongly built, but as nimble as rabbits. Including the 'shopkeeper', we were twelve in all. After our dinner we rested for a bit and then changed into more comfortable, short, padded jackets. We stuck daggers into our belts and tied ropes round our wrists. Pockmarks the Sixth and Pan Mingxun put pistols under their jackets – we only had two pistols altogether. Jiqing also stuck a forging hammer into his belt – it was not his own long-handled hammer, but his employer's short one. So we were transformed into a 'dagger group' – that was what the 'General Command for the Uprising' had called our provisional twelve-man combat group.

We had already reconnoitred every corner of the town in the short period while we were 'working' there: the enemy camp, the sentry posts and gun emplacements on the town wall. Now we were organizing a sortie to carry out our main task – that was the real reason why we had been 'working' here for nothing for the past few days. Soon after midnight, reckoning that the soldiers had already gone to sleep, Pockmarks the Sixth blew out the oil-lamp in the shop and cautiously opened the door. He poked his head out to look up and down the street. Then, turning round, he beckoned to us, indicating that we could all come out. I was the last out, quietly closing the door behind me.

We all separated and took different, prearranged routes to meet in a fixed place at a stretch of the town wall near the north gate – because several battlements had already collapsed and the sentries did not often come here on patrol. It did not take us too long to reach this assembly point, where everyone found their own place to hide. We kept our eyes and ears alert for any sound or movement inside or outside the town. I myself was crouching behind a pile of loose bricks from the collapsed battlement. I concentrated on looking out, as I was responsible for liaison and communication and had to report promptly whatever I noticed to our 'dagger group'.

Beyond the town there was a vast scene of checkered fields, mountains and hills hidden in the darkness. I could not make out the features of this impenetrable landscape, as they merged into the black curtain of the night. Here primeval peace reigned. As it was so quiet, however, one could detect the slightest movement, if one kept alert. As my eyes gradually got accustomed to the darkness, I could make out some movement in the distance. I began to distinguish an enormous formation advancing like a surging tide. Instead of the crashing sound of waves, however, it was approaching the town wall silently. As it came nearer the wall, I could clearly distinguish its shape.

This human tidal-wave was the countless number of the Peasant Self-defence Corps and volunteer forces. These men, armed with guns, red-tassled spears, fishing forks, cudgels, hoes, shoulder-poles, blunderbusses, sticks and other primitive weapons, had already reached the town wall. Heading them was a troop of strong young peasants armed with rifles on their shoulders. Alongside them was a group of unarmed men carrying ladders, cotton quilts, straw, thick tree trunks and heavy rocks. Some of them were gathering at the bottom of the wall; others were following the wall towards the north gate.

Suddenly there was a spark in their midst. I knew this was the signal to attack the wall, so I immediately reported it to members of the 'dagger group' hiding near by. We immediately divided into two groups, as we had planned, one grouping round me and the other following Jiqing to the north gate. Then I lit a bunch of matches and waved them to those below. The assault team there were galvanized into action and started their attack.

They followed the wall, which was only about twenty feet

high, and rapidly put up many ladders. We watched the strong and nimble young villagers climbing to the top of the wall one by one. They had wet straw and quilts on their heads to protect them in case they were suddenly fired on. When they reached the top of the ladders we let the ropes down, to haul them up the last stretch which the ladders could not reach. Thus in a flash a specially picked assault group of seventy Self-defence Corps members led by Liu Dawang had climbed to the top of the wall. Just as we were about to rush to the north gate and capture it, a sentry on guard in the street below suddenly discovered us and fired. But Pockmarks the Sixth, keeping watch beside us, reacted quickly and shot back. That was the end of the sentry – our 'shopkeeper' had shot him through the head. When we rushed to the north gate, we found Jiqing there already. He had dealt with two dozing sentries, using his forging hammer. He had slain them with just two blows, and without much noise. His group had immediately opened the town gate, and when we arrived it was wide open. The peasant forces surged into the town like a flood.

The next moment a thunderous din broke out from all around, as if the earth were cracking and the town was going to collapse. All the guns outside the town responded with a deafening boom, and on top of this was an echo of explosions, as if thousands of machine-guns and mortars were firing at the town – in fact, it was produced by fire-crackers lit in kerosene canisters. In all this confusion the Self-defence Corps and volunteer forces divided into three groups: one heading towards the Temple of the God of Fire in the south-west of the town – that was where the regimental headquarters of the county troops was located; another group set off towards the county government office – that was the headquarters of the whole county administration; the third group divided again into three sub-sections, each going to the other three town gates which had not yet been opened – later we found out that this was not necessary, as the armed peasants had already smashed two of them open with rocks and tree trunks as soon as they had seen the signal to attack. The fourth gate had been burnt down with firewood and kerosene and the sentries on guard there killed on the spot. These actions had been accomplished without too much difficulty, but they were vital. The peasant forces massing outside swarmed in triumphantly to occupy the strategic positions in the town.

The soldiers billeted all over the town woke up to find that they were completely surrounded. The peasants' armed forces had also opened the gates of their camp. Some of them did not even have time to dress or grab their guns and were scurrying away like rats. Others had got hold of their guns but not their ammunition belts, so they could not shoot. In no time the peasants had grabbed them and seized their weapons. The soldiers who fled into the streets could not distinguish their opponents in the dark. The streets were so narrow and they were in such a tight spot that they often ended up fighting one another. As they could not use their weapons in this situation they had to grapple with our men. The soldiers were mostly beaten by the peasants, who were used to manual work. This confused hand-to-hand fighting filled the dark night from the middle of the town right to the surrounding countryside. Around the town there were thousands of villagers, who made it difficult for the soldiers to escape over the vast expanse of the terrain. Most of them got a good beating, and when they had lost their guns all they could do was flee from the fray in all directions and eventually slip away.

This battle went on all through the night. It was not easy to distinguish the soldiers in the dark. The only way to recognize them was by their guns. Because they had all got up in a panic, they were not wearing their full uniforms. The peasant forces, though, were mostly interested in their guns, so they concentrated on seizing as many as possible in this battle. Luckily, they were all the latest model and easy to grab. The soldiers all valued their own lives more than their guns, so they just dropped them and fled pell-mell. The peasant forces just turned a blind eye and let them escape – because we did not yet have anywhere to accommodate prisoners.

By sunrise the battle was more or less over, and the peasant forces began to reassemble in the fields beyond the town. Our 'dagger group' had joined the battle after we linked up with the assault team. Our original formation was immediately broken up, and it became impossible to co-ordinate our activities. We just had to rely on our own individual strength and skill, trying to seize our opponents' guns. The only thing I could do in this situation was, of course, to hit them, trying to give them a deadly blow, in order to take their rifles. In this life-and-death struggle we could not spare enemy soldiers – some were killed in this hand-to-hand fighting. I felt a bit uneasy when I saw their bodies lying under the rising sun. In fact, I had never thought of hurting anyone before.

Actually, I am not so strong, but in this situation I suddenly got some superhuman strength from somewhere. I struck out left and right whenever I saw an enemy soldier. Perhaps I injured quite a few of them – I could not count at the time. Naturally I received many blows myself, but I was not knocked to the ground. On the contrary, whenever I was hit my strength seemed to increase and I had to fight the opponent to the death. I remember one short and skinny soldier who was dragging his gun along and trying to escape from the fray. I caught up with him in a few steps and gave him a hefty kick in the back, so that he fell down. To prevent him from fighting back, I quickly trod on his back and seized his gun, which I then used to smash his head with the butt until no sound came from him. Perhaps he was already lying among those corpses. Now, when the open fields had returned to their original peace and quiet, I recalled all this and it seemed like a horrible dream. I could hardly believe it myself: How could I have had such an experience in my short life?

In these crowded fields I turned to look at the ancient county town. It had not changed except for the red flags fluttering in the wind all over the wall. This scene showed us that the dark night was over and a fresh day had dawned. A fresh day, of course, meant that new tasks and new work lay ahead. The armed peasants, now assembled in these wide fields, were also stirred by the hope of this new day. Even though they had been fighting the whole night, they did not feel at all tired. On the contrary, they all felt extremely fresh and inspired. The first task was, naturally, to line up in ranks and count numbers. Next we had to collect the rifles and ammunition which we had captured from the enemy, besides the county government officials and army leaders whom we had arrested. The result of the count showed that we had lost nine of our men, including the old

farm-hand Wang Xiangzheng from Pheasant Nest; we had thir-
teen wounded, including Grandpa Whiskers – nobody had
asked him to join this operation, but he had insisted, 'to see
with my own eyes the power of the peasant armed forces'. He
had acted of his own accord, with the result that he had twisted
his left ankle and could not walk.

As for the enemy, the leaders of the troops headed by the
regimental commander had opened up an escape route, as they
were covered by a well-armed guard unit. The top official in
the county government, County Head Yao De-an, had become
terrified by the upheavals in the countryside during this period.
Added to this, there was the lax discipline of the troops garrisoned in the town. Blackmail, extortion and all kinds of other
crimes had closed down businesses one by one, so that the
county government finances had dried up. All these factors had
driven him to a mental breakdown, and he had to take sleeping
pills every night. That evening he had taken rather more than
necessary. The result was that when the Peasant Self-defence
Corps burst into his bedroom, they had to tweak his ear to pull
him out of bed before he finally opened his eyes. Now both his
hands were tied behind his back with a rope. He was tethered
to an elm tree by the road like a mule to show that he had lost
his political power. As for the precious arms and ammunition,
the booty was more than we had estimated, but still short of
what we should have got from this big victory: 392 rifles and 41
cases of bullets. Pan Xudong explained this shortfall when he
summed up the experience gained in the battle.

'The enemy troops finally opened two escape routes through
the west and south gates. They managed to escape, because the
road there runs through rather flat land and is difficult to block.
Comrade Pan Zaixing, who was in command there, discovered
that there was a machine-gun and mortar team among the
fleeing forces. He was afraid that they might put up a last-ditch
fight, mount a machine-gun and open fire, which would have
cost us many lives. So Comrade Pan Zaixing acted promptly
and resolutely and let them pass without resistance. Wang
Xiangzheng was in command in the area of the east and north
gates. The enemy troops there didn't have big guns, and they
were the first to be attacked and surrounded. Comrade Wang

Xiangzheng decided to engage them in hand-to-hand combat, and most of the rifles were captured there. Even though they were not as many as we had hoped, they'll still greatly increase our fire-power.'

To make this speech, Pan Xudong was standing on a table, which had been taken from Pockmarks the Sixth's shop to serve as a platform for the meeting. The Self-defence Corps and volunteer forces were formed up in ranks around the table, as in military order. Other villagers, who had come here to listen and join in the victory celebrations, were also gathered around. The general command had called this mass meeting right after the battle. Pan Xudong was not only summarizing the experiences of this battle, but also announcing future plans, which had been worked out before the victory. All the peasant fighters stood there valiant and proud, sporting leather belts, rifles on their shoulders and red ribbons pinned to their chests. The Self-defence Corps now carried the new, captured guns, instead of the primitive weapons and old farm implements, which they had handed over to the peasant volunteer forces. The county Self-defence Corps had originally possessed only 240 old rifles; the corps of neighbouring Mazhen county had even fewer, only 100 or so, making a total of only 340. Now, however, they had doubled in number – a veritable 'army'.

'We've won a great victory, but we mustn't forget the support we got from the peasant forces of our neighbouring county.' Pan Xudong was continuing his speech. 'Comrade Chang Je-an carried a heavy responsibility, commanding the peasant forces over there, with only a hundred old-fashioned guns and ten thousand peasant volunteers with only primitive weapons. He built fortifications beside the road leading from Mazhen county town to this town and prepared for battle, to cut off the county troops in case they were coming to reinforce the troops here. These measures gave us some protection, so that we could employ all our forces to attack the town. The reason I am mentioning this is to point out that our uprising was not an isolated action, but victorious only as a result of co-operation with the peasant armed forces of our neighbouring county. On a larger scale, our uprising is part of the future nationwide uprising. It will change the destiny of our country and all our lives.'

These last two sentences stirred our imagination and moved the countless peasants standing around the table. The wide stretch of land where we were gathered comprised the best rice fields. Now they looked bleak and desolate, because it was winter-time and they lay fallow. As soon as spring planting began, however, they would be covered with green crops, like an endless brocade, which would provide the villagers with ample food in the autumn. Now that the forces representing the landlords had been defeated in this region, these rich crops would naturally belong to the farmers. Realizing this, the peasants became excited and animated. All of a sudden I felt someone patting my shoulder. Turning round, I saw that it was Uncle Pan, who had slipped up to me.

'I've been looking for you,' he said, looking me up and down. 'I want to look at you. Fine, nothing has happened to you, I'm relieved to see.'

After this he went back to a row of self-defence troops not far from me. I looked around and saw Lao Liu standing quite a distance away among some women and old villagers, who had come from all around to see this spectacle. Perhaps he was busy treating them to his propaganda, so he had not noticed me. I did not want to go and interfere with him either. What surprised me was that Ho Shuoru was with him, first talking to a middle-aged woman next to him and then to Lao Liu. I only turned to pay attention to Pan Xudong when he suddenly raised his voice and turned to a new subject.

'We must consolidate our successes and continue to expand our power. We have to establish our own political power – a workers' and peasants' democratic government. We'll only be able to change our own lives when we've grasped political power. Usually we villagers didn't dare enter the "masters'" government office. We only went there to supply provisions and funds for the troops or pay a fortune to our "masters". There we were arrested and beaten, imprisoned and executed. Today we've relied on our own efforts to overthrow the "masters'" government office, to arrest the head of the government, Yao De-an, and to free the villagers who were imprisoned there! This proves that we have power, that the world has changed and that it belongs to the working people. We are going to elect the officials of our own government and have people who can represent our interests as committee members. We must all pluck up our courage and become masters! We must have our own proper army to protect our political power. The leadership has decided that this army will be composed of the Peasant Self-defence Corps, divided into two "routes". The Self-defence Corps here will constitute the first route, commanded by Comrade Wang Jiansheng; the second route will be formed out of the peasant volunteer forces in Mazhen county, commanded by Comrade Chang Je-an.

'With our own government and our own army, we can immediately start to reform the old social system which suffocated us for generations. This will ensure that we will no longer be insulted, discriminated against or oppressed, nor will we suffer from cold and hunger, be forced to sell our sons and daughters or wander around destitute. We will all have land, food, clothing and a roof over our heads. So the first task is to confiscate the landlords' property and land. We must carry out our land reform straight away, so that every peasant becomes a land-owner.'

As soon as he had spoken these words, the massed crowd erupted like a storm. This sound surged like a flood, higher and higher, spreading from the Self-defence Corps forces to the volunteer forces, then to the boundless crowd of villagers. The whole land and even the air seemed to be vibrating. The villages in the distance also seemed to have been affected, as we suddenly heard the distant sound of fire-crackers and gongs. The news of the victorious uprising had already spread like an electric shock to every corner of the county. Pan Xudong's words had expressed the villagers' centuries-old dreams, which could never be realized before. He could not go on speaking, though, because his voice had been drowned by the sounds of celebration and jubilation coming from all around. I only heard the last words of his speech.

'That's the end of this meeting. Tomorrow we'll assemble here again to celebrate the creation of the Workers and Peasants Democratic Government!'

When Pan Xudong got down from the table which had served as the platform, I realized that my duties as a member of the 'dagger team' were over. I suddenly thought of my mother – she must be missing me. Just as I was thinking of going home to tell her I was safe and sound, I turned round and saw Uncle Pan rubbing his eyes with his sleeve. When I hurried over to him, I discovered that he had tears in his eyes, but was making an effort to control himself.

'What's the matter, Uncle Pan?' I asked, surpised. 'What's the matter with you, when we're all celebrating?'

Uncle Pan did not answer, but sobbed quietly – he could no longer control himself. I was even more surprised because he had always resigned himself to his hard life, without a sense of bitterness. It seemed that he had been very slow to react in this respect.

'You're tired, Uncle Pan,' I said, supporting him. 'Come back to our house and have a rest. Mother must be missing you!'

Uncle Pan did not refuse, so I helped him move away from the crowds. He did not say a word on the way, as if he were deep in thought. When we reached Aunt Sunflower's home, the sitting room was filled with a joyous atmosphere. Aunt Sunflower, Sister Apricot and my mother were all busy making soup and boiling red eggs. As soon as Uncle Pan entered the room and saw this festive scene, he stood there dumbfounded. Seeing this, the three mothers were also surprised. They all stared back at him, as if he were a stranger. Then, to everyone's surprise, Uncle Pan was no longer able to control his tears. He looked rather like a big baby.

'What's the matter?' asked my mother. 'We've heard the news of the victory and we're overjoyed. What's happened to you?'

Now Uncle Pan at last spoke out with a sobbing voice.

'I don't know. I'm sorry, I'll dampen all your spirits. Ever since I joined the revolution I've been working wholeheartedly for this victory. But now that victory has really come, I don't know why, but I suddenly feel old! The more these young villagers rejoice, the older I feel! Such a great era! How am I greeting it?'

'You think too much, Uncle Pan,' said Aunt Sunflower. 'After such a hard life, you're now witnessing this day, when a new

279

life is beginning, so you should feel young. I'll tell you some good news. Just when you were seizing the county town, O Ran gave birth to a plump baby, a future ox-herd!'

This unexpected news suddenly overwhelmed Uncle Pan. His spirits revived and his wrinkled face beamed brightly, all smiles instead of tears.

'Where?' he asked impatiently. 'Where? Tell me, quick!'

'In the inner room,' answered Sister Apricot. 'Didn't you see us preparing sweet soup and boiling red eggs? We're just celebrating the birth of her baby!'

'Her baby is my grandson,' mumbled Uncle Pan. 'I saw O Ran growing up with my own eyes; for me she's almost like my own daughter. Now she's a mother, producing a new generation – double happiness! Right, I'm not old. Now it's time to start working for the next generation. I'll never be old!'

He cast aside all taboos and the traditional superstition that a man should not see a woman in childbirth, striding into the room where the baby was born. He was so impatient to have a close look at O Ran, whom he had seen growing up, and at the newly born 'ox-herd baby'.